Unraveling Secrets

BOOK 1 OF THE SECRETS TRILOGY

LANA WILLIAMS

Interior format by The Killion Group
http://thekilliongroupinc.com

CHAPTER ONE

London, May 1882

Abigail Bradford followed her quarry through the unfamiliar cobbled streets of the East End, her heart pounding with fear, wondering if she trailed a ghost.

"You're certain that's Simmons, miss?" asked Thomas, the brawny footman who also served as protector for her family.

"No. How could it be? Vincent Simmons was hung for murdering my father ten years ago."

Yet his tattered bowler hat bobbed above the crowd just ahead in the evening twilight, the man blissfully unaware of his pursuers.

Thomas had spotted a man loitering outside their Mayfair home last week and chased him off. The same man had returned two days later, allowing Abigail to catch a glimpse of him—and she'd nearly dropped to her knees. His was a face she'd never forget, one that still haunted her nights.

Thomas had followed him to a tavern then to his lodgings in Alsatia. Tonight, they'd caught sight of him making his way home from The Ox and Crown Tavern where he seemed to be a regular, according to what little Thomas had discovered.

Abigail stumbled on the uneven cobbles, her gait awkward in the oversized boots she wore.

"Miss, no offense, but you walk like a girl," Thomas grumbled. "Can you lengthen your stride?"

Abigail tried to do as he suggested, but the brown trousers she wore were a bit snug. The coarse shirt and wool jacket felt bulky on her slim figure. "Is that better?" she asked.

Thomas merely sighed. He'd been appalled when she'd insisted on coming along on this venture, advising her that a lady could not roam these rough streets. When she'd refused to stay behind, he'd procured a mismatched set of boy's clothes to disguise her.

At sixteen, she'd witnessed her father's murder when they'd interrupted Simmons burglarizing their country home. Now, a decade later, doubt warred with determination. She had to know if Simmons had somehow escaped the hangman's noose.

"Shall I grab him?" asked Thomas, his height allowing him to track Simmons easily amid the lively street.

Abigail glanced around nervously. "Let us find a more deserted area to confront him."

She and Thomas were out of their element here. A more secluded place would improve their odds. She kept the brim of her cap tugged low, leaving her free to stare at the foreign landscape, her senses flooded by the unfamiliar sights.

Dilapidated, soot-blackened brick buildings with broken steps and uneven doors lined the street, so different from the tidy, organized streets of Mayfair where they lived. Shouts and curses rang through the air and mingled with the clatter of horses and carts in the street.

People of all sorts thronged the sidewalk, jostling Abigail as they hurried by. Young boys with knee-length pants, suspenders, and bare feet hawked nuts at the door of a theater they passed, a musical lilt to their thick Irish brogues. An old grizzled man, his hat at a jaunty angle, carted a tray of hot elder wine for sale, calling out in a sing-song voice to entice customers.

The door to a tavern swung open as they walked by, giving Abigail a glimpse into the dim interior. Men, laughter, and music spilled out along with the scent of fried food, smoke, and ale.

"Stay close." Thomas grabbed her arm to keep her from being swept along by the tide of humanity flowing into the pub.

A bare-headed woman with gin-glazed eyes leaned against a doorway, her generous bosom framed by a dirty red shawl. She sent Abigail a wink and licked her lips. "I like 'em young. How 'bout a quick tumble?"

Abigail's face heated and she quickly lowered her gaze, but not before she caught the shock on poor Thomas's face.

"God help us," he muttered. "You should not be here."

"At least we know my disguise is a success," she offered with a stifled laugh. She refused to be daunted by this outing.

The footman shook his head as he moved closer to her side, walking at a steady pace through the crowded street. Fewer people wandered the streets as they traveled farther east.

"If Lady Bradford finds out—"

"We'll be home before she and my sisters return." At least Abigail hoped so. She didn't want them to discover what she'd been up to. As the eldest, the responsibility of finding out if Simmons had returned from the dead fell squarely on her shoulders.

"Perhaps I should carry the gun, miss," the anxious servant suggested.

"I know how to use it. Don't worry so, Thomas." She wished she could take her own advice. She touched her father's pistol tucked into the waistband of her trousers. Her skills were rusty but she was sure she remembered enough of her father's shooting lessons to protect Thomas and herself if necessary.

"We'd best catch him before he disappears into his lodging house just ahead," the footman advised.

Abigail nodded. Her stomach burned with nerves, her palms damp. She breathed deeply to calm herself but regretted it as the foul stench of rotted food and human waste burned her nose.

They closed in on Simmons as he passed an alley. Abigail motioned to Thomas, who dashed forward and grabbed his arm.

"Here now! Leave off!" Simmons protested as he tried to pull away.

Thomas held on tight and backed Simmons into the alley entrance before releasing him. "We need a few words with you."

"What fer?" Simmons asked angrily as he peered at them, no sign of recognition on his face. His voice was gravely as though from disuse. "I've no money if that's what yer about."

Abigail's heart raced as she stared at him, unable to believe her eyes. "Vincent Simmons," she called out to test her sanity.

He jerked in surprise, his hands clenched. "No. No, my name is Edward Smith."

She froze with disbelief. Had she somehow gotten it wrong? She stepped forward and tipped her cap back to better see his face in the faint pool of light coming from the street lamp.

His eyes widened as he got a good look at her. A small smile turned his lips, and he brazenly dipped his head in acknowledgement. "Good evenin' to ye, miss."

His recognition of her erased all doubt as to his identity.

"How is it possible that you live?" She shook her head, unable to believe her eyes, trying to grasp how he could've escaped. She'd testified at his trial, heard his sentence, and within days, received confirmation of his death. Yet here he stood. Fear spiraled through her at what he might want.

"I've no idea what ye mean." He shrugged carelessly.

"You were hung for murder," she persisted. Had there been some mix up at Newgate Prison?

"Vincent Simmons hung. As I said, my name is Edward Smith." He flashed a knowing smirk with his lie. "Ye won't catch me admittin' otherwise."

Anger at the pain this man had caused her family chased away her fear. She slipped a hand inside her jacket and felt the butt of the pistol in her palm. The solid feel of it reassured her. How she wished she could simply draw the gun, squeeze the trigger, and be done with the lying murderer before her.

Then it would be over.

Her family would be safe again.

Her fear would ease and her nightmares of losing all of her family would end.

What did it matter *how* he'd escaped the hangman's noose? She'd only be seeing his sentence carried out at last.

Yet she hesitated. Vengeance was not so easy.

Despite his crime, she didn't think she could pull the trigger and kill him in cold blood. That would make her no better than him.

She studied his face in the dim light, noting that the past ten years had not been kind to him. His once ruddy face was pale, his cheeks gaunt, making his nose all the more prominent. Lines etched his eyes and creased his mouth. A head taller than her with a thin frame and ill-fitting, ragged clothes, his eyes darted to Thomas then returned to her.

"I wouldn't expect to see a lady such as yerself 'round here," he said, the smirk still in place.

"And I didn't expect to find you skulking about outside our door of late."

"Well, I was just havin' meself a look-see. No harm."

"No harm?" Fresh anger washed through her until she shook with it. "You killed my father before my eyes ten years ago. What greater harm could you have possibly wreaked?"

Those few horrific moments had forever changed her family's life. It seemed only fair that they'd changed his as well.

"Ye got it wrong." He moved closer, his smirk fading.

"Stay where you are," Thomas warned him.

"What game are you playing?" Abigail demanded.

"Like I said, my name is Edward Smith, just released from Pentonville Prison."

Outrage filled Abigail. "That's a lie! I won't let you get away with it."

Simmons cocked his head to the side. "Vincent Simmons hung before witnesses. I admit to nothin'. And no one will believe ye since ye've no proof."

She swallowed hard, her heart sinking, for she feared he spoke the truth. How could she convince the police he lived when their records showed he'd been executed?

"Why are you bothering us?" Did he seek revenge for her testifying against him, or worse, did he plan to kill the rest of her family?

His eyes narrowed as he stepped closer still, keeping a careful watch on Thomas. "Since ye think ye know me, why don't ye give over what I want and I won't darken yer door again."

Baffled, she could only stare at him. "What could you possibly want from us?"

"The rock. I need it. I'll be back by yer place soon. Have it ready."

Doing her best to ignore his menacing tone, she told him the truth. "I have no idea what you're speaking of."

A knife blade flashed in his hand. Fear caught in her throat, choking her. Thomas muttered an oath.

"Yer a smart lady. Ye'll figure it out. Now both of ye step aside. I've got an appointment to keep."

Thomas cast Abigail a worried look but she kept her gaze on Simmons. Determination filled her. She would not lose control of the situation. She needed answers in order to protect her family or this man would ruin their lives again. Gritting her teeth, she pulled the pistol from under her jacket. The sound of the hammer cocking echoed in the alley. "We're not finished with this conversation."

Simmons' eyes widened. The surprise on his face was somehow satisfying. How good it felt to have turned the tables.

"You're not leaving until you explain," she warned, the pistol heavy in her hands.

He flipped his knife and caught it easily. "I'll stick this between yer man's eyes and snap yer little neck before ye can take aim. Now leave off."

She could see he meant every word by the way he moved and knew from what he'd done ten years ago that he was capable of it. Her heart pounded so loudly she could hear little else, but she refused to allow him to flee. She leveled the loaded pistol at him and tightened her finger on the trigger, willing her hands to hold steady.

"Try it," she bluffed, praying to God he wouldn't. "I'm quite good with moving targets.

Now tell me what rock?" She aimed the barrel at his heart.

Stephen Nolton, Viscount Ashbury, navigated the streets of the East End with ease, pleased with the results of the evening. His ribs hurt, his knuckles were bloody, but his opponent was in far worse shape.

The man wouldn't be so quick to take what wasn't his next time. In fact, Stephen was certain he would pursue a new line of work from this night forward. And that was exactly what Stephen wanted. One more person set on the path of right before he hurt an innocent.

The dark shadows that chased Stephen would be held at bay for another night. That was all he could do—battle each day to keep them back. To make up for his past mistakes. He sighed at the bleakness of his life, only to feel a sharp pain in his side as though prodding him to forget his own worries and focus on those who were truly in need.

As he neared the corner of an alley, a muffled curse sounded. The hair on the back of Stephen's neck rose. In recent years, he'd become adept at detecting trouble.

Angry voices grew distinguishable and Stephen eased forward, trying to catch the words and locate the speakers.

"Tell me what rock!"

Stephen frowned at the educated diction to the woman's voice—something completely out of place amidst the hopeless poverty of this neighborhood. He looked around the corner of the building into the alley where three shadows came into view.

The shadows of three men.

He studied the area more closely, trying to ascertain what was happening. The smallest—a boy judging by his size—aimed a gun at a man with a knife. The third man, dressed as a servant, stood just to the side of the boy. He couldn't see where the woman was, but it was the boy who caught his full attention.

Despite his obvious ill intent as he aimed the pistol, golden light hovered around his head and shoulders.

In Stephen's experience, a light-colored aura meant a good, honorable person. Yet this aura, speared with deep blue and yellow, defied description and left him speechless. The vibrant yellow meant success and intelligence. The dark blue indicated spirituality.

He doubted he'd ever get used to his ability to see auras, and rarely did he see anything but gray and black. But in the ten years he'd had the damned skill, never had he seen anything like this one.

The nervous servant's aura was gray and murky—the color he saw most often as people's auras were a mixture of their thoughts. The man with the knife had the imprint of the street on him—a worn, dirty jacket, a few days worth of beard on his thin, pale face, soot smeared on his cheek. His aura was dark with flashes of black permeating it, proof of bad intentions for certain. Auras told Stephen only a small part of the story, giving him clues to follow. The rest he had to discern by listening and observing.

"Answer me," the woman's voice demanded.

Not a boy after all. Even as Stephen processed that fact, the man with the knife lunged forward.

"No!" The servant yelled as he rushed toward him, using his hand to block his advance.

"Thomas!" she cried out. The gun she held quivered, just like her voice, but she quickly steadied both. "Get back," she ordered the knife holder.

Though she put on a brave front, she was clearly frightened and unwilling to fire her weapon. Stephen didn't blame her. Killing a man was no easy feat, nor was it easy to live with.

He stepped into the alley. "What goes here?"

As he feared, the lady swung the pistol at him. He held up his hands to show her he had no weapon. He preferred to use his fists when the occasion called for force. "Aim that elsewhere," he ordered.

"Who are you?" she asked as she moved the gun toward her intended victim. The bill of her cap cast a shadow over her eyes, but the delicate line of her jaw was visible. An overly large jacket covered her frame. Her disguise was quite effective and hid the majority of her femininity. Despite yielding the weapon, her aura remained bright and colorful. She held steady, obviously not allowing her fear to overwhelm her.

What on earth was she doing here?

"I was passing by and thought you might require assistance," he answered at last, then tore his gaze from the woman to glance at the man with the knife.

Her intended victim remained in place, trying to decide if he should fight or flee, the lady's wobbling gun seeming to add to his uncertainty. Stephen's presence helped block his escape route.

"You've interrupted a discussion of a personal nature," she informed Stephen. "Please continue on your way."

"Miss?" The servant held out his hand. Blood dripped from a deep cut across his palm.

She gasped, her gun trembling when she saw the blood. "Thomas, are you all right?"

"We'd best hurry this discussion along." The servant withdrew a handkerchief from his pocket to wrap around his hand.

"Answer me, damn you!" Clearly angry, she

steadied the pistol once again at her target.

Stephen lowered his hands and eased closer, watching the cornered man's aura to see what he would do next. The thoughts and urges people had, even if only temporary, shot out spears of color. The man's aura remained black as coal, his gaze fixed on the pistol. Not a good sign.

"Leave off," the man snarled at her. The knife he held glimmered in the faint light.

Though Stephen couldn't deduce what had brought the lady to this alley with a gun, her aura put him squarely on her side. She might have the more effective weapon, but her inexperience created a huge disadvantage. Stephen doubted she'd be able to pull the trigger, not with her aura.

Out of the corner of his eye, he saw the man lunge toward her.

"Christ." Stephen rushed forward to block him.

A shot echoed in the alley, disturbing the quiet of the night.

Stephen jerked, his arm no longer his own. Blinding pain speared through him, stealing his breath.

"Damn me! I've had enough." The intended victim plowed past Stephen, knocking down the footman as he flew into the street.

"Oh!" The woman cried as her pistol clattered to the cobblestones. "Sir, are you all right?"

Stephen dropped to his knees, shocked at the depth of the pain in his body. He'd known this night would come but hadn't expected it quite so soon.

"Thomas, help me," the lady demanded.

Hands held Stephen steady as he wavered, his vision narrowing until all he saw was her. "Didn't think...you'd do it," he muttered as he fought to catch his breath.

"I—I didn't mean to," the lady said. "I'm so terribly sorry."

Stephen groaned. So was he. Damn but it hurt. It was his blasted luck that she hadn't killed him instantly. That would've been far too easy an exit from this cursed existence.

"We need to get him some help, miss," the footman urged as he peered inside Stephen's jacket. "It's bleeding like a—" He seemed to think better on his word choice. "It's bleeding bad."

"I'll be fine. You two...see to your own safety." Asking for assistance of any sort was not in his vocabulary. Not even now. Once he gathered his wits, he would make his way home.

"We will not abandon you in your hour of need. Especially not since I caused your injury." After a long moment, she said, "I'm sorry but I can't take you to my home. I could never explain you to my stepmother."

"Yes. That might be...awkward." He wanted her gone, her and her bewitching aura. "Do not bother yourself."

"Don't be an idiot. Give us your address and we will escort you there."

She thought him an idiot? He wasn't the one who'd pulled the trigger. "No." He shook his head. No one came to his home. Ever.

"We are not leaving you here, sir." She pulled back his jacket and gasped. "Thomas, we need something with which to bind this."

Stephen looked down and saw what had the lady so upset. The bullet had struck just above his heart. His once white shirt was crimson. The metallic scent of it made him woozy. Somehow, knowing it was his blood pumping out turned his stomach, or perhaps it was the burning pain that did so. Either way, nausea had him clenching his jaw even harder.

Shaking hands removed his jacket and he caught his breath. Sweat beaded on his forehead as the pair shifted him about, each movement more excruciating than the last. Perhaps they were here to torture him, to make him suffer more for his past misdeeds.

"Hang on, sir," the woman said, her voice trembling. "We must first stop the bleeding. Then we will move you to safety."

With much effort, he tried to gather his thoughts, to focus on anything except the pain in his chest that dulled his senses.

His gaze caught on her.

Her cap tipped back as she worked, revealing an oval face framed by the elegant line of her jaw. Her eyes were enormous. He had the oddest urge to drag her into the light so he might see their color, for it was impossible to tell in the dimness. Her dark brows held a slight arch. Tendrils of dark hair had escaped her cap.

He couldn't understand what had drawn a lady like her to these filthy streets, but she didn't belong here.

"You should go." He closed his eyes.

"Hush," she said her voice gentle. "I nearly have it bound."

Hush. Warm memories filled him with that soft spoken word. How often had his mother said that to him? He missed her to this day. In this moment, more than ever.

"Sir? Sir?" The lady gave him a little shake, sending pain shooting through his entire body. "Tell us your address. Where shall we take you?"

"The Barbican. On Pall Mall," Stephen muttered.

Stunned silence greeted his request.

"You've just been shot and you want us to take you to a gaming hell?"

He nearly smiled at her incredulous tone. "Aye."

When his world faded, the image of her stayed, accompanying him into the darkness, forever imprinted in his mind.

CHAPTER TWO

Abigail waited alone with the unconscious man in the dirty alley, her panic rising. Thomas had left to fetch help. Already it seemed as though he'd been gone a lifetime. Every scuffling sound caused her heart to skitter as she glanced around to find the source. How could she protect the injured man if Simmons or anyone else came upon them?

His head was heavy in her lap as he lay on the cobbled alley with only his jacket beneath him and hers covering him. She checked the binding, made of Thomas's shirt, on the man's wound again. Blood seeped through the cloth, growing each time she looked. Worry and remorse had her fighting back tears. Oh, dear Lord, if this man died, she didn't see how she could possibly live with herself. Would she be arrested for murder?

She couldn't believe she'd shot him. The gun had gone off on its own, at least that's how it had seemed. The events had happened so quickly, leaving little more than a blur in her mind.

"Hang on, sir. Help is coming." She smoothed his soft, dark hair, unable to think of anything else she could do to bring him comfort. Rugged brows framed his eyes. He had a narrow, straight nose and a strong jaw. His hair was clipped short with a hint of sideburns. His tone told her he was well educated, though his clothing had seen better days. She couldn't imagine why he wanted to be taken to The Barbican.

A torch light appeared at the end of the alley, startling her.

"Is anybody down here?" The authoritative voice gave her hope that help in some form had arrived at last.

"Yes!" she called out. "Hurry, please! A man's been injured."

As he drew nearer, she saw he wore a constable's uniform. Relief poured through her.

"We had a report of gun fire," the man said.

Her father's pistol lay on the cobbles nearby. She swallowed hard as she stared at it. She couldn't quite bring herself to say that she'd pulled the trigger. "Yes, this man's been shot. He needs help. We must hurry."

"Good Christ!" The constable held the light aloft. "Lord Ashbury, haven't we told you no good would come of your antics?"

Lord Ashbury?

This man was a lord? But she was given no time to question the information.

Thomas returned with another constable and the men loaded the injured man into a waiting hackney. Abigail gathered their jackets and the gun, tucking the blasted thing back in her waistband then hurried to the hackney.

"He requested to be taken to The Barbican," she told the constable, "but perhaps you know where he lives?"

The constable stared at her, taking in her trousers with a puzzled frown. "We'd best take him to The Barbican if that's what he said. Mr. Farley will know what's best."

Abigail was hustled into the hackney, her lap providing a pillow for Lord Ashbury's head and the conveyance was soon rumbling toward Pall

Mall. One constable rode along to ensure their safe arrival along with Thomas.

She tried her best to cushion the lord from the jarring ride, but he was so big. His body took up most of the seat, leaving her tucked into the corner. The constable sat opposite them and helped to hold the lord in place on the narrow bench.

She cradled his head with her arm to prevent it from swaying as they turned a corner. The pleasant scent of bay rum clung to him. As unobtrusively as possible, she sniffed again, unable to resist the woodsy smell. A glance at the binding on his upper chest showed the movement was not doing him any good. She held him tighter, willing to do anything to help him.

At last they arrived at The Barbican. Four columns lined the front of the three-story granite building. Torches lit the flight of stairs that led to massive double doors where two men stood guard. Rows of curtained windows lined the upper floors of the building, giving no hint of what might be inside.

The understated elegance of the exterior matched Abigail's vision of a gentleman's club, but everyone knew the true purpose of the establishment. Why Lord Ashbury wanted to come here puzzled her.

The constable directed the driver to the side door of the imposing structure. He alighted and hurried to knock on the door three times, then paused and knocked once more. At last the door opened to reveal a tall, burly man who frowned at the sight of him.

A few words were exchanged and in short order, several men hurried to the hackney and carried the injured lord inside.

"You'd best go in as well, miss," the constable advised her. "Mr. Farley will need to know what happened."

She swallowed hard, wondering if the constable would soon arrest her for attempted murder. Heart pounding, she realized she had no choice but to accept the consequences of her actions.

Thomas followed her inside. She caught sight of dark wood, rugs from the Far East, and sparkling crystal chandeliers before they were escorted upstairs to a suite of exquisitely furnished rooms. What seemed to serve as a drawing room allowed her to glimpse into the bedchamber beyond where the still unconscious Lord Ashbury now lay in a massive four-poster bed fit for a king. Tears filled her eyes at the sight. Did he yet live? Surely someone had sent for a doctor.

An older man with a receding hairline, thick gray mustache, and the neat appearance of a solicitor left the lord's side, closing the bedchamber door behind him as he moved toward her.

"Miss, I hope you're able to shed some light on what happened." The man's gaze took in her attire, stopping on the blood that covered the sleeves of her jacket and her hands. "Are you injured as well?"

"No." She gestured toward the bedroom, still uncertain what to call the man. "That would be...his blood."

"Good God!" He shook his head. "What happened?"

"Well," she began, her heart racing. To her dismay, tears filled her eyes and her throat clogged with emotion. What else was there to do but admit the truth? "I shot him."

The man's eyes widened. "Why?"

"Well, I— That is to say, I—" Uncertain how she could explain, she looked at Thomas, hoping for assistance, fighting back tears.

"It was a terrible accident," her footman said, his fingers worrying the brim of his hat. "The lord came upon us in the middle of a...discussion with a third party and interceded."

"Oh?" The man appeared less than surprised.

"Will he be all right?" she asked, managing to push the words out past the lump in her throat. "Have you sent for a doctor?"

"Indeed. He'll be along shortly to advise us for certain."

Relief filled her at his words. "I am terribly sorry. I didn't mean to shoot him. As Thomas said, it was an accident." Did he believe her? Fear spiraled in her belly as she pictured being hauled away by the nice constable who'd escorted them here.

"I'm sure it was." The man sighed. "I'm surprised something like this hasn't occurred before now."

"Pardon me?"

"Never mind. If I could get your name in case it's needed?"

The door behind him opened and a servant stepped out. "Mr. Farley? He's asking for the woman."

Abigail's stomach clenched. She'd hoped for a brief moment that Mr. Farley was going to let her go. Now she feared the worst. Her throat dry, she glanced at Thomas before looking back at Mr. Farley, prepared to pay the price for her actions. After all, it had been her finger on the trigger.

No one else. Only her.

How often had she lectured her younger sisters about taking responsibility for their actions? She could do no less, no matter the dire consequences. She'd tried so hard these past ten years to take care of things, to keep her family safe from harm. Now she'd nearly killed an innocent man. Why had she thought she could deal with the problem of Simmons on her own?

Light poured out the open bedroom door as though beckoning her forward. With a deep breath, she straightened her spine, praying this night wouldn't end with her in Newgate.

Mr. Farley gestured toward the door. "After you, miss."

Stephen waited, willing the burning pain to ease long enough for him to see her one last time. The woman with the golden aura who had nearly caused his demise.

Though the throbbing ache was dreadful, he realized now that the wound was not fatal. He closed his eyes for a brief moment as regret filled him. His bleak existence would not end this night after all.

Since that was the case, he wanted two things from this wretched night: to know her name and to see the color of her eyes. That seemed small enough payment for the pain she was putting him through.

After what seemed like an eternity of waiting, she stepped into the doorway, her aura visible even at this distance. Rather than hesitating as he'd expected her to do, she walked forward until she stood beside his bed.

"How are you feeling?" she whispered, the brim of her hat casting a shadow over her eyes.

"Like hell."

If he hadn't been watching so closely, he would've missed her swallowing hard, the tremor of her fingers as she smoothed the bottom of her jacket.

"I am so very sorry. I never intended you harm."

"Too bad your aim was off," he muttered. "Then

we wouldn't be having this conversation."

"I'm afraid I don't understand."

"Never mind." He shook his head, trying to keep his foul mood from spilling onto her until he got what he wanted. It wasn't her fault she hadn't hit him where it counted. "What were you doing in Alsatia dressed like that?"

She lifted her chin. "I assure you I was on a necessary mission."

He stared, willing her to lift her head a bit more so the light would catch her eyes. Instead she dropped it.

She mumbled something but he couldn't make out the words through the sea of pain that threatened to drown him. "What?"

"I thought I was chasing a ghost."

Her words made no sense, but perhaps that was because of the pain that ebbed and flowed with each breath he took. He closed his eyes, fighting nausea.

"Your name?" he asked at last, not bothering to open his eyes.

A long moment of silence ensued before at last she answered. "Abigail Bradford...my lord."

Abigail. Of course. How appropriate. Curse her for telling him. Now he'd never forget it. Somehow he knew he was going to regret this, but he opened his eyes anyway. "Take off that dreadful cap."

She blinked then reached up to draw the thing off her head. A strange buzzing sounded in Stephen's ears.

Blue.

Her eyes were blue.

Why hadn't he realized they would be? The sparkling cobalt color suited her perfectly. Not just any blue, but the color of the sky in the spring, just before sunset. That amazing shade that made one take a moment to appreciate the sight. The dark ring of black surrounding the iris made the blue all the more stunning.

Her complexion was alabaster smooth, her face made interesting by her high cheekbones, an angled jaw, and a chin that held a hint of a dimple. Her hair was nearly black and pulled back from her face. Dark, arched brows added to her look of intelligence. Her nose was narrow, her lips bowed at the top.

But those eyes were what pulled at him. He would've been far better off without seeing them. Somehow he knew they'd haunt him in the coming days.

As he continued to watch her, he saw that fear lay in their depths. He frowned. Did she fear him?

"Will you be contacting the police?" she asked.

It took a moment for her words to register. He nearly laughed. Far be it for him to involve the law. They had a love-hate relationship. Was that her worry? "I won't contact them if you promise me something."

"What?"

"Stay out of the East End. You do not belong there." He clenched his jaw as his chest burned. He looked at her one last time, wishing he'd never met her, knowing he wouldn't forget her. "And stay the hell away from me as well."

"But I—"

"You are not safe. Not there and not here. Now get out!" Anywhere near him would only put her in danger of one sort or another. He didn't need another death on his conscious.

Her eyes widened as she backed away. Farley came forward to escort her out and the door shut behind them.

Stephen closed his eyes, hoping the doctor would arrive soon to give him something to numb the pain, both body and mind. Yet all he saw was a pair of large blue eyes.

Abigail.

How ironic that of the many things that haunted him, her and her golden aura would be the most disturbing.

Vincent Simmons hurried along the dark streets toward the workhouse, hoping he wasn't too late.

"Blast that woman," he mumbled under his breath. Why couldn't she hand over the bleeding rock and be done with it? But no, she had to make this difficult. He'd been so tempted to tell her the truth—that he was indeed who she thought he was. But he'd been warned never to admit to his previous name or their whole plot might be at risk. Rubbing it in her face served no purpose other than to make him feel better.

He glanced around nervously. Even a former inmate had reason to fear these streets. A man might slit your throat as much as look at you in this neighborhood. All layers of civilization were stripped bare. The trappings of humanity had stopped about two blocks ago. No warm glow lit the houses. No lace curtains softened the windows. Nothing but brick and coal dust lined these rough streets.

He slowed as he rounded the next corner and looked about cautiously, worried that his contact had given up on him.

"'Bout time ye showed yer face."

The gravelly voice had Vincent spinning to face him. "I appreciate ye waitin' fer me. Ran into a bit of trouble."

"Is that right? Trouble of the female kind?"

Vincent nearly snorted. "Female, aye, but not what you think."

"Yer loss. Be sure I don't regret waitin'."

"I'll make it worth your while. No worries on

that account."

The lad he spoke with couldn't have seen more than twenty years, but since those two decades had been spent on these streets, he might as well have been fifty. His battered hat was pulled low over his brow, leaving his dark, greasy hair to flatten tight to his neck. Though Vincent couldn't see much of him in the dark, he would never forget those flat, black eyes. The memory of them from their meeting the previous day made him shiver.

"Tell me again what yer lookin' fer," the young man said, hands at his sides, his body quiet as though holding his energy for more important tasks.

Vincent's source had warned him to be cautious as Mikey could be brutal and never hesitated to use his fists.

"I'm in need of a few boys. Preferably old enough to not miss their mothers overmuch, but young enough not to complain." That made the workhouses and orphanages the perfect place to find what they were looking for. No relatives asking what had become of them. They could disappear with no one the wiser.

"What fer?"

Vincent lifted his chin and puffed out his chest with pride. "To participate in a scientific experiment."

"Yeah. Right. By the likes of ye?"

"I'm an assistant to a very important scientist. I contacted ye on his behalf."

"Ye goin' te torture them?"

Vincent couldn't decide if Mikey sounded fascinated or horrified at the prospect. Most likely, a bit of both.

"No. No," Vincent hastily denied. He didn't want to risk getting on Mikey's bad side. "Nothin' of the sort. I'm afraid I can't divulge more than that. It's all very secret."

"Humph." The silence grew long, and Vincent worried the man would turn him down. "Ye won't cause them harm?"

Vincent nearly chuckled. To think that Mikey had a conscious came as a big surprise. That was a weakness Vincent might be able to use at some future date. "It's not our intent to cause them harm."

Sure, it might be a side effect of the experiment, but it certainly wasn't their intent. Especially since it wasn't easy to find 'volunteers'. If they could use them more than once, all the better. As his uncle had told him, a death or two for the betterment of science was more than a fair trade.

That was all well and good as long as it wasn't Vincent's death. He'd come as close to death as he wanted to when he'd narrowly missed hanging for murder. He didn't care to get that close again.

Vincent liked to think that his uncle's grand plans depended on him. He had no desire to become—how had his uncle put it? Oh, yes—a disposable asset. Vincent intended to be an important part of the plans and that started with finding 'volunteers' for the experiments.

"All right then. I'll see who's willin' to earn a few coppers."

"Excellent."

"Ye pay me now then I'll pay the lads."

Keeping most of it for yourself? Vincent wanted to ask but held his tongue. "Sure. I'll need at least two now. More later."

"I can only do one at a time. Otherwise, it will bring too much attention."

Vincent sighed. That meant more work for him. He'd have to keep the little buggers until they had enough to do the experiment. On the other hand, the last thing he needed was to draw attention.

"I suppose that'll do," Vincent said.

"Ye got a problem with it? Go find another."

"No, no," Vincent reassured him. "I can make that work. It's just not how I was plannin' it. That's all."

"Humph."

Vincent could feel the heavy weight of his regard. The greasy smoked sausage he'd enjoyed at the tavern earlier stirred restlessly in his belly, threatening to make a reappearance. He tensed, prepared to go for his knife if need be, though he doubted he'd have a chance against Mikey.

"Give me two days. I'll see what I can do."

Breathing a sigh of relief, Vincent reached in his pocket. "Here're the coins we agreed on."

Mikey snatched them from his hand. "I'm goin' to need this much again when I deliver."

Vincent sputtered in protest until Mikey stepped closer, his solid chest and broad shoulders reminding Vincent of an angry bull.

"Got a problem with that?" Mikey asked.

"I expected to do business with a man of his word," Vincent said. He had to take a stand now or the lad would triple the price next time. He couldn't have that. His uncle was working on a tight budget.

A long moment passed until Mikey seemed to realize that Vincent wasn't going to back down.

"Fine. We'll stick with the price we agreed to this time. But if ye need more, it's gonna double."

Vincent nodded. "Fair enough. Yer takin' a bit of risk with all this. And I'm grateful fer yer assistance."

"Just be sure ye leave me name out of it. I like to keep me business transactions to meself."

"Ye and me both." Vincent had decided long ago that fame was not for him. But he intended to gather a fortune as quickly as possible.

With luck, he'd have it before the end of the summer.

"Pleasure doin' business with ye, Mikey. See you in two days time."

The lad didn't answer. He turned away and disappeared into the night, leaving Vincent alone. At least he thought he was alone. After glancing about nervously, he hurried back the way he'd come, anxious to put this place behind him.

CHAPTER THREE

Abigail sighed with relief as she sank into the cushions of the carriage. Shopping was not her preferred way of spending an afternoon. However, her young sisters, at the age of fourteen, thrived on it.

Though twins, Sophia and Olivia were barely recognizable as siblings. Olivia was slim, strawberry blonde, and tall, much like their mother, Irene. Sophia was darker, shorter, and rounder, similar to Abigail's father. Their personalities were night and day as well, but the pair of them together created a force of nature.

They settled on either side of her in the carriage, chatting about everything from the ribbon they'd found to the new silk at the dressmaker's. Rarely did they complete a sentence, instead interrupting each other, their minds working in parallel.

"Did you see the pink? I thought it—"

"Divine. I completely agree. Although the purple—"

"Perfect. Yes. It would go so well with the white—"

"Taffeta. So true. And the—"

Abigail let their words swirl around her as she shared a smile with her stepmother who took her seat on the opposite cushion for their journey home.

With a slim figure and smooth skin, Irene was still an attractive woman despite being in her mid fifties. Her green eyes held intelligence, and her auburn hair was rich in color. Abigail adored her.

Abigail's striking combination of black hair and blue eyes were a bequest of her father's. She knew her looks caused Irene both pleasure and pain as they reminded her of her late husband. Abigail's birth mother had died of tuberculosis when Abigail was three. For many years, it had been just her and her father until he'd married Irene when Abigail was ten. Irene had served as both her mother and her friend ever since.

Moments like this, when her family was together and happy, were meant to be treasured. Which was exactly why she hadn't been able to bring herself to tell them of the return of Vincent Simmons.

Two days had passed since the night in Alsatia. She'd scoured the paper each morning, fearful of reading about the shooting of Lord Ashbury or even worse, his death, but no report had been filed.

Yet it was a night she'd never forget.

Her horror when she'd realized she'd shot him.

Waiting in that dark alley scared no one would come to aid them.

Images of the lord were emblazoned in her memory. The line of his brow, the strength of his jaw, the feel of him against her, the scent of him.

Not to mention him telling her to get out.

To stay away.

She swallowed back her hurt. He need not worry on that front. She hoped never to set eyes on him again. A more rude, insufferable man, she'd never met.

Yet his haunted green eyes, the slight bump on the bridge of his nose, and the scent of him were constantly in her thoughts.

She berated herself. Her worry over the *situation* had sent her stomach dancing that night, not *him*.

It was only those niggling questions from what little she'd learned about him that wouldn't let go. What had he been doing in that neighborhood that night? Why had the constable not been surprised to see him in such circumstances? What did he have to do with The Barbican?

"Abigail?"

Irene's voice jolted her back to the present. The frown on her stepmother's face told her this wasn't the first time she'd called her name.

"Are you all right? You seem very distracted of late."

She badly wanted to tell her the truth: *I'm distracted because I'm afraid the man who murdered my father is lurking nearby.*

But no. What purpose would that serve? For months after her father's death, all of them had startled at every little sound. Sleep had been impossible. Outings were a nightmare. Even after Simmons' hanging—or when they thought he'd hung, she corrected herself—their nerves had been on edge.

She needed to resolve the situation herself. Maybe her discussion with Simmons had warned him away and he'd realized her family was no easy target. She closed her eyes, saying a quick prayer that it was true.

"I've been a bit tired of late," she answered at last. "That is all."

"Then it's a good thing we're staying in this evening."

"Indeed." She smiled at the girls who had paused in their conversation to listen. "What would you like to do tonight?"

"I think we should help you pick a gown for the

Mortenson's ball." Olivia smiled mischievously, awaiting her reaction.

Abigail nearly groaned as a small knot of panic formed in her chest. She'd all but forgotten about the annual ball hosted by their mother's dearest friend to be held next week. Attendance was mandatory for Abigail.

Irene frowned at her and Abigail hastily smiled. "Excellent idea. I value your opinion."

"I still think you should order a new gown," Irene said.

"I'm sure one of the gowns I already have will do quite nicely. After all, it's not as if I'm a debutante desperate to attract the notice of a suitor."

Despite her stepmother's wish for her to marry, Abigail realized she was practically off-the-shelf. At six and twenty, she no longer compared to the fresh young innocents who'd be introduced this season. Besides, with the odd dent in her chin, the slight overlap of her two front teeth and her avid interest in financial matters, few men found her attractive. Those who had *she* hadn't found appealing.

Not one iota.

After all these years, she'd become convinced that the best place for her was continuing to care for her family. She was very good at it. At least she had been, until this latest development.

Luckily for her, the carriage drew to a halt outside their Mayfair home so she didn't have to argue the topic again with her stepmother. It was the one point of contention between them. Abigail had no desire for a husband, and Irene was certain she needed one.

Thomas, who served as both footman and coachman for their household, opened the door and Abigail was the first to alight.

"Did you see anything?" she whispered to him.

"No, miss. You?"

"Nothing. Perhaps our conversation with him succeeded in convincing him to stay away."

Ponsford, their butler, appeared at the door then hurried down the stairs toward them. One look at his distraught expression was enough to have Abigail's full attention.

"What is it?" she asked.

"Terrible. Just terrible." The old man, who was normally stoic, appeared very agitated. "Someone smashed in the garden door."

Abigail's stomach dropped. "They're in our house?"

Directly behind her came gasps from Irene and her sisters as they all gathered around Ponsford, including Thomas.

"Not any longer. I heard some commotion while I was downstairs in the kitchen. He must have heard me coming. I only saw the back of his filthy jacket and bowler hat as he ran out."

"Are you all right? Was anyone hurt?" Irene asked, her face ashen.

"Jenny, the maid, was struck from behind but seems to be recovering."

"Poor Jenny," Olivia said.

"Will she be all right?" Sarah asked.

"Cook is seeing to her. I fear the library is in a terrible mess."

"I can't believe someone would do such a thing in the middle of the day," Irene said.

Abigail shared a look with Thomas. Fear warred with anger. She had an idea of who the would-be thief was. If only she knew what the man wanted. The things he'd said in the alley had made no sense.

"Did you send someone for the police?" Irene asked.

Ponsford flashed a glance at Abigail before he answered. "Yes, my lady."

Abigail nodded. The butler was well aware that she'd spoken with the police about Simmons already. "Excellent, Ponsford. Well done. Let us see what the damage is."

She led the way up the front steps, pausing as Thomas reached for the door to open it for her.

"What will you tell the police, miss?" the footman whispered.

"The truth. Perhaps they'll take our previous complaint more seriously now," she said quietly, not wanting to alarm the rest of her family. She turned to Ponsford. "Are you sure Jenny is all right?"

"She's fine. A bit shaken up and a nasty headache is all."

"You didn't see anything more of the thief?"

"No, miss. Only the back of him. It happened so quick."

Abigail entered the foyer, noting that nothing was out of place there. She continued on to the library, the sight before her giving her pause. "Oh dear."

"Heavens," Irene whispered from behind her. "The thief tore the place apart."

Cold seeped down Abigail's spine as fear settled in a tight knot in her stomach. He'd obviously been searching for something. Her desk drawers had been removed and turned upside down, the contents strewn across the floor. Books from the shelves lining the walls added to the mess. Knickknacks were knocked over. Chairs had been upended.

"Oh goodness." Olivia stood just behind Abigail, peering into the room over her shoulder.

"I'm going to check on Jenny," Sarah said and hurried toward the stairs.

Olivia held Abigail's gaze for a long moment. "Don't worry about the mess, Abigail. I'll help you put your desk back together."

Abigail cleared her throat, reminding herself that now was not the time to fall apart. She squeezed Olivia's hand, grateful for her support. "Thank you. The police should be here soon. We won't touch anything until they have a chance to see it."

"Won't they want to know if anything is missing?" Olivia asked.

"Oh. Yes, that's probably true." Abigail forced herself to step further into the room. She couldn't help but search each corner to see if Simmons lurked there.

"You'll need to look through your papers, Abigail." Irene glanced at the items on the floor, her distress obvious. "Though I can't imagine him wanting any of those."

"Actually, if he was smart, that's exactly what he would've taken. I have some brilliant investment ideas jotted down. He could triple his money in short order if he—"

She caught the look Irene gave her and stopped mid-sentence. She was well aware of what her stepmother thought of her financial adventures. Never mind that her skills were creating a dowry for the girls. "I will check them. What of the ornaments? Was there anything of value in here?"

Ponsford stepped forward to point at the collection of small statues that lay on the floor. "Those are probably the most valuable ones in here. Odd that he didn't take them if he wanted something easy to sell."

That only confirmed Abigail's suspicion as to the would-be thief's identity.

"You sure you don't want me to put the furniture to rights, miss?" Thomas asked.

"No. I want the police to see how destructive he was first."

The doorbell chimed and Ponsford hurried to

answer it.

"We've never had any problems before." Irene shook her head. "I still can't believe someone would break in during the middle of the day."

The muffled sound of voices came from the hall.

"Would you prefer to speak to the police while I check on Jenny?" Abigail asked.

"You speak with them, my dear. You're so much better at that sort of thing than I."

Abigail breathed a sigh of relief, grateful she'd have the chance to talk to the constable without her stepmother there. She could hardly reveal who she thought the suspect was with Irene in the room. If possible, she intended to keep Vincent Simmons a secret from her family.

Surely the police would believe her now.

A constable in a dark blue frock coat entered the room. He had a thick red mustache and a round face. Abigail was pleased to see he wasn't the same person she'd spoken with at the police station the previous day about Simmons escaping his hanging.

He glanced about the room, not bothering with a greeting. "Quite the mess he left, eh?"

"Indeed it is." Abigail stepped forward. "I'm Abigail Bradford and this is my stepmother, Lady Bradford."

"Constable Jennings, at your service."

Irene dipped her head at the man's bow. "I'll leave Abigail to give you the few details we know. We do hope you'll be able to find the person who did this and put an end to it."

"We do what we can, my lady. But crimes like this are a bit of a challenge to solve."

Irene's eyes went wide at his words.

"Thomas, could you see that repairs are made to the garden door? We'll need a better lock on it as well." Abigail hoped that would calm her stepmother.

"Of course, miss. I'll see to that immediately."

"I'll leave you two to discuss this." Irene smiled politely at the constable. "I'm certain we can expect results with such a capable man as you on the case."

The man beamed at her words. "I promise to do what I can, my lady."

"Well then, that is all we can ask, isn't it?" She winked at Abigail as she left the room.

Abigail bit back a smile at her stepmother's obvious attempt to flatter the constable. With no man in their household, they had to do what they could to be certain they were treated fairly. Irene was not above plying her feminine charms, if necessary.

Ponsford closed the door behind Irene and Thomas, remaining in the room. Abigail appreciated his support. The old butler had been with their family since Abigail's birth and often served as her sounding board. He knew all about Simmons' return to their lives and was as frustrated as she at recent events.

The constable cleared his throat and withdrew a small notebook from his breast pocket. "Now then, perhaps you could give me what information you know?"

"Ponsford?" She nodded at the butler to share what he knew which he did in precise words.

"And that was when you arrived home, miss?" the constable asked when Ponsford had finished.

"Yes. I can't see anything that's missing, but I haven't gone through all my papers yet."

The constable laughed. "I doubt the thief was after those. He'd be looking for small objects he could easily carry and sell."

Abigail bristled, unable to help herself. "My papers are extremely valuable. They contain detailed information about—"

Ponsford cleared his throat and raised a brow, a sure sign that she should reconsider her words.

She drew a deep breath, resigned to keep to the topic at hand. "I'm sure you're right. But those statues are quite expensive and would've been an obvious item for him to take."

The constable followed the direction of her finger and reached to pick up one. "Humph. True enough. Perhaps that's when your man here interrupted him. Can you give me a description of him?"

"I'm afraid I only caught a glimpse of the back of him." Ponsford proceeded to give him the few details he knew.

"We do have a suspect we would like to have you investigate," Abigail said.

"Oh? Why didn't you say so? Has someone bothered you before? Made threats?"

"Indeed they have. Vincent Simmons. He's only recently been released from Pentonville Prison. Our footman can give you his current place of residence."

Constable Jennings scribbled as she spoke.

Again, Ponsford cleared his throat.

Abigail knew exactly what he was thinking, but she wasn't going to bother explaining about Simmons' escape from the death sentence he'd received. She'd tried that approach with the constable yesterday and failed. In truth, she was certain he'd thought her a loon.

"He might also go by the name of Edward Smith." That was the best she could do. She glanced at Ponsford to see him nod in approval.

"He has an alias? Quite ambitious for a petty thief."

Abigail debated saying more, but decided less *was* more in this case. She'd let the constable do his own research and hopefully at the very least put Simmons back in jail.

"How do you know this Simmons character?"

"Ah—" How could she explain it? "He knew my father."

"Do you have any evidence to support your claim that he's the one who broke in?"

She looked to Ponsford for help.

"He was seen outside the house just last week, lurking about," the butler said. "Very suspicious behavior."

The constable looked up from his notes to study the butler. "Perhaps Lord Bradford is available that I might speak with him."

"He is deceased," Ponsford told him. "Ten years past."

"My condolences, miss." The constable dipped his head. "Terribly sorry."

"Thank you," Abigail said.

"It's just you and the lady then?"

"And my younger twin sisters."

"A house full of ladies? I'm sorry to say that not having a man in residence makes you an easier target."

Ponsford cleared his throat again, obviously affronted at the constable's comment, but the policeman remained unaware of the butler's annoyance.

"I was told someone was injured?" Constable Jennings asked, glancing between them.

"Yes, our maid Jenny was struck from behind."

"I'll want to speak with her. And your footman as well."

"Of course. Do you want to examine the room further? Perhaps see if there are any clues?"

The man frowned at Abigail's suggestion. "No point in that. If you find something as you're tidying up the place, let me know. But if the thief broke in during the day, chances are he's experienced and wouldn't have made the mistake of leaving behind evidence."

Abigail was growing more frustrated by the moment. "Could you tell me what your next steps are? How do you intend to approach Simmons?"

"Now now, miss. No need to worry your pretty little head about such matters. Leave it to us. It's what we do. I'll let you know as soon as I discover anything of interest."

"When can I expect that?"

He smiled condescendingly. "When I contact you. Some things can't be rushed."

"I'm sure you'll do the best you can," she replied, wishing she could demand immediate action.

Funny how when a woman was demanding, she acted like a shrew, but when a man did so, he was merely someone who knew what he wanted. She wasn't yet ready to be called a shrew, but that day might come if she didn't hear back from Constable Jennings soon.

"Perhaps you could take me to where the maid and footman are?" the constable asked Ponsford.

"Of course. This way, please." Ponsford led the way out the door.

"Good day, miss." He bobbed his head.

"Oh, wait. One more thing." Abigail paused, deciding how best to word this. "My stepmother, Lady Bradford, upsets quite easily. I'd rather you spoke only to me of anything that develops."

"Very well. Good day."

Abigail frowned at his retreating back. Somehow she wasn't reassured by the constable's visit. She felt no safer.

A glance about the wrecked room had her biting her lip with worry. Yet she could think of nothing else she could do to keep her family safe.

Stephen paused as he attempted to don his shirt, closing his eyes at the wave of pain that tore through him when he tried to lift his arm. "Damn!"

"Do you truly think this wise?" Daniel Farley asked as he stood nearby, watching.

"What? Do you think I should lie in bed for the next month?" Stephen disliked the anger that spewed out but seemed unable to do anything about it.

"Resting for more than two days would hardly hurt. You were *shot* after all," he said dryly. "Not to mention the surgery to remove the ball."

Stephen held back a growl. The whole situation was so frustrating. All because of that blasted woman! He hated the pain and weakness that filled him, especially since all he could do was lay there and think of her.

"I'm all for you getting up and moving around a bit. I just don't see the need for you to go downstairs tonight. Chances are that someone will jostle your shoulder and since you've insisted on keeping your injury as much of a secret as possible..."

Stephen sighed. As always, Farley was the voice of reason. "Fine. I'll satisfy myself with walking around my rooms a bit."

"And perhaps eat a decent meal for a change," Farley suggested. "Proper nutrition will aid your strength."

"You're worse than my mother ever was."

"Since the dear lady is no longer with us, it's my job to look after you when you refuse to look after yourself."

Resigned to being stuck in his room for another day, Stephen walked to the window and pulled back the drapes to stare out across the city, doing his best to ignore the pain in his shoulder and the weakness in his legs.

Dusk settled over the horizon, disguising the soot-covered buildings with a golden glow. Soon night would fall in full, and with it came another sort of darkness all together. The darkness that mankind brought. When the lights went out, sinners showed their faces.

But this night, it would have to get on without him. Someone else would have to try to keep the villains at bay, to keep the innocent safe, to keep the ignorant unaware of the evils out there.

He let the drapes fall back in place, but that didn't block out his own dark thoughts. This would be his second full night inside. That meant the restlessness would start. His own demons would plague him. With no outlet, they would circle in his mind in an attempt to drive him mad. He'd found the only thing that worked to hold them back was to go out into the streets and find people in need of aid.

"One more night will do no harm," Farley said softly, as though he'd read Stephen's thoughts.

Farley knew all of Stephen's secrets, or most of them anyway. Having a business partner and friend like Farley to cover his back when he needed it and to leave him in peace when he didn't was more than Stephen could've asked for.

Certainly more than he deserved.

"You're right," Stephen agreed but without conviction. "It's only one more night."

He walked to the crystal decanter on the dresser and poured himself a brandy with his bad arm, just to push himself a little. Then he took the edge off the pain with a gulp of the golden liquid. It burned a path down to his belly, spreading warmth as it went.

"Shall I stay?" Farley asked. "We could play some chess if you're up to it."

Stephen glanced to the ivory chessboard that sat on a small table near the fire. The black and white intricately carved pieces did not beckon him this night.

"No need. I'll be fine. I think I'll go home for a few days on the morrow, assuming you can handle things here?"

"Of course."

"You should go down to the gaming room to see if you're needed."

"As you wish."

Though he knew he'd probably hurt Farley's feelings, Stephen did not call him back. He did not want company. He wanted to brood with a glass of brandy while he contemplated big blue eyes and a golden aura.

CHAPTER FOUR

Abigail hurried into the library two days later, anxious to hear what Constable Jennings had discovered. Her hopes were high that he had Vincent Simmons in custody and had uncovered how Simmons had escaped from hanging. Her nerves were frayed from being on the watch for the man everywhere they went.

"Good day, Constable."

The thunderous look on the official's face was less than reassuring. "I would hardly call it that, miss."

"Excuse me?"

"The police are very busy. We do not take lightly to those who send us on wild goose chases."

Dread curled in the pit of her stomach. "I'm afraid I don't understand of what you're speaking."

His red mustache twitched with indignation. "I'm *speaking* of you providing false leads."

"I did no such thing!"

The sound that escaped the constable's mouth was difficult to interpret. He withdrew his notebook from his breast pocket. "Did you or did you not suggest that Vincent Simmons was the man who'd broken into your home?"

"Well, yes, I have every reason to suspect—"

"Simmons was hung ten years past. How could

you have possibly seen him outside your home of late?"

She gritted her teeth in frustration. "I have no proof, but he told me himself that he did not hang. That instead, he switched places with another man named Edward Smith—"

"Ah, yes, let us discuss this Smith person." The constable flipped the page of his notebook. "Edward Smith boarded a ship to America the day after he was released from prison with his wife and three sons."

"What? No, that can't be." Abigail frantically tried to think of some way to prove her claim. "Simmons told me the police wouldn't believe me."

"So you're saying you've spoken with a ghost, is that it?" The constable's brows rose to the brim of his hat. "You're one of those, are you? One who communicates with the deceased?"

"Heavens, no! I'm telling you that Simmons is not dead."

"I examined his death certificate myself."

"It was forged."

"What proof do you have of that?"

"None, but surely it's obvious." Abigail wanted to throttle the man and his ridiculous attitude. Speaking with the dead? Who was the crazed one here? "If you'd only listen to reason—"

"Miss, I mean no disrespect, but I can't be wasting my time chasing after people who either no longer exist or who have left the country." He rose from his chair and tucked the notebook back in his pocket. "Someone obviously broke into your home, but since nothing was missing and we have no real leads, we'll have to close the case unless additional evidence arises. Good day to you, miss."

Shocked at the turn of events, Abigail could only stand there, mouth ajar, while the constable showed himself out. She'd thought she'd found assistance to protect her family and now she was left with no one to aid her. Again.

"Was that the constable?" Irene asked as she came into the library.

"Yes, but he was of no help whatsoever."

"Why? What did he say?"

The entire story nearly poured forth before Abigail caught herself. She still didn't want to tell Irene of the return of Vincent Simmons. She knew he was real even if the constable refused to believe her. But she didn't want her family to know that. "He said without evidence of some sort, there's nothing he can do."

"That's ridiculous. What are we to do now?" Her brow furrowed and her gaze darted about the room as though hoping to find a solution tucked in a corner.

Abigail forced a reassuring smile to her lips. "Thomas has put better locks on all the doors. I don't expect we'll have another break-in."

"I'm sure you're right." The worry in Irene's eyes belied her words.

Abigail was at a loss. Now what was she to do? Simmons was obviously not going away on his own.

The next morning, Stephen sat at the desk in his library, staring at the papers spread before him. No matter how hard he concentrated, he couldn't make sense of them. With a growl of frustration he sat back, annoyed that he couldn't focus.

The quiet of his town house on Park Lane was a welcome change from the noise and energy of The Barbican. His injury felt better today, but given his lack of focus, perhaps he needed additional time to recover. He'd hoped that a change of scenery would improve both his mood and his health. He well knew the two were often closely connected.

His home was his private sanctuary. No one visited here, not even Farley. Stephen kept his life at the gaming hell and his personal life separate. Not that he had much of a personal life.

He picked up one of the papers, hoping to hold back the darkness that loomed over him once again. It helped to stay busy, to keep his mind occupied, but that wasn't always enough to fend off the shadows.

The headache that throbbed at his temple often indicated the beginning of another bout of the despair that stole days of his life at a time. The thought of suffering through one now, in addition to the gunshot wound, was more than he could bear. He was certain the bouts were a side effect of the experiment that had gone wrong nearly ten years ago.

Before him in the center of his desk was an electromagnetic device—fine copper wire coiled with transducers at either end. The apparatus was a miniature version of the one that had forever changed his life. As he stared at it, memories washed over him from those days that seemed a long time ago and yet as if they'd occurred yesterday.

His first few weeks at Cambridge had been lonely, but soon he'd met Michael and Lucas. Previously only acquaintances, the three of them became inseparable, even sharing the same tutor, Professor Grisby. The professor had provided wise advice, extra assistance and lively discussions the three friends had enjoyed.

Professor Grisby had been fascinated with electromagnetism—the ability to create and control a magnetic force with electricity. His excitement over its potential to aid mankind had been infectious. He'd hoped to develop many practical applications with its power and had involved the three friends in his research. One of their first experiments had been using the force to bend metal.

The challenge with all of their tests over those two years had been trying to control the velocity. And that had been where things had gone awry in their last experiment. Stephen should've stepped in and stopped it. He'd realized the flaw in their plan but had hesitated and the transducer had surged with power; electric currents had struck them all.

The memory of the jolt still made the hair on the back of Stephen's neck rise. He'd never before or since felt that level of pain—a stunning force that had ricocheted through his body. He'd tried to piece together what had happened after he'd been knocked unconscious. His memory of the entire incident was hazy at best. He'd woken to find a jagged cut across his chest and a lump on his head from striking the table he'd stood beside. The floor was littered with debris, the room filled with smoke.

Dizzy, his head pounding, he crawled to Michael first. He shook his unconscious friend, scared he'd lost him. After hearing a moan, Stephen had made his way to Lucas who'd been even closer to the transducer. He'd shoved pieces of debris off Lucas but hadn't been able to rouse him. The pulse beating at the base of his neck had been the only sign of life.

Professor Grisby had stood near one of the coils, next to the switch that powered the device. Stephen finally located the professor sprawled on the floor. The sight was something he'd never forget.

One side of his mentor's face was marred beyond recognition. His hands were burnt severely and his leg was turned at an odd angle. Fear roiled in Stephen's throat as he'd put a trembling hand to the professor's neck, hoping for a pulse.

There'd been nothing.

He'd gone for help, but the doctor had not been able to revive the professor. He'd told Stephen it was for the best—the damage Professor Grisby had sustained would've made surviving difficult, let alone having a normal life again.

Lucas's physical injuries had taken months to heal, but his mental and emotional wounds festered. He'd left for Brazil soon after he'd been physically able with nothing more than a gruff goodbye. As a second son, his presence in England wasn't required. Stephen could only surmise that Lucas had decided a change of scenery would make life somehow more bearable. Whether he'd gained the ability to read auras, Stephen didn't know, for Lucas had refused to speak of it before he'd left.

Michael still lived in London, not far from Stephen, though he might as well live in America for as often as Stephen saw him. Michael pretended as if nothing untoward had occurred, as if they hadn't been damaged and left with abnormal abilities. But Stephen knew better. Michael could see auras of success and failure. He'd greatly prospered since the accident. Many in London believed he had the most amazing luck. He seemed to have adjusted well to the change as he moved about in society easily, at least as far as Stephen knew.

Stephen didn't blame Michael for denying his aura-reading, but didn't feel as forgiving about Michael denying him. Michael treated him like a distant cousin twice removed, making Stephen realize that Michael blamed him for the accident.

The last time they'd spoken at any length had been at the professor's funeral. They'd been stunned and sick with disbelief that they'd lost their mentor, that what had seemed such a simple experiment had resulted in his death. Watching the professor's family—his sister and her children—as they grieved at the funeral had been heart wrenching and doubled his own grief.

And his guilt.

Why hadn't he stopped the experiment when he'd realized it would fail?

Stephen spun the device in his fingers. He'd conducted a few experiments of his own since then, trying to re-create what they'd done that night on a small scale. He'd hoped to reverse the affects—remove the curse they'd all received— that had left him abnormal, living on the fringes of society. But so far, he'd had no success. Certainly not to the scale needed to recreate what had happened.

The scar he bore across his chest, not far from the gun wound, often pained him when the weather changed. Worse was the deep misery that buried him in darkness, always accompanied by a headache so severe he could barely function. In addition was the damned aura reading, which was impossible to ignore.

His life might be imbalanced, but it was the best he could manage with the hand fate had dealt him.

"Lord Ashbury?" Winston stood at the doorway of the library.

"Yes?" He frowned, surprised his butler had bothered him. Winston was well aware of his preference to be left alone.

"There's a young lady here to see you."

Stephen stared at him, unable to comprehend such an occurrence, certain there had to be some sort of mistake. "A lady?"

"Her name is Miss Abigail Bradford. She insists it's important she speak with you."

A ringing noise sounded in his ears. "Abigail?

She's here?"

"Shall I send her away?" Winston seemed as puzzled by the situation as he.

"No. No, show her in."

Before Stephen could contemplate the wisdom of his decision, Winston had disappeared and soon after, Abigail entered the library. Immediately he realized he wasn't prepared to see her again so soon.

Or ever...for that matter.

Five days seemed like nothing.

His heart pounded. His mouth grew dry.

If not for her golden aura and those cobalt blue eyes, he might not have recognized her. Gone were the trousers and worn jacket. In their place was an attractive slim-fitting gown of dark blue, the skirt artfully draped to reveal a pleated cream-colored underskirt. A clever hat matched her attire, graced with black feathers. The hat made her eyes appear even larger. Her pale cheeks held a delicate hint of rose.

How she'd ever managed to pass as a boy was a miracle.

"Good day, Lord Ashbury." Her eyes held steady on his.

Trying to gather his senses, he let the silence linger a moment longer than was polite. He needed to make certain she knew she was not welcome to visit him, especially not at his home. In fact, he'd told her to stay away from him when they'd last spoke. "Come to check on my health? Or lack thereof?"

"I'm delighted to see you up and about. You appear to be recovering nicely." Her smile was strained, giving him hope he was making his point.

"No thanks to you." He held her gaze, not bothering to return her smile.

"I wanted to apologize again. I didn't mean to

shoot you."

"But you were prepared to shoot the man to whom you were speaking?" Though he'd thought on it long and hard, he couldn't imagine why she'd been in the East End dressed as such and with a gun, no less. Perhaps if he appeased his curiosity, his mind would let it go. Then he could forget her.

"In truth, I only wanted to frighten him, but I have to admit I was tempted. It would've solved my problem which seems to be escalating daily." She swallowed hard. "That man was supposed to hang for killing my father."

Sympathy stirred deep within him, much to his regret. "He was never caught?"

"Actually he was. Caught and convicted and sentenced to hang yet somehow he escaped. How that happened remains a mystery."

"I'm sure the police would be quite interested to hear your story."

Anger flashed briefly across her face. "I tried that, but they've accused me of giving them false information. Among other things." She dropped her gaze, causing him to wonder of what else they'd accused her. Then he reminded himself it was none of his business.

"If a peer was murdered, the police will be certain to punish the culprit."

"They think they did. Their records show he hung ten years ago."

She didn't look crazed, but he had to wonder. If she was lying, her aura would darken, but at the moment, it continued to glow. Yet her story made no sense. "Perhaps you're mistaken. Maybe the man isn't who you think he is."

Her bottom lip quivered and those eyes grew even larger. "I saw him. I saw him murder my father. I will never forget what he looks like."

"No. I don't suppose you will." Stephen knew all too well that there were some things a person never forgot.

"Simmons—that's the man with whom I was speaking when you interrupted—admitted his identity."

A slim gray spear spiked through her aura. Now she was lying...or at least exaggerating. He waited to see if she'd admit it.

"Well, perhaps not in so many words. But he recognized me. He knew exactly who I was. He tried to give me some other name with the story that he was just released from prison. Why else would he skulk about outside our home if he were not the same man? Even worse, he broke in to our house three days ago."

"If all that is true, why would he bother you? Do you think he seeks revenge?"

She swallowed hard, her gaze met his again. "That is my worst fear."

The truth of her statement was reflected in the depths of her eyes. That vulnerability made him long to draw her into his arms, to comfort her, to offer his protection. But if she knew the truth about him, she wouldn't welcome his assistance. Far from it. "Your situation appears to be a difficult one. I wish you well with it." He sat down, grateful the desk was between them which forced him to keep his distance.

Now, if only she'd take his hint and leave.

Instead, she did the opposite. She sat in the chair on the other side of his desk, making herself quite at home.

"I'm afraid I have an appointment I must see to," Stephen said, unable to believe she'd sat down uninvited.

He couldn't help but admire the tenacity of this woman. That had to be the reason he hadn't thrown her out already. It couldn't be because of her golden aura, or her sparkling blue eyes, or that slight dent in her chin.

Nor could it be because somewhere, in the depths of his soul, he was grateful she was here, sitting in his library.

"I'm here to ask for your help."

"I thought you were here to inquire about my health." He no longer held hope that he could annoy her with his rude behavior but couldn't resist trying. Never mind that he was starting to enjoy the challenge she presented.

"I already told you I was glad to see you're healing well and all that." She waved her hand as she scooted forward on the edge of her seat. "But you see, I could think of no one else who could aid me."

The last thing he wanted to do was get involved with this woman in any way. Especially since after their brief meeting, he couldn't get her out of his mind. Imagine what might happen if he had more time with her. No. The best course of action—the only course of action—was to get her to leave his home. Now.

"I'm terribly sorry, but as I said, I must be going." He rose, careful not to jar his shoulder. "Your best course of action would be to contact the police. Perhaps if you speak with someone in charge, they'll be more sympathetic to your plight."

But she didn't budge. She kept her seat, those big blue eyes peering up at him from beneath her hat. "He broke in. Though we've replaced the locks, he could do so again. Please, my lord. I am begging you for help. I have no one else to ask."

"Surely you have some male relative you could prevail upon."

"There's only me, my stepmother, and my younger twin sisters. Uncle Reginald remains in the country. He does not care for the city or for us for that matter. There's no one else."

Abigail studied the lord, trying to determine

the best way to convince him to help her. He looked much as she remembered although seeing him in broad daylight in clean clothes certainly enhanced his attractiveness.

His green eyes, framed by dark brows, were all the more arresting set against his tanned skin. His straight brown hair swept to the side. While his expression was less than friendly, she couldn't stop the flutter in her stomach at the solid strength of him.

His clothing was modest but impeccable. She was certain his broad shoulders had more to do with his true form than his well-cut morning coat. A waistcoat of the same cloth was just visible in the coat's opening and a white shirt with a down-turned collar set off his dark skin. A knotted black silk neck scarf completed the suit.

His attractiveness and confident manner were appealing in a way she'd never before encountered. He appeared capable of handling anything, including forcing Vincent Simmons to leave her family alone.

He was exactly the sort of man she needed.

Or rather, what the *situation* required.

How could she get him to agree to do as she asked? Pleading with him seemed to have no effect. Perhaps cold, clear logic was the key.

"Since you interfered with my questioning of the man, it's only right you fix the problem." She eased back in her chair, prepared to make her argument. She ruthlessly shoved aside her guilt at shooting him. In some respects, that had been as much his fault as hers. Or so she kept telling herself.

"The only thing I interfered with was you putting a bullet through him."

"I was trying to get the truth out of him when you...got in the way." Everything had happened so fast. Would she really have pulled the trigger if

Lord Ashbury hadn't come along?

"I'm sure." He nodded as though pacifying her.

She held back her ire. Whether or not he believed her didn't matter. She rose to face him, desperate to convince him. "You are my only hope."

"You need the police, not me."

"Their lack of response has forced me to take action into my own hands."

He hesitated for the barest moment then shook his head. "I'm sorry. I can't help you. I bid you good day." He gestured toward the door as though he couldn't wait to be rid of her.

She promptly sat again, deciding he'd have to physically remove her if he didn't agree to assist her. She had no other options. "No."

"*No*? I don't believe you're in a position to refuse." He moved around the desk to stand before her chair, staring at her in disbelief.

"Aren't I?" With a smile, she looked up at him, waiting for him to realize she had no intention of leaving until he agreed to help her.

His eyes narrowed. "You are a very determined woman."

"I know what I need."

He leaned down, bracing his good hand on the back of her chair.

She jerked back as her world tilted. He was so close she could see small flecks of gold in his green eyes. Her gaze drifted down to his lips. Even as she watched, he drew nearer and her heart stopped. She instinctively tipped her mouth to meet his.

Perhaps she needed him even more than she'd realized.

In different ways than she'd first thought.

"Go to the police." He spoke slowly, enunciating each word. "Keep talking to them until you get someone who will listen."

A moment passed before the meaning of his words sank in. Surely her disappointment wasn't because he hadn't kissed her. No. It was because he refused to help, she reminded herself. Anger quickly replaced the disappointment.

"I've already told you. I did that," she snapped, annoyed with herself and her ridiculous response to this man. Her throat burned with the effort to control how she felt, how desperate she was to put Simmons and everything he represented behind her. "I need you." She swallowed and tried to make herself clearer. "I need your *help*."

She stared at him, trying to gauge his reaction. He was her answer. She was convinced of it. If only she could convince him. "Please."

His gaze held hers for the length of a breath then slowly lowered to her lips. Her breath caught in her lungs as heat curled through her, wrapping its tendrils around her.

He drew back and straightened with a grimace, breaking the spell. "I cannot help you."

Distraught, her thoughts ran wild as she tried to think of any means, fair or foul, to force him to help her. "In exchange for your assistance, I offer my silence about your nefarious activities."

"What?"

"Your association with The Barbican. That's hardly an appropriate activity for a lord."

He scoffed and turned away to pace the room. "Now you intend to blackmail me? Very unladylike of you." His light tone mocked the gravity of her threat.

"I will do anything it takes to protect my family. Anything." She tried to make her tone menacing, but wasn't sure what that should sound like.

He turned to look at her, his gaze resting just above her head. She resisted the urge to check her hat to see if it sat askew.

"While you are obviously adept at many things, blackmail is not your forte."

"How do you know what I'm capable of?"

"Let's just say I'm a good judge of character," he said with another glance at her head.

"It would be quite simple," she continued as though he hadn't already refused her multiple times. "I have the address of his lodgings and his favorite pub. It would only take a few moments of your time."

He hesitated and she hoped he was seriously considering helping her. Had she finally captured his sympathy?

"You want someone to warn him?" he asked. "That's all?"

She bit her lip, for in her heart she feared more than that would be necessary to make Simmons go away. But it was a start. "Yes. Precisely." She waited, her breath caught in her throat, hoping he would agree at last.

A long moment of silence followed. "Very well then. I'll see what I can do."

She jumped to her feet, so grateful that it was all she could do to maintain her composure. "Thank you so very much, my lord."

"But know this." His narrowed gaze met hers, her heart skipping a beat at the anger she saw there. "You will not visit my home again. Do I make myself clear?"

CHAPTER FIVE

Farley looked up from his desk as Stephen strode into his office at The Barbican. "There you are. I thought perhaps you'd decided to abandon me in favor of returning to polite society."

Stephen scoffed. "Hardly."

"I'm pleased to see that you're recovering so well."

In response, Stephen raised his arm, far from pleased with his progress. "It's coming along, I suppose."

"These things take time." Farley folded his hands on the desk as he watched Stephen pace the room.

How like Farley to refrain from asking where he'd been. "I have been wasting time chasing phantoms."

"Pardon me?"

With a heavy sigh, Stephen raked his good hand through his hair. "I'm sure you remember Miss Bradford."

Farley frowned for a long moment before his eyes widened. "The woman who shot you?" The look of shock on his face was almost comical.

"Indeed."

"And?"

"She came to my residence."

"No!" Farley well knew how little Stephen

cared for visitors of any sort at his home.

"She insists she needs my help."

Stephen explained the nature of her problem and how he'd reluctantly agreed to assist her. He left out the reason he'd consented as that still escaped him.

"Despite the name and address Miss Bradford provided, Vincent Simmons is nowhere to be found. No one seems to have seen or heard of him."

"Perhaps the police were right," Farley suggested. "Maybe she provided false information to you as well."

"No. I saw the man myself in Alsatia that night. He has her worried." The fear in her eyes had been all too real. That had been what had convinced him to aid her in the first place. Not that it had done any good.

"I hate to burden you with other issues." Farley tugged at the end of his mustache, a sure sign that something was bothering him.

"What is it?"

"We've received a report from one of the workhouses that several of the boys there have gone missing."

He and Farley had a network of 'associates' throughout the city who kept them informed of any unusual activity. These contacts ranged from children to the elderly.

"First it was only one, but now two more have disappeared."

"Did you check if Smithson or Rudley took them?" The two men, both owners of manufacturing plants, were notorious for abusing child labor laws. They'd been warned against it, but greed often took precedence over obeying the law. The small forms of children were ideally suited to fit into the narrow areas of the machines used in textile mills and the ventilation shafts of coal mines.

"Excellent idea. I'll send someone to make inquiries."

"Are they certain they didn't run away?" Often boys took it upon themselves to obtain jobs of a less than desirable nature to earn money. Anything to help their families get out of the workhouse. But that was often where the trouble started. If they started down that path at a young age, it was difficult to pull them back onto the right side of the law.

That was why Stephen chose to fund several workhouses and orphanages with profits from The Barbican. He also encouraged the children to attend school when possible and found legitimate places to employ them when they reached the proper age. By providing such opportunities, he hoped to keep them off the streets when they grew older. Doing so would give him less to do at night. The fewer thieves and cutthroats on the street, the better.

In truth, the auras of those struggling between good and bad tugged at him, especially in children. If he could help prevent them from being forced to choose a life of crime so they could help feed and house their families, it eased his own torment. Aiding others couldn't make up for the death of Professor Grisby or the injuries to his friends, but it helped chase away the shadows that haunted him at night.

"Lawrence is the one who reported it to me," Farley said, mentioning a lad who worked as one of their 'associates'. "He thinks trouble is afoot. He knew one of the boys quite well, and the boy had never mentioned any plans to leave."

Stephen considered what other action could be taken. A niggling sense of worry came over him. "I think Lawrence could be right. Have the other lads keep their eyes and ears open for more information. We'll make some inquiries of our own."

"Very well, my lord."

"I fear additional efforts on Miss Bradford's request will have to wait until we can track down those missing boys."

"As long as she doesn't intend to come after you with her gun again," Farley replied with a chuckle.

Stephen nearly shuddered at the thought. "Perhaps her ghost has disappeared on its own. Then she will no longer plague me." The idea of never laying eyes on the woman again should've pleased him.

Why didn't it?

Please advise the status of our project.
A.B.

There, Abigail thought as she reviewed the message she'd penned. Surely that was secretive enough. She hadn't revealed her identity or the nature of their association.

Three days had passed since she'd spoken with Lord Ashbury and she'd heard nothing.

Absolute silence.

Infuriating silence.

In truth, she'd expected the matter to be resolved by now. How long did it take to locate a criminal and give him a warning? Especially since she'd given him Simmons' name and address. She hoped a man involved in a gaming hell could manage such a thing with ease.

"Abigail? Are you ready?" Her stepmother's voice carried from the foyer into the library.

Abigail sighed. An afternoon spent shopping was not high on the list of things she desired to do. However, her sisters had decided that none of her gowns would do for the Mortenson's ball. The new one required another fitting this afternoon, and the girls insisted she needed to select the proper accessories for it as well. Abigail suspected the true reason they wanted to shop was to purchase something for themselves.

"I'll be right there, Mother."

As she watched her mother, Sophia, and Olivia walk out the door, she handed the envelope to Ponsford, the butler. "Please see this is delivered as quickly as possible."

Ponsford read the address then gave her a long look. "Do you think it wise to contact him? I thought we agreed that you'd keep your distance."

She'd told both Ponsford and Thomas of her decision to request Lord Ashbury's assistance for their problem. Ponsford, well connected to the servants' gossip that wound its way through the city, had cautioned her. Rumors circulated as to the lord and his activities, some describing him as odd while others called him dangerous. That particular description made her uneasy, but it also made him the perfect man for what she needed.

"We need to know if he's taken any action. I don't want him to forget."

"Very well, miss," Ponsford said with obvious reluctance. "I'll see that it's delivered."

Abigail hurried outside to join her family, giving a nod to Thomas who held the carriage door for her. She settled in beside her stepmother, letting the chatter of the girls flow around her. The day was overcast but pleasant enough for an expedition such as this one.

"Mother, are we going to the lace-maker's first?" asked Olivia.

"We'll be back in time for tea, won't we?" Sophia asked.

"Wouldn't it be lovely to use some ostrich feathers if we purchase new hats?" Olivia's hopeful expression made Abigail smile as she knew what Irene's answer would be. Irene doted on the girls but kept a firm rein.

"Feathers of any sort are not appropriate for a girl of your age." Irene shook her head.

"What about some striped ribbon?" Abigail suggested before Olivia could protest. "Perhaps you could tie an elaborate bow with it."

Sophia's blue eyes grew wide at the suggestion. "Yes, let us try that, Livie."

"Shall we pick up the hats first?" Abigail asked, well aware the girls would be more patient at the dressmaker's if they'd already made their purchases.

After several stops, they continued down Regent Street to the lace-maker's. Olivia still pouted about not being able to use feathers but soon forgot her disappointment at the many choices of lace. The girls contemplated options as though their very lives depended on their decision.

To pass the time, Abigail stepped outside for some fresh air.

Then she saw him. Vincent Simmons, as bold as could be.

Something about the way he leaned against a lamppost across the busy street caught her eye, for it was the same pose he'd taken outside their home. Her heart pounded and chills raced down her spine.

Acting nonchalantly, she turned and studied the samples of lace displayed in the window. She kept her head tilted down, but lifted her gaze until she could see Simmons' image reflected in the glass. His appearance was more respectable than when she'd last seen him. His jacket seemed fitted and cleaner, his bowler hat almost fashionable. But his posture and features, even at this distance, were unmistakable.

She bit her lip, considering what action she

should take. Thomas was with the carriage at the end of the crowded street, too far away to be of any assistance. Did she dare confront Simmons herself?

Anger washed through her. This should not be happening! She'd requested Lord Ashbury's assistance to take care of Simmons, yet here he was. In broad daylight no less. Lord Ashbury owed her an explanation.

Holding tight to her anger, she stepped back into the shop. "Mother? I'm going across the street to..." She looked over her shoulder to see what store she could use as an excuse. "To look for buttons. I'll be back directly."

Irene frowned. "Are you in need of buttons?"

"I thought they might have something the girls would like. I'll only be a few moments." She smiled brightly and gave a little wave, hoping she'd pulled off her small deception.

Without looking in the direction of Simmons, Abigail wandered down the street, pausing to look in several of the windows. At last, she crossed to the other side and made her way toward where she'd last spotted him.

"Abigail! What a pleasant surprise."

Abigail started at her name being called from across the crowded sidewalk. She caught sight of Catherine Vandimer waving and nearly groaned with dismay. "Catherine! How lovely to see you."

"And you as well in that rather...interesting gown." Catherine looked up and down the length of her.

Near Abigail's age, she was wealthy, attractive and on the hunt for a title but apparently not for friends. Her catty comments were annoying, and she had a well-deserved reputation as a gossip.

Catherine's father had only recently made loads of money from a South American mine. Now that she was an heiress, Abigail had no doubt

Catherine would soon be engaged to some titled lord who had no idea what he was getting himself into. In the mean time, Abigail felt a sort of kinship with her since she didn't fit into polite society that well either.

Catherine's timing today couldn't have been worse. Heart pounding, Abigail risked a glance over her shoulder to where Simmons stood.

Or rather, where he *had* stood.

Panicked, she searched the busy street but didn't see him anywhere. With a sigh of dismay, she turned back to Catherine.

Good manners dictated that Abigail visit with the woman when what she really wanted was to walk away. While she refused to sink to Catherine's level, she couldn't resist giving a subtle dig of her own. "Yes, well, we don't all have the time to dedicate to fashion that you do."

"If it's a matter of time, I'd be happy to share what I— Abigail? Whatever is wrong?" Catherine asked, as she noted Abigail looking around.

"I...I thought I saw someone I recognized." She knew he watched her still. She could feel his gaze on her, could feel his smile at having outwitted her once again. Blast him!

"Who is it? Perhaps I can help you search," Catherine offered.

Abigail's gaze caught Catherine's curious expression and realized how odd her behavior must seem. She didn't need the woman spreading rumors, not when she was trying to keep secrets from Irene.

"You're too kind." Abigail forced a smile. "Never mind. It's of no importance." She drew a breath and tried to act naturally. She'd be damned if she'd let Simmons know how much he upset her. She gestured toward the lace-maker's shop as she kept a vigilant eye on the area surrounding it. "Do come and say hello to Mother and the twins. They'll be delighted to see you."

Catherine seemed to relax as she discussed the lace she'd found at another shop whose products were apparently far superior to the store where Irene and the girls were. Abigail listened absently, the quality of lace the last thing on her mind.

She would not let Simmons hurt her family.

She would not let him intimidate her.

His stalking of her and her loved ones would end.

A visit to Lord Ashbury was now on her agenda for the afternoon. He'd better have a good reason for this delay. What could be taking him so long? If he wanted to lure Simmons into the open, all he had to do was spend some time in her company. In fact, she'd insist on it.

Or perhaps he'd already warned Simmons, but the murderer hadn't heeded his warning. She'd advise Lord Ashbury that he needed to be sterner and threaten Simmons with something. Anything.

Simmons would show himself again, and when he did, she'd be ready. With or without Lord Ashbury's help.

Stephen stepped out the side door of The Barbican into the damp London air. A thick fog had settled over the city shortly after midday and continued to retain its hold into the late afternoon with no sign of easing.

Another boy had gone missing from a different workhouse, bringing the total to four. Stephen intended to visit the place to see if anyone had seen anything. He and Farley's sources had yet to turn up clues. The matter was growing increasingly worrisome.

He glanced up and down the street only to stop short when he saw a woman alighting from a modest carriage nearby. Dressed in dark blue from head to toe, her face was hidden by a thick veil. She turned to speak with her footman, but they were too far away for Stephen to hear their conversation.

Not that he needed to. He knew all too well the identity of the woman. The golden glow of her aura gave her away. Longing filled him as he stared, his heart thudding rapidly. He pushed aside the feelings and blamed his thundering heart on the anger that filled him. She had no business taking the risk of coming near The Barbican. If she was seen here, her reputation would be ruined.

He strode forward, noting when she caught sight of him, her body freezing for a brief moment before turning to face him.

"What do you think you're doing?" he asked, torn between throttling her for taking such an unnecessary risk and pulling her into his arms.

"I came to speak with you," she answered.

"Have you no care for your reputation? Why on earth would you come here?"

"Because you told me not to visit you at your home again," she replied, her annoyance evident in her tone. "How else could I speak with you if I didn't come here?"

With a near growl, he glanced around to make certain no one had seen them. Satisfied, he gestured toward the carriage, careful not to touch her. Doing so would tempt him more than he could bear.

"I'm not leaving," she protested. "Not until I've spoken with you."

"You have spoken with me. Now go." He had no choice but to take her elbow to urge her into the carriage. Despite his glove, his fingers tingled at the contact. Imagine what would happen if he actually held her in his arms.

She dug in her heels and refused to budge. "I have something important to discuss."

"So important that you'd risk being seen at a gaming hell?" Her determination amazed him. Never had he met someone so focused on what they wanted.

"No one will recognize me." She paused to look back at him over her shoulder. "How did *you* recognize me?"

"If I knew who you were, someone else will as well." He hoped she wouldn't realize he hadn't answered her question. "Now get in."

"Not unless you come along as well. I must speak with you."

The footman cleared his throat, catching Stephen's attention, then tipped his head toward an approaching figure of a man.

"Very well," Stephen reluctantly agreed. Anything to get her off the street before someone saw her.

As Miss Bradford stepped into the carriage, Stephen turned toward the footman, noting he was the same servant who'd accompanied her into Alsatia. "Is she always this stubborn?"

"If you only knew," the footman whispered. "Not much can be done to stop her when she gets her mind set on something. Believe me, my lord, I've tried."

"I would suggest you try harder. Take us around the area."

Stephen followed the lady into the carriage, sitting opposite of her. Her sweet fragrance curled around him inside the enclosed space. The vibrant golden light of her aura disoriented him, making it difficult to gather his thoughts.

She pulled back her veil and tucked it into the brim of her hat. Those big blue eyes held steady on his. That didn't help him in the least. He refused to be distracted by the slight dent in her chin, by the ache of need filling him. The power she held over him surprised him. He wasn't quite sure what to do about it.

"Well?" she asked. "Have you any news for me?"

"If I had something to tell you, you would've received word."

"I saw him earlier today, so I have to assume you've done nothing thus far." The annoyance in her tone was quite obvious.

"Simmons came to your home again?"

"No. But he was outside the shop I was in on Regent Street this very morning."

"Did he approach you? Threaten you?" His blood chilled at the thought of her in danger.

"No."

Something about the way she drew out the denial had him questioning her further. "But you approached him?"

Heat crept up her cheeks even as she raised her chin. "What choice did I have? Besides, it was broad daylight on a crowded street."

"Need I remind you that this Simmons fellow is dangerous?"

The lord grasped Abigail's elbows and tugged her forward before she knew what he was about. The movement of the carriage turning a corner tipped her forward. Her breath caught as awareness rippled through her. His strength took her by surprise. It had been only nine days since he'd been shot, yet he showed no sign of weakness.

Those green eyes bored into hers as his fresh, clean scent filled her lungs. It struck her that, for the second time that day, she'd placed herself in danger.

"Did you not see the knife he held the last time you confronted him?"

"Ah..." How was she supposed to think when he loomed over her? His lips were close enough to—

"He could stick that knife in your side before anyone noticed he held it."

His hands held her waist to make his point. She jolted forward at the contact, her nose bumping his chin.

"Oh!" Her lips parted. She couldn't take her gaze off his mouth. His hands felt warm on her waist despite the layers that separated them.

He gave her a little shake as he spoke. "Do *not* approach him again."

She looked up into his eyes and tried to swallow. What had she been trying to say? Oh, yes. "Someone has to and you're not taking any action. I don't understand why you haven't yet spoken with him." Lord Ashbury didn't seem to realize how desperate she was to put an end to the threat that Simmons represented.

"For one, Simmons vacated the lodging house you discovered and hasn't been seen at the pub. Secondly, a more pressing matter is now requiring my attention."

She drew in a breath to steady her nerves only to catch his clean scent once more. It reminded her of the sea with a hint of bay rum. Compared to the foppish dandies she'd met who smelled of strong cologne in an effort to mask other odors, Lord Ashbury smelled refreshing. She looked up at him from beneath her lashes, hoping to hide his affect on her.

What on earth was wrong with her?

A mere look from this man had her fumbling like a young girl, uncertain of herself. And when he touched her—regardless of the layers of clothing that separated them—awareness speared through her to her toes. The sensation was very unsettling, not to mention unfamiliar, but oh, so intriguing. No man had ever made her feel anything like this.

He rubbed his forehead as though he had a

headache before scowling at her. "I did not promise a particular schedule."

"If you can't find him, simply say so. There's no need to become defensive."

The glare he gave her would've withered others, but luckily she was no fainting wallflower. "Perhaps we should locate him together," she suggested, her enthusiasm growing as the idea took hold.

"I'm experienced in such matters. You may rely on me to take care of it."

"You must forgive me for failing to trust you," Abigail said. "After all, I only have your word."

"That should be enough."

"Hmm. I would suggest we plan some sort of outing for the morrow to see if Simmons appears."

"No."

"Probably not Regent Street again. What of Hyde Park?"

"Miss Bradford—"

"Or perhaps Piccadilly would be better?"

"The two of us seen together will only complicate matters."

She frowned, not sure what he meant. "How so?"

"I'm an unattached gentleman and you a lady. If we're seen together in public, certain conclusions would be drawn."

"Oh, but—"

"We wouldn't want the *ton* to latch on to the notion that we are involved in any way."

She bit her lip, pondering the ramifications of what he'd said.

"I would remind you," he continued, moving to the edge of his seat, "that your visit here today is highly inappropriate."

"True." She blinked and eased back, suddenly uncomfortable with his proximity.

"I think it best we don't meet again." He

tapped his gloved finger on her nose. "And do *not* confront Simmons."

A spark of awareness flashed through her, mingled with fear.

But she couldn't afford to let him intimidate her. "I will do what I see fit—"

A small smile played at the corner of his mouth. "Do you never cease arguing?"

She stiffened when his lips took hers, shock holding her still. The heat from his lips melted her from the inside out. A tiny moan escaped her mouth and he groaned in response.

Her anger slipped away and desire took its place. All thoughts flew from her mind and she could only feel. Much more than simple heat spiraled through her.

So this was desire...

For so long now, she'd thought herself incapable of feeling it.

She tilted her head, wanting more of what he offered. His hand cupped her cheek, the other holding her arm, steadying her from the sway of the carriage. With more courage than she'd thought she had, she reached up to rest her hand on his broad shoulder, careful that it wasn't the one she'd shot.

For a long moment, she allowed herself this pleasure. She allowed herself this longing for things that could never be. This man was not for her, but that didn't mean she didn't wish he was.

He eased back, breaking the fragile moment that she'd never forget.

She opened her eyes and couldn't stop a smile from spreading across her face. She knew exactly why he'd kissed her, and while a small part of her was sad that it wasn't because he desired her, she was grateful he'd tried to distract her from her purpose. It had been a lovely distraction and had taught her something new about herself. She was capable of passion. How wonderful to know.

"You are a very clever man, Lord Ashbury. Of that I have no doubt. But you will not be rid of me so easily."

CHAPTER SIX

The next morning, Stephen sat astride his black gelding, tapping his riding crop against his leg as he waited near the entrance of Hyde Park, still not certain how this meeting had come to pass.

He'd said no.

In fact, he'd said it several times. Yet here he was. Something about Abigail made her impossible for him to resist. He admonished himself for thinking of her with such familiarity but he couldn't seem to help himself.

His mood lightened as he saw her riding toward him, her footman following behind. She sat well in the saddle, and her taste in horseflesh couldn't be faulted. The chestnut gelding with a white blaze on its face and matching white stockings tugged at the reins, but she held them with a firm hand.

Stephen had great sympathy for the servant trailing her as he now knew this woman refused to listen to anyone's requests for caution. For some odd reason, he found himself admiring that quality about her.

Her riding outfit was tailored to mimic a man's suit, a deep shade of rose with cream-colored piping that made her skin glow. The taut material formed to her every luscious curve, the side saddle rounded her hip, and once again he found himself thinking things about her that he shouldn't. A matching hat sitting at a jaunty angle completed the ensemble. Her black hair was pulled back into a tight chignon with not even one loose strand dangling to tease him. Yet he realized the slender column of her neck was the true temptation. Nibbling there would be a sweet beginning. Did her luminescent complexion extend to the rest of her body?

The image the thought created made him stir with desire, their heated kiss still fresh in his mind. Her innocence had been obvious, equal parts warning and allure. He couldn't say why she appealed to him, but something about her struck him like a flame to tinder.

She waved and smiled at him. He was proud of himself for refraining from returning her wave. Instead, he surveyed the area—anything to cool his blood.

"Good morning, my lord."

He dipped his head in acknowledgement while sternly reminding himself of their purpose here. "Have you seen Simmons?"

She glanced over her shoulder at her footman who shook his head. "Not yet. Beautiful day, don't you think?"

He glanced up at the sky, not having noticed the weather. Clouds were scattered across the pale blue expanse, but the sun prevailed, an unusual event in the spring. "Indeed. Shall we?"

He led the way then slowed for her to ride alongside him.

"You could at least act like you're here to enjoy the day rather than searching for someone."

He raised a brow at her. Did she truly think that necessary?

She shook her head. "You're as bad as Ponsford."

"Who is Ponsford?"

"Our butler. He is constantly raising his brow at me."

"Then you make a habit of doing inappropriate things?"

"According to him," she said ruefully.

"And what of your stepmother. Does she find your behavior untoward?"

"She'd prefer me to be more traditional. Luckily, the twins take much of her attention."

Though more questions crossed his mind, he held them back. There was no point in learning more about this woman or her family. Within a few days, his association with her would end. The thought did not please him at all.

"What of you, my lord? Do you have siblings?"

"No."

"Parents?"

"Deceased."

She gave an exasperated huff. "Has no one versed you in the art of small talk?"

"I'm not here to visit with you. I'm here to find Simmons."

"There's no reason we can't enjoy a friendly conversation while we see if he appears."

He said nothing, hoping she'd take the hint. Conversing with her wouldn't be wise. The more he knew about her, the more he wanted to know. He needed to keep his distance from her if he wanted to keep his sanity.

The park was busy with people in carriages, on horseback, and on foot. Ladies were well dressed in riding attire with matching ornate hats, ostrich plumes dancing with the movement of their horses. Men wore dark coats, top hats and brandished riding crops, all taking in the scenery nature provided as well as the interesting parade of people.

Abigail's footman rode a respectable distance

behind them and seemed to watch carefully for Simmons as well.

"Couldn't you pretend as though we're conversing?"

"Why? You don't seem to care what people think." Already he could feel the stares of others. It bothered him that she didn't try to better protect her reputation.

"Abigail?" a feminine voice called out from behind.

Stephen turned to see an attractive lady riding toward them.

"Catherine. Two days in a row. How surprising," Abigail said with a laugh, color high in her cheeks.

The woman looked with wide eyes between him and Abigail as introductions were made.

Miss Catherine Vandimer seemed to be Abigail's age. Her aura was a muddy brown, confirming his first impression of her—outwardly friendly but inwardly unpleasant. Another member of the *ton* whose thoughts did not match her behavior. A fraud for certain.

Stephen didn't remember meeting her before, but she acted as though she was acquainted with him. He never went to balls or other events as the only purpose for such affairs was to find a wife, and that was not possible for him. Not with his secrets.

"When I spoke with you yesterday, you never mentioned your acquaintance with Viscount Ashbury."

Miss Vandimer's smile and obvious interest made Stephen certain he'd been the topic of their conversation. He nearly smiled. It seemed Abigail had been making some inquiries of her own.

"Didn't I?" Abigail glanced at him as her aura dimmed. Clearly she was uncomfortable at the conclusions her friend seemed to be drawing.

Miss Vandimer's speculation about their relationship was obvious. She had a hard edge to her, a brittle beauty betrayed by the tightness of her smile and the calculating look in her eyes.

Her kind was common in society, putting her own desires above anyone else's, intent on trapping the most eligible nobleman to whom she could latch on. Stephen dismissed her, his attention returning to the search for Simmons.

Abigail quickly changed the subject. "Are you out to enjoy this fine day?"

"Actually I'm meeting someone. There he is now." She smiled over her shoulder.

Stephen looked to see who was joining her. Surprised, he drew a slow breath. Perhaps America wasn't so far away after all. Michael Drury, Lord Weston rode toward them. His eyes narrowed when he saw Stephen.

"Ashbury."

"Weston." Stephen couldn't help but regret that their once close friendship had been reduced to awkward, one-word greetings. No aura was visible around Michael. Stephen had never been able to see it. He could only conjecture that it was because they'd both been affected by the accident.

Abigail's curiosity rose as she watched the two men, the tension in the air palpable. What history did they have that made them so wary of one another?

"You're already acquainted?" Catherine asked with her usual forthrightness.

"Old friends," Lord Weston responded. His clipped words made Abigail think they weren't friends any longer.

"Old indeed," Lord Ashbury added, a note of regret to his tone.

Catherine laughed nervously. "Well...Abigail, I don't believe you've met Viscount Weston?" She sent an intimate smile at her riding partner.

Lord Weston was an attractive man, near Lord Ashbury's age, with riveting blue eyes and black hair.

"A pleasure, I'm sure," Lord Weston said with a smile, making an effort to be friendly, which was more than Abigail could say for Lord Ashbury. "Amazing weather for May, isn't it?" he asked as he glanced around the park.

"Indeed," Abigail agreed as she glared at Lord Ashbury.

"I do hope the sun stays out for a time," Catherine added, but rather than admiring the bright day, she smoothed the deep blue skirt of her riding habit.

Abigail wondered if she thought the sheen of the material was more flattering in the sun then berated herself for being petty. As though she'd read Abigail's mind, Catherine took a long look at Abigail's riding attire.

Before she could criticize it as she often seemed to do, Abigail decided to change the subject. "Are any of you attending the Mortenson's ball?"

Catherine gave a sidelong glance at Lord Weston before answering. "I hope to, but our schedule is just so busy right now. My father and I have many invitations to consider."

Abigail caught herself before rolling her eyes. Instead, she glanced at Lord Weston to see his reaction to Catherine's unsubtle way of claiming popularity.

He gave Catherine a charming smile. "You'll have to let me know if you're attending so I can plan accordingly."

Catherine giggled and batted her lashes. "Of course."

For heaven's sake. Abigail decided she needed to escape before she said something to Catherine about her ridiculous behavior. Abigail looked at Lord Ashbury, hoping he would add to the conversation or better, suggest they be on their way.

"And what of you, Lord Ashbury? Will you be coming since Abigail will be there?" Catherine's question made Abigail's cheeks heat with embarrassment.

"I fear I'm already engaged that evening."

Catherine cast her a pitying look. "That's too bad. Lady Bradford will be there. Or perhaps you've already met her?"

Lord Ashbury didn't answer. Abigail could only guess what gossip Catherine might start spreading after this encounter. The last thing Abigail needed was for Catherine to speculate about her relationship with Lord Ashbury to her stepmother.

"Miss Vandimer, shall we be on our way?" Lord Weston asked, as he gave Abigail an apologetic smile. Whether it was for Catherine or Lord Ashbury's behavior, Abigail wasn't certain.

Within moments, the pair had bid her goodbye and rode off across the park, ignoring Lord Ashbury completely.

"That woman is irritating." Abigail watched Catherine tip her head back and laugh at something Lord Weston said.

"So it seems."

"Ah, he speaks." She turned to glare at her companion.

"Talking is often overrated."

She had to admit he had a point. Catherine was a perfect example. "Is Lord Weston an old friend or a former one?" she asked, noting his grim expression as he watched them leave.

"Depends on who you ask." Stephen's expression was unreadable, his gaze still on the departing couple as he raised his gloved hand to rub his temple.

"Do you have a headache?"

He dropped his hand abruptly. "No."

Exasperated at his obvious lie, she returned to the topic at hand. "Couldn't you at least pretend to be civil?"

He raised a brow in surprise at her question. "She's your friend. Not mine."

"Yes, but—"

"You've shown no regard for propriety. Therefore, I must conclude that it doesn't matter to you. In which case, what she thinks of me or us riding together doesn't matter either."

"Perhaps I should catch up with her and ask her not to speak of...us," Abigail suggested, still worried that Catherine would say something to Irene. Her stepmother didn't need any encouragement in that area.

"That would only make matters worse. The damage has already been done. She's a person of few scruples and wouldn't think twice at stepping over you to improve her own station in life."

Abigail looked at him with wide eyes, making him realize he'd said too much. "How interesting that you'd say such. Catherine wasn't truly rude. Most people are fooled by her, much like Lord Weston. I had no idea you were so insightful."

He tried to think of a plausible explanation for his comment but none came to mind. At times, he forgot he knew more about people's intentions than he should. Miss Vandimer's aura and mannerisms had shown malice, only a mild case of it perhaps, but malice none the less. The best they could hope for was that she was so diverted with Weston she'd forget about them.

At last with a shrug, he offered, "Never mind. I'm only guessing." That part was true at least. He could only tell that her intentions were not good.

Long after that moment, he continued to feel the weight of Abigail's stare. The woman was too observant for her own good.

The next morning, Mr. Nesbitt, Abigail's ever efficient solicitor, tidied some papers before handing them to her. "I think you'll find this of interest."

Abigail sat back in the chair of his office as she perused the documents. Doubt filled her as she read further. "Brazilian railway stock?"

Mr. Nesbitt shrugged. "You did ask for something with a chance for a high return."

She bit her lip. Catherine's father had made a fortune in a similar investment of late, but that didn't make her any less wary. "I am interested in a few investments that might offer a quick return for a higher risk, but this isn't what I had in mind. Would you invest your money in it?"

He stroked his generous mustache with one finger as he gave serious consideration to her question. She wondered if he'd grown the mustache and sideburns to make up for his receding hairline. He'd been gray-haired for as long as she could remember, but he looked much as he had fifteen years ago when she'd first met him. Her father had often brought her along to their meetings even though her stepmother had thought it highly inappropriate.

Mr. Nesbitt had served as her father's trusted advisor and had continued on as hers since her father's death. Soon after her father's funeral, he'd taken her aside and confirmed that her father's title and estate would go to her Uncle Reginald. That had come as no surprise, but then Mr. Nesbitt had gone on to explain the income from the inheritance would also go to her uncle and asked how she wanted to handle the debts her father had incurred that were not part of the estate.

Shocked, she hadn't known what to say or how

to proceed. She'd realized he'd come to her rather than Irene as her stepmother had been both distraught over her father's death and consumed with the twins. After much consideration, Abigail had decided to sell a few of her father's things that weren't entailed to pay the debts and create a small savings for them to live on.

She and Mr. Nesbitt had held weekly meetings to decide what to pay off first as well as how to invest the little money they had. She'd read everything she could on making investments and found she had an aptitude for finance. Mr. Nesbitt had proved to be an excellent advisor, but she listened to her own instincts first.

She'd soon paid off all her father's debts and provided a stable income for her family. The dowries for her sisters were growing as well. She enjoyed the challenge of it and knew the benefits outweighed the drawbacks. No matter if her unusual interest had chased away potential suitors. Her enthusiasm for the topic often resulted in her conversing about it. Few men appreciated her comments, but despite her mother's protests, she refused to hide her enjoyment of financial matters. She wasn't willing to give it up for anything or anyone.

"This sort of investment might carry more risk than necessary," Mr. Nesbitt admitted at last.

"I agree. I'd prefer a business venture closer to home. Let me think on the matter further and see if something comes to me."

"Might I inquire as to how the other matter is progressing?"

"Simmons?" Abigail set the papers on her lap with a huff. "Lord Ashbury is proving very difficult to deal with." She'd told Mr. Nesbitt of Lord Ashbury's involvement in the gaming den after swearing him to secrecy. She considered her solicitor both a friend and confidant, especially since they had no male relatives to guide her.

"He's reputed to be a bit of a loner, a man who walks his own path," Mr. Nesbitt offered.

"That is certainly true. My logic seems lost on the man."

Mr. Nesbitt chuckled then coughed politely in an attempt to hide his amusement at her frustration. "My apologies, miss. I'm certain your determination alone will persuade him to comply with your wishes."

"I'm starting to doubt that. I only want Simmons out of our lives. But it seems the task I asked Lord Ashbury to perform is not as simple as I'd hoped."

Simmons hadn't made an appearance at the park the previous day. Waiting for him to show up was unsettling to say the least. She'd even caught herself looking over her shoulder all the way to Mr. Nesbitt's office this morning.

"All the better that you involve someone like Lord Ashbury for the task, wouldn't you say?"

"Perhaps. I've never met a lord who acts as he does," she admitted. He never did what she expected. Was that why he unsettled her so?

"Lord Ashbury withdrew from society for the most part since that terrible accident. Happened at Cambridge, I believe. About ten years ago."

Abigail leaned forward, her attention caught. The man might be infuriating, but she couldn't get him out of her mind. "What accident?"

"I don't know many of the details, other than what was reported in the newspaper. He and his friends were injured and their professor killed when an experiment they were performing went awry."

A shiver ran down her spine. "What sort of experiment?"

He tugged at one end of his mustache. "No one seems to know. Rumors flew as to what they were doing. Something to do with electromagnetism I believe."

Her father had been killed about that time. How odd that they'd both had such a traumatic event occur so close together. "What sort of injuries did Lord Ashbury receive?"

"The paper didn't say. Whatever happened not only killed their professor, but seemed to end any friendship between the three men."

"Was Lord Weston one of the three?"

"Why yes. I believe he was. How did you know?"

"Only a guess." Abigail remembered the chasm between Lord Ashbury and Lord Weston from the previous day all too well. She couldn't help but wonder what had occurred to sever their ties. "Lord Ashbury seems to have recovered from any injuries he received."

Mr. Nesbitt shrugged. "Sometimes the worst injuries are not of a physical nature."

The documents lay forgotten on her lap as she thought of the darkness she'd sensed in the lord, of his secretiveness, of his frequent headaches. Mr. Nesbitt might be more right than he could've guessed.

CHAPTER SEVEN

Stephen stepped out of the fog-shrouded night and entered the Bull and Boar Tavern, a popular establishment in the East End. Though he braced himself before going into such places, the onslaught of auras with urges and thoughts spearing through them was overwhelming.

The air reeked of onions, unwashed bodies, and smoke. The crowd was thick on this night, and voices rose and fell as men argued over everything from the price of tea to who could whistle the loudest. Apprentices, clerks, dock workers, old and young alike drank ale and ate sausage rolls or porkpies. The few women there were either brazen with the hope of selling more than drinks or hardened to the lurid promises addressed to them.

The multitude of people and auras pressed in on him. Already a dull pounding had begun in his temple and nausea threatened. He paused, closing his eyes for a brief moment to shut out the images and regain his balance.

"Step aside," a man said as he pushed past Stephen toward the bar.

Stephen mumbled an apology and continued into the pub. Members of the *ton* were unlikely to recognize him should they happen to lower themselves to visit the dimly lit pub. His brown suit was dusty, out of fashion and had seen better days. A bowler hat sat low over his brow. He slouched a bit, shuffled his feet, and kept his chin down.

As best he could, he blended into the crowd, noting Farley and one of their associates had already arrived. Several times each week, they visited this tavern or another like it to collect information just as they did at The Barbican. Dreadful deeds were not limited to either the rich or poor.

While The Barbican carried a thin veneer of civility, the East End didn't bother with such frills. Stephen had long ago learned that establishments such as this one were best approached in two's or three's. As was their normal pattern, he didn't sit with Farley but instead found a place with his back to the wall a short distance away.

Stephen used his aura reading ability to help them decide whether to investigate people or situations further. If a black spike appeared in the aura of someone who looked as if they were up to no good, then he and Farley would watch them carefully, eavesdrop when they could, and follow them if necessary to see what they were up to. Sometimes they uncovered plots to commit murder, arson and other atrocities. Other times they merely stopped a brawl. And often, what they'd seen amounted to nothing. No matter the outcome, he felt compelled to do what he could to prevent people from hurting themselves or others.

Somehow, aiding those in danger made his own life more bearable.

With luck and persistence, they would soon gather rumblings on the missing children and Simmons, both of which were proving to be troublesome problems with little information.

In the light of day, when well rested, Stephen

could see that all their efforts and the risks they took were worthwhile. He knew they made a difference when they thwarted a thief's plans to steal or a swindler's intent to cheat. But some nights, all their attempts to stop the dark side of men seemed pointless; too few against so many.

Farley caught his eye and looked deliberately at a table of five men who leaned forward, talking intently. The tension in their faces spoke volumes. Stephen nodded to let Farley know he understood.

Stephen casually sipped his ale as he studied each man at the table. A heavyset Irishman by the look of his red hair and pale skin eyed Stephen suspiciously. Stephen let his gaze travel across the crowded pub before returning to the table. Unfortunately, he was too far away to hear much.

One of the men at the table held himself back from the group, not engaged in the discussion. His aura was lighter than the rest. The red-haired man's aura seemed to hold the darkest thoughts of any of them.

Stephen had developed patience over the years, waiting to see if what he saw in auras was confirmed by the expressions and conversation of the people involved. He glanced at his drink just as the red-haired man looked at him again. Stephen kept his gaze down, straining to hear anything of value without appearing overly interested.

"I'm tellin' ye, we need to consider the merits of forming a union."

"Yeah, but I don't want to be on the wrong side of things."

"And what side would that be?"

"I dunno. That's why I'm waitin' to see."

"We can't afford to wait, Jimmy."

The rest of the conversation was lost to Stephen as voices from a nearby table rose in song. He caught Farley's eye and touched his chin, indicating he wasn't sure yet but the group warranted further observation. Next Farley tipped his head toward two men sitting on the opposite side of him.

These two were a little easier to read. By the look of their dark auras and the sidelong glances they cast the woman serving them, Stephen surmised they intended to take more than she was willing to give.

He touched the lapel of his jacket, and Farley nodded in response. Those two would be watched carefully. Stephen guessed they'd try to accost the woman when she left the tavern after closing. Either he or Farley would remain to make sure the men behaved themselves.

He and Farley had developed their signals over the course of time. Farley wore an old suit and adjusted his accent to match the harsh neighborhood, looking more like a clerk than the manager of a successful gaming hell.

While Farley was an expert boxer, Stephen preferred *savate,* a French street fighting technique that allowed for kicking in addition to punching. On the rough streets of the East End, Stephen needed all the advantages he could get.

He'd met Farley at a local tavern almost seven years ago and, after realizing they had mutual interests, had soon worked out a business arrangement to their satisfaction. Farley had his own reasons for helping Stephen. His youngest sister had been accosted and brutally beaten on her way home from her job at the tea factory when Farley was only sixteen. Since then, Farley had learned to fight and had taken the law into his own hands more than once.

He'd worked with Stephen for over a fortnight before finally questioning his method of routing out those who truly intended harm. Rather than being shocked when Stephen had reluctantly explained, Farley had been fascinated. That had been the one and only time Stephen had confided his ability to anyone. The feeling of vulnerability was not something he cared to repeat.

The evening passed as the tavern's customers came and left, but the two men who watched the serving woman remained. The red-haired man and the others at his table left as well, taking their volatile argument over forming a union with them. Stephen hoped the man's dark aura had more to do with his worry over unfair working conditions than any foul intent.

A young man with blond hair and blue eyes caught Stephen's attention, his aura dark and heavy. At Stephen's sign, Farley befriended the man.

"Ye look like yer in need of another pint. Let me buy one for ye," Farley offered with a smile.

The young man looked at him suspiciously. "What's it to ye?"

"Nothin'. Just being friendly is all." Farley signaled to the barkeep for another ale. He retrieved it from the chipped mahogany bar and slid it in front of the man before turning away.

It never paid to act too anxious to hear someone else's troubles as it roused suspicion. The man stared at the pint for a few moments before taking a long drink. Then he rose to stand at Farley's table. "Thank ye."

"Think nothin' of it. Have a seat." Farley shoved back an extra chair at his table. "I saw the craziest thing down by the dock this morn."

Before long, Farley had him laughing at his ridiculous story involving a dog chasing a flock of geese only to turn tail and run when one of the geese decided to return the chase. As he drank a second pint, the young man shared the reason for his foul mood. He'd just been fired from his job.

"I was thinkin' about paying the bastard back for lettin' me go. Got a wife and babe to care fer." He stared morosely at his drink.

"Aw, don't be doing something that wouldn't make yer young one proud," Farley said. "Another job will come along."

"Not bloody likely. I've searched everywhere I can think of."

"You go talk to Watford at the warehouse on Sharp Street. He might have something for you," Farley offered.

Stephen hid a smile at the hope that lit the young man's face. At least one problem had been averted tonight.

He shifted his attention to the other tables around him. Over the course of the evening, a couple of conversations mentioned the missing boys, but no one seemed to have any additional information.

Stephen watched a group of three men whose auras shifted from gray murkiness to black spikes as the evening passed. Stephen drew as near as he dared but caught only bits and pieces of what they said. He'd nearly given up on hearing anything of interest when he heard the words "boys" and "experiment" uttered by one of the men. They all left soon after.

Curious, Stephen rose to follow and signaled for Farley to keep an eye on the men who still watched the serving woman.

Stephen exited the tavern, shutting out the rousing notes of 'The Parson and the Chamber Maid' as he closed the door and stepped onto the dark, foggy street. As he looked for the men, he shifted his shoulder to ease the tightness there. Though it was healing, the gunshot wound still hurt and his stamina had not yet returned in full. In addition to his injury, a crowded establishment always took its toll, but one filled with the people from this neighborhood with their suspicious minds and ill intentions was exhausting.

He rubbed his forehead in an attempt to ease the ache there, hoping he could quickly find the men who'd been talking in the tavern.

His step hitched as he realized someone watched him. As casually as possible, he surveyed the street through the mist. Several carriages and cabs passed by and many people went about their business but none seemed to pay him any mind. He paused just beyond the hazy gas street light to gain a better view.

The sound of a shoe on the cobblestone behind him had Stephen spinning around in time to see a fist plowing toward him. He narrowly dodged the blow when another smashed into his side, knocking his hat to the ground.

"That'll teach ye to mind yer own business!" His thick Irish brogue identified him as the red-haired man from the tavern.

Stephen's years of training as a *savateur* took over. Acting on instinct, he drove his fist into his attacker's jaw. The man staggered back as Stephen spun to heel kick his other assailant.

"Bloody hell! Watch out fer 'is feet!"

The barrel-chested Irishman refused to give up and seemed determined to damage Stephen's face with fists like hams. Luckily, his next punch swung wide.

The other man tried to circle behind Stephen. "If yer thinkin' to bilk us, ye best think again. Yer like don't belong 'ere."

"Last time I checked, I was free to drink wherever I please," Stephen answered as he waited with his hands at the ready to see what the men would try next. He silently cursed them for interrupting his pursuit of the one lead they might've had for the missing boys.

"Ye said he'd be an easy mark," the red-haired

man's cohort said as he lowered his fists. "I'm not stayin' for this." He retreated into the foggy night, ignoring his friend's angry curses.

The remaining man threw his fist again. Stephen blocked it with his forearm, using the man's own momentum to shove him away.

"Mind yer own business, damn you!" Cradling his arm, the man hurried off after his friend.

He took a slow breath to calm his racing heart then straightened his clothing. As he bent down to retrieve his hat, a sharp pain shot through his shoulder. He lifted the lapel of his jacket to make sure the damned injury wasn't bleeding again but couldn't see anything in the dim light.

He should've realized they'd look at him suspiciously if they thought he was listening to their discussion about whether to form a union. Even talking about it was seen as a threat by some businesses.

Awareness shot through him again, and he shifted to see if one of his attackers had returned.

The only thing he spotted in the fog was a sleek black carriage rolling to a stop across the street. The red velvet curtain was pulled aside as though the passenger watched him. The coachman hopped down, and Stephen immediately recognized Abigail's brawny footman.

"Bloody hell." He glanced around the area once more, but the two he'd followed out of the tavern were nowhere in sight.

Stephen crossed the street. "Thomas," he ground out. "I thought we agreed you'd try harder to control her."

"You've a fine sense of humor, my lord. Glad to see those men didn't beat that out of you," the footman said as he opened the carriage door.

"You could've come and helped," Stephen suggested, rather annoyed that he hadn't.

"Didn't look like you needed assistance."

Thomas grinned.

Stephen stepped into the carriage, latching the door behind him. Abigail's fragrance filled the small space, a welcome reprieve from the scents of smoke, ale and sweat that surely clung to him from the tavern.

Why did she insist on letting the filth of this area touch her? No good could come of it.

"Are you all right?" she asked, her honeyed tone pulling at him along with her scent.

"Fine," he gritted out, determined to resist her allure. He'd dreamed of her again last night and those images teased him now.

"What was that all about?"

"A minor disagreement." He eased back in the corner of the seat opposite her, wincing as his shoulder throbbed with pain. "What are you doing here?"

"I think that would be obvious."

He narrowed his eyes. "Perhaps you could enlighten me anyway."

"You've advised me that I am not to visit you at your home or your...business establishment. What other recourse is left to me but to follow you to someplace where I can speak with you?"

"I'm certain I told you not to come to the East End again either."

"I remained in my carriage. It's not as if I am wandering the streets."

"That hardly keeps you out of harm's way." He had to make it clear that she wasn't safe in this part of the city. Logic had no affect on this woman. If anything happened to her—he didn't want to finish the thought.

"So you're not going to tell me why you were brawling when we came upon you?" she asked.

"Nothing that involves you." He knew he spoke bluntly but couldn't help himself. It annoyed him that she'd seen him in what amounted to a street brawl.

"Do you often get in fights?" She sounded cross at the idea of it.

He heaved a sigh. "At times, they are unavoidable in my line of work."

"Then I suggest you seek a different occupation."

As if it were that easy, he thought. "What was so bloody important that you found me here?"

The dim glow cast by the carriage lamp created an intimacy he would've preferred to avoid. After the events of the evening, a part deep inside him strained to be closer to her, to absorb her golden light and soothe his darkness. The temptation of her surrounded him until he could hardly breathe. Her face was hidden in shadows but he didn't have to see her expression to feel her displeasure. Perhaps that would help him keep his distance.

"My apologies for interrupting your evening of drinking and brawling, but two days have passed since I've heard anything from you."

"When I have something to tell you, I'll contact you. Following me serves no purpose."

She huffed in response. "Are you telling me you *still* don't know of Simmons' whereabouts?"

Stephen's frustration pushed him to the edge of his seat. "I'm sure you remember me mentioning other problems that have arisen which occupy my time. Perhaps you could consider for a moment that the world does *not* revolve around you."

She sat forward as well until her face was mere inches from his, not backing down. He tried his best to ignore the fact that her reaction was exactly what he'd hoped for. That she'd push him beyond the bounds of gentlemanly behavior, and he'd be left with no choice but to touch her.

"My family's safety is at stake. I have difficulty believing anything you're doing in some disreputable pub could be more pressing."

Her gaze dropped to his lips, and the fragile restraint he had on his desire for her snapped. Before he could think twice, he took her mouth with his.

She tasted so sweet, as though she'd just drunk a golden elixir blended specifically to entice him. Her lips curved to fit his. They were soft and supple, and he lifted his hand to caress her cheek. Her skin was just as smooth and silky as he'd remembered.

She responded to his kiss tentatively at first, as though uncertain what she should do. He'd caught her by surprise, of that he had no doubt.

He waited, expecting her to shove him back and put him in his place. Instead she tilted her head and deepened the kiss. Desire speared through him, almost painful in its intensity. It had been so long since he'd felt like this, since he'd been with a woman who stirred him so.

Her hand touched the back of his neck, curving around the sensitive skin at his nape, her gloved fingers running through his hair. Her touch was pure magic, at once soothing him and making him yearn for more.

He opted for more, plundering, parting his lips to taste her more fully. She stilled at his sudden invasion then opened her lips to return the favor. Her ardor added to his own until his head swam with her sweetness.

His hands sought her body of their own accord, finding their way beneath her cloak. The feel of her slim waist only made him wish for the barriers between them to be gone. He lingered there, then raised his hands until his fingers grazed the swell of her breasts.

At last he pulled away before he couldn't any longer, before he went further than he could bear. He rested his forehead against hers as he attempted to slow his hammering heart and rein in his passion before he took her on the seat of the carriage.

He drew back to look at her. Sure enough, her aura held a rosy glow, making her all the more beautiful. But under that rose color was the golden light that had captured his notice the moment he'd met her.

A reminder of why she was not for him.

She deserved a man who could honor that golden glow with a marriage proposal and a normal family life, something he could not offer. Not with the darkness buried inside him.

Clenching his jaw, he lowered his hands, unable to resist trailing a finger along the curve of her cheek and the slight indentation of her chin as he let her go. "You must stay away, Abigail. You are not safe here."

Her blue eyes assessed him for a long moment. Her expression held only candor, no deceitful fluttering of her lashes, no coy smile. "I'm not supposed to visit your home or The Barbican. I'm not supposed to follow you here." She gestured with her hand as she spoke. "What exactly do you expect of me?"

"I expect you to stay home where you'll be protected. Have patience and we'll see this resolved."

From the thin line of her lips, he knew she didn't care for his answer.

"No leads arose at the tavern I was just in, but I will find him. Simmons is known by a few, but none seem to know him well. He isn't moving with the same people he was before his time in prison and he's using other names besides Edward Smith."

"How can I protect Mother and the girls while you search? Locked doors aren't enough to stop him." Her anxious tone spoke volumes.

Stephen understood her worry, but if the man hadn't harmed her or her family yet, it was doubtful he would. On the other hand, the missing children he'd been searching for might already be dead. The threat to them was unknown. It wasn't fair that he had to choose between the two, but life wasn't fair. He'd learned that long ago. He had to pick the bigger evil to pursue.

"Post additional footmen at the doors night and day. Take more of them with you when you go out."

"Do you have any idea how impractical that is? How many footmen do you think we have?"

"It's only temporary. Until we locate Simmons."

"What am I to tell my family?"

"Tell them you've heard vandals are in the area and you want extra protection."

She looked appalled at his suggestion. "I don't want to lie to them."

"Haven't you already?" He sat back. "If they aren't aware of Simmons and the threat he poses, you've obviously been withholding information. Omission *is* a lie."

"I only did that to protect them. To make certain they don't worry. I'm not certain what else to do." She chewed her lower lip, and he could tell that some idea was forming in her mind.

He braced himself, for he was certain he wouldn't like it.

"We should work together." She offered the suggestion in a rush as though it were brilliant.

"What?"

"Together. Follow the leads as a team. It would be much more efficient."

He stared at her, shaking his head. Where did her outlandish ideas come from? Perhaps she'd read one too many novels. "No."

"Why? I think it's truly a sound notion. We'll

find him in no time." Her enthusiastic tone held such hope.

"No."

"Yes." There was that hope again.

"*No*."

"I have the time which you don't, and you have the leads, which I lack. It makes perfect sense."

He placed a finger along her lips to stop any more ridiculous notions she might come up with. "Listen well. We're working on your problem each and every day. I'll let you know as soon as we have something of interest to report. I expect you to go home and stay out of harm's way. Do you understand?"

She drew a breath to argue.

"Abigail," he murmured softly.

Her crestfallen expression was more than he could stand.

What was he to do with her? He removed his finger and placed a lingering kiss on her sweet lips, being careful to keep his desire reined in.

"Have patience. I will be in touch." He was out the door before she could protest. He cast one more look at her, appreciating her beauty in the soft glow of the carriage light and did his best to ignore her disappointment.

He escaped into the foggy night with the barest hold on his sanity, certain he'd be chasing her in his dreams that night.

What crazed notion would she come up with next?

CHAPTER EIGHT

Abigail perused the growing crowd at Lord and Lady Mortenson's ball. The annual May celebration was a favorite of her stepmother's, and therefore not to be missed, at least not according to her Irene.

Stunning in a shimmering gown of gray silk with a fitted rose-colored underskirt, Irene chatted nearby with Lady Mortenson as Abigail tried not to look at the clock again. She was certain it was malfunctioning as the hands hadn't moved.

In truth, this wasn't the first time she'd experienced that phenomena since she'd seen Lord Ashbury three days past. She'd had trouble focusing on anything, and time seemed to crawl at a snail's pace. All she could think of was the way he'd held her as though he'd *needed* her. That lovely swirl of sensation in the pit of her stomach when she was near him. The heat of his lips on hers. Just the memory of that feeling made her mouth go dry and her body tingle in the oddest places.

This revelation had forced her to rethink the image she held of herself. She drew a deep breath and couldn't help but smile at this new knowledge.

Abigail Bradford was capable of passion.

For years, she'd thought herself flawed. She'd danced with men, had her hand held by men, even suffered a kiss or two.

And felt nothing.

Lord Ashbury had changed all that. She'd yet to determine what was different about him that caused her reaction. Perhaps some scientific explanation existed for the chemistry between them, but the sensation felt too good for her to be concerned about the mechanics of it. She couldn't help the giggle that bubbled up in her throat, spilling onto her face, which caught the attention of her stepmother.

Irene halted mid-sentence to stare. "Abigail, are you well?"

The heat of a blush crept up Abigail's cheeks. "I'm fine. It's terribly warm in here, don't you think?"

Irene continued to watch her as she resumed her conversation with Lady Mortenson, so Abigail tried to think of something less distracting.

She bit back a sigh as she caught sight of Lord Brighton approaching. The wealthy lord annoyed her to no end with his condescending attitude. He considered himself quite the catch and had made it clear that he thought men were far superior to women. Abigail had found it amusing at first that he'd sought her out when he believed education of any sort was wasted on women. She'd never bothered to hide her enjoyment of learning, especially of financial matters. But his snide comments at her interests grew more irritating each time she spoke with him.

His ridiculous attire proved money didn't buy good taste. Tonight he wore an orange-striped silk waistcoat with a matching cravat. Orange wasn't becoming with his ruddy complexion, but she was convinced no man could wear the color well. She wondered if he wore a corset to encase his ample form as he often seemed short of breath.

She pretended her attention was riveted on the opposite corner of the room with little hope it would dissuade him from speaking with her.

"Miss Bradford! Such a delight to see you this evening."

"Lord Brighton." His blond hair was parted with precision down the middle and his sideburns covered a good portion of his jaw. His nose was overly long and his thin lips did little to hide his yellowed teeth.

He greeted her stepmother and Lady Mortenson then returned his attention to her.

Abigail had done everything she could think of to discourage the lord but he seemed intent on attempting to court her. The man was unable to take 'no' for an answer. She cast a look at Irene, wondering if her stepmother had encouraged Lord Brighton to pursue her.

How she wished Irene would understand that she didn't want a traditional role of wife, even if it was to a rich husband. After working long and hard to learn how to manage their income and make wise investments, she had no desire to hand their money, or her freedom, to a husband.

She needed to make Irene understand that Lord Brighton was not for her. The idea of being trapped into a marriage with someone she neither liked nor respected made her shudder.

"That's a lovely gown you're wearing," he said, his breath reeking of onions, as he gestured toward her deep burgundy gown.

"I fear it clashes terribly with your waistcoat," she said, covering her nose with her gloved hand.

He frowned down at the orange atrocity straining at the buttons, then back to her. "I hardly think—"

"No need to take affront. I'm merely stating a fact." She turned her attention back to the crowd, hoping that if she ignored him, he'd go away.

Dancers filled the floor and Abigail eyed them with longing. Gowns in a wide array of colors glided past her, glinting in the soft light. Though she loved to dance, she'd learned not to overindulge in it. Dancing encouraged things like courting. If the proper distance wasn't maintained, or if one danced too many times with a particular partner, rumors circulated. While she was considered off-the-shelf by most of the *ton*, she couldn't ignore the rules completely.

"I say, Miss Bradford, would you care to dance?"

If only Lord Brighton would view her as no longer eligible for marriage. She searched for an excuse to deny his request for he was not an accomplished dancer. Rather than allowing her to follow his lead, he used his strength to move her where he thought she should go—an unpleasant sensation for certain. "I fear I twisted my ankle earlier," she lied with little remorse.

"Abigail!"

The familiar female voice proved a welcome distraction. "Catherine, delightful to see you again." A delight because it would distract Lord Brighton. She wasn't averse to throwing Catherine in his path.

"Have you met Lord Brighton?" Abigail asked.

"Not formally." Catherine turned with a polite smile to the lord whose face lit with interest.

Abigail made the introductions, relieved to let the burden of small talk fall to Catherine. Her ploy didn't last long as Catherine moved to stand on the opposite side of her, distancing herself from the annoying lord.

"Have you seen Lord Weston?" Catherine whispered as she scanned the throng.

"No. I don't believe so. Has he caught your interest?" She couldn't contain her curiosity.

"Oh, yes. I'm trying to make certain I've caught his." Catherine gave her a sly smile.

Abigail almost felt sorry for the lord. Did he realize what he was getting himself into?

Catherine's mannerisms suddenly changed to that of a fluttery debutante, complete with a giddy laugh. Abigail stared, wondering what had caused her drastic change in behavior.

Then Abigail saw Lord Weston approaching and the reason for Catherine's transformation was explained, but nonetheless distasteful. It seemed so deceptive to capture a suitor by pretending to be something you weren't.

An unexpected pang of longing filled her. What would it be like to have a man like Lord Weston seek her attention? But it wasn't Lord Weston who filled her mind. She reined in her overactive imagination. There was no point in wishing for things that would never be.

"Good evening, ladies," Lord Weston said as he approached, his gaze dropping to Catherine's bosom. Abigail couldn't blame him the way Catherine thrust her abundant breasts forward.

Lord Weston was handsome with intelligent, assessing blue eyes and dark hair. His black jacket was set off by a white shirt and deep blue waistcoat, so different than Brighton's.

Abigail could see why he held Catherine's interest, but she wondered what in Catherine held his. She was attractive enough, Abigail supposed, but she just wasn't very...nice. There was no other way to put it. In Abigail's opinion, what lay on the inside of a person was as important as the outside.

Lord Weston's attention turned to Lord Brighton and he frowned, staring at the lord intently. He seemed less than pleased by what he saw. Perhaps it was the orange waistcoat that offended him. Then he seemed to catch himself and smooth out his expression.

"You remember Miss Bradford?" Catherine asked.

Lord Weston smiled. "Of course. Are you enjoying the ball?" His gaze caught on her hair rather than her face.

She had the urge to pat her carefully arranged locks to see if they were out of place. How peculiar that Lord Ashbury often did a similar thing.

"Yes, thank you." Before she could say more, a shiver of awareness ran down her back, giving her pause.

A murmur rose through the crowded ballroom, and she turned to see what had caused the sensation.

Perhaps her imagination had gotten away from her after all.

Her breath caught at the sight of Lord Ashbury striding toward her. Much like Lord Weston, his evening attire was subdued but flawless. His expression was typically grim, but that didn't matter. Those green eyes were locked on her, making it difficult to do anything other than blink.

And try to remember to breathe.

People turned to look as he passed, but he ignored them, his attention fastened solely on her. Her stomach dipped as though she'd spun too fast. The solid strength of him, the intensity of his look made her heart thunder. She couldn't help but wonder at the myriad of feelings his mere presence created within her.

His gaze at last took in the people surrounding her. His eyes narrowed as he noticed Lord Weston.

"Weston."

"Ashbury."

The tension between them filled the air.

Catherine glanced between the pair curiously, then slipped her arm through Lord Weston's with a possessiveness that seemed unwarranted. "Weren't you going to ask me to dance, my lord?"

Lord Weston looked down at her and made a visible effort to lighten his mood. He patted her hand. "Indeed."

"Miss Bradford, Brighton." Lord Weston nodded at each of them and guided Catherine to the dance floor, completely ignoring Lord Ashbury.

Abigail looked up at him to see his reaction to the not-so-subtle snub. His mouth twisted, and he gave a small shake of his head.

"I say, what was that all about?" Lord Brighton asked Lord Ashbury.

"Ancient history."

Not so ancient, Abigail thought. If she had to guess, she'd say the wounds created by their rift had not yet healed. Though she longed to know what had occurred after the accident to drive them apart, she refrained from asking. Now was not the time.

"How do you mean?" asked Lord Brighton.

Abigail couldn't believe the audacity of the man. Before Lord Ashbury could respond, she turned her back on Brighton and asked, "What brings you here, my lord?"

He looked at her, his gaze catching on her hair, much like Lord Weston's had. This time, she couldn't help but pat the upswept strands to see what might be amiss. "Is my hair coming down?"

He frowned then glanced at her hair again. "No."

"Then why does everyone keep staring at it? First Lord Weston and now you."

Stephen allowed himself a smile. Although Abigail did have lovely hair, he doubted that was why Weston had been staring at the top of her head. He wondered what Weston saw when he looked at Abigail's aura. Was it anything like he saw? So beautiful with gold and blue lights that he wished he could capture it in a glass ball to look at it always? Something about those vibrant colors around her gave him hope.

Or perhaps it was her.

With a huff, Abigail reached up with a gloved hand and touched her hair again. "What is so amusing?"

"Nothing." He glanced at Lord Brighton who seemed quite puzzled by their conversation but showed no sign of leaving them. The orange waistcoat on the man was hideous. When the lord stared at the low neckline of Abigail's gown and his aura shot with black, Stephen had had enough.

He supposed there was no other way to have a private moment with her. He offered her his elbow. "Would you honor me with this dance?"

Those amazing blue eyes lit with delight, making Stephen wish he'd asked her for no other reason than to please her. "That would be lovely."

He took hold of himself. He wasn't here for her enjoyment or his own. Only for the business they shared.

"But I thought you hurt your ankle," Lord Brighton said with a distinct whine to his voice.

"It's feeling better now." Her color high, she turned to Stephen. "Shall we?"

Stephen watched her to see if her ankle was truly injured as he led her to the dance floor, but detected no sign of pain. He held her as lightly as possible, all the while berating himself for the position in which he found himself. Surely he'd learned by now that being this close to her was pure torture. He'd been wrong to think the crowded ballroom would make any difference.

She moved with grace, her dark hair gleaming under the lights of the softly lit ballroom. The strands were twisted in an intricate manner then

pulled back to tumble in curls down her neck. A
neck that begged to be kissed. She fit him
perfectly, following his movements as though
they'd danced many times before.

He rarely attended balls or other social events.
The crowds here were nearly as painful as the one
at the Bull and Boar Tavern. Just as many held
desperate urges and his head pounded in
response. Yet as he focused on Abigail, the
distractions faded, lessening his discomfort. The
simple act of holding her seemed to settle the
restlessness deep inside him.

As they spun to the music, Abigail let out a
laugh of delight. "You're very good."

He couldn't help but smile at her enjoyment.
More easily than he expected, he pushed the sight
of other people's auras and their urges aside and
focused on her. The beauty of the moment, of
Abigail, soaked into him. Everything else became
a blur. Her gaze held his and even the sounds
around him faded.

Her responsiveness to his every step on the
dance floor made him wonder how responsive
she'd be in his bed. Would she follow his lead? Go
where he guided? Desire spiked through him at
the thought.

When she tipped her head back and laughed, it
was all he could do not to pull her close and
devour her.

Heady with need, he knew he had to stop, to
end this torture. Yet he couldn't. This sort of
pleasure came into his life—his lonely existence—
so rarely; he couldn't bear for it to end when it
had only begun.

All too soon, the notes of the music faded, and
they were forced to stop. He enjoyed the feel of
Abigail in his arms, their bodies scandalously
close for a long moment, before at last he released
her.

What had made him think he needed to seek her out at the ball? He could never again be part of this world. He might have kept his involvement in The Barbican hidden, but if he moved in these circles, it wouldn't remain that way. Far worse, if polite society knew of his aura reading, he'd be considered a freak, an oddity better displayed in Covent Garden alongside the fat lady or the elephant man. Not to mention what Abigail would think.

He was unfit to be a husband. He couldn't allow his desire for this woman make him forget.

"Is something amiss?" Abigail's eyes were full of concern.

If only she knew how truly amiss things were. He mentally slammed the door on his longing for things that could never be and put his mask firmly in place. He needed to return his focus to the business at hand.

"We've found Simmons' new lodgings. It's being watched and we hope to locate him within the next day. I thought you'd want to know."

The brilliant light in her cobalt eyes dimmed, much to his surprise. He thought she'd be pleased with the news.

"Is that why you came here?" she asked, her tone flat.

He frowned. "I rarely attend balls."

"Yes, I know."

"Abigail—"

"Tell me more of his lodgings." She seemed to be all business now.

"He isn't there often according to the sources we've found, but we'll catch him upon his return."

"Good."

"I'll keep you apprised of any further progress."

"Of course."

Blast the woman! Why did he feel like he'd disappointed her? What did she want him to say?

That he'd come here expressly to see her? Well, he had. But for her sake as well as his own, the reason had to be to advise her of the latest development in their pursuit of Simmons. After all, he well knew if he didn't she'd seek him out. And look at what had happened the last two times she'd done so.

"Enjoy the rest of your evening." He bowed and left her with her stepmother.

"And you as well, my lord." She turned away without a backward glance.

The evening passed with excruciating slowness for Abigail once Lord Ashbury had departed. Dancing with him had left her longing for more, but she knew all other partners would fall short. Then again, it wasn't really dancing for which she longed.

The way she felt when she was with him was indescribable. Something about him drew forth a yearning deep within her. His slow smile started in his eyes then crooked the corner of his mouth before becoming a smile in full. But it was worth waiting for.

When she was in his arms, she could think of nothing else. She feared he'd forever ruined dancing for her. They'd moved as though they'd been made for each other. He had an effortless grace with an innate rhythm that made the waltz a true joy.

Or perhaps she'd just felt as if she were floating because of the way he made her feel, not because of how he danced. She sighed at the thought.

Though she told herself over and over she was glad he'd reminded her that their relationship was only business, she couldn't quite convince herself. The pleasure had gone out of the evening and she wanted nothing more than to go home.

"Mother, are you planning on staying much longer?" Abigail asked, hopeful that she might be ready to leave.

"I'm rather enjoying myself, dear. Aren't you?"

"Yes, of course," she lied. "I just wondered how long you'd like to stay."

"Who was the man you were dancing with earlier?"

"No one special." Her heart felt heavy at the answer for he wasn't—he couldn't be.

Irene smiled as she glanced past Abigail's shoulder. "Perhaps you'd like to dance some more. I know how much you enjoy doing so."

Abigail's heart leapt to her throat. She spun to see if Stephen had returned.

Lord Brighton stood behind her, smiling broadly, yellowed teeth in full display.

Disappointment speared through her, followed by dread. Something about him made her uneasy.

"Now that your ankle is better, may I request the honor of this dance?" Lord Brighton's expression was confident.

His certainty alone irritated her.

"Abigail, do grant Lord Brighton's request. He's asking so nicely," Irene implored her.

She turned to stare at Irene, wondering what on earth had gotten into her. Why was she pleading Lord Brighton's cause?

Left with no choice, she reluctantly nodded her acceptance.

The music swelled and the dance began. He stepped on her toe twice and kept such a firm hold on her hand that her fingers were numb. His performance, or rather lack thereof, was all the more noticeable after her dance with Lord Ashbury.

She escaped Lord Brighton as quickly as possible only to catch sight of Lord Thompson moving in her direction. She couldn't stand another meaningless conversation with an overdressed dandy who acted as if he did her a great favor by showing interest in her.

With a quick word to Irene, she slipped out the garden door into the cool evening air. She watched through a window as Lord Thompson arrived at where she'd been standing moments before and searched the crowd for her.

She sighed with relief at the near miss then gave a startled gasp when warm hands grasped her arms from behind.

"I knew you'd eventually follow me outside. I'm glad I waited for you."

The strong odor of onions made Abigail turn her head away. "Lord Brighton, I didn't realize you were out here."

He laughed as he turned her around to face him, keeping a tight hold on her. "I don't believe you, but play the innocent. I must say I find that appealing."

She stepped back only to come up against the high, brick garden wall. A flutter of panic tumbled through her, but she pushed it away with anger. "I must return to the ballroom. Mother will wonder where I've gone."

"I think your mother might approve of us having a little time to ourselves. I've been waiting for this opportunity all evening. I'm not about to let you sneak off now." He moved closer, one finger trailing up and down her arm.

Trying not to inhale his obnoxious breath, she pushed him back. "You're taking liberties I don't appreciate. I'm going back inside."

He seized her again, the feel of his gloved hands on the bare skin of her arms repulsive. "Not before you bestow a kiss on me, my dear. You've teased me all night."

"I have not and I resent you saying so. I was

merely being polite. Let me be clear—I'm not interested in pursuing any sort of involvement with you." Again she shoved him back, but he didn't budge.

"You may not be interested in me, but I'm interested in you. I don't mind your bookish ways overmuch. Intelligence is occasionally an asset in a wife, as long as you keep it to a minimum. We'd make an excellent match." He held her tight, trapping her arms between them, and attempted a kiss.

Abigail turned her head and his lips landed on her cheek. She held on to the anger that poured through her at his forward behavior and tried to shove him back but he didn't budge.

"Cease this madness at once!" She struggled against him, shocked at how strong he was, unable to believe him capable of this. "What sort of gentleman are you?"

He laughed—a very unpleasant sound. "The kind who takes what he wants. Just the man a headstrong woman like you needs."

"Let me go!" She wrenched one hand free and managed to punch him in the stomach, but as she suspected, he wore a corset. The blow did nothing to deter him.

"I admit I occasionally like it rough," he said with another laugh. "But your independent streak will be a thing of the past once I'm through with you."

Fear rushed through her and she fought his hold in earnest.

"Easy now," he chided. "We'll soon be interrupted by Lord Thompson, your mother, and Lady Mortenson. I fear I'll be forced to propose and you'll be forced to accept."

Panic, hot and liquid, surged. She looked him in the eye, determined to make herself clear. "I will not marry you and nothing you do or say will coerce me."

He shoved her back against the wall, the force stealing her breath, the violence of his attack shocking her. "You'll do as I say or pay the price." He kissed her again, this time finding his target. His tongue filled her mouth, the taste gagging her. Then he drew back and squeezed her breast through the fabric of her gown.

"Leave me be!" She lifted her knee, aiming for his groin, but he blocked her attempt.

"Such a fighter. That makes me want you even more." Again he shoved her.

This time, her head struck the brick and a black haze filled her vision. Stunned from the impact, she felt his hands at the neck of her gown followed by the cool night air on her naked breast. He pinched her nipple painfully.

"You are a beauty, Abigail. Too headstrong by far. I can't wait to tame you in proper fashion."

Abigail struggled harder, realizing Lord Brighton might very well succeed in his attempt to compromise her. But he anticipated her every move. Terrified, she tried to clear her head enough to determine a way to escape him.

Without warning, his bulky form was torn from her. She searched the darkness, dreading the sight of her stepmother's horrified expression.

CHAPTER NINE

Rage coursed through Stephen as he shook Brighton like a rag doll. How dare the lecher put his hands on Abigail.

"Leave me be," Lord Brighton cried.

"You bastard." Stephen let go of Brighton's jacket and plowed his fist into his jaw.

Brighton howled in pain, but Stephen wasn't finished. He repeated the hammering twice more until Brighton crumpled to the ground. He bent over Brighton's inert form, ready to do more damage.

"Stephen?"

Abigail's trembling voice pulled him out of the red haze that filled him. He hesitated before looking at her, not wanting to see the disgust and horror her expression would surely reflect after what she'd witnessed him do.

Before he could utter an apology, she stepped toward him, her expression filled with relief. Then she stumbled, and he swept her into his arms. Her face was as pale as the frost at dawn. Regret washed through him as he realized he could've prevented this.

"I'm sorry, Abigail," he whispered. "I saw Brighton's ill intent in the ball room, but I thought it overzealous lust. I never believed the man would orchestrate something like this."

He heard voices approaching and could think of no explanation to the scene that would not create a scandal.

"Please, don't let them find me," Abigail murmured as she wrapped her arms around his neck.

He needed no further urging to carry her to his nearby carriage. He'd left the ball by the same door as Abigail then had watched her through the window like some lovesick schoolboy before at last walking away. But while waiting for his carriage, he'd been unable to shake off his unease and returned to the garden entrance to find Brighton accosting her.

His footman hurried forward to hold open the carriage door. "Can I be of assistance, my lord?"

"Find Lady Bradford and advise her that her daughter isn't feeling well and is returning home."

Stephen stepped into the carriage and settled Abigail on the seat beside him, her head buried in his shoulder. "Are you all right?"

She kept her head down and nodded.

He eased back so he could look at her in the soft lantern light, searching her face to make sure she spoke the truth. "What were you thinking? What possessed you to be outside with that blundering fool? Surely at your age you know better."

"I went out by myself in order to avoid Lord Thompson." She winced as she touched her head.

The blood on her fingers caused an odd pressure in his chest. He wanted to hold her tight and never let her go, keeping her safe in his embrace. "You shouldn't go anywhere alone. Especially not with Simmons lurking about."

"It isn't my fault Lord Brighton concocted some crazed plan to force me into marriage."

He cursed himself once again. If only he'd watched Brighton closer. "What plan?"

"He said my stepmother and several others would soon find us in a compromising position so he'd be *forced* to propose and I'd have to accept."

Stephen wanted to shake her, to make sure she realized what a near miss she'd had. "Why would you go outside by yourself in the first place?"

She glared at him. "The same reason you did, my lord. To escape the crowded ballroom."

It was hard not to sympathize with her when she stated it like that. "Next time, take an escort with you. If not Brighton, Simmons could've been waiting in the garden for you."

She gave an unladylike snort. "At times, an escort is impossible. My head hurts." She pressed her hand to it again.

"Not as much as Brighton's."

"There is some comfort in that." She looked up at him. "Thank you. I'm not certain what I would've done if you hadn't come along."

How remarkable that she wasn't appalled at the beating he'd given Brighton, that she hadn't turned and run when she'd witnessed the violence of which he was capable. He cleared his throat, trying to keep his mind on their conversation rather than the flood of emotions coursing through him.

"You'd be engaged. To an idiot."

"I would've refused."

"The choice wouldn't be yours," he argued.

"In case you haven't noticed, we live in modern times."

He shook his head. "You underestimate the power of society and its opinion of you and your entire family. Ruination is no easy path to walk."

"Yet here I am alone in a carriage with you."

"No one saw us."

As she winced again, Stephen's anger softened. "You're right. This is not your fault. That lies squarely with Brighton. But you must be more careful." He lifted his hand to cup her cheek.

"Brighton is not the first to try to manipulate me."

"Nor will he be the last." He wanted to say that she was a beautiful, eligible woman whom any man would be lucky to call his wife. But he kept his words to himself.

She sighed and rested her cheek in his palm. "It's very tiresome to be on guard from such things. Especially at my age."

The thought of some man putting his hands on her enraged him all over again. He closed his eyes for a moment to tamp down his anger. "You are far from on the shelf. I'd suggest you find a husband who can offer you protection."

"I don't intend to marry."

"Why?"

"It's a long story."

"I believe we have time." He gently brushed a strand of her hair off her cheek, wondering if she trusted him enough to share a part of herself.

"I have a rather unique...endeavor," she whispered after a long pause.

"Oh?" He couldn't imagine what *endeavor* would prevent her from marrying.

"I—I make investments." She dropped her gaze as though she didn't want to see his reaction to her confession.

He frowned, still not quite understanding. "Investments? Of a financial nature? As a hobby?"

"It's not a hobby," she retorted, her irritation obvious. "My father did not leave us in the best of financial circumstances when he died. With no male heir, his title went to my uncle, who is not the generous sort. We needed income." She shrugged as she looked back up at him. "I have a gift for picking successful ventures, you might say."

"You are clever, aren't you?" That fit perfectly

with what he knew of her. Intelligence shown like a beacon out of her blue eyes.

She gave a small, embarrassed laugh. "Men do not appreciate discussing such things with a woman. A husband would never allow me to continue my work. I assist not only my family, but our servants and a few other acquaintances as well. Plus he could take all the money I've earned for his own purposes. I cannot allow that."

He rubbed his thumb along her soft cheek. "The right man would understand. Perhaps even help where he could."

"Not the men I've met. Lord Brighton is a good example."

"He's a poor example of a man." He shook his head, wondering what other secrets she had.

"I intend to build our wealth so we can provide a dowry for the twins. And I want to advise others on how to invest their money. Do you know how many widows there are who have no idea what to do or how to do it? They stuff their money under the mattress or in an old teapot because they don't know what else to do." The passion in her voice was undeniable.

"I had no idea," he admitted. He'd never thought on the subject overmuch.

"At any rate, I have no intention of marrying as a husband would spoil my plans."

"I don't agree with you but I do respect your desire to help others. Did your parents' marriage lead you to this conclusion?"

"No, but I've come to realize theirs was the exception. Uncle Reginald is horrible to his wife and she says nothing. Uncle Herbert writes out a schedule for Aunt Lottie. I find it all quite ridiculous. Women have no rights once they marry."

"So you'd like to keep your freedom."

"Wouldn't you?" Those blue eyes implored him

to understand.

"What sort of things would you do without the restrictions a husband might place on you?" He was curious to hear what she'd say. He'd never met a woman who said and wanted the things she did.

"I would—" She hesitated for a moment, lowering her lashes, then lifting them again, staring at his mouth. "I would kiss you and not worry over the consequences."

His heart stopped. He could only watch as she drew closer, slowly, haltingly. Her breath fanned across his cheek. Yearning welled through him until at last her lips found his.

He'd been so sure he was strong enough not to let this happen again.

But no.

He'd underestimated her power over him. Her lips were soft and warm and pressed gently against his. Her golden light was so appealing compared to the darkness he often endured.

She eased back to look into his eyes. "I don't want to remember Brighton when I go to sleep tonight. I'd much rather dream of you."

Unable to deny her request, he took her mouth with his, until she sighed and her whole body relaxed against his. Though his desire for her was almost painful in its intensity, he held back, reining in his passion. He wrapped his arms around her, holding her with care, offering comfort.

She grimaced in pain, arching her back.

Stephen loosened his hold. "I'm sorry you're hurt." It made him want to pummel Brighton all over again.

"My back. My head. Damn that man." Abigail grasped his arms as he released her. "Don't let go. Please." She laid her head on his shoulder and burrowed. There was no other word for it.

"No. I won't let go." His heart squeezed as he uttered the promise.

A soft tap sounded at the carriage door, and Stephen heard his footman's voice. "I've delivered the message, my lord. Shall we proceed?"

"To Miss Bradford's residence, please."

Soon the carriage swayed. Abigail remained in his arms, her head tucked under his chin, her lavender fragrance teasing his senses, her soft form pressed against his.

He did the only thing he could—he held her gently and told himself to let tomorrow take care of itself.

Life took twists that one never expected—like holding the very person you could never have.

The next morning, Abigail snuggled deeper into her pillow, reluctant to rise. She was sore from the bump on her head and the bruises on her back, physical reminders of last night's events.

Emotionally she felt far worse. Humiliated, angry, and somehow more fragile than ever before. She'd always believed herself strong and capable, but never had she gone through what she had last night.

The new feeling of vulnerability made her question her hopes for the future. Part of her wondered if her mother and Stephen were right. Perhaps she should consider marrying. A husband would provide protection. It was highly unlikely that she'd ever have to worry about being accosted if she were married.

A knock sounded at her bedroom door before she could ponder exactly why the idea held so little appeal.

"Come in."

Irene peeked in, concern evident in her expression. "I came to see how you're feeling."

A mixture of fear and embarrassment poured through Abigail. Had her mother found out what had truly happened? Then Abigail remembered Stephen telling his footman to deliver the message that she was ill. Relief made her light-headed. She'd prefer no one learn what had occurred.

"Ah—better I think. A little tired and a bit of a headache still." That much was true, she thought as guilt tapped on her shoulder.

Her mother sat on the edge of the bed and studied Abigail with a critical eye. She put a hand to her forehead. "You're pale, but no fever. Why don't you rest in bed this morning and then see how you feel?"

The comforting presence of the woman who'd been both her mother and friend for so many years brought a lump to her throat. For a long moment, she was tempted to let her tears flow and tell her everything.

"What is it, Abigail?"

Yet all the years of protecting her could not be overcome so easily. Instead, Abigail found herself asking, "Did Lord Brighton speak with you?"

A knowing smile came over Irene's face. "As a matter of fact, yes. Did he say something to you?" The hope in her voice made Abigail squirm.

"I realize you only want what's best for me," she said, trying to find some way to make her mother understand, "and that you'd like for me to marry. But I do *not* welcome his interest."

"But—"

"Please don't encourage him." Though tempted to tell her exactly what the lord had done last night, she couldn't see a purpose to it. "I don't care for him at all. He'd be the last man I'd want to spend any time with, let alone the rest of my life."

"I see." Irene stared at her, obviously trying to read between the lines. "I realize he isn't young or handsome, but he is wealthy. He could take care of all of us. You've carried the burden of that for far too long."

Frustrated, Abigail tried to think of a way to make her understand. "We can take care of ourselves. We don't need a man for that. Especially not Lord Brighton."

"Did he do something inappropriate?"

"Yes, and I told him in no uncertain terms his advances were not appreciated." Not that he'd listened to her, but there could be no doubt he'd received Stephen's message. "I believe he now understands my feelings on the matter."

Irene frowned. "I hope nothing I said made him act rashly."

She took Irene's hand. "I wish you'd understand that I don't want to marry."

"I only want you to have—"

"What you and Father had, I know, but what you shared was so special that I doubt many people have that chance."

Irene squeezed her hand. "As long as you promise not to completely rule out marriage if the right man should come along."

Abigail smiled, unable to keep the image of Stephen from popping into her mind. He made her heart beat faster, of that there was no doubt. She'd told him of her interest in financial matters and he hadn't batted an eye. But she didn't think he was interested in marriage any more than she. "Yes, I promise, as long as you promise not to encourage anyone else to approach me."

"That's fair." Irene leaned forward to press a kiss on Abigail's temple and squeeze her shoulder. "I'm sorry you're feeling poorly, dear. Stay right here and rest. I'll have Eloise bring up some warm chocolate."

"That would be lovely. Thank you."

Sophia and Olivia arrived with the hot drink and sat on either side of her for a time, concerned that she wasn't feeling well. Their presence gave her such comfort, but when their governess arrived, they departed, leaving her alone with her thoughts again.

As she enjoyed the chocolate, Abigail couldn't help but imagine the story Lord Brighton would circulate for his injuries. The idea of running into him next week or even next month made her feel worse.

Would he try something again? She shuddered at the thought. Last night had been a narrow escape. If she wanted to remain independent so she could continue to manage her family's investments and help others manage theirs, vigilance needed to be her constant companion. The next time, Stephen wouldn't be there.

She'd be forever grateful to him for rescuing her otherwise she might be betrothed this morning. She frowned, trying to remember what he'd said as he'd carried her to the carriage. Something about how he'd seen Brighton's ill intent. Whatever had he meant?

With a sigh, she closed her eyes, embarrassment heating her face as she thought of her forward behavior in the carriage. Then she realized she didn't care. She'd do it again if given the chance. Stephen was unique as was her reaction to him. She might never again meet a man like him.

Strong.

Virile.

Passionate.

And she mustn't forget dangerous. The manner in which he'd dealt with Brighton with such ease made her shiver.

Dangerous indeed.

He kept a distance between himself and others, and that was something with which she was familiar.

She would never again risk losing someone she loved. She'd decided that soon after her father had been killed. The pain of losing him had been unbearable. While she refused to turn over all her hard-earned income to a husband, her decision to never marry hinged even more on her desire not to be hurt again.

To date, she hadn't met anyone who'd changed her mind. In fact, the men she'd encountered confirmed to her that she wasn't meant for marriage.

A marriage of convenience had never been an option she'd seriously considered. Convenient for whom? Certainly not for her. Besides, her stepmother and the twins still needed her.

Yet without the protection of a husband, she was vulnerable to what Lord Brighton or any other hopeful suitor imposed upon her as Stephen had said. A dismal thought for certain.

A knock at the door interrupted her thoughts.

"Miss? You have a visitor," said Eloise with a smile.

Dread filled her. Surely Lord Brighton wouldn't have the gall to come. "Who is it?"

"Lord Ashbury."

The air left her lungs in a whoosh. How unexpected. Her cheeks flooded with heat. Her heart beat furiously.

"Shall I have Ponsford send him away?"

"No! No." She sucked in a breath. "Tell Ponsford I'll be down shortly."

"Of course, miss. I'll be right back to assist you."

As soon as the maid shut the door behind her, Abigail scrambled out of bed, breathing deeply to calm herself. "Oh, dear!"

What on earth was Stephen doing here? Her mind spun at the possibilities. A flutter of longing curled deep within her.

Abigail put a hand to her forehead to see if she had a fever after all. She must be coming down with something. No other excuse explained the heat flooding her entire body.

Shoving the unfamiliar feelings aside, she hurried to her wardrobe, wondering what to wear. She still hadn't been able to decide by the time her maid returned. "Which one, Eloise?"

"Perhaps the yellow? You look lovely in that." The maid pulled out the gown to hold it for Abigail's inspection. Her brown eyes twinkled with excitement, making Abigail realize how unusual the situation was.

Rarely—no, never—did she have male visitors.

"Excellent idea. Did you see him? How did he look?" Abigail asked as Eloise assisted her with her stockings and chemise.

"Ponsford? He looks fine, miss."

"Not Ponsford. Lord Ashbury."

"Oh. I didn't see him. Ponsford had already showed him into the drawing room."

With quick efficient movements, Eloise fastened her corset then reached for her camisole. Finally she drew the gown over Abigail's head and began to arrange her hair.

"I hit my head last night," Abigail said as she touched the bump, "so please be careful."

"Oh, miss, that's a terrible goose egg! No wonder you have a headache this morning."

With a gentle touch, she arranged Abigail's hair into a loose chignon. "There you are, miss. You look lovely."

Abigail studied her reflection in the mirror with a critical eye. Her face was pale and shadows marked her eyes, but little could be done about that. She drew a deep breath to calm herself, surprised to realize she was trembling. Surely Stephen was only here to make certain she was recovering from the previous night's events.

Very kind of him actually.

How odd that 'kind' was a word she'd use to describe him despite the violence she'd witnessed last night.

Uncertain what to expect, she made her way down to the drawing room where Ponsford stood immobile in front of the closed door. The butler made no effort to open it for her.

"Are you going to let me in?" she asked warily.

"Do you realize the identity of your visitor?"

Abigail narrowed her eyes, wondering where this conversation was going. "Lord Ashbury?"

Ponsford raised a brow—the right one of course. "I do believe he's the very person we agreed it would be best if you avoided."

Abigail had forgotten that. "Oh. Yes. Well..."

"He is a dangerous man, miss," he whispered.

The image of him beating Brighton came to mind. "That's true, but he's helped me tremendously."

"He located Simmons?"

"Not yet. He might need assistance with that."

Ponsford looked down his nose at her. "That shouldn't require your involvement."

"Well—"

"I don't believe it wise to associate with him."

"I know, Ponsford. Truly I do. But some risks may be necessary to protect our family."

With a scowl, he put his hand on the doorknob. "There's one more thing you should know."

"And that is?"

"Lady Bradford is in there with him."

Abigail stared at Ponsford, her stomach sinking to her knees. "Oh, no."

CHAPTER TEN

"I saw you at the Mortenson's ball last night, did I not?" Lady Bradford offered Stephen a polite smile.

"Briefly." He wondered how long he'd have to wait until Abigail arrived to save him.

"When did you and my daughter become acquainted?"

"Only recently." He could feel the woman's curiosity, even see it in the streaks of her aura, but he didn't intend to answer her questions. He'd leave that to Abigail.

"Hmm. Well, it's very kind of you to drop by even though it's rather early for visiting."

He gave what he hoped was a charming smile at her reprimand but didn't rise to the bait, waiting to see if she'd berate him further for not following social rules. In truth, he was out of practice. He couldn't think of the last time he'd called upon a lady.

"I believe she'll be down shortly."

"Thank you," he said.

"Lovely weather we've been having."

"Indeed." He'd never been adept at the art of small talk and since the accident that lack had worsened. The difference between people's thoughts and what they said was distracting, to say the least. It made it difficult to keep track of conversations.

The door opened and Abigail rushed into the room, ending the awkward silence. For that he was grateful. She looked back and forth between them as though worried about what topic they were discussing.

She wore a gown of golden yellow, but that seemed a poor description of it. The warm, sunny color flattered her luminescent complexion and enhanced her aura. He could hardly take his eyes off her. Relief filled him as he realized she looked quite recovered from last night's incident.

He rose to greet her, taking her hand in his before he realized what he'd done.

"Lord Ashbury. This is...unexpected." Her tone held a reproof he found amusing.

Stephen almost wished he hadn't made this visit, but what he had to tell Abigail couldn't wait. It was the least he could do after the previous night's events.

"Abigail, I didn't realize you and the viscount were so well acquainted." Lady Bradford's brows rose as she waited for an explanation.

For the first time since he'd met Abigail, she had no immediate response. In fact, she nearly squirmed as she tugged her hand from his. "We were...introduced a week or two ago." She looked at her stepmother as though to see if her response was sufficient.

"Oh?"

She shifted as though still trying to keep the squirming urge at bay. Apparently some of her thoughts were dark as her aura smudged with gray.

Stephen had learned over the years that the more often someone acted on their negative ideas, the darker their aura became. One of the reasons he was here was to make certain that never happened to Abigail's brilliant aura. That alone was worth the uncomfortable situation in which he now found himself.

"So nice of you to drop by, Lord Ashbury." Abigail's glare conveyed the opposite of her words.

He smiled, pleased last night had not damaged her spirit. Deciding the time had come to proceed with the reason for his visit, he turned to Abigail's stepmother. "It was lovely to meet you, Lady Bradford."

The woman remained still for a long moment, as though deciding whether to comply with his subtle request for a few moments alone with her daughter. At last she rose, her eyes alight with curiosity. "A pleasure to meet you as well, my lord. I hope we'll see you again."

Stephen dipped his head, neither agreeing nor disagreeing.

Lady Bradford turned to her daughter. "I trust you'll be along shortly, Abigail?"

"Of course."

The lady left with one last glance over her shoulder, leaving the door open wide.

Abigail waited a moment before walking to the door to peek out then pushed it nearly closed. When she turned back to him, her expression changed to irritation, something he was getting used to seeing.

"What on earth are you doing here?"

"I came to inquire as to how you're feeling."

Her cheeks flushed pink as did her aura. "I'm—I'm a bit bruised but fine."

He waited to see if she'd offer more. He could only imagine how upset she was. He'd spent a restless night and ventured to guess she'd tossed and turned as well.

She shrugged, clearly uncomfortable with the subject. "I fear the next encounter I have with Lord Brighton will be rather awkward, but I don't intend to let that keep me from my normal activities."

Even the mention of Brighton's name angered Stephen. He clenched his fists in an attempt to rein in his temper. "That's one of the reasons I'm here."

A frown marred her brow. "What do you mean?"

"It seems that Brighton is planning to leave London."

"Truly?" The hope that lit her face justified his early morning visit to Brighton's home.

"Indeed. He'll be gone for some time." He could nearly see her mind process his news.

"I heard nothing of this last night."

"I believe it's a new development."

"Is he spending some time at his country estate?"

"Actually, he's leaving for the continent."

"What did you do?" Her eyes narrowed.

"Pardon me?"

"You heard me. What did you do?"

She'd come to know him better than he'd realized, but he didn't intend to confirm her suspicions. He had no desire to darken her golden light with the details of his exploits.

But he wouldn't lie to her either. "I merely had a few words with him."

"On my behalf?"

Stephen shifted, now the uncomfortable one. He couldn't quite tell what she was thinking. Surely she wouldn't be angry with him for taking care of this matter. The woman needed someone to protect her and if she refused to find a husband, he had to serve in that capacity this time. Their acquaintance would soon end and someone else would be responsible for her.

The thought caused him to scowl.

"Yes," he said at last.

Wonder spread over her face and she stepped

forward to grasp his hands. "No one has ever done something like that for me."

In that moment, Stephen understood how challenging her life had been since her father's death. A young girl who'd had to grow up quickly and become the head of her family. No chance for the frivolity young ladies of her station should enjoy. No hand to guide her or shelter her from the harshness of the world. No male relative to protect her.

All the more reason she needed a husband. If only he could make her see that. An honorable man who would love her for her independence, not try to squelch it.

He released her hand to cup her cheek. "A man such as he has no business claiming the title of gentleman. Nor should you be forced to encounter him at a ball or some other outing."

"I confess the notion worried me. What exactly did you say to him?"

Stephen shook his head. He would not sully her with the details of the meeting. How Brighton had stumbled back in fear and groveled. "You must promise me this. You will be more careful in the future. You will not wander about alone *anywhere*. You will not go to the East End or any other inappropriate neighborhoods."

"I hardly think—"

"Abigail, if not Brighton, some other man could easily repeat what happened last night with a far worse outcome."

She frowned and dropped his gaze. He could tell the realization had already occurred to her, no matter that she didn't like it. "Yes, well, I plan on being much more careful."

"That might not be good enough."

"What would you have me do?"

He gritted his teeth and said what needed to be said, no matter that he didn't like it. Hated it, in fact. "Marry."

A faint flush filled her cheeks as her eyes widened and her mouth opened in surprise. "Is that a proposal?"

Shock coursed through him, stealing his breath. The idea of having Abigail at his side night and day filled him with a longing so deep, he could hardly think. "No!"

"Then what do you mean?" She seemed almost angry at his denial. Or was she disappointed?

"I'm merely repeating that a husband would offer the protection you need."

"But not you." She lifted her chin as she said it, as though daring him to disagree.

He swallowed hard. He had no right to the feelings he had for Abigail, for the desire with which his body betrayed him when she was near, for the fierce protectiveness he felt for her. She deserved so much more than he. "Not me," he said at last.

"I see."

He couldn't let it go at that. He didn't want her to think the blame lay with her. With an attempt at a wry smile, he said, "Marriage is not an option for a man such as me."

She tilted her head to one side as though his response puzzled her. "How so?"

"You've seen my...shall we say unusual occupation. Not a good fit for a wife and family." Not to mention his headaches, the bouts of deep despair that slid over him, and oh, yes, his cursed aura reading ability. But he intended to keep those secrets.

"You do seem to live dangerously."

Relief filled him as he realized she grasped his problem.

"But I would think that the right woman would understand, perhaps even help you in your endeavors," she said with a bright, knowing smile.

How dare she use his words from last night back at him?

"I hardly think you can compare your hobby of investing with my—"

"Do *not* refer to my interest as a hobby." The thin line of her lips told him he'd found a sore spot. "It provides us with a stable income, thank you very much."

"How clever of you."

"I know of several investment opportunities you might be interested in." She blinked up at him with those big blue eyes.

"I'm certain you do," he gritted out between clenched teeth. How had she turned the conversation so quickly?

"Perhaps with better use of your money, you wouldn't need to involve yourself in the gaming house."

He breathed deep before he indulged in the urge to kiss her silent again. That seemed to be the only method to get her to stop talking.

"You see," she said, obviously warming to her subject, "investing is rather simple if you consider the advantages and disadvantages of each investment opportunity and weigh them carefully."

He closed his eyes, hoping for patience. He didn't dare kiss her in her own home. Her mother was no doubt right outside the door.

"I'd be happy to share what I've learned with you."

Patience showed no sign of arriving. That meant he had to leave. He walked to the door with his jaw clenched, hoping to escape before he did something he'd regret.

"Where are you going?"

Without a backward glance, he shut the door behind him with a satisfying click. The gasp on the other side of it was almost as satisfying.

He'd been wrong to think the woman could marry. She'd drive her husband mad within days of the nuptials.

He nodded at the tall, elderly butler who stood in the foyer. Stephen paused, looking carefully at him.

"My lord?" asked the man.

"Ponsford?"

"Yes."

"She has the craziest notions."

"Yes, my lord," he said, his voice so matter-of-fact that Stephen realized the butler had probably been privy to that information for years.

"We need to keep a close watch over her."

The servant held his gaze. "Not an easy task."

"No, but over the next week, it will continue to be necessary. Of vital importance, in fact."

Ponsford nodded. "Yes, my lord."

Stephen couldn't help but smile, for he knew he'd have assistance watching over Abigail.

"Best of luck to us both," he muttered as he walked out the door. "We're going to need it."

Two days later, Abigail perused the shelves at the small bookstore on Truckford Lane, her nerves humming. She'd received a cryptic message from Stephen requesting she meet him here but he had yet to make an appearance. She hoped he planned to tell her Simmons had been found and successfully warned off. If that were true, she intended to propose they change their relationship to something of a more personal nature: an affair.

Her stomach dipped at the very idea of it. To calm herself she picked a book from the shelf before her and paged through it.

The shop sat on the edge of respectability and, from what she'd seen, its customers were a mixture of the affluent and the middle class.

Based on the interesting collection of books offered for sale, all patrons seemed to share a serious love of reading.

Abigail returned the book to the shelf and walked through the narrow aisles with their tall shelves and stacks of books. Stephen's choice of a meeting place was quite clever. The layout offered privacy. They were unlikely to run into anyone they knew here due to the location of the bookstore. And she couldn't help but be touched at his thoughtfulness of selecting a place she would enjoy browsing. Books were one of her favorite things.

She bit her lip as her mind returned to thoughts of Stephen.

An affair.

The idea sent shivers down her arms. She'd thought about it from every angle. It made perfect sense. Neither of them wanted to marry, and while she was certainly no expert, they seemed to have a certain spark.

Who was she kidding? A spark?

She'd never felt this deep sense of longing before in her whole life. It was an ache that poured through her entire being from head to toe when she was near him.

Or when she thought of him.

And especially when she dreamed of him.

Somehow, she was certain this was a once in a lifetime opportunity. At the age of six and twenty, she'd had the chance to meet many men yet had never felt anything like this. She wanted the chance to explore these feelings. Since she didn't want to marry and neither did Stephen, delving into a passionate affair with him seemed the perfect solution.

She'd spent hours determining the proper way to suggest it, but in the end had decided the words would come to her along with the opportunity.

Just the thought of talking to him about it made her stomach flutter.

She'd dressed carefully for the occasion in a gown of blue a shade darker than her eyes. Her hair was twisted into a loose chignon topped with a little hat. She knew she looked her best. Irene had even complimented her as she left the house, supposedly for a meeting with Mr. Nesbitt.

As she paused to study the binding of another book, she reminded herself she need only convince Stephen of the benefits of her plan. He'd see the logic of her suggestion; she was sure of it.

What on earth was keeping him?

"May I help you find something, miss?" A small mouse of a man stepped forward, his shop apron streaked with dust and ink, and a pleasant smile on his face.

"I'm only browsing, but I must say, your collection is quite impressive."

The man beamed with pride. "I try to offer books on every subject a customer has ever inquired about. If I don't have it, I find it. If I can't, I contact an author who I think is capable of writing about a particular subject, and together, we publish a book to answer that need."

"What a clever idea." Her mind flew with the possibilities.

"I realized several years ago that if one person was interested enough to look for a book on a topic, someone else would be as well. Of course, those books are only available in my shop."

"Exclusivity, of course. Brilliant."

"It's worked out well thus far. We recently expanded and need to do so again soon. It's always a bit of a struggle between wanting to offer a larger selection and having enough revenues to make changes. Can't do one without the other."

"Do you have investors?"

"Good day, Miss Bradford. I see you've met Mr.

Larson."

The sound of Stephen's voice so near had her spinning around in surprise, her heart racing at the sight of him. His black morning coat fit his broad shoulders impeccably. A gray silk waistcoat contrasted with his white shirt and black neck scarf.

As always, it was his eyes that drew her— those green eyes that held more secrets than one person ought to have. She longed to lift the dark depths from them, if only temporarily.

Would he allow her to?

She pulled her thoughts back to the conversation and smiled at the shopkeeper. "Not formally."

Stephen introduced her and advised Mr. Larson that they wanted to browse. Soon they were left alone to wander among the rows of books.

"So you have news?" she asked, anxious to hear if anything more had occurred with Simmons. She bit her lip, hoping Stephen would tell her the threat of him harming her family was gone.

"Some," he said as he took a book from a shelf and glanced around as though to ensure no one overheard them.

Worry settled in her stomach, smothering her hope as she studied his serious expression.

"As you know," he continued, "we found Simmons' new lodgings and posted a man to watch it. Oddly enough, it took several days before Simmons showed up."

"I haven't seen him following me or my family either." She told herself there was no need for the sense of foreboding that filled her.

"We wondered where he'd been as well. Once he made an appearance, we decided to follow him rather than confront him so we could see what he was about."

Her unease bloomed. "And?"

"He made several stops, including a baker, an apothecary shop, and a butcher."

"That doesn't seem unusual."

"At the butcher, he bought cheap cuts of flank but far more than one man could eat. He purchased a dozen loaves of bread from the baker. At the apothecary, he obtained a large quantity of a sleeping remedy."

"How odd. Does he have family elsewhere to whom he's taking supplies?" Somehow she'd never imagined him with loved ones.

"Not that we've found. Then we followed him to a warehouse near the docks. Not exactly a place where relatives would be living."

Abigail was silent for several minutes while she thought over the information. "What do you make of this?"

"I think he's involved in something bigger than harassing you and your family."

The idea surprised her. "Such as?"

"I don't know, but I intend to find out. I wanted you to be aware of the situation as I'm having him followed until we know more."

She sighed as disappointment seeped through her. She'd been afraid that had been the point he was making, but she knew he was right. If Simmons was involving others, they needed to discover his plan and with whom he was working.

"I don't think Simmons has the wherewithal to mastermind a grand scheme on his own," added Stephen, watching her closely.

"Which means he's under the direction of someone else."

"Yes, and I want to know who."

"How long do you expect it will take before you can put an end to all this?" The stress of constantly being on watch for Simmons was wearing on her. She was ready to move forward with her life, and she'd hoped to begin today.

"I wouldn't think long now that we've found him. The good news is that since we're following him, there's little risk of him bothering you without us knowing about it."

"Unless you lose him."

"Unlikely, but yes," he admitted. "We know where he's staying at least part of the time, and where he's purchasing supplies. Whatever he's doing, I'm certain he's up to no good. With a bit more time, we'll know what it is and stop him. Consider the delay a way to help others."

"I can't help but worry he'll approach us again."

"We'll do everything we can to make sure that doesn't happen." He paused, his gaze resting above her head for a long moment.

She opened her mouth to ask if her hat was crooked when he set down the book, took her elbow and escorted her to the rear of the store. He glanced around to make sure they were alone.

"I realize I'm asking much of you, but it might help if we knew more about what happened the day your father was killed."

Abigail's heart squeezed. While time had eased the raw edges of her grief, it hadn't truly faded. Witnessing her father's violent death at the age of sixteen had forever changed her life. She still found it difficult to discuss. However, if recounting the events could help in any way, she'd tell Stephen all she could.

"Father and I were at our country estate in Kent. Mother had remained in London with the twins. We'd been visiting a local squire that afternoon, and when we returned, we went into the library so Father could retrieve some papers." Abigail shivered as the memories of that day flooded her mind and heart.

"Simmons stood near the desk with papers and

books strewn all over, the room torn apart. Father demanded to know what he was about."

She folded her arms across her middle to hold the pain inside. "The police said later he'd broken a window pane and unlatched a door." Her gaze met Stephen's to see if he wanted her to continue.

His expression held sympathy and concern. "Then what happened?"

"Simmons drew a knife as Father charged toward him." She could still see the bright flash of it and feel the fear that had shot through her. "Simmons demanded he back away. Father told him to drop the knife. Neither complied. Then Father grabbed for the knife. They struggled, yelling and knocking things over. Simmons gained the upper hand and stabbed Father. Simmons ran when one of our servants came in."

The picture was so vivid in her mind that she had to fight the burning lump in her throat. "Father staggered and fell to the floor. I couldn't stop the blood. So much of it." She stared at her gloved hands, still able to see the crimson soaking his white shirt, coating her hands as she tried to make it stop.

Stephen took her hands and held them tight. "How terrible."

"Father must've realized how badly he was injured, for he grabbed my arm and pulled me close. He..." she closed her eyes as tears choked her, "he said I was to take good care of Mother and the girls. Then the light in his eyes went out. I shook him and pleaded with him, but he didn't come back."

"I can only imagine how difficult it is to remember that day. Did you determine what Simmons was after?"

She swallowed and drew a shaky breath. "No. The police thought it was just a burglary."

"Can you think back to when you first saw

Simmons? Was he searching a particular area or looking at something specific?"

Abigail tried to picture the room. "Books and papers were scattered about. The drawers had been pulled from the desk and upended."

Stephen put his arm around her and drew her close. His presence comforted her in ways she hadn't imagined, soothing her grief. With the calmness came the memory of Simmons standing at the desk, several rocks from her father's collection in his hands. That image brought a reminder of Simmons' words.

"He wants a rock! He told me so the night I confronted him in the alley. That's what he was holding when we came into the library that day."

"A rock?"

"Collecting them was a hobby of my father's."

Stephen frowned. "Did his collection contain anything of value?"

"I've no idea. He enjoyed gathering specimens and speaking with fellow collectors. I know he had several from other countries and all different types."

"Do you still have the collection?"

"Most of it. We had to sell a few of his things when he died. The rest of the collection is in our library. That must be why Simmons broke in—to continue his search."

"Interesting that upon being released from prison, Simmons immediately comes to look for this rock. May I see the collection?"

"Certainly."

Stephen touched her cheek gently and she wanted nothing more than to lose herself into his arms, to ease the pain of her memories with the passion she was certain she could find in his embrace.

But the time had not yet come to propose the idea of an affair to him, much to her disappointment. Her enthusiasm for the idea had been diminished by memories of her father. With a deep breath, she pulled back her emotions and her memories.

"Are you all right?" Stephen asked as he trailed a finger along her cheek, his gentleness disarming her meager defenses.

"I'm fine," she said, nearly meaning it. His tender regard made her heart squeeze. Perhaps the moment wasn't right today, but soon, she'd convince him to have an affair with her. Her blossoming feelings for him demanded no less. "You're right. We should try to discover what else Simmons is involved in. Other people's lives may depend upon it."

He clasped her hand and gave her a smile. "I'll let you know what transpires."

CHAPTER ELEVEN

"This is not a wise plan," Stephen said as he watched the entrance of Newgate the following evening.

Night had fallen, bringing with it a dense, damp fog which added to the eerie atmosphere that had always surrounded the prison the few times he'd visited.

He turned once again to stare at the boy's attire Abigail wore. He couldn't help it. The bulky jacket wasn't flattering, but her snug trousers reminded him that she was long-limbed and rounded in all the right places.

"Yes, it is. We've already discussed it." She tugged the brim of her cap lower as though she, too, was uncomfortable with her attire.

"How I let you convince me to come along escapes me." Stephen pulled his gaze back to the large, grim granite building, trying to ignore her presence and focus on the task at hand.

Abigail had pleaded with him to accompany him when he'd informed her of the meeting. Next time, he'd remember not to tell her about such things until after the fact. He was no match for her brand of logic or those amazing blue eyes. Who could say no to her?

Gas lamps lit the narrow wooden door of the prison entrance. The iron teeth at the top seemed to threaten any visitors brave enough to ring the bell. The structure had a hopeless air to it and was an unpleasant spot to linger near. He hoped the guard Farley had located would soon arrive so he could get Abigail away from the dismal place. The man had worked there when Simmons had been convicted and supposedly hung for murder.

"Of course I had to come. I want to hear what this guard has to say. Why does that seem so unreasonable?"

"Let's see. Perhaps because you're a lady? Or because your stepmother would faint dead away if she knew what you were about. Or it might be that—"

"Yes, yes. You've made your point." She glared up at him, the bill of her cap casting a shadow over her blue eyes in the dim light. "But I haven't changed my mind."

"Nothing so logical for Miss Bradford," he muttered.

"What was that?"

"Never mind. Remember, you promised to let me do the talking. If you utter even one word, you'll ruin your disguise."

"So you've told me," she said, her tone impatient.

"Forgive me, but the idea of you staying quiet for any length of time seems unlikely."

"If you ask the questions I wrote down, there'll be no need for me to speak. Did you bring the list?"

He pulled it from his coat pocket for her inspection.

"Well then, I'll remain as quiet as a mouse."

"I think this is our man," Stephen said. "Stay behind me so he doesn't get a good look at you."

An older man in a dark uniform with a ring of keys dangling from his pocket shuffled toward them. His shoulders hunched even further as he glanced around before approaching them. "You be the guv lookin' for information?"

"Yes."

The warder peered at Abigail warily, making Stephen's nerves draw taught. "Who's this?"

"No one of import." Stephen moved to shield her from view, cursing himself for allowing her to be there.

"Let's see the money first. You're askin' a lot to remember somethin' that happened nearly a decade ago."

Stephen drew some notes from his pocket and the guard reached for them. "Hold off. Half now and the remainder will be yours if we're satisfied with your information."

The warder muttered but pocketed the money.

"What can you tell us about Vincent Simmons' release?"

"I believe you've got your facts wrong. Vincent Simmons hung for murder three days after he was found guilty. That was ten years past."

Stephen heard a protest behind him and reached back to hold Abigail in place. "So the records say, but you and I know better."

The man gave a sly smile. "A man named Edward Smith was sentenced to ten years for burglary that same day. He served his time at Pentonville."

"And?" Stephen prompted before Abigail tried to speak.

"Rumor has it that Smith took Simmons place with the executioner in exchange for money to take care of his wife and children. Very noble of Smith, don't you think? I wonder if his widow thought so. Course some said he was dyin' from consumption anyway. He certainly was thin enough and had a nasty cough. Mayhap it was true."

Stephen had suspected something like this had

occurred. At times there was no justice in the world. "Who arranged for the switch?"

"Don't know, but a murderer of a nobleman don't get off that easy on some guard's say-so."

"A name would be of value to us." Stephen pulled out another note.

The guard swallowed hard as he stared at the money. "You didn't hear it from me."

"Your identity will remain a secret."

"All right. Near as I can tell, it was Charles Nulty, the Chief Warder. But some say more than him was involved."

Stephen pondered what little he knew of the man, surprised he'd succumbed to bribery of any sort. Or perhaps it had been blackmail that had persuaded him. Information could often be used as leverage on the best of men.

He felt a poke in the back and turned to find Abigail pointing toward the list tucked in his pocket. Lord, but the woman was relentless.

Without bothering to consult the list, he turned back to the guard. "I have a difficult time believing Simmons had the intelligence or the wherewithal to arrange all this."

"Someone on the outside did and provided the money for it as well."

"Who?" Stephen prompted.

The warder shook his head. "If anyone knows, they're not sayin'. One of the prisoners heard Simmons braggin' about how he had connections in the scientific world but he wasn't what I'd call a reliable source."

Stephen glanced to Abigail to see if this meant anything to her but she shook her head. "Why would a scientist want Simmons?" he asked the warder.

The guard shrugged. "No one seemed to know."

"We need a name."

"There isn't one. I already tried. I figured you'd

be willin' to pay extra for that but either no one knows or no one's talkin'."

Stephen studied the man's aura, but could see no obvious sign of deceit, which reinforced Stephen's own instincts. There was no point in pressing the man further.

As though he read Stephen's thoughts, the warder said, "I need to be goin' now." He held out his hand for the rest of the money.

Stephen paid him. "If you come across more names, send word through the man who contacted you. He knows how to reach me."

"Don't count on it. Don't know who else I'd ask. Nice doin' business with you, guv."

Stephen watched the warder disappear into the shadows of the building as Abigail moved to stand beside him.

"Why didn't you make him give us a name?"

"He had no name to give."

"How do you know? He was probably lying."

"Let's just say I have experience in these matters." Stephen gestured at the hackney that awaited them at the end of the street and breathed a sigh of relief, knowing he'd soon have Abigail safely ensconced in her home.

"Odd that Simmons is searching for a rock and was rumored to be tied to a scientist. It makes no sense," she said.

He remained silent, pondering the information. It was starting to make sense to him, but he wasn't yet ready to share it with her, not until he discovered more.

"What is our next step?" she asked.

Stephen shook his head. Abigail's persistence never ceased to amaze him. "We'll determine a list of potential people who were in a position to arrange the switch then investigate what scientists Simmons could have been involved with. Perhaps we can dig up more on Charles Nulty."

The silence between them grew long but it was comfortable. The darkness of the hackney's interior and the muffled hooves of the horse on the street created an intimacy Stephen knew he should fight. Abigail's scent was sweet—lavender if he wasn't mistaken. The warmth of her body pressed against his heated him from the inside out, especially when he envisioned her inappropriate attire.

Damn those pants.

She sighed and relaxed, leaning against him. The small movement stopped all his thoughts save one. He shoved it away and counted the lamp posts along the street, anything to stem the desire flooding him.

She wound her arm through his, and he swore he could feel her breast resting on his arm despite the thick jackets between them. He gave up on the lamp posts and tried desperately to remember all the Latin phrases he'd struggled through in school.

She rested her head on his shoulder with another sigh, snuggling closer.

Damn.

What was he to do?

The same thought as before the lamp posts came to him, and this time, he couldn't stop from acting on it. This time, there was no anger between them. Only pure desire.

He drew her into his arms and slowly lowered his mouth to hers, giving her the chance to refuse him. Part of him hoped she would, for he had no right to kiss her.

Instead, she lifted up to meet him halfway. That small gesture of acceptance released the floodgates of his desire. He kissed the edges of her lips then delved his tongue into the sweet depths of her mouth. She responded with eagerness, wrapping her arms around him as though she never wanted to let go.

He pushed off her cap so he could touch the soft strands of her hair. When that wasn't enough, he ran his hand along her side, down her hip to cup her bottom tucked so tightly in the trousers.

A moment passed before he realized the hackney had halted. He pulled back, attempting to gather his wits as he realized they'd arrived at her home.

She drew back as well, the dim light revealing the tendrils of dark hair framing her face, her lips full from his kisses. He closed his eyes for a moment, forcing his desire back.

He considered apologizing, but realized he didn't want to. "Good night, Abigail."

"Good night," she said softly. A dark flare appeared in her golden aura as she smiled and trailed her hand along his cheek then grabbed her cap.

As he watched the door to her home close behind her, he couldn't help but wonder what thought had crossed her mind.

He was certain it involved him, but he didn't think he'd like it, given the dark spear in her aura.

With a sigh, he gave the driver his address. He had to find a way to maintain his distance from her. Cozy hackney cab rides were no longer an option.

Abigail paced her bedroom in her nightgown, too restless to sleep after the events of the evening. To learn that someone had been paid to take Simmons' place was disturbing news. Why? Who was Simmons so important to that he would arrange for such a thing?

None of it made any sense.

It certainly confirmed what Stephen had

already determined—Simmons was not working alone.

She paused by her window to search the area below but nothing was visible in the dark. It was unnerving to know Simmons was still out there and wanted something from her. Since she hadn't given it to him, she had to assume he'd be back for it.

No wonder she couldn't sleep.

Stephen's ideas for additional inquiries on the switch seemed logical but unlikely to provide them with real answers. How many people would remember what had taken place that long ago?

She took comfort in the knowledge that Stephen was having Simmons watched. With luck, he'd get to the bottom of the situation before Simmons had a chance to follow through on his plans, whatever they were.

Thoughts of Stephen caused a peculiar feeling in the pit of her stomach. Leaning on him in the carriage had comforted her at first, but then her awareness of him had bloomed. There was no doubt her attraction to him was deepening each time she saw him.

Tonight, as she'd bid him goodbye, she'd realized she didn't have to worry about broaching the topic of an affair with him. Instead, she would simply let their attraction take them there.

The very idea of it made her tremble.

As she saw the situation, she had two options. She could be forthcoming and tell him exactly what she wanted. That seemed such a cold way to approach what should be, dare she say, hot?

Or—

Her breath caught as heat coursed through her. She could seduce him. She bit her lip as the idea formed more clearly. He'd hold her as he had earlier, kiss her, even caress her, and at last she'd know what it was like to make love.

To be a woman in truth.

She couldn't think of a better man to give her that experience. No one else could make her heart pound with a simple look and that slow smile. No one else could make her head spin with his kisses.

Now she need only determine the proper timing and arrange a few other details. She could ease into it; plant the seed of desire in their next meeting or two. An affair would follow naturally. That would make it a simple process, she thought with a smile. One she looked forward to. A welcome distraction from the worry of Simmons.

She need only find her courage to make it a reality.

The next afternoon, Stephen surveyed the rocks and minerals displayed on the desk in Abigail's library. With much effort, he kept his gaze on the specimens rather than Abigail. A difficult task considering the pale blue gown she wore with its low-cut neckline, something highly unusual for this time of day. Or perhaps he was more out of touch with society and fashions than he'd thought.

For the tenth time, he reminded himself that the purpose of his call was to inspect the rock collection, not ogle her.

He'd been certain her stepmother would be home, but Lady Bradford and her two youngest daughters were out shopping.

"Your father had an extensive collection," he commented, tearing his gaze away from tempting curves of her breasts. The sweet pink of her aura caused his own passion to rise.

"Yes," she said as she bent forward and lingered in that position to reach for an obsidian rock, her curves drawing his gaze again. "Grandfather gave him a few items when he was young and Father collected many more over the years."

He held his breath, wondering if she'd spill out of the low neckline. Once she'd straightened, he forced his gaze from the perfection of her breasts to look at the rock she held.

She rubbed the black, shiny surface back and forth slowly with her thumb. Her pink aura deepened to rose even as she looked at him from beneath her long lashes.

Was she trying to drive him mad?

"He brought back many from his travels," she added.

"Did he have a particular area of interest?" Stephen realized he held an oddly shaped conglomerate.

"Anything unusual, I suppose." She pointed to the books on a nearby shelf. "He studied all he could find on the subject and loved speaking to anyone who shared his...passion."

He swallowed hard, trying to cool his ardor. The way she'd spoken that word in her honeyed tone made it difficult to think. Out of the corner of his eye, he saw what looked to be a meteorite—a flat gray stone on the opposite side of the desk. "Do you know much about them?"

"Not really. He catalogued the collection but I'm not certain where that information is." She frowned as though trying to remember. "He was very excited about a particular meteorite he found while in India. That happened only a few months before his death. He also received a rather unique specimen from a fellow collector in Brazil."

Stephen walked around the desk to pick up the one he'd spotted. "Is this one of them?"

She took it from him, her fingers trailing along his palm. "I'm not sure. It might be. Do you collect as well?" Her bright blue eyes distracted him once again. Her bare fingers lingered in his palm as she handed the stone back to him.

He stared at her, his mind blank for a long moment. "I only dabble, but I once assisted someone who took great interest," he said at last. Professor Grisby had been an avid collector. He'd had a special interest in meteorites. In fact, before his death, he'd been searching for a particular lunar specimen said to aid in the conduction of electricity. He'd been certain it would help their experiments with electromagnetism and give them the even conduction for which they'd been looking.

"My stepmother and I have talked about donating the collection to The Society for the Science of Rocks and Minerals, but neither of us has had the heart to part with it." She sighed as she looked over the stones, her aura dimming. "I thought I'd put father's death behind me, but now that Simmons has returned, it seems to have brought it all back."

The quiver in her voice tugged at him. "I'm sure that's only natural. Not only did he die a violent death, but you witnessed it. That must make it all the more difficult." Stephen told himself he had no other choice but to draw her into his arms, unable to resist offering her some small measure of comfort.

She nestled into his embrace, her head on his shoulder, her warm form melding to his as though she were made for him. He could feel the tension in her body ease as he continued to hold her, running his hands along her back. "I'm sorry this is so painful for you."

She'd grown up with the weight of responsibility on her shoulders. Her desire for independence was a lonely path and he wondered if she'd realized that. She was turning her back on the very thing he couldn't have—a family.

He understood why in some respects, but he

didn't think she'd counted the many advantages a marriage with the right person could bring her.

She lifted her head to look at him, her eyes full of unshed tears. "Thank you."

"For what?" he asked, his hands pausing in their rhythm, hoping those tears wouldn't fall. He couldn't bear it.

"For understanding. For helping me with Simmons. For everything." She smiled tremulously. "What started as a simple quest was no such thing, I fear."

"Yes." The mention of the reason for their relationship doused him with reality and reminded him to maintain his distance. He eased her from his arms, bracing himself when her smile fell, hoping the tears wouldn't follow.

It wasn't his place to offer comfort or question the path she'd chosen for her life. Each time he met with her seemed like a test of his fortitude, of his ability to resist temptation—a test he had no intention of failing. Nothing good could come of indulging his affection for her except for temporary pleasure and that would end in hurt.

He did his best to push aside the black hole of darkness that opened before him at the thought of the lonely days ahead when the temptation of her had been removed. There was nothing to be done about it except move on, and the sooner the better.

"We've followed Simmons several times to a warehouse near Hook Lane and Blackwall Road close to the docks but haven't yet discovered why he's going there. The buildings and streets in that area are a maze which has made it difficult to track him."

Abigail sighed. "I have to confess it feels as though two steps are taken backward for every step forward."

"If we can't resolve the case soon, we'll form another plan. Perhaps set a trap of some sort."

"That's an excellent notion."

The excitement in her eyes made him nervous. Even as he stared, dark spears appeared in her aura. Now what was she thinking?

"I could be the bait for the trap. We could get the word to him somehow that I have the rock he wants." Her enthusiasm gained momentum. He could see her ideas swirling through her aura. "When shall we plan it? Perhaps tomorrow? Where do you think would be the best place?"

Stephen held up his hand in an attempt to slow her down. "You'll not be luring him anywhere. That is not an option."

"Why ever not? I think it would be quite effective."

"But not safe."

"You'd be nearby, would you not?"

"My presence wouldn't prevent Simmons from drawing that knife of which he seems so fond."

"Oh."

He watched as her enthusiasm for her idea deflated like a dirigible tangled in a tree.

"I would feel better if I were assisting you in some capacity," she said. "Surely you could use another pair of eyes watching for him." Her hopeful expression was difficult to resist.

"Abigail, I would not risk even so much as a hair on your head." He reached out to run a finger along the black, silken strands just above her ear, enjoying her reaction as her eyes widened and her breath caught. "We will discover what he's up to soon enough along with who else is involved. But we will not risk any harm to you."

Those fathomless blue eyes held his and, for a long moment, he thought her in agreement.

"I appreciate your concern. Truly, I do."

He sighed, bracing himself for her argument. From past experience, he knew it would be a sound and logical one.

"But at times such as these, reward cannot be gained without risk. Please know that I'm prepared to do whatever it takes to capture Simmons and put an end to the nefarious plan in which he's involved."

He marveled at how she could take him from desire to anger in a moment. A remarkable skill for certain and quite effective. "I appreciate your willingness to sacrifice yourself."

Her cheeks colored at his words.

"But we'll leave sacrifice to others. I have people working for me who are skilled in such matters. There's no need to—"

"I have to disagree." She lifted her chin, those blue eyes determined. "It's me he's after."

"That may be, but he can't have you." It took him the barest moment to realize how proprietary he sounded. This woman twisted him in knots—physically and mentally and verbally. His only option was to leave before he did something he'd regret.

"You will remain home or escorted by your footman at all times. You will not take any chances. Do you understand?"

Her reluctant agreement to his request made him doubt her sincerity right along with the dim color of her aura.

As he walked out of the house moments later, the meteorite in his pocket, he couldn't shake the uneasy feeling that came over him.

CHAPTER TWELVE

Abigail pondered the message from Stephen for the fiftieth time as she sat at her desk in her bedroom after breakfast.

Delivered two days ago, the note was vague at best.

Developments have arisen. More to follow.

S.

Yet nothing had followed. Why bother to send a note that said so little?

After worrying endlessly about what developments he referred to, she'd sent a message of her own yesterday, but he'd not bothered to answer. Waiting was driving her crazy. There had to be something else she could do.

Simmons hadn't been sighted for days now, but if anything, that made her more nervous. With everything Stephen had discovered, she had no doubt Simmons was plotting something terrible.

But what?

For the first time, she considered explaining the entire situation to her stepmother. She couldn't be with her family all the time. Poor Ponsford and Thomas had been on guard for weeks now and it was wearing on all of them. If Simmons wasn't caught soon, she'd have to tell Irene, though she dreaded the idea. Irene and the girls would be terrified.

No, she decided. That had to remain a last resort.

She'd promised her father she'd take care of her stepmother and the twins. That included not worrying them unless absolutely necessary. In this case, ignorance was bliss.

She rose from the desk more determined than ever. She had no choice other than to research the situation herself. Sitting here was accomplishing nothing. Obviously, something had gone awry, and it was up to her to discover what.

She'd take the proper precautions of course. No need to be rash, but a visit to the area by the docks Stephen had mentioned was in order. She considered taking Thomas with her but decided against it. The brawny footman would only draw attention and she wanted to remain in disguise. She need only avoid Ponsford as her stepmother and the twins were going out soon. Then she'd conduct her own investigation with no one the wiser.

Stephen strode into the dining room, anxious to hurry through breakfast so he could call upon Abigail. He'd already delayed longer than he should've, but he'd been trying to keep his distance. Each time he saw her, his feelings deepened. He could no longer trust himself when he was near her. Yet if he didn't advise her of their progress regarding Simmons soon, she'd do something drastic despite promising otherwise.

As per usual, the morning paper awaited him at the table. He sat and unfolded it as a footman arrived with eggs, hot rolls, bacon and a steaming cup of coffee.

He glanced through the headlines as he started on the eggs. Two bites into his meal, the fork clattered to his plate.

The headline read: *Reclusive Scientist Soon to Reveal Electromagnetic Experiment Results*.

Alarm spread through him as he read on, his appetite gone. The article was brief, mentioning a mysterious unnamed scientist who'd prepared sizable transducer coils held in a vacuum with the intent of making the electromagnetic waves self-propagating. His newly discovered technique allowed the waves to maintain velocity and therefore ensure a more even transfer of energy.

The writer was obviously a skeptic for he went on to say how other scientists had tried similar experiments without success.

One of those previous scientists had been Professor Grisby.

He read the ambiguous article several times, trying to pinpoint what bothered him. As the reporter stated, several other scientists had conducted such experiments. The professor hadn't been the only one. It wasn't unusual for multiple scientists to do similar experiments at nearly the same time. Often it was a matter of who published their results first to determine who received credit for the discovery.

Professor Grisby had nearly completed such an article at the time of the accident. He'd been certain the experiment would succeed and the only thing left to do would be to document the specifics in order to claim the discovery for his own.

Stephen started to set the paper aside but stopped. He couldn't shake his unease. Hadn't he learned over the years never to ignore the intuition that seemed to strike when trouble was near? The feeling he had now was no different. Harm would certainly befall someone if he walked away from it.

With reluctance, he pushed back the chair, paper in hand. The time had come to visit an old friend, or as Abigail had so aptly put it, a former friend.

He doubted Weston would be pleased to see him.

"Ashbury, this is an unexpected...surprise."

Stephen clenched his jaw at the lack of welcome from Weston. He'd anticipated it but that didn't make it easier to hear. Not for the first time, he wished he could see his friend's aura. Any sort of assistance to measure his thoughts would've been helpful. "Isn't that the nature of a surprise? To be unexpected?"

Weston didn't seem to appreciate the insight if his grim expression was any indication. He sat down at his ornate desk and drummed his fingers along the immaculate surface. "To what do I owe the honor of this visit?"

"Did you see this morning's paper?"

"I only had time to peruse the financial section. Why?"

Rather than answer, Stephen held out the paper folded to the article in question.

Weston took it and scanned the headline. "Electromagnetism? I would've thought you had lost interest in the subject. I certainly have."

"The article reminds me of someone."

Weston narrowed his eyes. "Who?"

"Professor Grisby."

With a scoff, Weston looked back at the paper. "Oh, please."

The derision in his voice stung. Stephen wondered if he really was losing his mind. First the headaches, then the melancholy. Now he was imagining things.

"I only ask that you read it."

Weston sighed then proceeded to do as he asked. At last, he said, "Many scientists are interested in electromagnetism these days. It's become quite the rage."

"But isn't it odd that this particular scientist is a recluse and refuses interviews?"

"Hardly. Most scientists are far from socially adept."

Frustrated, Stephen tried another avenue. "The vacuum transducer described is very similar to the one Grisby built."

"There aren't enough specifics here to determine that. Ashbury, what is it you want?" Weston asked, clearly annoyed by the discussion.

Stephen ran a finger along the inside of his collar which suddenly felt tight, wondering if he dared speak his mind. "Is there any possibility this scientist is Professor Grisby?" He knew it made no sense, yet he couldn't shake the feeling.

"Have you gone mad?"

Doubt and despair speared through him. "Perhaps." In truth he worried the dark mood that came more and more frequently might be a preview of insanity. "All I ask is for you to tell me this is not Professor Grisby."

"This is not Professor Grisby." Weston handed back the paper. "In case you've forgotten, he's dead."

"So there's nothing in this article that makes you uneasy?"

"Other than the fact that another scientist might lose his life while trying to control electromagnetism? No."

"But—"

"Ashbury, I've done as you asked. I hate to be rude but I have an appointment." He stepped around his desk, obviously intent on seeing him to the door.

Despite Weston's reassurances, Stephen's unease remained. He couldn't shake the feeling that something was amiss. Rather than taking

Weston's hint to leave, he remained where he was and read the article again. Weston was right. The simple words on the page described several other scientists. Why did he think of the professor when he read it?

Weston stood beside him and tapped the paper Stephen held. "I'm telling you, that can't possibly be the professor. We saw his body that night. We attended his funeral. We watched his sister and her family grieve. Surely you haven't forgotten that."

"No." Their grief was something he'd always remember. Professor Grisby's sister had sobbed uncontrollably. The sound had broken his heart. Her oldest child, still a young girl, was the only one who'd remained composed. Despite her dry eyes, her grief was palpable. The sag of her shoulders, the grim set of her mouth, her large, empty brown eyes staring straight ahead. The devastation seemed to have shaken her world.

"Then you know this has nothing to do with Grisby."

Stephen stared into Weston's eyes, trying to absorb the surety Weston had, but failing. "I'm going to see what more I can discover."

Weston shook his head. "You are the most stubborn—"

A knock at the door interrupted him.

"What is it?"

A servant stepped into the room. "A messenger has arrived for Lord Ashbury."

Stephen frowned. He couldn't imagine why any of his messengers would come here to speak with him. "I'll let you be on your way," he told Weston and moved to the door.

Weston followed him. "A messenger?"

He paused to look at his friend, surprised at his sudden interest. "Must be from one of my associates. We're in the middle of investigating a few problems."

Before he got to the door, James, one of the lads who worked for him, stepped forward, hat in hand.

"Sorry to bother you, my lord, but the man we've been watching for arrived at the warehouse near the docks. You said you wanted to know immediately."

"Well done." Stephen turned to Weston to say goodbye, regret filling him at the loss of his friend, wishing things were different. "I apologize for interrupting your morning."

Weston frowned. "Who have you been watching for down there?"

"No one you know. I'll bid you good day." Stephen moved toward the door.

"That's a rough area."

"Indeed."

"You're not going there alone?"

"James will be with me." Stephen looked at Weston, wondering what was going through his mind.

"He's a boy." Weston pointed out the obvious.

"He's tougher than he looks." Stephen nodded at the lad. The hope he held that Weston might assist them was a fragile thing.

Weston tugged on his watch fob to check the time. "I can't possibly accompany you. I'm already late."

Stephen pushed back the disappointment with a polite smile. It should be enough that Weston had considered it. "Of course." The loss of a friend, of someone he'd thought he'd always be able to count on, still hurt. "We'll be on our way."

"Wait." Weston stuffed the watch back in his pocket and ran a hand through his hair. "I don't think you should go down there without more support."

"Are you offering to accompany us?"

Weston sighed. "I suppose I am."

With a smile and a lightness in his heart, Stephen gestured toward the door. "I'd appreciate your assistance. I'll explain along the way."

They arrived near the dock in Stephen's carriage, but stopped short of Hook Lane, the area where Simmons had been seen. Stephen didn't want the carriage to draw attention.

"So this Simmons person is bothering Miss Bradford?" Weston asked as they alighted.

"Yes. We finally located him only to realize he's involved in something far larger than threatening Miss Bradford. He's been on a spending spree of late which indicates he has access to money. He's buying enough food for a group of people. Whoever he's working for had sufficient funds and connections to arrange for the switch of the two prisoners at Newgate. Someone willing to wait ten years for Simmons to be released from prison. All of that suggests a large operation. Simmons isn't smart enough to succeed in such an endeavor alone. At any rate, he needs to be stopped. The danger to Miss Bradford and her family cannot continue."

"Ah, yes. The delectable Miss Bradford. She seems to be at the heart of this matter."

Stephen glared at Weston, but held his tongue. Weston's description of her as 'delectable' angered him more than it should. He couldn't possibly be jealous.

"What ho," Weston said with a smile. "The lady is the true issue here. Has a woman at last captured your attention?"

"Weston, please. Focus. James will outpace us if we don't hurry along." Stephen was willing to say anything to silence his questions.

Weston chuckled but walked faster. "What is

Simmons after? Why does he bother Miss Bradford?"

"He told her he wants 'the rock' but hasn't been descriptive enough for her to know to what he's referring. Her father had a rather extensive rock collection, so we're assuming Simmons is after something in that."

"Interesting."

"One of the specimens in his collection is a lunar meteorite."

Weston stopped and grabbed Stephen's arm. "Grisby searched for that type of rock prior to his death."

"Indeed."

"Do you think it's the same type Grisby wanted?"

Stephen nodded.

"Quite the coincidence," Weston murmured.

"Isn't it?"

"That explains why the newspaper article upset you. You've already got the professor on your mind."

Stephen didn't bother to respond, grateful Weston had made the same connection he had. Perhaps he wasn't losing his mind after all.

They continued on, winding their way through the crowded, narrow street. Dock workers, clerks, and all manners of people went about their business, paying little heed to them. Carts piled high with goods jammed the lane with their drivers hollering to clear the way. James looked back once or twice to make certain they followed.

"Right over there, my lord." James stopped and pointed across the street.

The two-story brick and wood building had seen better days. The high windows were coated in soot and grime. The boards were rotting in places. Two huge doors sealed the front of the building with a large padlock and chain, visible even from where they stood.

"Picking that will be quite the challenge," Weston observed. "And me without the proper tools. I trust you have yours?"

Stephen smiled, knowing full well Weston didn't possess such tools. "I do, but I don't want to risk being seen. Is there another entrance, James?" he asked.

"Yes, around back. There's a smaller door on that side."

"Let's take a detour. I don't want to risk Simmons spotting us."

The trio backtracked through the muddle of people and buildings and at last drew within forty yards of the rear entrance. They paused to study the area which was nearly deserted except for two boys.

Stephen recognized Hubert, another of their associates, who was tucked in the corner of a nearby entryway, munching on a cone of chips. The other boy slouched against a doorway two doors down and seemed oddly familiar. The boy shifted, and something about his stance caught Stephen's attention.

"Christ!" Shock stole his thoughts.

"What?" Weston asked, looking again at the two street urchins.

"Miss Bradford," Stephen ground out, anger pouring through him.

"Where? The two boys..." Weston's voice trailed off as he watched a moment longer. "Impressive. I wouldn't have looked at her twice if you hadn't recognized her."

"Blast the woman! Her impatience is unbelievable."

As they drew closer, the rear door of the warehouse burst open. Simmons rushed toward Abigail. Apparently he'd recognized her as well.

Stephen's heart stopped as he sprinted toward

them. His feet felt mired in mud as he watched the scene unfold. He knew he couldn't reach her in time.

Simmons grabbed Abigail before she had a chance to flee. He started to shake her, but caught sight of Stephen and Weston bearing down on him. He jerked Abigail in front of him so they both faced Stephen. Simmons' knife blade gleamed as he pressed it to her throat.

Abigail's gaze met Stephen's, and he could see the fear that gripped her.

"Stay back," Simmons called out. "Ye don't want her hurt."

Stephen's footsteps slowed. "Let her go," he demanded.

Simmons smiled. "Leave off or I'll slit her throat."

Weston grabbed Stephen's arm and brought him to a halt. "Do as he says," he whispered. "We outnumber him by far so we'll free her soon enough."

Abigail's frightened gaze held Stephen's as Simmons backed away. Stephen had never felt so helpless. The pair disappeared around the corner of a narrow alley.

Hubert darted out from the entryway in which he'd hidden, fright etched in his face. "I'm sorry, my lord. It happened so fast. He had that pig sticker and—"

"No fault lay with you, Hubert," he reassured the boy. "Stay here with James."

"No! I want to help."

"Me too!" James added.

Stephen hesitated for only a moment. He didn't want anyone else in danger but the more eyes they had looking for Simmons and Abigail, the better. "James, take the far side of the building, and Hubert, take the other. If you see them, follow but keep your distance!"

The two boys dashed away as Stephen and Weston sprinted toward the alley where Simmons had dragged Abigail.

As they passed the door from which Simmons had emerged, it opened again. Two large men stepped out, blocking their path.

"Where do ye think ye're goin'?" One of the ruffians towered over Stephen, blocking the sky from view.

"You didn't mention this part of today's outing," Weston muttered from beside him.

"Wasn't planning on it myself."

"You get the bigger one."

"Of course," Stephen reluctantly agreed. Hoping to use the element of surprise, he hooked his booted foot behind the large man's ankle and shoved him back.

The man didn't budge.

All too aware of time passing and Abigail being taken farther and farther away, Stephen tried again, this time adding his fist into the equation. His opponent staggered but caught his balance.

He glimpsed Weston landing a blow on the smaller man and hope brought him strength. He slapped the man's fist away then boxed his ears. The big man staggered back, no doubt distracted by the ringing in his ears. Stephen delivered a quick uppercut to his chin followed by a swinging kick to his abdomen.

The man tottered for a brief moment before crumpling to the ground. Stephen turned to see Weston standing over his adversary who showed no sign of moving.

"You'll have to tell me where you learned to fight like that," Weston said as he brushed off the lapel of his jacket.

Stephen merely nodded, then tore down the alley where Abigail had disappeared. Weston's booted footsteps pounded right behind him. At the mouth of the alley, Stephen slid to a halt and looked up and down the busy street but could see no sign of them.

"There!" Weston pointed toward the docks.

Abigail seemed to have gathered her wits and had become a dead weight, making progress difficult for Simmons. Stephen nearly smiled at the sight. Simmons had no idea what he was in for if he managed to take her. The lady was a force unto herself.

With Weston behind him, Stephen darted around workers, carts, and horses, following as closely as he dared. He spotted Hubert approaching Simmons from the other direction. The boy gave Stephen a quick nod to acknowledge he'd seen him, then pulled his hat down low and hurried along. Hubert rammed into Simmons as though he hadn't been watching where he was going.

Simmons lost his grip on Abigail, and she slid to the ground. Simmons turned to yell at the boy, threatening him with his knife.

Hubert held up his hands, palms out. But rather than moving out of the way, the boy turned and stumbled, managing to maneuver himself between Simmons and Abigail.

Simmons grabbed the lad and shook him. Then he stared at the street urchin for a long moment. Simmons appeared to recognize the lad. Stephen quickened his pace, trying to weave through the crowded thoroughfare to reach them.

Abigail started to crawl away, hat in hand, which caught Simmons' attention. He stepped in front of her and shoved her back with his boot while still grasping Hubert's jacket with one hand, his knife in the other. Hubert lurched forward as though Simmons' movement had unbalanced him, but the way he put his shoulder into it, Stephen knew it was an act.

"That boy's going to get himself killed!" Weston said.

Simmons shoved at Hubert again, obviously desperate to grab Abigail before she escaped. But the lad didn't budge. The snarl on Simmons' face said his patience had come to an end. He stabbed Hubert in the abdomen.

"No!" Stephen yelled, but he was still too far away to be heard above the din of the street.

Hubert's shock at his injury lasted only a moment, then fury took over. The boy punched and kicked to defend himself, landing a solid blow to Simmons' leg.

A few passersby stopped when the scuffle crossed their path and within seconds a small crowd had gathered, partially obscuring Stephen's view. One man cheered for Simmons, while another shouted encouragement to Hubert. No one attempted to stop the madness. The crowd seemed anxious for the fight to continue, making it even more difficult for Stephen and Weston to reach them.

Stephen lost sight of the action as the press of bodies closed around them. "Save the boy," he called to Weston. "I'll find Abigail."

He waded into the crowd, his heart in his throat, hoping he could save her before Simmons used that knife on her.

CHAPTER THIRTEEN

Fear and anger warred inside Abigail. She lashed out at Simmons with her feet, anything to draw his attention from the boy. Her reward was a kick to her thigh. She grunted in pain but didn't stop.

She refused to let Simmons harm the lad any further, not when he'd been trying to save her. Using her heavy boot, she struck out again with all her might. Simmons cursed at her as he staggered back. She struggled to her feet, appalled at the cheers from the crowd encircling them. Couldn't they see the boy had been stabbed?

Desperate to find someone to aid her, she scanned the mob. The crowd parted briefly, and she caught sight of Stephen elbowing his way toward her. Relief flooded through her. She looked back to the boy and saw Lord Weston approaching him. Tears filled her eyes as she realized help had indeed arrived.

Simmons spotted the two lords as well. His foul language and knife divided the crowd quickly. Disappointed onlookers booed as he fled the scene.

"Stop him!" Abigail cried out, but no one listened, probably because of the bloody weapon he waved about. Within moments, he'd disappeared.

"He's getting away," she told Stephen as he

reached her.

Another boy appeared at Stephen's side, bouncing on his toes, eager to help. "I'll follow him, my lord."

"All right, James, but stay back. Do *not* let him see you." The lad took off before Stephen had finished speaking.

He turned back to Abigail and pulled her into his arms for a long moment. She felt him draw a deep breath, making her realize how worried he'd been. At last he eased back to study her face. "Are you all right?"

"'Tis the boy who was stabbed."

"But are you hurt?"

"Only bruised." She raised a hand to straighten her cap only to realize how much she was shaking. Now that Stephen had arrived, her racing heart started to slow, the knot of fear in her stomach loosened, but her leg throbbed from Simmons' kick.

"Get back," Lord Weston called out to the crowd, and people began to disperse. "Go on about your business!"

"Let us get you and Hubert to safety," Stephen said, his arm still around her as he guided her forward.

Hubert's pale face shook Abigail to the core. She watched in dismay as he put a hand to his stomach and his fingers turned red with blood. When he caught sight of it, his breath came in shaky gasps. Lord Weston supported him as he faltered.

Images from her father's death mingled with the sight of Hubert, bringing tears to her eyes. She started toward him, fear coiling inside her once again.

Stephen stopped her, those green eyes steady on hers. "Abigail, you must be strong. If Hubert sees you upset, he'll think his injury is worse than it is. Stay strong for me, all right?"

She blinked through her tears, holding Stephen's gaze as she attempted to calm down. After another deep breath, she glanced at Hubert, and the sight of his shaky smile helped clear her mind. "Yes. Yes, of course."

"Had to be the hero, didn't you?" Stephen patted the boy's shoulder in a show of affection once they reached him. "I suppose you'll want extra pay for this."

Herbert's face flushed as he smiled up at Stephen. "All in a day's work."

"I can't thank you enough for saving me," Abigail said, doing her best to keep her composure and not stare at the blood staining his shirt.

"It was nothin', miss. Didn't really think he'd use that poker. Least not on me." He pressed the handkerchief Weston had given him on his injury.

"Hubert, I believe I told you to stay back. You're only supposed to gather information, remember?" Stephen asked. "Not put yourself in danger."

"I'll remember that from now on, my lord," Hubert said, his smile still in place.

"Can you walk?" Stephen asked the pair of them.

Hubert nodded.

Abigail did so as well, hoping her legs would hold her. Now that everything had quieted, she realized her entire body ached. But she was grateful to be alive and out of Simmons' clutches.

"Keep your hat on and your head down," Stephen told her. "I'd rather polite society didn't hear of one of its own brawling in the street." He looked at Hubert. "Let us take you to my home and send for the doctor."

"Excellent notion," Lord Weston said, then supported Hubert's elbow and led the way toward the carriage. "You'll have quite the story to tell the other lads, won't you? Say, what is that building over there?"

Lord Weston continued to chat about random topics Abigail thought strange until she realized he was trying to keep Hubert's mind off his wound.

Luckily for Abigail, it worked for her as well.

"You and I are going to have a long discussion once we see to Hubert." The grim set of Stephen's mouth filled her with dread.

"Ah...I believe my stepmother is expecting me soon." Abigail latched onto the excuse, certain the conversation would not be a pleasant one.

"Very well. I'll escort you home and we can talk there. Perhaps Lady Bradford could join us."

Abigail blanched. "You're right. We can visit at your residence." The last thing she needed was to have her recent activities revealed to her stepmother. She felt bad enough as it was.

"I thought so." He watched her limp for a long moment, a scowl on his face. "Are you quite certain you're all right?"

"More so than Hubert."

"Simmons could've very well stabbed you, too."

"I'm extremely grateful he didn't." She resisted the urge to put her hand to her throat where Simmons' knife had cut her. In truth it hurt, both from the blade and his arm. Her thigh held a bone-deep ache where he'd kicked her. She could only hope he had a limp as well.

She'd thought luck had been with her when she'd spotted Simmons near the address Stephen had mentioned. She'd followed Simmons to the warehouse and decided to watch the entrance to see what he was up to. It hadn't taken her long to realize she wasn't the only one watching the building. Knowing Stephen already had someone in place made her realize how stupid she'd been to doubt him. Of course he was on top of the situation. Why had she worried about it?

She'd been careful to remain hidden from view. At least she'd thought she had. When Simmons had come running out of the entrance straight toward her, she'd frozen with fright. Obviously, she was not well equipped to deal with that sort of situation. Her trembling body attested to that fact.

As they walked toward Stephen's carriage, she couldn't help but continue to look for Simmons, fearful he'd sneak up behind them or jump out from a building they passed. She was grateful when they were safely ensconced in the carriage.

Hubert winced from pain as the carriage swayed, and Abigail's guilt mounted. She was well aware his injury was her fault. Her reckless actions had put him in danger. The boy's pallor increased; his breathing was shallow, and sweat beaded on his brow. All caused her worry to deepen.

The ride to Stephen's residence on Park Lane passed in a blur as she watched the red stain growing on the white handkerchief Hubert pressed against his wound. Stephen and Lord Weston spoke of mundane matters, but their conversation no longer distracted her.

When they arrived, a flurry of activity ensued. A doctor was sent for while Hubert was made comfortable in a guest room. Lord Weston departed with the promise to see what additional information he could discover. Stephen disappeared into his library with two of the other lads who worked for him to apprise them of what had happened. Apparently they were friends of Hubert's and concerned over his injury. In short order, the doctor arrived, seeming to be a very capable man. He hardly batted an eye at Abigail's attire.

Then the activity halted, leaving Abigail to

wait in the drawing room alone, anxious for word of Hubert's prognosis. She paced awkwardly, her injured leg complaining with each step, but the pain seemed a minor penance for what she'd done.

How could she possibly live with herself if her rash action of investigating the warehouse caused the boy's death? The longer she waited, the more convinced she became that his injuries were life-threatening.

At last she collapsed in a chair, her hands covering her face as she tried to hold back her tears.

The door to the drawing room opened and she looked up, hoping with all heart the doctor had arrived with good news.

Her chest tightened when she saw Stephen, his brow creased with worry.

She put her hand to her heart, wishing she could somehow change the events of the day. "Is Hubert all right? Please, just tell me. Will he live?"

"Of course he will." Stephen closed the door behind him and knelt before her to gather her into his arms as she started to cry. He should've realized how worried she'd be as she waited here alone.

But even as he held her, he tried to shore up his guard against her anguish. How was he to maintain any sort of distance when she was crying? Watching Simmons drag her away at knife point had taken years off his life. Even the memory of it had his heart squeezing.

He pushed aside the image and attempted to reassure her. "The doctor says he'll be fine in a few days. The blade didn't penetrate any vital organs."

Rather than reassuring her, the news seemed to break the fragile hold she had on her emotions. She burst into sobs, her slim body shaking with them.

Defenseless, Stephen held her tighter. "Shh. He's going to be fine. Didn't you hear me?" His words only seemed to make her cry harder.

"I—I'm—so—rry!" She clung to him for dear life, as though she'd never let him go.

He drew a deep breath to keep his thoughts focused on consoling her, but her sweet lavender scent filled him. Traitorous desire curled through him.

Ruthlessly shoving it back, he simply held her, rubbing her back through the coarse men's jacket she still wore. He did his best to give her the comfort she sought. His fingers strayed to the curls that had come free of the knot at the back of her head, then to the delicate skin at the back of her neck. Somehow that seemed to soothe them both.

When her sobs subsided to shudders, she pulled back to look at him, her blue eyes luminous. "You're certain Hubert will be all right?"

"Yes. He's resting comfortably."

"I never meant for any harm to come to him. Truly."

"I know." He shook his head. "But you mustn't take such risks with yourself or others. What possessed you to go down to that warehouse?"

She closed her eyes, regret etched in her face. "I wanted to know what was going on. Why it was taking so long. What Simmons could possibly be up to in that building."

"Didn't you receive my message?"

"Two days ago."

"I told you I'd let you know when I discovered more." He gave her a little shake. The day could've ended in tragedy. He could be mourning the loss of her right now. Anger pulsed back through him at the thought. "We can't simply barge in and ask what they're up to. These things take time."

She lowered her damp lashes. "I fear patience is not one of my strengths."

He placed his finger over her lips to stop her from saying more. "You nearly lost your life today. Never will you take such a risk again."

Her blue eyes reflected distress as she looked up at him but he held firm. "Promise me," he demanded.

At last she nodded, and he removed his finger. "Don't underestimate Simmons. Remember, he's capable of killing and may do so again. I'll post a guard outside your home."

"That's not necessary. We'll—"

"You'll what? You haven't even told your family of the danger you're in, have you?"

"I won't unless I absolutely have to. It took years after Father's death for us to feel safe. I vowed we'd never live with that sort of fear again."

"Abigail, you don't have to protect your family alone. Let me help you."

Her breath hitched as tears once again filled her eyes. "I can't tell you how much that means to me."

Her strength, intelligence, determination to protect her loved ones, and even her blasted independence all combined to create this beautiful woman whom he admired and respected.

But what he felt for her was so much more than that.

Emotion swelled through him, and he was helpless beneath the onslaught. His gaze dropped to her lips and the lure of them proved too much. He took her mouth with his.

Heat filled Abigail as Stephen's lips met hers. A lovely eddy of sensation unfurled inside her, and she melted against him. His strength felt so good, so right.

Her heart raced when he drew back to look at her for a long moment, those green eyes full of secrets. He moved his hands to cup her face, his touch gentling as he melded her lips to his once again.

She moaned and lifted her hand to cover his.

This was heaven! Of that she had no doubt.

His tongue, hot and wet, danced along the seam of her lips, and she opened to welcome his invasion. The spinning inside her deepened, spearing into the very core of her.

"Abigail," he muttered against her lips.

She could only sigh as liquid heat filled her. A gentle tug released her from her bulky jacket. The cool air contrasted with Stephen's warmth. Her body trembled inside and out.

His hands moved to her waist, then shifted to her ribs. His thumbs rose to just beneath her breasts and she caught her breath as he kissed her again. She ached everywhere he touched her and everywhere he didn't.

"Stephen—"

"Yes. I know. We must stop." He leaned his forehead on hers and drew a long slow breath.

"No." That was the last thing she wanted. This was the opportunity for which she'd been hoping. "Surely one more kiss will cause no harm."

He opened his eyes to look at her, their depths drawing her in, making her want to do something—anything to ease the shadows there.

She pressed her lips to his, pouring her heart into the kiss, hoping he'd let her in.

He hesitated for the briefest moment, then wrapped his arms around her as though he'd never let her go. "One last kiss to remember," he murmured.

Her heart fluttered at his words. Surely it wouldn't be their last. She kissed him again, eager to persuade him otherwise. To seduce him if she could.

Instead of meeting her lips, his mouth trailed along her jaw, slowly down her neck, lingering at the sensitive spot below her ear that she hadn't realized was there.

With great care, he kissed the spot near the cut Simmons' knife had made. "I'm sorry he hurt you," he whispered.

His lips continued to her collar bone and warmth pooled low in her belly, her breasts tingling. "Oh, Stephen."

"Yes."

"I need..." Her voice trailed off as she tried to put words to what she felt, to what she wanted. "I need more."

"Yes. More," he agreed and at last his lips captured hers.

Deep and hungry, his mouth moved over hers with a thoroughness that intoxicated her. She startled as his fingers touched the bare skin of her waist. Gently, he eased her shirt off her shoulder and kissed the bruise forming there.

Eager to keep pace, she unfastened his morning coat and waistcoat and pushed them off his arms. He shed them without complaint. Then she untied his neck scarf and he quickly removed it. The soft linen of his shirt felt marvelous over the contours of his muscled chest. His strength excited her yet made her feel weak.

"Abigail." Her name was half groan, half sigh.

She smiled. How extraordinary that her touch could make this powerful man tremble. With shaking fingers, she unfastened his shirt, revealing the binding on his shoulder where she'd shot him. Remorse filled her at the sight.

He lifted her chin to look in her eyes and smiled. "Don't regret that. It brought us together."

Smiling now, she returned her attention to his

chest. With a gentle finger, she traced a long, jagged scar that ran beneath the bandage, diagonally across his chest. "What happened here?"

He caught her hand and pulled it away as though he didn't care to be reminded. "It was a long time ago."

She pressed her lips to the scar, wondering what horror had befallen him to leave such a mark. But she let it go and continued her exploration. The wiry hair on his chest felt marvelous, his flesh hot beneath her touch.

"My turn," he whispered, then removed her shirt, leaving only the thin linen of her chemise between them.

She hadn't donned her corset with the hope she'd look less feminine in her boy's clothes and now was grateful she hadn't. All her thoughts fled as he trailed his fingers along her ribs, and at last brushed the tips of her breasts through the thin linen of her chemise. Longing spiraled through her and she arched her back.

"Yes," he encouraged and filled his hands with her breasts, kneading them gently.

She wanted to give him the same glorious sensations flooding through her and started with the sculpted firmness of his chest. He was beautiful. She stroked the pebbled hardness of his nipples in wonder.

One of his hands remained at her breast while the other lowered and worked at the fastening of her trousers. He helped her ease them off and they fell forgotten on the floor.

"I only want to touch you," Stephen murmured in her ear. "Please."

"Oh, yes," she agreed, reveling in the sensations flooding through her. She'd never felt anything so right.

He kissed her again, long and slow, as his

fingers found the bare skin of her waist and belly beneath her chemise, circling lower and lower. He eased apart her thighs and moist heat spread through her. She ached with need, but for what she wasn't sure.

"So soft," he whispered, his mouth moving along her neck and ear as he continued to kneel before her.

She writhed against him, searching for more of the pleasurable torture.

"You're so beautiful," he said, then took her mouth with his, demanding she respond. Still his fingers worked their magic, moving lower.

All thoughts vanished. Only feeling remained, igniting her. Her breath came in gasps as he touched her center, seeking the dampness there.

"Oh!" she cried out, stunned that he could create such amazing sensations within her.

He continued to touch her, enchanting her into a vortex of need. "Let go, my sweet," he muttered between kisses. "Just let go."

She tipped her head back, unable to do anything except what he asked, to trust him in this moment.

Her world spiraled, then burst. Waves of pleasure poured through her, over her, under her. She delighted in the onslaught of sensation, knowing she was safe in Stephen's arms.

Stephen watched as Abigail's aura glowed, her passion enhancing the golden light with vibrant pinks, her whole body infused with it. He ached so badly that the mere brush of her leg against his trousers pained him.

Still he continued to kiss her, to murmur in her ear as she made the journey back down to earth. How he longed to have gone with her. But that could never come to pass. He had this moment and intended to hold onto it for all he was worth.

She opened her eyes, her expression of wonder bringing a smile to his face. He took no small measure of satisfaction in knowing he'd brought her such pleasure.

"That was..." Her loss for words only made him smile broader.

She shifted, bumping against his body. She frowned at his hardness and, before he could stop her, pressed her fingers on him.

The breath whooshed out of his lungs at her touch. He jerked her hand away.

"But what of you?" she asked. "I would bring you pleasure too."

"You have, Abigail. You have." He wove his fingers through hers to make certain they stayed in his.

"Not enough, surely." Her blue eyes searched his face.

"As much as I can handle at the moment."

She stretched up to kiss him, wrapping her arms around his neck. Desire resurged in an instant, and it took every ounce of his self control to loosen her arms and stand.

But she came with him.

Her warm, soft body against his made him try desperately to remember why he was pushing her away. The lady had no idea what havoc she was wreaking.

"I would finish what we started, Stephen."

"That's impossible."

"Why?"

The throbbing in his loins made it difficult to form words that would make her understand. Hell, it was difficult for *him* to understand. "I can't give you what you want...what you need. There are things about me you don't know."

She trailed a finger down his scar again and his breath caught. Could she read his mind? That damned scar was a visible reminder of the day his life had been forever altered. If it weren't for that terrible day, perhaps things would be different.

But regret served no purpose.

"There's nothing you could tell me that would change my mind," she said. "In fact, I've wanted to ask you..."

Dark shades appeared in her aura, and he knew he wouldn't like what she was going to say, yet he had to ask. "What is it?"

"I—I have a proposition for you."

A dark spear appeared in her luminous pink aura. He waited silently while she worked up the courage to ask him whatever crazed notion she'd come up with.

"I would like to have an affair with you."

"No." He forced out the word despite the longing that surged through him, despite the fact that he ached for her body and soul and wanted nothing more than to have her as his own, if only temporarily.

Those blue eyes blinked at him, her hurt obvious. "Why not?"

"You deserve more than an affair." He retrieved her shirt from the floor and handed it to her, hoping she'd dress before he changed his mind.

"But an affair is what I want."

He scoffed as he buttoned his shirt. "You can't possibly know that."

"I think I know my own mind." She pulled on her shirt.

"You'll change your mind. Believe me." She'd soon meet a man she cared for and they would marry. He had no doubt of that. And it would not be him. He donned his waistcoat, hoping the barriers of clothing would prevent him from taking up where they'd left off.

"If you're not interested, just tell me." She

fastened her shirt and pulled on her pants.

"Abigail, I'm not trying to hurt you," he said, yet he could see he already had. That lovely rosy glow in her aura had faded to ash. "Your offer is tempting."

"I don't understand. I thought you wanted me." A single tear hovered on her eyelash as she looked up at him.

He smiled wryly. "I do. More than you can possibly know. But if we give way to...this." He gestured between them, unwilling to name what he felt for her. "The consequences would outweigh the benefit."

"I don't see how."

"Then you must take my word for it."

She stood staring at him and he knew she wouldn't let it go.

"You deserve more than serving as someone's mistress."

"I'm not asking to be your mistress. I'm only suggesting we further explore our passions."

Bloody hell! How could he make her understand? He ignored her comment and continued, "It makes no difference. You'd have to lie to your family. If your stepmother found out—"

She blanched at the thought. "I hardly think she'd discover us."

"Of course she would. If not her, someone else." He pulled on his jacket, well aware his jerky movements showed his frustration. "Why are you so eager to throw away the chance for marriage and a family?"

"I've told you. I have no intention of marrying." She turned her back to him to pick up her jacket.

"A union with a suitable man, one who would be your protector, your friend, your lover, would be far different than you think."

She stepped forward to caress his cheek. "I would like to have that with you."

"Without the formality of a wedding?"

"Are you asking?" She smiled at his silence. "Do not worry, my lord. I'm well aware you have as much of an aversion to matrimony as I do. That's why it puzzles me that you question my plan to avoid it."

"Mine is not an aversion." He clenched his jaw, wondering how he could possibly explain that he was not fit to be a husband without revealing too much. He didn't want to tell her about the looming pit of darkness inside him that he couldn't always escape or the risks he took to save others that put his life in danger. "There are reasons I am not a suitable husband for anyone."

"Such as?"

"I cannot say."

She tilted her head to the side, examining his features. He did his best to keep his expression even, his emotions in check, his mask firmly in place.

"Does it have to do with the scar on your chest? Or perhaps the headaches you frequently have?" She reached up to touch his temples. "I'd lay odds that you're getting one this very moment."

His mind raced. Had he been so obvious in her company? What else had she found out? He stepped back. He couldn't allow her to get so close to him. "I believe we were speaking of you. I'm afraid I must decline your proposal. Think harder on the risks of what you're suggesting. If we were caught, you'd be ruined. As would your sisters' chances of making a good match."

She frowned at his words. At last he seemed to be getting through to her. "But—"

"For better or worse, you have a family who loves you. Do not let them down at this late juncture. Not after all you've done for them."

She bit her lip, and he hoped she was taking his advice seriously.

"You should reconsider your choice to never marry. It's a lonely path you seek." He moved to the door before her hurt expression changed his mind. "I'll send for a carriage to see you safely home."

She remained where she was, and for a moment, he feared she'd refuse to leave until he agreed or carried her out.

"May I see Hubert first?" She met his gaze.

"Certainly." He opened the door, hoping his sanity would return once she left. "Winston?"

His butler appeared. "Yes, my lord?"

"Miss Bradford would like to see Hubert. Then order the carriage and have her taken home."

"Of course, my lord." The butler stepped back from the door, awaiting Abigail.

Stephen turned to her, hoping his expression didn't reveal his feelings. "I will keep you apprised of all activities and a guard will be watching your home. Please do not take any more unnecessary risks."

She placed her cap on her head, tucking the loose strands inside. If only he could tidy up his feelings for her as easily. "I'll be anxiously awaiting word from you," she said.

He nodded. In truth, there was nothing left to say.

CHAPTER FOURTEEN

"I can't believe we're doing this." Weston paused to scrutinize the deserted street in the faint light of dusk.

"Nor can I," Stephen responded, certain he had a different meaning than his friend. If someone had suggested a few days ago that he and Weston would be skulking about near the docks together at Weston's behest, he'd have called the keepers from Bedlam to fetch them both.

While nothing was resolved between them, Stephen preferred to think they were on their way to mending the rift between them. At least something positive had occurred, despite the events earlier that day.

"No one seems to be around," Weston observed.

"Perfect. Let's see what's inside."

Weston had suggested they search the building as soon as possible, much to Stephen's surprise. Now, Weston led the way toward the rear entrance Simmons had exited earlier that day. A lock hung on the wooden door that hadn't been there before.

"This should be fairly simple," Weston said as he removed a small leather case from his pocket.

Stephen watched in surprise as he pulled out a lock pick. "You amaze me."

Weston smiled. "We all have our secrets, don't

we?"

"Indeed." Stephen's curiosity was peaked, but now was not the time to compare notes on their experiences over the past ten years.

He kept watch while Weston focused on the lock. In a matter of moments, Weston stood and gestured toward the door. "You first."

How often had they taunted each other with that phrase during their university years? Pushing aside the fond memories, Stephen listened carefully as he opened the door a crack but was greeted only by silence.

The interior of the building was lit only by the last bit of dusk that came in from a narrow row of windows along the top of the far wall. The building felt empty as well, lacking any sense of the energy that people emanated.

"Anything?" Weston asked from behind him.

Stephen shook his head and opened the door farther, pausing to let his eyes adjust to the dim interior. "There doesn't seem to be much in here."

The large open space was empty except for a few broken wooden crates and tarps stacked to one side.

Weston walked forward cautiously, his boots making little sound on the stone floor. The far corner held a series of three doors, all closed. Being the methodical man he was, he moved toward the closest one and looked inside. "Empty as well."

Stephen let Weston continue his exploration while he lit the lantern he'd brought. Holding the light aloft, he examined the crates on the far side of the room. The markings were those of a well known shipping company that transported all manner of goods. It was difficult to tell what they'd held.

Weston returned to his side. "All the rooms are empty. The only thing I found was this." He handed Stephen a small brown bottle.

Stephen moved the lantern closer to read the label. "Dr. Sand's Sleep Elixir. Safe for all ages."

"Does it make any sense to you?" Weston asked.

"Simmons bought a large quantity of a sleep remedy at an apothecary shop. Perhaps he has trouble sleeping."

"I'd suggest he try a new line of work instead. I'd lay odds that this contains opium. Quite unhealthy."

Stephen gestured toward the crates. "Not much help here either."

"It might be worth an inquiry at that company. I should have some time on the morrow to see if I can discover anything interesting."

"It's unfortunate that James lost Simmons' trail earlier. Our search would've been easier."

Weston moved a short distance away, examining the floor. "Bring the light over here."

Stephen drew nearer and saw the outline of a large, thick circle on the dusty floor. Together, they moved around the rest of the warehouse and found an empty spool of wire and two more circles. The three imprints were the same size and distance from the center of the room.

A memory came to Stephen of another room many years ago, when a stormy night had changed their lives forever. Three large circular transducer coils had stood in the lab, spaced ten paces apart. The current they'd generated had nearly killed them all.

He refused to voice his thoughts for fear he truly was losing his mind. There wasn't enough evidence to support his suspicion.

"These look familiar," Weston said as he studied the circles.

"Yes, they do." An uneasy feeling spread through him.

Weston's gaze caught his. "This is rather alarming, don't you think?"

"Bloody bleedin' buggers!" Vincent Simmons rubbed his aching thigh as he arrived at their new location. He shifted the loaves of bread to search for the key in his pocket. He wasn't sure if he cursed those who awaited him inside, those who'd caused him to waste half his day changing locations, or those who had made his leg throb like a bad tooth. "Blast them all."

The day had been long and hellish.

First he'd spotted Miss Bradford outside the warehouse. What could he do but confront her? It had seemed too good of an opportunity. He'd held hope that he could force her to take him to get the rock.

But as soon as he'd gone near her, those two lords had come on the run. Damn if one of them hadn't been the same man who'd shown up in the East End the first night Miss Bradford had followed him.

Left with no choice, Vincent had dragged her off for his own safety. *Christ, but that had been a mistake.* Between her and that street urchin attacking him, his leg pained him so much he could hardly walk.

Then he and his uncle got into a terrible argument. As if any of the events of the day had been his fault. His uncle had called him a fool for not realizing Miss Bradford found his whereabouts. Then his uncle had insisted they move the entire operation—no easy task. That had required additional men who'd required extra pay to keep their mouths shut.

Lucky for Vincent that a few of those sort always seemed to be roaming around near the docks. They'd finally gotten everything, including the damned kids to the new location. As if all that wasn't bad enough, they'd run out of food for the little buggers.

At last he managed to shove the key in the lock and open the door. A foul odor hit him in the face. The bucket in the corner obviously needed to be emptied. This day just kept getting worse.

"Get back, ye filthy things," he called out as he entered the room.

"Let us out of here," one of the boys demanded.

"Hush up. Ye'll see this project through to the end." Vincent had known the burden of taking care of the brats would fall on him. They were a pain in his arse. Food, a place to sleep, a place to piss. The list was endless. No wonder his own mother had deserted him. Children required too much effort. Having someone dependent on you day after day wore a person down.

But before his uncle could proceed with the experiments, they needed a few more kids. Unfortunately, Vincent had been forced to end his relationship with Mikey, who'd been supplying them with the 'volunteers'. The man had said people were asking questions, and it was too risky for what they were paying him. He'd wanted ten times as much when he'd handed over the fifth and sixth boys.

Now Vincent was at a loss as to how they could get a few more children to assist them. He'd picked up one on the street the other night, but you didn't see that very often any more. Not with all the reformers roaming about London.

He threw the loaves of bread at the boys. "Share it amongst yerselves. This is all ye'll be gettin' for a time, so make it last."

Nothing was going according to plan. He laid the blame squarely on that Bradford woman. The time had come to take action on that front, no matter what his uncle said.

Abigail hobbled into the dining room the next morning, wishing she could've stayed in her room. Every bone in her body ached, every muscle seemed to have stiffened overnight. Her high-necked gown hid the cut she bore from his knife. Her hair covered the bump on her head. Each and every bruise on her body made itself known as she moved.

She felt much worse than she had the previous day, both emotionally and physically. Her maid had been horrified when she'd realized the extent of Abigail's injuries. She'd sworn Eloise to secrecy, telling her she'd fallen and didn't want to worry her family.

"Abigail? Whatever is the matter?" Her stepmother looked up from her tea.

"Are you all right?" Sophia asked, her toast forgotten on her plate.

"I've twisted my ankle," Abigail replied. She'd thought long and hard on an excuse. The worst of her injuries was her thigh where Simmons had kicked her. Though she'd tried, she couldn't walk without hobbling along. Since she couldn't think of a believable excuse for that injury, she'd settled on a twisted ankle.

"How ever did you manage that?" Olivia asked.

"A misstep on a stair. Clumsy of me, wasn't it?" She kept her attention on the sideboard, carefully selecting what she wanted for breakfast. She'd come to realize she was a poor liar and the less eye contact she had with her family, the better.

Perhaps Stephen was right—if she had to continually lie, her stepmother would eventually find out.

"Were you wearing shoes with heels?" Sophia asked. "I must admit they make walking much more difficult. Why just yesterday I turned my ankle."

Abigail smiled. Sophia was a good bit shorter than Olivia and always wore shoes with small heels. "Perhaps my choice of footwear was part of the problem."

"Should you be abed?" Irene asked as she watched Abigail's awkward gait.

"I fear it will only stiffen more," she said as she helped herself to eggs and toast though she wasn't hungry. She couldn't stand to be alone with her thoughts...or rather her disappointment...any longer. Despite Stephen's reasons for not finishing what he'd started, only one thing was clear to her: he'd rejected her. That hurt, no matter how she tried to convince herself otherwise.

"I hope you've nothing pressing to do today."

"I've a meeting scheduled later with Mrs. Weatherly to discuss a new investment." Abigail was quite proud of the widow's progress and her growing confidence in financial matters. She hoped a discussion with her would serve as a distraction from everything else.

"Are you certain you feel up to it?" Irene asked.

"If you have to go out, you could have Thomas carry you, Abigail," Sophia suggested with a giggle.

"Or how about that handsome lord who was here the other day? Surely he'd be willing to assist you," Olivia added.

The twins erupted into laughter even as Abigail felt her face heat with embarrassment. If only they knew just *how* he'd assisted her the previous day. She drew a deep breath to slow her pounding heart at the memory of his hands on her, of his lips—

"Now girls," said Irene, wrenching Abigail's thoughts back to the present, "your sister is obviously not feeling quite the thing. No need to tease her when she's not her best."

Abigail sat, determined to enjoy her sisters' lightheartedness after the dark events of yesterday. Life was precious and should never be taken for granted. Mornings like this when they were all together and enjoying each other's company were to be cherished.

She nibbled at her toast as the girls chattered about their lessons. The previous day's activities had been tiring, and she'd had a restless night. Each time she'd fallen asleep, she'd relived Simmons dragging her through the street. When she'd woken, her mind had been flooded with those moments in Stephen's arms.

"Are you feverish?" Irene asked as she watched her.

"No, I'm fine."

Nothing was wrong other than the memory of a simple kiss that had led to so much more. Wasn't that what she'd told Stephen? That she wanted more? What was wrong with her that she still did, even after he'd turned her away?

With effort, she forced those memories to the back of her mind. There was no point in regret. She couldn't take back her actions and in all honesty, she wasn't sure she wanted to. She'd had no idea she was capable of that sort of desire.

For so many years, she'd thought herself frigid, unable to feel anything deeply. She'd thought that perhaps the loss of her father had scarred her for life. The brief touches she'd shared with men over the last few years had meant little. Nothing in fact. Not even one tiny flutter in her stomach.

Yet Stephen had only to look at her and she burned like a flame in a gas lantern.

Though hurt at his rejection of her request for an affair, she wasn't completely surprised. Perhaps he was trying to be a gentleman. At any rate, the idea of not pursuing her relationship with Stephen further was unacceptable. After all these years, she'd at last discovered a man who stirred her senses in every way. She wasn't willing to let that experience pass. Not yet.

Her thoughts were interrupted by Sophia and Olivia who were excited about a gathering they'd been invited to attend that afternoon. Abigail wasn't sure if they were animated about the party or the idea of escaping lessons for a few hours.

Abigail nodded at the appropriate time when her opinion was consulted about what they should wear, but her thoughts remained on Stephen. Would a different tactic be more successful with him? What might have happened if she hadn't stopped to ask him about having an affair, but used seduction instead? She was sure he felt something for her, some kind of desire.

While she intended to spend her future alone, shouldn't she have a night to remember? A night that would make her a woman in full and give her memories for a lifetime?

"Abigail."

The exasperated tone to her stepmother's voice caught her attention.

"That's the third time I've called your name." Irene's eyes narrowed in concern. Or was it suspicion?

"I'm sorry. I confess I'm a bit distracted this morning." Abigail tried a smile, hoping to appease her.

"I would like to speak with you privately after breakfast."

The girls hushed. Irene rarely requested such meetings and never in that tone.

"Of course."

In short order, the girls departed for their lessons with curious looks.

Irene studied her for a long moment. "You know I love you like my own daughter..."

Abigail smothered a sigh. This was definitely

going to be a lecture.

"But your recent behavior is highly concerning." Irene held her gaze for a long moment. "You were so strong when your father died." She reached out to take Abigail's hand. "I leaned on you when you should've been leaning on me. It was hard to remember how young you were when you acted so mature."

"That was a difficult time for all of us. We got through it together." She squeezed Irene's hand, wondering where she was going with this conversation.

"Yes, we did. But I have to wonder if I've allowed you to become too independent. I'm not always certain you act in your own best interests."

Abigail frowned. "I've always put the welfare of the family first. You and the girls have been my top priority."

Irene leveled her a stare. "Exactly. You are a young lady. Yet you act like the head of the family. You've never had a chance to be normal."

"Normal?" Offended, Abigail had to question her. "I'm not certain I understand what you're saying."

Irene sighed as she released Abigail's hand. "My concern is your secretive behavior of late. You're leaving the house without mentioning to anyone where you're going. You did it again yesterday. And now you're injured and I have to think it's far more than your ankle. Are you rebelling because I burdened you too much when you were younger?"

"No." Abigail hardly knew how to react to her question when it was so far from the truth.

"I feel like you're keeping something from me."

Abigail's heart thundered. This was her chance to share the burden of Simmons' return, to tell her of the threat he posed. She could even tell her of her attraction to Stephen and the tumult of emotions she felt.

But all the years of protecting her could not be changed so easily. The business with Simmons might be over any day. Wouldn't revealing it to Irene now be selfish? They'd been so close to catching him yesterday. Why worry her? Abigail knew herself to be the stronger of the two of them and had years of proof of that.

Stephen had a guard hidden nearby to watch the house. Thomas and Ponsford continued to watch over them as well. If they remained vigilant, Simmons couldn't cause any harm. She'd just make sure they took extra care in the next few days.

She released a long, slow breath and pasted on a feeble smile. "I took a tumble when I hurt my ankle. I confess my shoulder is sore as well. I'm just rather embarrassed at my clumsiness. That is why I didn't want to tell you the extent of my injuries."

Irene watched her and Abigail could practically see her weighing what she'd said. "I would like to think that you would come to me with any concern you might have."

"Of course," Abigail agreed.

"Hmm...I hope so." Irene tapped a finger on her lip. "There's something different about you this morning. Are you certain that's all that happened yesterday? Were you with Lord Ashbury?"

"I—ah—" Guilt and shock warred within Abigail.

"Do you have any sort of affection for him?"

"We have more of a...business relationship," she offered, hoping to appease her.

"Business?" Irene made the word sound rather distasteful. "Please tell me you're not attempting to convince him of the merits of some new investment scheme you've found."

Abigail dropped her gaze. Maybe she should've

told her the truth, but she could hardly explain that she'd almost been compromised, but not quite. She'd almost made love, but not really. That she was still trying to find some way to convince Stephen to cooperate.

"Honestly, dear, I don't think that wise. Men hate being told what to do and heaven forbid if he realizes how intelligent you are."

"Oh!" Abigail could only stare. Where did Irene get such ideas?

"I know your financial endeavors are important to you but do try to hold your tongue around him. Men of his ilk like to be the one giving advice."

"I—"

Irene patted her hand. "You promised me you'd be willing to explore your feelings if they should arise. After all, he might be using business as a ruse to get closer to you." She studied Abigail closer. "Should we have a more detailed discussion about intimacy? I always assumed you'd come to me if you wanted to know more details."

"No need." Abigail could only imagine how red her cheeks must be.

"You *do* know you can speak to me about anything? That I'm always here for you? That I love you dearly?"

"Indeed I do and I'm extremely grateful for it. I love you, too."

Irene released her hand and smiled. "Enough of this conversation." She rose, smoothing the front of her gown. "I suggest you rest today. The less you walk on that ankle, the better."

Abigail smiled with relief at the change in the subject. "You're right. What of you and the girls? Do you have plans other than the gathering this afternoon?"

"I believe it's our only outing for the day."

"Is Thomas driving you?"

"Unless you'll need him," Irene said.

Relieved they'd be well protected, Abigail shook her head. "No, I'll remain home today. Perhaps Mrs. Weatherly can visit me. Shall we plan on dining together this evening? Perhaps we can convince the girls to play for us."

"That would be lovely. I look forward to it." Irene paused beside Abigail's chair. "You're certain you're all right? You really do seem...different somehow."

It took all of Abigail's resolve to maintain her composure. Why now, after all these years, did her stepmother choose to be quite so insightful? "I'm fine. Truly."

"By the way, there was a ruffian lingering outside the kitchen entrance this morning. I had Thomas send him on his way. We don't want people lining up at the door seeking handouts."

Abigail's stomach plummeted. The man had been sent by Stephen as an additional guard. She could only hope Thomas or Ponsford had remedied the situation since they were aware of the man Stephen had sent.

Lying was always so much more complicated than one anticipated. How was she going to manage to keep the whole problem a secret even for a few more days?

CHAPTER FIFTEEN

Weston paced Stephen's library the next morning, his steps jerky with tension. "If this is some sort of hoax, some trick to get us to reveal ourselves..."

Stephen sat slumped in his chair, tired from his night's work. He rubbed his hands over his eyes, trying to grasp why Weston was so riled. "Reveal what?"

After he and Weston had finished their foray into the empty warehouse, he'd met with Farley at the gaming den and solved a few problems there, among them stopping a lord from cheating at cards. He and Farley had then visited the East End again in hopes of finding something about the missing children. The leads on that case had dried up. The conversations and activities at several taverns had yielded little. A man had taken a disliking to Farley at one of the bars, and they'd had to create a diversion to avoid a fight.

On nights like that, he was tempted to let events unfold without him. Trying to find reasons to prevent people from acting upon their impulses without appearing a crazed lunatic was no easy task. At times people were grateful for his interference. Others became frightened of him as they feared he could read their minds. Still others became outraged at his meddling, certain he was spying on them.

In the few hours he'd had to rest afterward, sleep had eluded him. Dark, dragging despair had nipped at the edges of his mind, making slumber impossible.

As he watched Weston pace, Stephen shook his head. More people had been in his home, his private sanctuary, in the past two days then in the past five years combined. Weston had come of his own accord this morning. How had that come to pass? He wasn't sure if his exhaustion was the problem, but he couldn't determine what his friend was going on about.

"Don't be a fool." The look Weston cast him would've withered a weaker man.

"Ah." At last, light dawned on him. "You're referring to our aura reading abilities." He waited, wondering if Weston would actually admit to anything. Weston hadn't discussed his ability to read success or failure since he'd first revealed it before the professor's funeral. "No one knows anything about us or our odd talents. Besides, we found nothing at the warehouse."

Weston stopped and stared at him as though his brain was addled.

"What? Three rings on the floor can hardly be called actual evidence," Stephen argued.

"Hmm."

"Have you told anyone about your..." Stephen hesitated on the proper term to use.

"Ailment?" Weston finished. "No, of course not. Why would I?"

Stephen shrugged. "With Lucas in Brazil, there's only the two of us. I've told only one person, someone I'd trust with my life." Farley would never betray him. "So how could it be a hoax to draw us out? Who would bother?"

Weston spun away to look out the window.

"Did you discover anything about those empty

crates in the warehouse?" Stephen was certain something else had raised this level of unease in Weston. His mood was significantly more agitated than when they'd parted ways the previous night.

"Nothing of interest. However, I did find out the lease on the building is under the name of Leon Smith."

Stephen thought on the name for a moment, trying to determine why it sounded familiar. "Wasn't Professor Grisby's middle name Leon?"

"Yes."

"That's a bit of a coincidence."

Weston turned back to look at him. "Surely you remember I don't believe in coincidences."

"Interesting that they could move things out of the warehouse so quickly."

"Yes. Those circles on the floor, what exactly did you think of when you saw them?"

"Probably the same thing you did."

Weston picked up the small transducer coil from Stephen's desk and held it up.

Stephen nodded. "But where did they move them to?"

Weston rubbed the bridge of his nose. "I have no idea. Nor did anyone share information when we asked around. If they were transducer coils, they'd be large and heavy. Someone should've noticed them being loaded and hauled away."

Stephen frowned. "Were you by chance dressed normally when you made inquiries?"

"What do you mean?"

"You tend to be dressed in the height of fashion. The knot in your cravat puts most to shame."

Weston touched the item in question. "I hardly think a person's answer differs when questioned by a man with a properly tied neck scarf than..."

"Than someone who looks less like a well-to-do lord and more like their own kind?" Stephen finished when words seemed to elude Weston.

Weston scowled. "Perhaps you're right. However, unlike your Miss Bradford, I don't happen to possess a disguise that would make me look like I live on the streets."

Stephen's stomach lurched at the words 'Your Miss Bradford'. "She's not mine."

Weston raised a brow. "I beg to differ. At any rate, I'll see if I can come up with more suitable attire and return to the area near the warehouse to make additional inquiries. Would you care to join me?"

"Perhaps. Send word when you're going and I'll see what I can arrange. If I can't come, I'll send Farley with you. He's extremely helpful in these situations. It might be worthwhile to search the warehouse again in the light of day."

"Good point," Weston said. "I also spoke to the man who wrote that article you found in the newspaper. He had nothing more to offer other than confirming that the scientist who's making those claims is very secretive. A recluse. He knows nothing more than what he wrote."

Stephen nodded, then opened a drawer in his desk, took out the meteorite he'd taken from Abigail, and tossed it to Weston.

"It's heavy."

"I believe its density is part of its appeal."

"Along with its magnetic properties." Weston turned it over and over in his palm. "The fusion crust is easily identifiable just as Professor Grisby described."

"I wish I was clearer on what Grisby thought it would do and how he intended to use it with the coils."

"He was rather vague on that, wasn't he?"

"In hindsight, one might even think he didn't trust us enough to reveal those details," Stephen offered.

"Or perhaps he didn't think three university students would be interested enough to care."

Stephen shrugged. Weston had a valid point. The three of them had thought the experiments more of a lark than serious business. They hadn't really believed anything significant would come of the tests.

Weston sat in the chair opposite Stephen's desk and leaned forward. "You don't truly believe he could've survived the accident, do you?"

"How could he? Lucas nearly didn't survive. There's no possible way Grisby did. We both saw his body. He had no pulse." Stephen tapped his fingers on his desk as he thought it over. Again. "All I know is that something is awry and I'm determined to get to the bottom of it."

"Have you told Miss Bradford of the reason this stone is so desirable?"

"No." Guilt filled him at the admission but he reminded himself it was for her own protection. "The less she knows the better."

Weston shook his head. "I hope you know what you're about. Do you have a plan in mind?"

"One involving the stone in your hand."

Weston tossed it lightly up in the air and caught it. "Excellent idea. Perhaps Professor Grisby wasn't the only one searching for a meteorite like this."

Winston, Stephen's butler, opened the door with a smile, his blue eyes twinkling. "Good day to you, Miss Bradford."

"And to you, Winston."

Abigail's stomach whirled as though she'd spun too many times while playing blind man's buff. The thought of seeing Stephen again after their passionate interlude the previous day had her emotions in a tumult. How did one act the day after? Pretend as if nothing untoward had occurred? Or be prepared to pick up where things had left off? She wished she knew the proper etiquette for this sort of meeting.

"I'm afraid Lord Ashbury is not at home at the moment," the butler said, as he stepped aside for Abigail to enter the foyer.

She sighed, whether from relief or disappointment, she wasn't certain. In truth, she wasn't yet prepared to see Stephen. "Actually, I've come to visit Hubert if I may." She held up a box of candy. "I brought him a little something."

"How kind of you, miss. He's a bit restless, so your call will be a welcome distraction."

Guilt flooded her. "Is he in pain?"

"Some, of course, but I think boredom is the worst of his symptoms at the moment," he said. "However, the doctor advised that rest is imperative."

Winston led the way to the top floor of the house where Hubert was ensconced in a comfortable room. The boy was propped up on the pillows, his face still pale, but his expression lit up at her arrival.

"Good day to you, Hubert. How are you feeling?" Abigail asked.

"Fairly well, miss. And ye?"

"Thank you, Winston," she told the butler as he left the room. She settled in the chair near Hubert's bed and looked over her shoulder as though to ensure they were alone, then whispered, "I confess I'm a bit sore."

Hubert chuckled. "Nothin' like a street brawl to test yer skills."

Abigail shook her head, still shocked at the events of the previous day. "It was certainly a new experience for me. Do you hurt much?"

"Nah. Ain't too bad if I stay still. It's a bit borin' is all." The scowl on his face spoke volumes.

"Resting will help you heal."

"I think I'd be fine back on the streets, but Lord Ashbury says otherwise," he grumbled.

"It's impossible to argue with him. I'd advise against it."

Hubert nodded. "He's a standup lord. Ain't no doubt. He offered to replace my income while I'm laid up."

"Very generous of him." Abigail was impressed by Stephen's thoughtfulness.

"I'm not so certain about his other idea."

"Oh?" Abigail waited, curious as to what that might be.

"He wants me to go to school."

Abigail's heart expanded another notch. Bless Stephen for encouraging the boy. "That's a wonderful idea."

Hubert shook his head as though he couldn't imagine doing so. "If it was anyone else but his lordship suggestin' such a thing, I'd tell them to bugger off. But his lordship has a gift fer judgin' people."

"How do you mean?"

"He can tell if..." Hubert narrowed his eyes as though deciding how best to explain.

But she was desperate to hear it. "He can tell what?"

He shrugged. "If someone has good intentions or not. I'm not sure how to describe it. But he's helped some of the other kids from the workhouse. Saved them, in fact. If not for him, they'd have ended up in some terrible factory or out on the streets like meself."

"How so?"

"He takes in as many of the young ones as he can at the orphanage he sponsors, but the older kids—those he deems worthy—he helps get them in schools or jobs. He's spot on at pickin' the good ones. Some of the kids already settled on a life of crime. They've no interest in learnin' a proper job. They'd prefer pickin' pockets or the like. They'd turn their backs on ye without a second thought."

"Oh?"

"But his lordship can tell those with just a glance. I don't know how, but he's right every time."

"Amazing." She thought back to previous conversations with him, what he'd said about both Catherine and Brighton.

"We've been tryin' to figure out how he does it but with no luck. It's a right mystery, it is."

"Unbelievable." He hid this all from society whereas other gentlemen involved in charitable activities bragged of their social responsibility. Why? And how did he so accurately determine those he could save and those he couldn't?

"I brought you a little something." Abigail handed him the box. It seemed so inadequate compared to what he'd done for her. "I know it's not much."

Hubert tore into the wrapped package with glee. "Chocolates? Oh, thank you, miss. What a treat. The other lads will be jealous and I'm not willin' to share."

Abigail smiled, happy Hubert was so pleased with her token. "Don't eat them all at once. You'll end up with a stomach ache."

Hubert nodded around a mouthful of one of the sweets.

"Your bravery saved my life." Tears clogged her throat as the terror of that moment claimed her again. She'd thought Simmons intended to kill her just as he'd killed her father. "Simmons would've succeeded in dragging me off if not for your valiant efforts."

Hubert swallowed the mouthful he chewed. "But miss, I think ye forgot somethin'."

"What do you mean?"

"After I saved ye, ye saved me. We're even."

Abigail frowned, bewildered by Hubert's statement.

"Ye were kickin' that man like a mad woman, no offense. If not for ye, Simmons might've done me in."

"He's right." Stephen's deep voice came from the doorway. "Your efforts distracted Simmons from further harming Hubert."

Abigail's face heated as she looked at Stephen, her heartbeat quickening. "I thought you were out."

"I've just returned. Winston informed me of your visit to Hubert." He moved to stand beside her chair.

Her stomach quivered at his proximity. His green eyes held hers for a long moment, stealing her breath. She could only wonder at the thoughts behind them.

"She brought me chocolates!" Hubert held up the box to Stephen. "Would you like one, my lord?"

"No, thank you. You deserve every one," Stephen told the boy with a smile.

Hubert dipped his head and smiled.

Abigail drew a long breath. Despite her nervousness at speaking with Stephen, she had even more questions for him after her visit with Hubert. "If you have a moment, may I speak with you privately?" she asked Stephen.

"Of course."

She rose and bid the boy goodbye with a promise to visit again soon, then followed Stephen down to the library. She couldn't help but stare at him in the light of the new information she'd received as she took a seat before his desk.

"What is it?" He frowned when she watched him, wondering if she dared ask what was on her mind.

"I have a few questions."

"Oh?"

She decided to ignore the warning in that one word. "I feel you've been less than honest with me."

"How so?"

Was it just her imagination or did he look uncomfortable at her accusation? Surely that was a sign of guilt.

A knock on the door interrupted them. A young maid peeked into the room. "Shall I bring tea, my lord?"

"No," Abigail answered.

"Yes," Stephen said at the same time.

She looked at him with frustration. "We're in the middle of a discussion."

"Tea is conducive to discussions, I'm told."

She was sure he was attempting to delay her questions.

"Yes, Sally, please bring us tea." He turned to Abigail. "Perhaps sandwiches as well?"

With a huff, she said, "Very well then."

"Excellent." He thanked Sally, who departed. "Now you were saying?"

"I was asking—"

"I hope you're feeling no ill effects of yesterday's events?"

Abigail couldn't help the heat as it rose in her cheeks. Did he refer only to the fight with Simmons or to their interlude? She decided to assume the former. "A bit bruised but fine."

"Good. Allow me to advise you of the new information we've discovered."

"Oh?"

Grateful he'd diverted her attention, even if only temporarily, Stephen said, "Weston and I paid a visit to the building Simmons was frequenting, but unfortunately we found it empty."

"Why would Simmons be in an empty building

that long? I waited outside for hours."

Stephen sent her a look of disapproval. "Don't remind me. At any rate, it appears the building was emptied sometime after our encounter with Simmons."

"Perhaps we could discover who leases the building—"

"Weston has. From what we can tell, it was leased under a fictitious name. He's digging deeper but it will take time."

Abigail leaned back in her chair, her shoulders wilted. "Will every clue we obtain lead to a dead end? I fear this will never end, that Simmons will never be stopped." Not only did her expression hold defeat, her golden aura was smothered in gray.

Unable to stand her despair, he rose to take her hands in his and pull her into his arms. Never did he want her to lose hope, for if she did, he feared his own fragile hold on that elusive feeling would cease. A life without hope was no life at all.

She'd come to represent all good things in this world, and he needed her to remain just as she was. He could only offer her temporary comfort because once Simmons was stopped, Stephen's time with her would end. Once again, he'd be left to his lonely existence. He hoped he could fill the void of losing her with the memories of their time together.

That had to be enough.

"Abigail," he murmured, studying her bright blue eyes, wishing he could make things right with a snap of his fingers. "Hold on for a little longer. We will see this thing through."

"How much longer?"

"I'm not certain. But we're getting closer each day. If we capture Simmons when we next spot him, we might lose our chance to stop something far worse."

"Worse than him harming my family?"

"We're trying to make certain it doesn't come to that. But we need additional information. Can you manage for a few more days?"

She bowed her head. "You've no idea how much I wish this to end. For life to be normal once again."

"I do understand. It's your decision. I'll do all I possibly can to protect you, but if you want me to catch Simmons and warn him off now, I will." But he knew that wouldn't be enough.

Men like Simmons couldn't be stopped by a few words. His aura was dark as night, and the information they'd gathered thus far confirmed Stephen's suspicions. While he couldn't predict the future, he knew from his ability and past experience that a plan was in the making.

A long moment passed as he waited, wanting nothing more than to keep her in his arms, to hold her and comfort her, to tell her everything would be all right.

But he couldn't promise her anything more than he already had.

At last she met his gaze again. "If Simmons is involved in something—something that could hurt others, then he must be stopped." Even as she spoke, the gray smothering her aura lifted. Not completely, but it abated.

And for now, that was enough.

"We'll take every possible precaution—"

Abigail placed her hands along his shoulders and his words fled. "Yes, I know. You'll do your best."

She tilted her face up to his, and the blood in his head rushed down. The desire he'd reined in forged ahead. Her sudden change of mood was disconcerting. He could only hope she didn't intend to ask him to finish what they'd started the previous day because he feared at this moment, he'd readily agree.

"You see, it all comes down to one thing." She studied his face as she trailed a finger across his cheek toward his lips.

His breath halted as spears of pink and rose colored her aura.

"I trust you." She lifted up onto her toes and kissed him.

For a brief moment, he simply basked in her words and her affection, receiving what she gave him. Then his own desire took over. He wrapped his arms around her and hungrily demanded more. He clung to her like a drowning man holding fast to a rope.

A knock on the door startled them both.

Abigail backed up and dropped into her chair, leaving Stephen standing there with his mind blank.

The maid entered the room with the tea tray and set the items on the low table at the end of the room which had a small sitting area. "Will there be anything else, my lord?"

"That will do, Sally. Thank you."

Stephen's gaze returned to Abigail, wondering if she cared to continue where they'd left off.

She seemed to have recovered quicker than he. With grace, she rose and patted his arm as she walked toward the sofa and chairs near the table. "May I serve?"

He watched her, trying to determine if she was attempting to make him crazed or if that was just a side effect of her actions. With a deep breath, he sat beside her on the sofa, determined to regain control of his longing for her. "As you wish."

She placed a variety of sandwiches and biscuits on his plate and prepared a cup of tea for him as well.

Stephen sat back, trying to work up an appetite for something other than her.

"Now then," she said as she took a sip of her own tea, "I believe we were discussing you not being forthright with me."

Were they? He couldn't quite remember.

"Hubert shared some interesting information."

"Oh?" He tried to think what secrets the lad could possibly know.

"He's excited about your suggestion that he attend school."

Stephen breathed a sigh of relief. How could she take affront with him not telling her that? It had only happened yesterday.

"He told me how many other children you save."

He didn't think they'd had that long to visit.

"Hubert also mentioned something about an orphanage that you help support."

Stephen gritted his teeth, wondering what else the boy had said.

"He mentioned you finding employment for some of the children in the workhouse." She nibbled a biscuit. The movement of her lips made it difficult to think. "Is all this correct thus far?"

He dragged his thoughts back to her words, trying to foresee any potential damage in admitting to what she'd already discovered. Still, after all these years of keeping secrets, he could not bring himself to admit to anything. "Hubert must be feeling better if he was so inclined to chat."

"I have to wonder why you have an association with the gaming den." She sipped her tea then tilted her head to the side as though she pondered nothing more than the proper word to describe the color of the fabric covering the sofa.

He had to force himself to remain still instead of fidgeting like a boy caught in the act of stealing a biscuit from the kitchen.

"The only possible conclusion is that you use

the profits from the gaming den to help fund the orphanage." Her eyes narrowed as she honed in. "You take money others insist on throwing away and use it to help those in need."

"Hmm." Her conjecture was amazingly accurate. No one else of his acquaintance had come to that conclusion. Then again, she was one of a very few who knew of the gaming hell.

"Most of those you rescue from the workhouses are children."

He nearly groaned as he realized she wasn't done.

"But it sounds as if you're rather selective in choosing those you deem worthy of helping. According to Hubert, you have an uncanny knack for determining which children would actually benefit from your assistance."

A tight band wrapped around his chest. This was what he'd feared. Abigail was an intelligent woman who had a great deal of information about him.

Her gaze held his. "Don't deny it. I know something more is going on." Her eyes widened as though she'd just remembered something. "The night Brighton attacked me, you said you'd seen his ill intent. You seem to know things before you should. How is that possible?"

Damn. She'd unraveled his secrets after all.

CHAPTER SIXTEEN

The silence grew long as Abigail held Stephen's gaze. He couldn't tell what she was thinking, whether she judged him poorly or thought him mad.

He'd wondered himself over the years.

Did he admit the truth? Or should he deny it all?

"Surely you don't intend to lie to me? Not after everything we've been through." Her soft words caught in his chest, creating a warmth he found unbearable, for he knew it couldn't last.

He dropped her gaze as he set down his cup. He'd delighted in Abigail's company since he'd known her. She was a bright, beautiful woman, and she twisted him into knots with just a glance from under her lashes. She was both clever and relentless. He must never forget that.

If he bothered to deny the truth of what she'd pieced together, she'd find evidence to prove him a liar. She'd watch him like a hawk for verification of what she thought true. Therefore, he had to conclude it was a waste of time to lie.

Weak logic, he berated himself. In truth, he had no desire to lie, not to her. He was tired of hiding, of avoiding connections to others for fear of having his secrets discovered, of having no one with whom to share his life.

Still he hesitated. If she thought him mad, it would strike a blow he wasn't sure he could survive. Dare he risk it?

For the first time, he was willing to try.

"Nearly ten years ago, I was at Cambridge with Michael Drury, Lord Weston, and Lucas Stanby, Lord Berkmond. We were all mentored by a professor highly interested in electromagnetism."

He cleared his suddenly dry throat. "He taught us much on the subject, and we conducted an experiment in his lab with large transducer coils we'd built. But something went awry. Not only did the experiment fail, but our professor was killed, and all of us injured."

"That must've been terrible."

He rose to pace before her. Even after all these years, it was difficult to revisit the details of that night. "Indeed it was. Lucas nearly lost his life. Michael stood behind him and was struck by the explosion as well."

"The scar on your chest?" Abigail asked.

"Yes." He rubbed the mark that would forever serve as a reminder. "Michael's is worse."

He glanced at her to find her expression a mixture of concern and curiosity. He hoped it didn't change to horror or pity when he revealed the rest.

"Within hours, I realized something more had changed. Something in our basic makeup had been altered by the electromagnetic blast."

Abigail frowned. "How so?"

He turned to face her so he could watch her expression. "I suddenly had the ability to see auras."

"Auras?"

It had been hard for him to understand and believe. He could only image that it would be doubly so for anyone who'd never experienced the ability firsthand. "Each person has a...light, a field of energy, that hovers an inch or two around their body, especially their head and shoulders."

"Oh, yes. A clairvoyant woman gave a demonstration of it at a meeting for the Society of Psychic Investigations last year."

He shuddered at the thought of giving a demonstration of his own abilities. "I see mainly good and evil in auras. If someone is overall a good person, they have a light-colored aura. If someone is bad, it's dark. Many people appear gray to me, but if they think about something or intend to do something, it changes."

"That's why you're always looking at my hair," she said as she touched her hat.

He smiled. "Yes. It's difficult at times not to be distracted by what I see."

"The night of the Mortenson's ball, you saw Brighton's ill intent in his aura?"

He grimaced at the memory. "Yes, but obviously not clearly enough."

She scoffed. "You saved me in case you forgot. What of Lord Weston? Does he see the same?"

"He sees success and failure."

"Fascinating." She bit her lower lip as she processed what he'd told her.

The sight made him want to do some nibbling of his own. "I'm not sure I'd put it quite that way."

"And your other friend, Lord Berkmond?"

"I don't know. He refused to speak of it and left the country as soon as he was able."

"Your...gift is what allows you to determine which children you assist. You give them a chance for a better life."

"Yes. I can't help them all but—"

"You help as many as you can." She tapped her adorable chin with a finger. "And the headaches?"

"A side effect of either the aura reading or perhaps the electromagnetism. I'm not certain."

While he was willing to tell her some things, he couldn't tell her everything. Revealing his aura reading held enough risk. He couldn't speak of the severe headaches and deep despair that came over him more and more frequently.

"Dealing with people in general is difficult," he continued, "but crowds are especially so. It's like walking through a room of people with signs above their heads telling you what they're about to do. If people have an urge to do something harmful, their aura spikes black. Except they don't always act on their thoughts."

"And therein lies your frustration."

He chuckled, but he knew it wasn't a pleasant sound. "Indeed. Walking by someone who intends to do something wrong, evil even, has proven impossible for me."

"What *do* you do?"

He shrugged as he halted before her. "Stop them when I can. It's far from exact. People change their minds. Sometimes they might think terrible things but not act on them."

"That must be difficult indeed."

"I can only use my best judgment of the situation. I look at their environment and their physical appearance. Are they losing money in a card game? Are they fingering their pocket or some other place they've hidden a weapon? Do they look desperate enough to take action?"

"It sounds impossible."

"I'm often wrong."

"But not always. How on earth do you stop them?"

He studied her expression, looking for the derision and doubt he'd expected but saw only curiosity. "Interrupt them. Distract them. Get their attention on something else."

"And if that fails?"

"I try to remove them from the situation." The

perplexed look she gave him nearly made him chuckle again. "I tell them I need help with something or that I heard someone was looking for them outside or any such foolishness."

Abigail rose to stand before him. "That all sounds impossible. How can you help people who don't necessarily want to be helped?"

"I can't. Nor can I walk away."

"I don't think I'd be able to walk away either. I suppose you have to help as best you can and trust that it's enough." She put a hand on his chest. "Why do you own the gaming den?"

"I won it in a bet. Another attempt to stop someone from doing something they shouldn't. Now, with Mr. Farley's assistance, it's used to fund the orphanage. And at times, it provides us with information on people involved in, shall we say...illicit activities."

"How clever of you. Do you turn those over to the police?"

Stephen laughed. "Rarely. The police don't always appreciate my efforts."

"So you can tell whether people are lying? That's why you didn't press the Newgate warder for more information. You realized he didn't have anything else to share."

"Yes, but it doesn't always work that way."

"That's amazing." She smiled up at him. "What did you see in my aura the night we met?"

Something deep inside him loosened. "An amazing golden light that I would recognize no matter what disguise you wore."

Astonishment spread into her blue eyes. "When I tried to visit you at the gaming den, I was covered from head to toe. But it was my aura that you recognized! Are auras that unique?"

"Yours is." He didn't tell her he'd never seen anything like hers before, that it turned rose when her thoughts strayed to passion, that even now, the edge of it was tinted pink. Her acceptance of what he'd shared made him realize what a treasure she was.

"I'm sorry again for the problems I caused yesterday." Color flooded her cheeks, making him wonder to which problem she referred. "So much time had passed since I'd heard from you, I thought you'd been distracted by other business and forgotten about me."

"Impossible." How could he forget anything about her? He ran his fingers along the softness of her cheek, unable to resist touching her. "But you must promise to be more careful. If you're going to leave the house, have Thomas accompany you or send me a message. I don't want you harmed."

She nodded. "I will. It's just that I'm very anxious for Simmons to be stopped."

"I know. Soon."

"I hope so."

"As do I, but the situation is far from resolved. In fact, evidence mounts each day that Simmons is involved in something more, a devious business that could take time to discover in full. Warning off Simmons might not be enough. Not if he's working for someone else. I know this delays the very thing you want. I'm sorry for that."

She nodded then sighed. "Stephen?" She slid her hand along the lapels of his jacket.

Rather than answer, he put his hand over hers and kissed her, certain that was what she'd been about to ask him for. The sweetness of her mouth caused his worry to slip away. Her passionate response brought forth his unfulfilled desire from the previous day in spades.

"Yes," she murmured and wrapped her arms around his neck.

He forgot about everything except the woman in his arms. He pulled her tight against him, reveling in the feel of her curves. This time, he didn't see how he could walk away from her. Not this time. He needed her desperately.

His heart racing, he pulled back to look at her, to see if she felt half of what he did.

Her desire showed clearly in her face, in her aura. "Would you," she paused to trail kisses along his jaw, "please," another on his neck, "make love to me?" Her tongue swirled in his ear. "Now?"

He hesitated, battling with his desire to have her versus his desire to protect her. Yet how could he resist when she put it so simply? "God help me. Yes."

Euphoria poured through Abigail. She'd been so worried he'd say no, that he'd leave her in this state of frustrating heightened awareness. That the pool of sensations swarming low in her belly would find no relief. Worse yet, that she'd never know what it was like to make love with him. Now more than ever, she knew it had to be with Stephen.

She kissed him to reward him for his answer then pulled back. With trembling hands, she removed the pin holding her hat and placed it on the desk, all the while keeping her gaze on him.

She reached back to unfasten the neck of her gown.

"A moment if you please." He strode to the door and locked it then returned to her with that slow smile she loved, making her heart squeeze. "May I assist you?"

She turned her back to him, enjoying the feel of his fingers against her, the sensation of cool air as he freed her from her gown. He slowly unlaced and removed her corset. Perhaps not as efficient as her maid, but his touch lingered in the most sensitive spots and felt nothing like Eloise's. Abigail's nerves fluttered when at last she stood before him in nothing but her linen chemise.

Slowly, she turned to face him, torn between embarrassment and desire, worried that he'd find her unattractive. His gaze trailed down her body and she couldn't help but wonder what he saw. He paused on her breasts, and her nipples hardened in response.

"Abigail, your beauty stuns me." He frowned and bent to gently kiss the cut along her neck. "Damn him for hurting you."

With determination, she pushed her embarrassment aside and raised her hands to her hair, well aware that her breasts strained through her chemise, leaving little to the imagination. She loosened her chignon, shaking out the long black strands as she continued to watch him, enjoying his reaction.

"Christ." As though he could take her torture no longer, he stepped forward, tossing aside his coat and neck scarf, and pulled her to him. "You are a siren," he muttered.

She tipped her head back and smiled, reveling in the knowledge that she could stir him. "Am I?"

His kiss confirmed her power.

The feel of his muscled torso under her hands made her ache. "And my aura? What color is it now?" she asked.

He leaned back and looked around her head and shoulders. "A vibrant rose found only in the perfect sunset."

His poetic description sent a tiny thrill through her. He ran his hands along her hair, tucking a lock behind her ear, then cupped each of her cheeks. "I want to see all of you. Now."

Emotions she'd never known before filled her, desire heavy deep inside her. She wanted to please him, and so did as he asked. She loosened the ribbons of her chemise and pulled the thin garment from her shoulders and let it float to the floor.

"Yes," he murmured, his fingers following a path along the sensitive flesh she revealed. Down her collarbone, to the tip of her breast, along her belly, then lower still. He touched the bruise coloring her thigh with gentle fingers and shook his head.

"Your turn," she demanded with a smile. She made quick work of removing his shirt, pausing to run her hands through the wiry hair of his chest, to trail her fingers along his scar, careful to avoid his bandaged injury. His muscles quivered in response. Next she moved to the waist of his trousers.

"Hold." He closed his eyes as though overwhelmed for a moment, then took both her hands in his. "Abigail, are you certain? I must know, for I—"

She put a finger to his lips. "Yes. I have absolutely no doubts. Can't you feel how right this is?"

He searched her face for a long moment before gathering her into his arms. "Yes," he agreed and sealed his words with a kiss.

She ran her hands along his shoulders, marveling at the solid feel of him. As he eased her down on the sofa, she wrapped her arms around him and kissed the hollow of his throat where his pulse beat frantically.

"So beautiful," he whispered as he trailed kisses along her neck, down to her breasts.

He took one into his mouth, his tongue swirling around the tip, shooting spears of sensation all the way to her toes. First one, then the other, causing her to gasp in surprise and delight, even as she realized his fingers glided low over her belly. She moaned, hoping he'd repeat what he'd done the previous day.

"Abigail, you're so beautiful." He lifted his head to watch her as his fingers touched the most intimate part of her.

As though performing a dance she didn't know, her hips swayed and thrust to his movements, sensations building within her. "Stephen, please."

He rose to unfasten his trousers, dropping them carelessly to the floor.

"Oh, my," she said as she stared at his form.

His body looked as though a sculptor had carved the cords of muscle, paying attention to detail along the hard planes of his stomach. She could see where the hair that started on his chest narrowed on his stomach and trailed down as though to point to his manhood. It stood erect, so different and so much...bigger...than the statues and paintings she'd viewed. How could the artists have portrayed it so wrong?

"You have the softest skin," he whispered as though trying to distract her from her surprise. He lay beside her on the sofa and continued to use his mouth and fingers to build her passion higher. His member pressed her thigh, surprising her with its heat and hardness. She hadn't reached the advanced age of six and twenty without some knowledge of the workings of intimacy, but that hadn't truly prepared her for the actual act, for the feelings building inside her mind and body.

Anxious to please him, she reached down and ran her fingers along his stomach, stretching until she felt that unfamiliar part of him. The breath left his lungs in a rush, giving her pause until she realized her touch stirred him as much as his moved her.

Too soon, he pulled her hand away and wound his fingers through hers as though to hold her in place. "I must have you."

"Yes." The longing he created within her demanded fulfillment.

He rose over her, settling between her legs, his manhood pressing against the very core of her.

She raised her knees, pleased at the sensation of his weight on her. He pressed into her center, and she could feel her tightness stretching to allow him entrance. Doubt filled her as she realized it simply wouldn't work.

"Stephen?"

His harsh breathing was her only answer as he reached down between them to touch her. As desire spiraled higher within her, he pushed forward, filling her.

"Oh!" The sharp pain took her by surprise.

He froze, nothing moving except his chest as his breath came fast.

"I don't think—"

"No. Don't think." He kissed her, the heat of his lips easing her concern.

After a moment, she realized her body had accommodated his size, leaving pleasure in the wake of pain. She tilted her hips experimentally, anxious to see what other feelings she might experience.

With a moan, he drew back only to thrust into her. Again, her hips danced with his as though caught in an ancient ritual unknown to her. Layer built upon layer until she couldn't bear it. At last, he touched her once again and the star she rode burst.

Stephen thrust into her one last time, his moans mingling with hers. She held him tight as she floated back down, her heart slowing, beating in time with his.

Satisfaction and happiness mingled through her as she enjoyed Stephen's naked body against hers. "That...was glorious."

He lifted his head, the gold flecks in his green eyes glittered as he studied her expression. "Indeed."

"I had no idea," she said with wonder.

He smiled as he shifted to rest his weight on

his elbows, his finger tracing her brow. But his smile soon faded and his gaze shuttered.

"What is it?" she asked, not ready to lose their close connection.

He shook his head and moved to her side on the sofa, pillowing her head on his shoulder, wrapping her in his warm embrace. He kissed the top of her head and her heart squeezed.

She basked in the moment, unable to stop the images of more times like this running through her mind. Times spent at his side, cuddled in his arms, visiting about their day, or in the throes of passion. Then she realized exactly what she was fantasizing about—a lifetime with him.

How had this happened? How had his presence in her life grown to include a future? A lump formed in her throat when she realized the irony of the situation. She'd found a man worthy of making her change her mind about marriage, but he had no interest in a life with her.

"It wasn't necessary for you to accompany me." Abigail glanced up at Stephen as they walked down St. James Street. One of her housemaids, Emma, trailed behind them. Abigail's pace was slowed by the lingering pain in her thigh.

"Forgive me if I disagree." He perused the street, clearly keeping an eye out for Simmons.

Stephen seemed in an odd mood today. The shadows under his eyes spoke of a sleepless night, and she couldn't help but worry it had to do with them making love. It tugged at her to think he was so troubled that it stole his sleep.

The street bustled with shoppers, everyone ignoring the dampness of the day. The sun was not to be found, too stubborn to show itself. A good day to stay home with a bracing cup of tea.

"I don't like shopping. I don't see how you can."

"Perhaps it's not shopping but the company of my companion I'm enjoying," he suggested with a smile.

Abigail's stomach dipped and her cheeks warmed at his comment. Now that they'd made love, she wasn't sure about the nature of their relationship. No longer strictly business nor did she think they were having an affair. She could only hope their interlude hadn't been a onetime occurrence.

"I do appreciate that Thomas is home with my stepmother and the girls rather than following me." Stephen's appearance on their doorstep in response to the message she'd sent about her intended outing had surprised her.

"And the other guards."

"Assuming Irene hasn't sent them away again."

He told her he'd posted a second guard nearby with the hope that at least one of them would always be able to keep watch despite her stepmother interfering with his plans.

Stephen shook his head. "I still think you should tell her the truth."

"I thought about it many times. In fact, I almost did. But it seems like we're nearing the end of this whole problem. Why worry her if Simmons is no longer a threat in a day or two?"

"Hmm." Stephen's noncommittal response was less than reassuring.

Again she ran through the advantages and disadvantages in her mind. No, she was certain she'd done the right thing. "If the situation changes or somehow worsens, then I'll tell her."

"As you wish."

If he only knew of the warm feeling that spiraled through her at his words. Pushing aside her longing, she consulted the list of items her stepmother had requested. When Abigail had heard her planning an outing with the girls to pick up a few needed things, she'd quickly offered to go in her stead. Irene had looked at her as though she'd lost her mind, but Abigail had convinced her she wanted some fresh air.

She'd nearly decided against bothering Stephen for such a minor excursion, but in the end had sent him a message and was glad she had. Any time in his company was time well spent. She hoped to find the right moment to suggest they meet again at his home for another...interlude, but so far, it'd been too difficult to manage such a private conversation while out in public.

Or perhaps she just hadn't found the courage to do so yet.

"The apothecary is next," she said. They'd already completed two stops and had one remaining.

"I'll keep watch outside."

Abigail and her maid entered the small shop that her stepmother frequented on a regular basis. "Good day to you, Mr. Skryme."

"Miss Bradford. How delightful."

The shopkeeper was a tall, thin man with gaunt cheeks, thick brows, and permanent dark circles under his eyes. Abigail wondered if he had trouble sleeping. If so, surely one of the concoctions in the bottles behind the counter would cure him.

"What might I assist you with?"

He spoke in a slow manner, enunciating each word with great care. His cadence amused Abigail, but the prophecies the man liked to expound gave her the shivers. The last time she'd been in his shop, he'd told her of an evil omen spreading due to the growing flocks of crows in the city. Each time she'd seen a crow after that, she'd wondered if what he'd told her was coming to pass.

The man could spread prophecies faster than a costermonger.

Abigail avoided looking at the snakes in bottles and the stuffed alligator strapped to the rafters and instead studied her list. "Lady Bradford requested some Grasshopper Pills for headaches."

"Certainly. Will there be anything else?" Mr. Skryme asked as he plucked a tin from a shelf.

"She wondered if you could recommend something for a stomach ailment."

"A stomach ailment. Interesting." He put his index finger to the corner of his mouth and looked at the ceiling as though searching for an answer there. "How long has the stomach been a problem?"

"The past two days believe."

"I have just the thing." He folded his lanky form down to peer in a drawer under the counter. "I anticipate many more will soon be seeking assistance with such ailments."

"Oh?" Abigail hid a grimace. Surely he wouldn't bring up the flocks of crows again.

"Indeed. Did you perchance see the moon last evening? I fear we can expect dour happenings over the course of the next three days."

The sound of a door squeaking in the back of the store interrupted Mr. Skryme's expansion of his prediction.

He frowned at the sound. "One moment please, Miss Bradford." The man rose and walked slowly through the doorway to the backroom.

Before Abigail had time to wonder what had occurred, Mr. Skryme came hurrying back, his eyes wide.

Abigail's breath caught as she realized something was terribly wrong.

"I fear—"

"Shut yer trap, old man!" A gruff voice sounded

from behind the apothecary owner.

Mr. Skryme flew forward, landing on the edge of the counter, revealing an unwelcome face.

"Miss Bradford. We meet again," Simmons said with a broad smile as he stepped from behind Mr. Skyrme.

Abigail backed up as her maid, Emma, squeaked with fright. Simmons wore the same brown suit and matching bowler hat she'd last seen him in, but his face and clothes were smeared with dirt and grime.

"What do you want?" she demanded even as her heart pounded.

He studied her from head to toe. "Yer dressed a bit different than the last time I saw ye. Hope I didn't damage ye much."

Abigail didn't bother to answer. She glanced over her shoulder to make certain Emma was behind her then risked a glance out the shop window, hoping to get Stephen's attention.

"Lookin' for yer protector?" Simmons asked. "Yeah, I saw him out there. He seems to be everywhere ye are. He's got people watchin' every damned place I want to go. How's a man supposed to do his business with so many eyes followin' him?"

"We could resolve all this if we stepped outside and spoke with Lord Ashbury." Fear made her chest tight, making breathing difficult. She eased back another step.

"I think not. Yer the one I want to speak with. Think those guards posted at yer house are goin' to protect ye?"

"Why do you insist on bothering us?"

"I want the rock. I've told ye that, but still ye don't hand it over."

"I have no idea to which rock you're referring." Abigail moved farther away, hoping she and her maid could get close enough to the door to make a run for it.

"I think ye do, and I'm growin' weary of the lies." His eyes narrowed as he leaned forward. "If ye don't get it for me, I'll be comin' to collect it. And next time I pay a visit ter yer house, I won't be so friendly. Blood will be shed, just like with yer father."

Emma gasped as Abigail's vision filled with flashes of memory, stealing her ability to think. Fear made her feet leaden. She glanced at Mr. Skryme who appeared stunned from the invasion of his shop. No help would come from that quarter.

Simmons cocked his head to the side. "Ye best stop backin' up or I'll have ta—"

He stared at something out the window then scrunched his shoulders like a turtle retreating into its shell. "Damn me."

Abigail turned to look behind her to see Stephen enter the shop just as Simmons bolted for the back door.

"Bloody hell." Stephen glanced at her. "Are you all right?"

"Yes. Yes, of course."

But she was speaking to his back as he sprinted after Simmons. The rear door slammed, leaving silence in its wake.

Abigail looked at Mr. Skryme, who still leaned on the counter where he'd landed.

"I say, what was that all about?" he asked.

"Part of the omens you mentioned," Abigail muttered.

"Pardon me?"

"Never mind." She sank into a nearby chair to ease her trembling legs, hoping her heart didn't beat its way out of her chest.

CHAPTER SEVENTEEN

Two streets away Stephen stopped, unable to locate Simmons. He'd lost him in the crowded thoroughfare.

"Damn."

He leapt up the front steps of a nearby building and scanned the area, searching for a fleeing figure wearing a brown bowler hat.

Nothing.

On this busy street, Simmons could easily have removed his hat, slowed his pace and blended in with the other people on the sidewalk.

Frustrated, Stephen turned to make his way back to the apothecary. Though tempted to search further, he couldn't risk leaving Abigail alone. Simmons was clever enough to circle around for her. That was something Stephen wouldn't allow.

He entered the shop, listening carefully to see if any conversation sounded unnatural. Only the even tones of Abigail and the shopkeeper greeted him. He glanced around the corner to catch sight of her. If her aura looked similar to when Simmons had appeared, he'd know danger was near. It had turned a muddy blue and thinned in places, and he'd known something was terribly wrong.

Now she stood, nodding politely to whatever the shopkeeper was telling her. She glanced at the stuffed alligator out of the corner of her eye then turned away. Her maid waited nearby.

Abigail's beauty here in this simple shop gave him pause. Her vivid blue eyes radiated intelligence. Her black hair shined in the light adorned with a clever hat set at an angle. He could envision her removing it as she had yesterday. If only she knew how erotic her disrobing had been. He knew he should regret making love with her, yet how could he? Never had he burned with desire as he did for her.

Afterward, his pleasure had dimmed knowing that he couldn't let it happen again. He had to keep her at a distance for both their sakes. If she were to get with child, they'd be forced to marry. He couldn't allow that. She wasn't his to keep. He wasn't fit to be a husband, especially not to a woman like her. If she were bound to him, her golden light might be forever smothered by the darkness inside him.

Still, he couldn't help but admire her as she chatted amiably with the shopkeeper as though the encounter with the man who'd killed her father and now threatened her family was of little consequence. She caught sight of him, and her face lit with relief.

"Are you all right, my lord?"

"Yes. Although I fear I lost our quarry in the crowd."

Her disappointment was palpable. He knew how much she wanted this whole situation to be over.

She shook her head. "He must've been following us. He knew you were out front." Alarm flooded her features. "You don't suppose he's going to my home..."

"No. My guess is that he'll retreat to determine a new plan."

"Oh, dear." Abigail's gaze scanned the room as

if it would tell her what that plan might be.

"May I inquire if all is well?" The shopkeeper's question seemed to pull Abigail back from her thoughts.

"Thank you for your concern, Mr. Skryme. And for allowing me to wait here." She picked up the wrapped items from the counter and handed them to her nervous maid.

Stephen watched the shopkeeper, trying to determine how upset the man was. His aura was a muddled gray but held a hint of blue. Stephen hoped that sign of intelligence meant the man was not overly wrought from the events of the last few minutes.

"No damage to you or your shop?" Stephen inquired.

"None at all. Thank you, my lord."

"You might want to keep that back door locked." He bid the man good day then opened the front door for Abigail as her maid followed.

"This will outdo his worry over the moon and the crows," Abigail said.

Puzzled, Stephen looked down at her as he offered her his elbow. "I don't understand."

"Nor do I. The man has more omens and prophecies to tell than he has remedies to sell. Today's events will give him something else to talk about."

Stephen smiled as he searched for any sign of Simmons. He was still annoyed that he'd missed spotting the man. "Do you think he'll share the excitement with Lady Bradford when she shops there again?"

Abigail halted to stare up at him in dismay.

"I fear you're going to have to apprise her of the issues that have arisen after all," he suggested.

"Oh, no." Her shoulders wilted as her gloved hand fluttered up to her collarbone, and her aura dimmed. "I suppose you're correct."

Stephen guided her aside so they weren't halting the other passersby, her maid waiting at a discreet distance.

"If I tell her, I..." Her loss for words pulled at him. "I've failed my promise to my father." Her blue eyes filled with unshed tears. "I promised to protect them and I haven't."

Stephen drew her arm tighter to his side, the only way he could offer comfort in such a public place. "You haven't failed anyone. No harm has befallen them."

She shook her head, clearly not convinced. "The mention of Simmons alone will frighten Irene. To learn that he's made threats all for some sort of rock—"

"Did he mention the rock again? Did he describe it?" Warning bells sounded in Stephen's mind.

"He asked for it, and I told him to be more specific. He insists I should know, but I don't. Do you think it could be the one you have?"

"It might be." He had to find a way to lure Simmons out of hiding without putting Abigail at risk.

Dread pooled in the pit of Abigail's stomach as she sat with her stepmother in the drawing room later that evening.

Sophia and Olivia were safely ensconced in their room. Apparently they were quite enjoying the new novel that was all the rage among their friends and were anxious to continue reading. Abigail had been delighted to realize Mr. Larson from the bookstore where she'd met Stephen had published the book. She'd already made arrangements to invest in his bookstore and looked forward to speaking with him personally about expanding it.

But right now, her concern was how to tell Irene that Vincent Simmons was not dead. She was having the worst time forming the words. She feared Irene would collapse in tears, much as she had when any other bad news had been delivered.

"Abigail?"

She looked up to find Irene's green eyes on her, brows puckered with concern.

"Whatever is the matter?"

Tears rushed into her eyes before she could stop them.

Immediately Irene rose and sat beside her. She put an arm around her shoulders and rested her head against Abigail's. "Tell me, darling. What's wrong?"

"We have a problem." Abigail forced out the words.

Irene drew back to look into her eyes. "What sort of problem?"

Abigail took Irene's hand in her own. She swallowed the lump in her throat, determined to find the courage to tell her. "Vincent Simmons did not hang for Father's murder."

"That can't be." Her stepmother's face paled as she sank back in the settee. "We received confirmation of his death."

"Somehow he switched places with another man who hung in his stead. He was released from prison nearly three weeks ago."

"How could that have happened? We must notify the police so they can arrest him again."

"I tried, but they don't believe me. Their records show he's dead. I've argued to the contrary, but to no avail."

"He's the one who broke into our home, isn't he?" Irene put a trembling hand to her mouth.

"I think so."

"Oh, dear heavens! What could that devil

possibly want from us? He already took your father."

Her upset made Abigail wish she could take back her words. But she couldn't. Irene needed to be informed for her own safety, so Abigail made herself continue. "He says he wants a rock from Father's collection."

"You've spoken with him?" Irene asked, her eyes wide with shock.

"Yes." She shared some of the details without elaborating on Stephen's suspicions that something more was underfoot.

"Abigail!" The tears in Irene's eyes spoke volumes. "You must be careful. I simply couldn't bear to lose you, too."

"You won't. I promise." She couldn't help but put a hand to the high neck of her gown that hid the cut from Simmons' knife. "Lord Ashbury has been assisting me with this...problem."

"Oh." She looked almost disappointed at this news. "That's very kind of him, but I'd rather hoped something else was bringing you together."

Abigail lowered her gaze. She had no idea how to respond. She decided it best not to. She could only deal with one issue at a time.

"Until we eliminate the threat of Simmons, I'd like you and the girls to go to the country and stay with Uncle Reginald." It was the only way Abigail could think of to keep them safe.

"To Kent? But that's where he killed your father!" Irene's eyes filled with tears, and the sight squeezed Abigail's heart.

"Simmons is in London, so you'd be safe in Kent. I'll send Thomas with you along with some other—"

Irene shook her head. "We're not going anywhere without you."

"I need to stay and see this through. Please take the girls and go," Abigail pleaded.

"I'm not leaving you here alone."

Abigail hadn't realized how stubborn Irene could be.

"Lord Ashbury will watch over me. I'll send word as soon as the problem is resolved."

Irene rested her hand on Abigail's shoulder. "We'll be safe if we stay together. I do realize you shield me from many of the troubles you face on behalf of our family, but not anymore."

"Mother—"

"I will not hear of you dealing with this alone. From now on, you'll allow me to help with the dilemmas that arise. We will work through any problems together. Including this one."

Abigail hardly knew what to say. This was the last result she'd expected from the conversation. She'd thought her stepmother would welcome escaping to the country rather than risking a confrontation with Simmons. A heavy weight inside Abigail eased. "If you remain, you must promise to take extra precautions."

"Of course, if you promise me the same."

To have her stepmother's support meant more than she could've guessed. "We'll both be careful," she agreed.

"Now then, let us discuss this further over a glass of sherry, shall we? I find myself in need of sustenance."

She rang for Ponsford who appeared so quickly that Abigail wondered if he'd been listening outside the door.

"Bring us two glasses of sherry, Ponsford. And the bottle as well."

The butler raised a brow in surprise but nodded. "Of course, my lady."

"I cannot fathom that Simmons managed to change places with someone." Irene shook her head at the idea. "What could he want with this rock?" she asked as though they discussed nothing more than tomorrow's schedule.

"I've no idea. Lord Ashbury looked through Father's collection and found one he thought interesting. But we still don't know why Simmons would want any of them."

"Didn't your father have a list of them somewhere? Perhaps that would give us insight," Irene suggested as Ponsford returned with the sherry and poured two glasses. "He was forever going on about their qualities. I think he jotted down many of them."

"I haven't been able to find that list. It seems to have disappeared." She and Ponsford had searched the library for it earlier.

"Hmm. Why don't you show me which rock Lord Ashbury thought might be the one in question? Perhaps that will jog my memory."

"He took it with him."

"Why?" Irene frowned at her as she sipped.

"I don't know. He didn't say." Abigail shivered as a trickle of unease passed through her.

Irene sipped again. "You're aware he has the reputation of being...shall we say, a man who walks his own path, are you not?"

Abigail felt Ponsford' gaze on her as well. She hadn't forgotten that he considered Stephen dangerous. In all honesty, there were times when he was, but never toward her. "Yes."

"Do you think he's trustworthy?"

"I do." She avoided looking at Ponsford as she took a drink. Surely she couldn't be wrong.

Irene gestured to Ponsford to refill her glass. "Did he think the rock valuable?"

"He didn't say."

"But he thinks that particular stone might be the one Simmons is after?" Irene took another healthy swallow much to Abigail's amazement.

"I don't know. I do believe he intends to formulate a plan to flush out Simmons, but I don't think he's yet determined the details."

"That's all well and good, but what are we to do if Simmons comes here and demands the rock again?"

Abigail set down her glass as doubt filled her. What would they do? Perhaps she'd better get the rock back from Stephen just in case.

Stephen stood at the interior window of his office at The Barbican, watching the people at the tables in the gambling hell below. The men ranged from earls to barons and everyone in between. The prince had even graced the establishment once or twice, not that Stephen would ever repeat that information to anyone.

Discretion was a necessary element in this line of business. Stephen appreciated that since he had secrets of his own to keep. Sharing one with Abigail had left him feeling off balance and unable to think clearly. He was no longer certain how to proceed with their relationship.

Farley appeared at his side, his suit impeccable, his long gray side burns clipped precisely. "Anyone we need to worry over?"

"No. Not yet at any rate. Although the lord with the gold waistcoat should be limited in the bets he places."

"Very well." Farley stepped out to send word down to the floor manager to advise him.

Stephen turned away from the window to pace his office, his thoughts in turmoil. Another boy had disappeared from the workhouse. Vanished was a better term, for no trace remained of any of them. According to his information, there were now eight missing, all boys. He couldn't understand how no one had seen anything regarding them. Surely someone had noticed the boy talking to a stranger or some other clue.

Farley had spoken with many of the people at the workhouse, but no one appeared to be involved. To think none of the boys had returned was alarming indeed. Stephen had to wonder if they still lived.

He also needed to determine a way to deal with Simmons before he made another unexpected appearance. He hadn't come by any of the places where he'd previously been sighted. Not having him under watch made Stephen nervous.

Stephen was certain the meteorite was the rock Simmons was after as there was nothing else as unique in Abigail's father's collection. But Stephen wasn't about to hand it to Simmons. Not until he found out who was really behind all this.

Farley returned to the room. "Are you going down to the floor tonight?"

"No, I'll be leaving shortly."

"You seem to be spending less and less time here." Farley's gaze remained on the crowd below, leaving Stephen to wonder at his thoughts on the matter.

"You have everything well in hand. My presence is no longer required."

At last, Farley's gaze met his. "Perhaps your talents are better used elsewhere."

"My 'talents' are not leading us anywhere." Stephen told him of Simmons' appearance at the apothecary shop.

"He might've taken Miss Bradford out the back door if you hadn't realized what was happening. You have your aura reading to thank for that," Farley insisted.

"It would've been better if I'd caught him." Stephen ran a hand through his hair. "There's been nothing more on the missing boys. I can't seem to gain any ground on that either."

"You'll remember I accompanied Lord Weston on another search of the warehouse Simmons was in."

"And?" Stephen turned to look at him. He'd forgotten about it.

"I found this in the same room where Lord Weston discovered the sleeping remedy." Farley pulled a small worn leather pouch from his pocket. He upended the contents into his palm.

"Jacks?" The pointed metal objects and ball were a game most children had played at some point in their lives.

"Indeed. Well worn by the dents and nicks. An inexpensive version," Farley commented as he turned the jacks over to examine them.

Stephen frowned, wondering what those had been doing in that room of the warehouse. "I don't see how this has anything to do with whatever Simmons was doing there."

"I'm not sure if they're a clue or an unrelated finding." Farley shook his head as he returned the jacks and ball to the pouch. "I still can't believe none of the children at the workhouse saw anything. Those kids have their eyes and ears open all the time."

"Yet they told you they knew nothing."

Farley frowned. "Would they have a reason to lie? Some acted strangely, frightened even, when I questioned them, but I thought that normal under the circumstances. For all they know, there's a murderer on the loose who preys on young boys."

Stephen thought it over. "It's possible someone's threatened them."

"That would explain why none are willing to talk."

"Perhaps the wrong people questioned them."

"Who would you suggest?"

"Let's send one of the boys in our employ to speak with them. Perhaps they'll have better luck."

"Excellent suggestion." Farley nodded. "They'd

be more likely to share information amongst themselves. We could also offer a reward for any information."

"Bribing children?" Stephen smiled. "I'm shocked, Farley." That sort of thinking was exactly why he admired Farley. The man had excellent strategizing skills.

"I'm certain the end justifies the means in this case. What are our next steps with Simmons?"

"I believe we'll plan a trap. Somehow, we'll need to spread the word that we have something he wants," Stephen said.

"Are you referring to the stone or Miss Bradford?"

Anger coursed through Stephen, surprising him with its intensity. "Using Miss Bradford is not an option. The meteorite should prove sufficient." He worked to keep the emotion out of his voice.

"I meant no offense."

Farley watched him closely, but Stephen merely nodded in acknowledgement. How could he explain his reaction to Farley when he didn't understand it himself? The protectiveness he felt for Abigail...hell, who was he trying to fool? The *growing feelings* he had for her refused to be smothered. Instead, they blossomed each time he saw her. He had no idea what to do about it.

"I wonder what he wants with rock." Farley caught his gaze. "Do you have any inkling?"

Stephen considered telling him about Professor Grisby's search for a similar stone, but decided it was irrelevant. The professor was dead, and they couldn't afford to make mistaken assumptions about why Simmons might want the damned meteorite.

"I intend to find out before we offer it up, but we have to hurry before he does something rash. I refuse to put Miss Bradford or her family in harm's way."

Abigail sat in the drawing room, enjoying a moment of peace and quiet with some reading. She'd met with the staff earlier and given them an update on the joint investment she'd made on their behalf. Their funds were accumulating nicely and that had the servants excited about the venture.

While at Mr. Larson's bookstore the other day, she'd picked up a small but fascinating book on neuro-hypnotism. The author was a Scottish physician who'd used the technique on himself to relieve pain. For some reason, she found the topic intriguing. She knew Stephen suffered from headaches and wondered if the practice could somehow help him.

Irene entered the room with the girls directly behind her, putting an end to Abigail's solitude.

"Mother, you promised!" Olivia stomped her foot as Irene sat on the settee beside Abigail and picked up her embroidery.

"I don't think it's a good idea to go out today," Irene said as she sorted through a basket of colored thread.

Knowing full well why Irene refused to allow the girls to leave the house unless absolutely necessary, Abigail felt obligated to intercede. "Did you finish the book you were reading?" she asked the girls.

"Yes," they answered together.

"It was very good," Sophia added.

"Then you'll be pleased to know that we're investing in the company that printed it."

"Really?" Olivia looked interested at the news. "Does that mean there will be another in the series soon?"

"Indeed," Abigail said. "But these things take

time."

Olivia looked less than pleased at the news.

"We're tired of being inside." Sophia flopped down on the settee between Abigail and Irene.

"We don't have lessons today and we want to go out," Olivia said. "Look." She pointed to the window. "It's not even raining."

The morning light streamed in the windows of the drawing room, beckoning them with its warmth. It was indeed a lovely day.

Abigail and Irene had come up with every possible excuse to curtail their activities over the past two days. Even Abigail was beginning to feel stifled. She'd heard nothing from Stephen since the apothecary.

She glanced to Irene and raised her brow, wondering if they should relent. Irene met her gaze, seeming weary of the girls' arguments.

"I could accompany them," Abigail offered.

"I don't know," said Irene, her hands quiet in her lap as she thought it over.

"Why are we always staying home now?" Olivia asked. "Please, Mother. I can't stand another day inside."

"Yes, Mother. Please!" Sophia's long lashes fluttered over her big brown eyes and Abigail was certain Irene would give in. Who could possibly resist Sophia when she used her charm?

Irene turned to Abigail. "What do you think?"

"I think it's a fine day for an outing. Girls, get your hats and cloaks." Abigail waited until they departed before saying anything more. "I'll take Thomas and one of the guards with me. Ponsford will be here with you along with the other guard."

Irene closed her eyes as though Abigail's words only worried her more.

"Olivia and Sophia will make us crazed if we don't allow it."

"True," Irene admitted with a sigh.

"I'll be extra careful. Besides, the sunshine is inviting," Abigail said. "Are you certain you don't wish to come with us?"

"I believe I'll admire it from inside."

"Very well." Abigail smiled. "We won't stay out long."

In a flurry of activity worthy of an overnight adventure rather than a simple outing to the park, the girls returned to the foyer then followed Abigail to the carriage. They didn't seem to notice how carefully she and Thomas scanned the area or that a new footman traveled with them.

From past experience, Abigail knew a public place wouldn't prevent Simmons from making contact. The man was certainly clever when it came to using opportunities. If he approached her again, she'd force him to describe the rock he wanted. She needed to know if it was the same one Stephen had taken.

The only reason she could think that Simmons would want a rock from her father's collection was because it was valuable. Yet if that was the case, why didn't he just ask for money?

"Stay close," Abigail warned them once they arrived.

"Are you certain you wouldn't rather have some privacy?" Olivia asked with a mischievous look upon her face.

Sophia giggled.

"No. I'd like you to remain nearby," Abigail answered, unsure what the girls were going on about.

"Well," Olivia continued with a sly smile, "if a certain someone was going to meet you here, we wouldn't want to be a nuisance."

Abigail's cheeks heated as she realized they referred to Stephen. Where did the girls get such ideas? "Stay close, please."

Still giggling, they led the way. Thomas and

the other guard, a brawny young man, followed behind Abigail. The park was busy today with many people out enjoying the fine spring day. The girls skipped ahead, stopping here and there to greet friends, often pausing to whisper in each other's ear. Abigail could only hope they weren't plotting anything.

As they continued along the path, the girls moved farther ahead. She called out to them, but they didn't hear her. With a worried glance to Thomas, she walked faster, hoping to catch them. Her skirt and the other people strolling along hampered her progress. She wove through the crowd, nodding politely as she saw acquaintances. Then she lost sight of the girls completely as they walked past the large sculpture of Achilles that stood in the park. Fighting off panic, she hurried toward the sculpture, hoping to find them lingering nearby as they were wont to do.

But the girls were nowhere in sight.

Thoroughly panicked, she stopped and looked back. "Thomas?"

"I can't see them either, miss. Shall I run ahead and make certain they're all right?"

"Yes, but not too far. I don't want us all separated."

He hurried away, stepping off the path to avoid the crowd.

Abigail glanced back to make sure the other guard was still there. He gave her a polite nod, his gaze continuing to scan the area.

Her heart pounded with fear. What on earth were the girls thinking when she'd specifically told them to stay close? She wobbled between fearing the worst—that somehow Simmons had taken them—to less dour circumstances—that they were having a bit of fun hiding from her.

As she was about to send the other guard for help, she caught sight of Thomas escorting Sophia and Olivia toward her. Both looked put out at the interruption.

"Abigail, whatever is the matter?" asked Olivia. "Thomas insisted you need us."

Torn between anger and relief, Abigail's hands shook as she reached for them. "I asked you to stay close when we arrived. Don't tell me you didn't hear my request."

"We weren't far," Sophia tried to assure her.

"We were only having some fun," Olivia added.

A motion caught Abigail's gaze just past Thomas's shoulder. She gave a startled gasp at the sight of Simmons a short distance away. "Oh, dear heavens."

Thomas glanced at her and immediately spun around, searching for the cause of her fright. He, too, must've seen Simmons, for he took off at a run, the other guard immediately behind him.

"Whatever is wrong with Thomas?" Sophia asked.

Olivia kept her gaze on Abigail. "You're as pale as a ghost."

Sophia took her arm. "Are you quite all right?"

"I'm fine. I believe Thomas saw someone he knew." She hoped the answer would pacify them so they wouldn't ask further questions. She willed her pounding heart to slow.

"So he chased after him?" Olivia shook her head. "That seems inappropriate."

Sophia stared at where Thomas had disappeared, her brows puckered. Abigail knew she didn't believe her explanation.

"Girls," she began as she realized what a close call they'd had, "I asked you to stay nearby. Why did you get so far ahead of us?"

Olivia gave her a sheepish look. "We were hoping you were meeting Lord Ashbury. We thought we saw him and wanted you to have some time together."

"Yes, and we didn't want to be in the way of your budding romance," Sophia added earnestly. "You need all the help you can get with him."

Abigail stared at both of them, certain they'd lost their minds. "Lord Ashbury is not interested in me...that way."

Olivia waved away Abigail's denial. "We've seen the way you look when you speak of him."

"He came for a visit the other day," Sophia added.

"And you've been gone more than usual," Olivia continued. "Not to mention how secretive you've been."

"So we assume you're keeping company with him," Sophia said. "We thought we saw him and that you had arranged to meet him here."

Olivia patted Abigail's hand. "We've no doubt he'll form an affection for you. You're pretty and smart. How could he possibly resist?"

Abigail shook her head. While she appreciated their faith in her, she couldn't believe the conclusions they'd drawn. "You're both mistaken. I need you to be careful over the next few days. There is a—a stranger lurking in our neighborhood, and I don't want him coming anywhere near either of you."

Sophia looked to where Thomas had gone again. "Does this stranger have anything to do with the man whom Thomas is chasing?"

Uncertain how much to tell the girls, Abigail put an arm through each of theirs and started onto the path again. "I'm sure Thomas will be along soon. Let's return to the carriage to wait for him."

By the time they returned home, two frustrated guards included, Abigail had recovered from her fright.

Another, stronger emotion had taken its place—anger.

Simmons had eluded them once again. She now knew he was still watching the house. The guards might be keeping him at a distance, but they weren't preventing him from spying on them and most likely looking for a chance to approach—a very unsettling notion that lay heavy on Abigail's shoulders.

What if Simmons had done something to the girls?

She couldn't get the thought out of her mind.

After seeing the girls safely inside, she gave her stepmother a brief update and spent several long minutes reassuring her. By the time Irene calmed, Abigail decided to pay a visit to Stephen.

Her patience had come to an end. Something needed to be done. Now.

CHAPTER EIGHTEEN

Abigail had Thomas take a long route to Park Lane to see if anyone followed. She breathed a sigh of relief when he thumped the roof of the carriage to let her know he'd seen nothing and was proceeding to their destination.

At Stephen's home, a young footman she'd never seen answered the door. When she asked to see Stephen, a look of panic crossed the man's face. "I'm sorry, but he's not receiving."

She frowned. "I believe he'll make time to see me."

The man's eyes grew wide as though he was trying to think of what else he could say. "I'm sorry, miss, but he's indisposed."

"He's ill?"

Winston entered the hall from the back of the house. The footman seemed quite relieved at his arrival. The butler's ever-ready smile looked a bit strained. "Good day, Miss Bradford."

"Hello, Winston. Is Lord Ashbury unwell?"

"He is certainly not feeling his best." A wary expression crossed the butler's face, making Abigail wonder what was going on. "I'll inquire if he's able to see you. Perhaps you'd like to wait in the drawing room?"

"Thank you." Perplexed at what could be wrong with the strong, virile man she knew, she withdrew to the drawing room where she paced, her concern growing by the minute. She needed to speak with him.

A loud crash sounded from a nearby room.

Within moments, Winston entered, his smile gone, his jacket askew on his shoulders. "It would be best if you left, miss."

Abigail stared at the butler, trying to determine what on earth was happening. "He refuses to see me?"

Again the butler hesitated. "He is *unable* to see you."

That made her even more certain that something was wrong. "I see. Thank you, Winston." She stalked past the butler and out the drawing room. But she had no intention of leaving.

She strode toward the library door.

"Miss Bradford." Winston hurried after her.

She held up her hand, palm out. "I take full responsibility, Winston. You should take this opportunity to have tea, don't you think?"

The butler shook his head, obviously unhappy with the turn of events. "He's not going to be happy with either of us, miss."

Abigail waited, her hand on the door knob, until Winston had taken his leave. She drew a deep breath to rein in her emotions then opened the door.

The curtains were drawn, leaving the room cloaked in darkness. The air was stale and made her wonder how long Stephen had been in there. Pausing to allow her eyes to adjust to the dimness, she moved toward the drapes and drew one back.

"Get out." The angry words spewed from a chair before the empty fireplace.

"Stephen?" Shock held her to the spot. How could the man she thought she knew speak to her with such rudeness?

"Where the hell is Winston?" His tone was gruff and anything but welcoming.

"He's indisposed," she said, letting her own anger color her tone.

He scoffed. "Then you'll have to show yourself out." His face was hidden by the wing of the chair in which he slouched. One of his long legs stretched out before him, but he didn't bother to rise. A nearly empty decanter and half full glass sat on the table beside him.

"Why are you sitting in the dark?" She moved closer, unable to guess what had him acting so oddly.

"I am not receiving."

"So I was told."

"Then go!" he barked.

Curiosity drew her forward, though a voice in her head suggested she do as he bid. She stepped around the edge of the chair, but could see little of his face in the shadows. "What's happened?"

"Nothing. I suggest you leave. In fact, I'm certain Winston would highly advise it."

"Are you in a mood?"

"When am I not?"

The sharp tone of his voice tugged at her and against her better judgment, she remained where she was.

"Go, damn it. Get out." He waved his hand toward the door.

"As soon as you tell me what's wrong."

"Bloody hell." He bolted up from his chair to loom over her. "What part of 'leave' do you not understand?"

She stiffened, her heart racing as she was forced back a step. She hardly recognized him. His face was ashen beneath the stubble of whiskers. Deep circles lined his pain-filled eyes. "I understand the word quite well, thank you."

Stephen turned away but not before she saw a flash of pain cross his features. That made her even more determined to discover the reason for his distress. He strode toward the door, jacket off, his shirt unbuttoned at the neck, not even properly tucked into his trousers—a far cry from his normally neat appearance. His state of dishabille made her feel like she spoke with a stranger.

He stuck his head out the door. "Winston!" He waited a moment before trying again. "Winston! Bloody hell. The place is crawling with servants until I need one. Show yourself out."

"You only have to tell me what's wrong and I'll go."

An impenetrable wall of silence was her only answer. But he rubbed his forehead as he moved back toward her, telling her that at the very least, he had a headache.

"Stephen."

Her soft whisper of his name struck him to the core. The dark void that held him in its grip loosened its hold for the barest of moments then came rolling back over him. He gritted his teeth to keep the blackness from spilling out on to her. What could he say to get her to leave before he said or did something they'd both regret?

Every few months, a dark gaping hole appeared in his psyche and lasted for several days. Of late, the spells had become more frequent and more difficult to fight off. When they struck, he couldn't sleep, had no appetite, and as Winston put it, raged like a wounded bear, striking out at anyone within reach. No wonder all the servants hid.

He'd yet to determine what triggered the bouts. They had to be another side effect of the electromagnetic blast, for he'd never had the problem before. The spells descended on him in the early hours of the morning and were impossible to shake off. It was like drowning in a pit of despair. His head pounded so hard he felt blinded by it. The only thing he could do was close himself off until the demons departed.

His deepest fear was that these spells were the first sign he was losing his mind and soon he'd be left with nothing but cold, pain-filled darkness. The fear of existing in the endless black void with only a headache to keep him company was more than he could stand.

"Go. Please," he bit out with his back turned towards her, holding his head, hoping it wouldn't explode.

"Let me help you." Her soft voice pierced through his darkness, beckoning him like the flickering flame of a candle.

Then hopelessness crashed through him again. "You can't. No one can."

"I would try."

The pounding in his skull dragged at him. He sat back down and held his head in his hands, eyes closed. "Nothing helps," he gritted out. "Not drink. Not sleep. Nothing."

He felt her presence directly before him, her sweet lavender fragrance enveloping him. Her fingers tentatively ruffled his hair, sending warmth trickling deep inside him.

He opened his eyes to find her kneeling before him. Those blue eyes seemed to reach out, grabbing hold of something within him. Again, he felt the flutter of her hands in his hair, then along the tight cords of his neck. He knew he should push her away, but couldn't find the strength. Instead, he closed his eyes and enjoyed her touch and the brief respite it gave him.

Her breath caressed his cheek and was soon replaced by the softness of her lips. "Let me help you."

The warmth inside him grew from her whispered plea. Her fingers ran along his eyebrows, soothing his aching head. With a slow, fluid movement, she eased him back into his chair. "Will you let me try?"

He found he couldn't deny her. Her presence alone seemed to lift some of the black cloak weighting him down. He wanted to tell her she held his very sanity in her grasp, but instead he gave the barest of nods.

She rose and moved behind him, her movements revealed by the rustling of her gown. Again he felt her fingers along his brows and nearly moaned in relief from the reprieve of his pounding head, even if it was only temporary.

"I have an idea to aid you." Her words were soft, spoken in a soothing tone. "You'll have to keep an open mind."

He couldn't concentrate long enough to guess her intention.

"Focus on the sound of my voice. On the feel of my hands. Breathe slowly and deeply. Relax." She paused between each instruction, giving his mind and body time to obey. "Clear the thoughts from your mind until all you see is gray. Never-ending soft gray."

The rhythmic cadence to her voice made it easy to follow her directions.

"Relax each muscle in your body, starting at the top of your head, moving down to your shoulders, to your chest."

Oddly, his muscles twitched as though completing her instructions of their own accord. He let them, doing his best to keep only gray in his mind as she continued.

"Now imagine floating before you is a crystal orb. It carries a soft, golden light."

He could see it perfectly. It was beautiful. He wanted to reach out to touch it, but the sound of

Abigail's voice telling him to relax kept his hands at his sides. The orb turned slowly, moving gently as though bobbing on the current of a river. Its golden light reached out to him like soft rays of sunshine, warming him. He could hear the sound of Abigail's voice but couldn't quite capture her words.

As he focused on the orb, he caught a glimpse of something in the smooth reflection of its surface. He concentrated harder, but the image faded. With effort, he relaxed again and the image grew stronger until at last he saw a beautiful woman inside the orb. He knew she represented warmth, everything good, and all hope in his world. She smiled and reached for him, enveloping him in a comforting blanket and all was right with the world.

Her name was Abigail.

Abigail was scared to death. What on earth had she been thinking? Hypnotism was nothing for amateurs to meddle in. The fact that she'd read a book on the topic hardly made her an expert.

"And now you'll awaken when I say your name."

She hadn't even finished the book yet. She had no idea how to bring Stephen out of this meditative state other than what she'd once seen at a performance in Covent Garden.

But she'd had to try to help him. She couldn't walk away when he was in so much pain. It surprised her that he'd relaxed enough for hypnotism to work. He had such a strong mind that it seemed an unlikely outcome.

Now she knelt before him, looking at his relaxed countenance as he leaned back in the chair. His dark hair fell across his forehead. That delicious stubble graced his jaw. Those long lashes lay still. He appeared to be sleeping. But she couldn't leave him this way. She'd read that much in the book. The doctor advised against using hypnotism as a method of inducing sleep as it wasn't safe to leave people in a hypnotic state for long periods of time.

"Stephen." She spoke his name with firm conviction, hoping it would be enough to bring him back.

Her patient gave no response. Panic whirled inside her. She waited a moment, thinking perhaps it took longer than she'd expected.

Still nothing.

She lifted her hand and cupped his cheek when his eyelashes fluttered.

"Stephen." Relief made her light-headed as his green eyes opened. She drew a long, slow breath to ease her pounding heart. "How do you feel?"

His brow creased. "What the hell was that?"

She blanched, realizing her efforts had been for naught. Her feeling of relief was quickly replaced with dismay. She'd hoped to help him and had only made matters worse. When would she learn to let things be?

"I'm terribly sorry. I—"

"Abigail."

She looked back to see an odd expression cross his features.

He lifted his finger and ran it along her cheek, his expression puzzled. "Did you hypnotize me?"

"I believe it's described as more of a meditative state." The way he regarded her with such intensity unnerved her. She still couldn't tell if he was angry or something else. "How is your headache?"

He blinked several times. "Gone."

Relief made her slightly giddy. "And the...other?" She wasn't even sure what to call the dark mood that had smothered him.

He seemed to take an internal assessment before answering. "I believe it's gone as well."

She studied his face to see if he told the truth. Though exhaustion showed in the shadows beneath his eyes, the tension in his face had eased.

His hand covered hers where it rested boldly on his thigh. Her cheeks flooded with embarrassment as she realized how intimately she was touching him, that she knelt between his legs.

Oh, dear heavens!

"I'm sure you're very tired. I should be going now and let you rest." She couldn't bring herself to meet his gaze, but as she tried to pull her hand out from under his, he wrapped his long, warm fingers around hers.

"Not so fast."

Her stomach danced. Her gaze caught on the open neck of his shirt where his skin was visible. Desire speared through her as she imagined kissing the hollow of his throat where his pulse beat. Something about that vulnerable spot drew her.

"Abigail."

Her gaze jerked up to his, certain he'd guessed her wayward thoughts.

"How did you learn to do that?"

Embarrassed, she decided there was nothing to be done except tell the truth. When he realized what a fraud she was, she had no doubt he'd be angry with her and rightfully so. "I found a book on the subject at Mr. Larson's bookstore. The author suggested if you focus both mentally and visually, you can enter a meditative state. He advised that it can be used for pain and other ailments."

Stephen stared at her.

"Truly. In fact, the author, a Scottish physician, used it on himself to treat his rheumatism pain." Abigail knew she was babbling, but she couldn't stop. "I'd thought to suggest it to my solicitor who suffers from a similar ailment, but then here you were..."

When Stephen remained quiet, she tugged her fingers out of his and rose. She reminded herself that he'd already yelled at her. Surely she'd already suffered the worst he could deliver. She shook out her gown to remove the wrinkles— anything to keep busy as she tried to think of something else to say.

Stephen stood as well. Before she could step back, he took both her hands in his, and kissed the back of each in turn. "You are an amazing woman."

"Oh. Well. Thank you." She was breathless with surprise at his gesture and pleased he wasn't angry after all.

He drew her closer. "No. I would like to thank *you*." He put his finger under her chin and touched his lips to hers. "Your talents never cease to surprise me."

"I'd be happy to lend you the book if you'd like." She lifted her mouth to his, hoping for another kiss.

His gaze held hers for a long moment, their seriousness giving her pause. "I don't think you fully understand what you did."

"Oh?"

"You saved me." His words hardly had time to register before he took her mouth with his.

The intensity of his kiss caused her heart to stutter. Never had she been kissed like this, as though he branded her as his own. A tide of desire swept through her and she clung to the moment. The feel of his lips on hers, the taste of brandy on his tongue, the rough stubble along his jaw, all merged to overwhelm her. His arms held her so tightly, she was certain he'd never let her go.

"Thank you," he whispered. His hands moved to grip her upper arms then pushed her gently back.

She stumbled, barely able to stand after the onslaught of his kiss. Her body felt cold, bereft of his warmth. His action thoroughly confused her.

He gave her a stiff smile, his jaw clenched. "I truly appreciate your assistance." He turned her toward the library door. "You've given me a gift that I did not deserve, and I—" He shook his head as he escorted her into the hall.

That was it? One moment he said she'd saved him and now he was showing her out? That's all his kiss had been—gratitude?

Before she could form a coherent word, she stood outside on the front step disoriented and very much alone.

Thomas hopped down from the carriage. "Ready, miss?"

"I suppose so." She glanced back at the door, still unable to fathom what had happened.

So...very...odd.

Stephen leaned against the door and closed his eyes. He'd told her the truth. The pounding in his head was gone. The dark despair had passed. In its place was an ache that demanded satisfaction.

That he'd found the strength to put her out the door was astounding. In truth, he'd wanted nothing more than to carry her to his bed and remove her clothing layer by layer so he could thoroughly enjoy her.

He'd savor every inch of her luminescent skin, then press his lips to her softness, find every nook and cranny that made her moan.

He'd make her his again.

Yet after what she'd just done for him—lifted him from one of his worst bouts ever, he couldn't repay her by giving in to his own desires.

No, he'd done the right thing.

They couldn't possibly indulge in an affair. Nor could he offer her marriage. How could he ever be a decent husband when he risked his life on a regular basis, when he suffered from the terrible headaches and the despair that so often accompanied them?

The best option for her was to find a man who'd care for her and marry her and give her the family she didn't yet realize she wanted.

The thought of her with a husband and babe made him ill. He feared the situation was worse than he'd thought.

Abigail was winding her way into his heart.

"My lord?" Winston's voice came from the end of the entryway. "Are you still...indisposed?"

Stephen opened his eyes to glare at him. He had half a mind to send him packing for allowing Abigail into the library. Lucky for Winston that it had ended well. "Yes, but for a different reason entirely."

"Excuse me?"

"Never mind. I don't understand it either." He heaved a sigh of frustration and made his way up the stairs, adjusting his trousers and reciting Latin phrases along the way.

The next morning, Abigail made her way to Mr. Nesbitt's office in Old Square with Thomas. They both watched for Simmons, Thomas nearly as nervous as she.

The tension of the situation was wearing on her, but she had no idea what more she could do. Until Simmons was caught, she had to make the best of it. Staying locked inside was not an option.

She had a life to live, including business to conduct. Somehow, hiding away seemed like letting Simmons win.

Perhaps she should try some self-hypnosis of her own to relieve her stress. She still couldn't believe it had worked on Stephen. Unfortunately, she'd forgotten to tell him of Simmons' appearance at the park so had settled instead on sending him a message this morning. While a cowardly way to inform him, it was as much as she could manage after the events of yesterday. Her uncertainty of how to handle their changing relationship added to her worry. She didn't want to become overly dependent on him.

As she reached for the door of her solicitor's office, it flew open. She jumped back, startled, nearly losing her balance.

"Miss Bradford!" Mr. Nesbitt exclaimed. "I'm terribly sorry." He reached out to take her arm, his hand shaking.

"Whatever is the matter?" Abigail had never seen the calm, collected man so overwrought.

"My office was broken into."

Abigail's thoughts immediately jumped to Simmons. The coincidence was too great. It had to have been him. "Have you sent for the police?"

"Yes, yes. I was just looking outside to see if they'd arrived." His shoulders sagged, and he gestured inside. "Whoever it was left a terrible mess but, please, do come in."

Abigail entered with Thomas directly behind her.

Though the foyer appeared undisturbed, the door to Mr. Nesbitt's office stood ajar, the wood near the jam in splinters. Abigail looked into the room and realized what had the solicitor so upset. Papers were strewn everywhere. Shelves had been broken. The desk drawers sat askew, some removed completely. The thief's search had been destructive, leaving a mess in his wake.

"I can't imagine who did this or what they were looking for. I keep nothing of true value here." Mr. Nesbitt shook his head. "I don't know yet if anything is missing. I didn't want to go through things until the police have a look."

Guilt sat heavy on Abigail's shoulders. Though she knew this was not her fault, she still felt as though she were to blame. Yet another person in her life had been affected by Simmons. "I can't help but wonder if this has something to do with me."

Mr. Nesbitt's eyes went wide. "Whatever do you mean?"

"We have not yet stopped Vincent Simmons. His actions grow rasher each day. I wouldn't be surprised if this was his doing."

"Why would he search my office?"

"I don't know. Looking for information on my family perhaps? It seems too great of a coincidence that you and I both had a break-in of late." She bit her lip, deciding against telling him of the rock for which Simmons searched.

He took off his glasses and polished them on his handkerchief with shaking hands. "I can assure you there was little here that pertained to your investments. In fact, I had taken your file home with me last night to prepare for our meeting this morning."

Abigail took some comfort in that. "The less he can find out about us, the better." She eyed the muddle. "It will take hours to put all your files back together. I'm terribly sorry about this."

He looked up in surprise. "Miss Bradford, it isn't your fault. You haven't done anything."

"And therein lies my worry." She'd been so caught up in her personal relationship with Stephen, so intent on avoiding the awkwardness that was sure to come next time she saw him, that she hadn't told him of Simmons showing up in the park. And now this had happened.

"What was that?" he asked.

"Nothing."

"I'm afraid we'll have to reschedule our meeting. I did complete the documents needed for the investment in the bookstore." He reached for a pile he'd set on a nearby table and handed them to her. "Those are the only papers of which I know the whereabouts. I hope the police hurry. The chaos is driving me mad."

"I'm sure they'll arrive soon. I'll return the papers at our next meeting." She turned to leave.

"Miss Bradford, do be careful. You must take all possible precautions in case Vincent Simmons truly is behind this." Mr. Nesbitt held her gaze. "He's dangerous."

"Yes, indeed he is." Of that she had no doubt. She needed to speak with Stephen about the latest development. If Simmons was growing more aggressive, then they needed to do so as well. Whether Stephen agreed with her or not remained to be seen.

CHAPTER NINETEEN

"My lord?"

Stephen looked up from the newspaper he read at his desk in the library. The sparkle in his butler's eyes was rather alarming. "Yes?"

"Miss Bradford is here to see you."

He set down the paper, his heart picking up its pace.

His butler's fondness for Abigail had grown even more since her performance the previous day. Winston's admiration for her was one more dent in the shield Stephen had built to keep her at a distance. He'd hoped to delay another meeting with her as long as possible. At least until he'd regained some control. Until he could trust himself to be in the same room with her and not make love to her.

But apparently a day could not pass without her visiting him. How could he maintain his defenses? "See her in."

Before he could rise, she burst into the room.

"You do realize your daily visits will cause people to talk," he said as he stood.

Those blue eyes stared at him nonplussed. She obviously had other things on her mind. "We have much more important matters to attend to than gossip, my lord. I fear Simmons has struck again." The tremor in her voice alarmed him.

"What's happened?"

She sat down in the chair before his desk, much to his relief. He had high hopes of keeping the large piece of furniture between them. Yet he realized the desk was no guard against his growing feelings for her.

The tilt of her head, the dent in her chin, the way she bit her lower lip, all appealed to him in a way he'd never felt before. Even her determination charmed him. He pushed aside his thoughts as she explained the incident at Hyde Park the previous day as well as the visit to her solicitor's.

"There's no proof Simmons was behind the break-in," Stephen felt obligated to point out.

"Please. I don't believe in coincidences."

"You and Weston."

"Pardon me?"

"Never mind. I'm relieved to hear your sisters were unharmed."

She put a gloved hand to her mouth as though to hold back her emotions. "Yes. But the sight of him anywhere near them..."

"I understand." It tore at his heart to see her upset. He ran his fingers through his hair, frustration mounting at the situation. "What of Mr. Nesbitt's office. Was anything missing?"

"He's still checking and has promised to let me know as quickly as possible." She took a deep breath. "You must see that the time has come to take action. This can't continue."

"We have been taking action. With a little more time, we'll be able to resolve the entire situation." Dread coursed through him as he saw her golden aura dim.

"Are you reading my aura?" she asked.

He blinked, realizing he'd given himself away. "I was simply admiring your hair."

Her eyes narrowed. "I don't believe you."

He shrugged. At least he'd succeeded in distracting her, if only momentarily.

"As I was saying," she continued as she glared at him, "More aggressive action is needed. Simmons is running rampant. I cannot allow him to hurt the people for whom I care."

Stephen leaned forward, resting his elbows on the desk, hoping he could instill some caution and reason in her. "Abigail, I realize you're frustrated by what you see as a lack of progress, but I'd remind you of how much we've learned already. A slow and steady path—"

Abigail bolted to her feet. "Slow and steady has gotten us nothing!" Her chest rose and fell with her upset. "We *must* do something more else Simmons will be knocking on my door, knife in hand, to take what he wants by force."

Stephen couldn't deny what she said. He wanted nothing more than to remove the threat to her and her family. Yet his instinct told him they needed more information—who Simmons worked with, what they intended. But how to keep Abigail and her family safe *and* stop the wheels Simmons had set in motion?

Knowing he might regret the question, he asked, "Do you have something in mind?"

She drew a deep breath. "We lure him to a place and time of our choosing."

"How?"

Another dark surge flared in her aura, making his insides twist. "By using me. We'll get a message to him that I'll give him the stone he seeks in exchange for his promise to leave us alone."

"His promise?" He let doubt shade his tone.

She nodded but her confidence faltered.

"You'd accept the *promise* of the man who killed your father?" Though he didn't want to hurt her, he had to make her see the truth in order to keep her safe. "You'd trust *him* to keep his word?"

Her chin lifted. "If the only reason he bothers my family and friends is because of the bloody rock, then yes. I suggest we give it to him."

"And if he doesn't keep his word?"

"I don't believe it will come to that." Her back was ramrod straight, her shoulders stiff.

He could see he wouldn't reach her this way. A new tactic was needed. He leaned back in his chair. "What do you think he wants with the rock?"

"I've no idea, nor do I care."

"Surely you're curious."

She blinked several times. "In truth, I haven't thought about it overmuch."

"A murderer," Stephen said, noting her flinch at the term, "works for someone who bribes officials at Newgate to allow him to switch places with another criminal. He then serves ten years in prison, and upon his release, one of the first things he does is seek out a rock he claims to be in your possession."

With a huff, she sat back in her chair. "All I want is for him to go away. For my stepmother and sisters never to be confronted by him. If giving him the rock will protect them, so be it."

"But why does he want that particular one?" He stepped around the desk despite his good intentions to keep away. How could he when he only wanted to gather her in his arms and reassure her?

"I assume because it's valuable. Perhaps it contains some rare ore or something. I don't really care why."

Stephen leaned down, putting his hands on the arms of her chair, his ire rising at her obstinacy. "What if he somehow uses it to hurt others?"

Her gaze lifted to his, not backing down. "How? How can a rock hurt anyone?"

"If it's used as part of something else."

"Such as what?" The disbelief in her tone made him realize how outlandish the whole scenario sounded.

He stepped back, berating himself for not being more forthright with her, for not sharing his suspicions about the scientist involved in electromagnetism. But he feared that if he told her everything, this determined, impulsive woman would seek her own solution to the problem. That would place her in even more danger. The best he could do was offer the tip of the iceberg. "I think the rock Simmons wants is a rare lunar meteorite said to possess qualities useful in science."

Abigail scoffed. "I have a difficult time believing Simmons is interested in science." She held up her hand as Stephen opened his mouth to protest. "And, yes, I do remember the prison warder telling us Simmons bragged that he had ties to a scientist."

"I'm not saying Simmons is the one who's involved in science. But it appears the person he's working for is," Stephen argued.

The scowl on her face spoke volumes and nearly made him smile.

"Weston is helping me track down the true name of the person who leased the warehouse Simmons was at. We hope to unearth additional information in the coming days."

"That may be too late." She rose and moved to stand before him. "What if we give him the rock and then follow him? We could see where he takes it."

Stephen shook his head. The thought of her anywhere near Simmons again made his stomach turn. "That carries far too much risk. Simmons has already proven his ability to disappear on the streets. Abigail, we have plans in place to lure out

Simmons, but we need more time to ensure he doesn't slip through the trap we set."

"I still think—"

A knock sounded at the door and Winston appeared. "Lord Weston is waiting outside in his carriage. He says it's urgent that you join him."

"Of course. I'll be right there." Stephen's excitement rose. "With luck, this will lead us to the true mastermind of the plan."

"I want to come with you."

Stephen took hold of Abigail's arms. "No. It's too dangerous. I want you somewhere safe. Return home and I'll send word if anything arises."

"But—"

"Have patience, Abigail. We're nearly there." Without a second thought, he pressed his lips to hers for a quick goodbye. The sweetness of her mouth ignited a flame before he could pull away. With a groan, he plundered for a brief moment, stunned at the passion that arose when he touched her.

He drew back, wanting nothing more than to stay. Yet the desperate desire he had for her was exactly why he had to go. "I'll let you know if we find anything."

A dark surge showed in her aura, giving him pause. "You'll go home?" he asked.

"Of course," she said. But she didn't meet his gaze.

"Abigail, I promise to advise you of what we find as soon as I can." Guilt shot through him, for he knew he couldn't tell her everything. He reminded himself it was for her own safety.

She nodded.

Somehow, her agreement didn't reassure him in the least.

"He's not going to like this, miss." Thomas

shook his head as Abigail explained what she wanted.

"With luck, he won't know. We're only going to follow them long enough to find out where they're going." She stepped into the carriage and took a seat. "Hurry. We don't want to lose them."

"He'll have my head," Thomas muttered as he secured the carriage door.

"In whose employ are you?" For heaven's sake, how had Stephen become such a big part of their lives that her servant worried what he'd think?

"Yours, miss," came his muffled response.

Thomas's lack of enthusiasm for their task did not help her nerves. In truth, he was right. Stephen would be furious if he found out. She hesitated, wondering if she was doing the right thing. Yet she couldn't shake the feeling that Stephen wasn't telling her the full truth of the matter. How could she determine how best to protect her family if she didn't have all the facts?

She only wanted to see where they were going. That should be enough to tell her the type of information they'd discovered. She and Thomas would follow at a safe distance. There shouldn't be any harm in that.

The carriage jerked forward, leaving her to wonder if Thomas had done so on purpose.

If Stephen had been more forthcoming, perhaps she'd be content to wait for word from him, but that hadn't been the case. A more secretive man she'd never met.

She touched her gloved hand to her lips, remembering the way his kiss had sent her head spinning. Maybe she could blame her impetuous behavior on temporary insanity. She shook her head. If she were honest with herself, she'd admit that her feelings were more than temporary. Much more.

So many things about Stephen appealed to her.

The way he smiled with his eyes before amusement curved the corner of his mouth. The way he gave her his complete attention when they spoke as though what she said was truly important to him. His many acts of kindness for the children who crossed his path. He was a complicated man full of secrets and layers which both fascinated and maddened her.

She closed her eyes and admitted the truth—she'd become far too dependent on him. That needed to come to an end. Though she could no longer envision her life without him, he seemed intent on keeping a wall between them.

A glance out the curtained window of the carriage told her they were once again moving toward the East End. The hard look of the streets gave her pause. The risks of this neighborhood were nothing with which to be trifled. Their carriage, while understated, would still draw unwanted attention.

Torn, she tried to weigh the danger against the benefits as the carriage slowed and drew to a halt, taking the choice out of her hands.

Rows of soot-blackened brick buildings stood on both sides of the street. Some boasted curtains while others lacked even that small touch of home. Laundry stretched across lines outside the upper stories of the buildings. The street was nearly deserted except for an old woman who walked by at a slow gait, her back bent with age. Two young men hurried past the carriage, laughing as they went and giving them sidelong glances.

Was this Stephen's destination? If so, who lived here? She looked for Stephen's tall form but could see little from her window.

Thomas jumped down from his seat and came to the window. "Lord Weston's carriage dropped them off near here before continuing on. I don't know which building they went in. Somewhere on the right I think."

"I wonder who lives here."

"I'm not sure, but we can't stay. Trouble will come looking for us if we do." He glanced about nervously as he spoke.

A man leaned against a nearby building, watching them from beneath the brim of his hat, hands stuffed in his pockets. As Abigail watched, he pushed himself upright and started their way.

"Oh, dear." She'd taken a gamble out of desperation to protect her family, and now they'd have to pay the price.

Thomas sighed and moved to block the carriage door. Abigail eased back and narrowed the opening of the curtain.

"What's the likes of you doin' round here?" The stranger asked Thomas.

"Waiting for someone."

"And who would that be? An earl?" He gestured toward their elegant carriage and then laughed at his jest.

"Never you mind. We'll be gone soon enough," Thomas advised the man.

"Perhaps I can help ye find who yer lookin' for." The man rocked back and forth on his heels. "For a price of course."

"Sure. A man's got to earn a living, doesn't he?" Thomas's accent had changed to one more suited to the streets.

"Are ye waitin' for a gentleman?" asked the stranger.

"Maybe even two." Thomas flipped him a coin.

"They're in that buildin' over there." He pointed to a lodging house two doors down.

"Who lives there?" Thomas held another coin between his fingers.

"Sorry, mate. No one I know. Can't help ye with that." He pocketed the coin Thomas had given him and strolled away, whistling between his teeth as he returned to his post.

Thomas edged closer to the carriage window but his gaze scanned the street. "Now what, miss?"

"Let us go before our presence draws more attention."

A large thump sounded on the roof of the carriage, causing it to rock. Abigail's heart pounded in fear. "What on earth?"

"How can we help ye?" A deep, gruff voice asked from above.

"You can start by getting off the carriage," Thomas answered angrily.

"Me and me mates fancy a ride," the voice answered. "How about ye give us one?"

Several rough looking men gathered around the carriage. Abigail's heart pounded. What had she been thinking? If Thomas was hurt because of her foolish actions, she wouldn't forgive herself.

She kept as quiet as possible, not wanting the men to know she was inside. Somehow she was sure that wouldn't help the situation.

"Come on. Give us a ride," one of the other men chimed in.

"No. Can't be missing my duties. The lord will have my head if he comes out to find me gone."

"Well then, how 'bout we leave ye here and take the carriage?"

The men laughed.

Abigail tensed further, realizing just how many had gathered around.

"Ye helped Willy over there. Throw a few coins our way."

"That was a legitimate transaction. He offered me information and I paid him for it. What do you blokes have to offer?" Thomas asked.

The carriage rocked again. Abigail braced herself to keep from being thrown to the floor.

Panic shot through her. She couldn't think of any way for her and Thomas to escape.

"Tell us what yer lookin' for." The deep voice came from above.

"I'm waitin' on my master. He's in that building over there."

From the narrow part in the curtain, Abigail could see he pointed to the opposite side of the street. Well done, Thomas, she thought. The last thing Stephen and Weston needed was to exit the building to find a group of thugs awaiting them.

"Enough with this. Hand over yer money."

"I don't have much."

In her narrow field of vision, Abigail saw the man Thomas had paid earlier slink into the very building in which he'd said Stephen and Weston were. How naïve of her to think he'd told them the truth. Stephen and Weston probably weren't anywhere near here.

She and Thomas were in serious trouble and she was to blame. She shouldn't have risked following Stephen and Lord Weston.

"He's lyin'. Boys, empty his pockets!" They rushed forward.

Thomas threw a solid punch at the first man who grabbed him but another took his place. From her narrow line of vision, Abigail flinched as he plowed his fist into Thomas's stomach. The footman bent over from the blow, groaning in pain.

Abigail searched frantically around the carriage for something to use as a weapon and came up with a parasol. She shoved open the carriage door, catching one of the ruffians in the back and sending him flying.

"Enough! All of you get back." She stepped down, keeping the sharp tip of the parasol pointed out as she moved to defend Thomas.

"What do we have here?" A burly man jumped

down from the top of the carriage.

"A lady by the look of her," added another.

"A pretty lady, ye mean." The man whistled as he elbowed one of his cohorts in the ribs.

Six in total surrounded the carriage. Abigail kept one arm on Thomas and her back to the carriage. Fear made her limbs tremble, but she refused to leave Thomas to fend for himself.

Thomas straightened and looked at her in disbelief. "Please get back in the carriage, miss."

"I'm not leaving you out here by yourself," she whispered.

The footman shook his head and reached for the handle of the door. "Please do. I beg your pardon, but you're not helping matters."

"Don't be ridiculous." She turned to look each man in the eye. "Now then, I'm going to ask you politely to please depart. Go on about your business and leave us alone."

The leader held the lapels of his jacket. "Not until ye give us yer valuables."

"In exchange for what?" Abigail asked. The longer she could prolong conversation, the better. She needed time to think of a way out of this.

"In exchange for us lettin' ye live," a man proclaimed.

She hid her fear, determined to keep some fragile hold over the situation. "You'll have to do better than that."

"Ain't ye a bold one," the leader said as he licked his lips. "I like 'em like that."

He stepped forward, and Abigail shoved the umbrella tip into his chest with all her might. "Back. Away."

The man yelped in pain, rubbing his chest as his face turned red with anger. "Enough of this. Get 'em!"

Thomas immediately lunged for the leader, landing blows on the others blocking his path.

Abigail swung and poked her parasol, determined to inflict as much damage as possible. A hand gripped her wrist. She stomped on the offender's foot. Someone grabbed the parasol and, though she struggled, he wrenched it from her grasp, twisting her arm painfully in the process.

Thomas fought like a mad man, but their opponents were too many. Both she and Thomas were soon held fast, the leader of the group chortling in glee.

"I believe I mentioned you shouldn't get out of the carriage, miss," Thomas muttered, his eye swelling and his lip bleeding.

Abigail said nothing, swallowing down her panic. How could she have possibly sat in the carriage while Thomas was beaten? She had to stay calm and try to remove them from this situation, but how?

CHAPTER TWENTY

Stephen shook his head with frustration. He'd held high hopes that finding Simmons' new lodging would provide them with a lead. "This seems to be another dead end."

Weston nodded. "You're right. There's nothing here."

The narrow room was stark and filthy and could hardly be called lodging. The thin walls were covered with mold and didn't hold back the noise of the neighbors let alone the weather. The only furnishings were an iron bedstead with a dirty mattress and a table with one broken chair. A tattered jacket and cap hung on a peg by the door. The place was dismal. No wonder Simmons spent little time here.

"Unless you count the rats," Stephen added as he took note of one scuttling out of sight.

Weston gave a mock shudder. "I don't."

"Nor do I." He lifted the mattress on one end, then the other, to see if anything was hidden there. A filthy wad of cloth was tucked at one end of the bed frame.

"What is that?" Weston asked as he drew near.

"Most likely nothing," Stephen said as he felt something hard in the center and unrolled the bundle.

"A rock?"

"A very unusual rock," he added, holding up the dark red discovery. "Simmons is quite the collector."

"Do you recognize this type?" Weston took it from Stephen to examine it.

"No."

"This gives us another puzzle to solve."

"Why would Simmons have a rock hidden under his mattress? Not to mention that he continues to ask Miss Bradford for hers." Stephen's frustration mounted. They seemed to discover one unrelated clue after another. "What is Simmons involved in?"

"Something that entails an empty warehouse with circles on the floor and rocks. That's not much information with which to make any connections," Weston said.

"Our clues are growing but not our solutions. We'll take it with us."

He moved toward the door, but stopped to examine the jacket that hung there. A quick search revealed nothing in the pockets. He knocked off the cap as he replaced the jacket. "Rather small cap."

"More like a boy's size, wouldn't you say?"

Stephen examined it closer. "First the jacks in the warehouse and now this cap. You don't think the missing boys and Simmons are related, do you?"

"I'm starting to wonder," Weston said.

"Let us be done with this place." Stephen replaced the cap and led the way out the door only to stop abruptly at the sight of a man lurking in the hall.

"Excuse me." He wrung his hands as he approached.

"Yes," Stephen said, dread filling him for no reason. He could tell the man meant no harm by his aura.

"Ah..." The man licked his lips nervously. "There's a carriage outside."

"Yes. Go on." Had something happened to Weston's carriage?

"A lady and her servant are out there. I think they might be waitin' for ye. They're in trouble. Serious trouble."

Weston came up behind Stephen. "What's this?"

"My worst nightmare," Stephen replied. He tore through the hall and down the stairs as fast as humanly possible, fear stealing his breath. He burst out of the building to see the man had not exaggerated the situation.

"Good Lord. What is Miss Bradford doing here?" Weston asked breathlessly from behind him.

Stephen didn't bother to answer as he watched the lady in question thrust and parry her parasol before it was jerked out of her hand. His heart leapt to his throat as one of the men grabbed her. Rage filled his vision.

"Release them," he demanded as he approached the group surrounding Abigail and her footman.

Abigail's face was pale and pinched with fear. The sleeve of her gown was torn. Thomas looked angry, his face bruised and swollen.

"Release them at once," he repeated as he strode forward, taking comfort in the knowledge that Weston had his back.

The man with the parasol in his hand spun to face him, his aura black as night. "Mind your own business. This doesn't concern you."

"Oh, but it does," Stephen disagreed. Two of the larger men moved to block his path. Without hesitating, Stephen struck one with his elbow then spun to kick the other in the stomach.

"Watch out!" Abigail's shout had him turning

in time to see his first opponent draw a knife.

Without pause, he struck the knife out of the ruffian's hand with the heel of his hand and followed with a low sweeping kick to knock the man off his feet. He looked behind him to see Weston overcoming one of the other men.

Those holding Abigail and Thomas glanced at each other then released their captives abruptly. One ran off. The other moved behind the man with the parasol, whether to lend support or hide, Stephen wasn't sure.

Abigail stepped forward to wrest the parasol out of man's hand. "I'll take that."

"Here now. No need to get rough. We were just havin' ourselves a bit of fun." The man eased back, his palms outstretched before him. "No harm done."

"No harm?" Abigail was obviously outraged by the man's words despite the tremble in her voice. "Look at my footman! And you broke my parasol." Her hands shook as she held up the drooping canopy to prove her claim.

"Sorry." He kept a wary eye on Stephen and Weston then hurried away with the remaining men.

Weston raised a brow in inquiry, but Stephen shook his head. He had no desire to chase them down and leave Abigail and Thomas alone.

Within moments, Stephen, Weston and Abigail were safely ensconced in her carriage. Thomas insisted on driving despite his injuries. Weston's carriage followed behind, his coachman disappointed to have missed all the action.

The silence was thick with tension. Stephen knew he needed to calm down before he spoke to Abigail. No doubt she'd have some logical explanation for her outrageous behavior. The way she continued to put herself at risk made him crazed. What if they hadn't been there to save her? He pressed his hand to his chest at the growing ache there.

"So," Weston said, looking briefly at Stephen before turning his attention to Abigail, "fancy meeting you in this neighborhood."

Abigail tightened her lips, and for a long moment, Stephen held hope that she'd remain silent.

If she knew what was good for her.

She heaved a sigh and he closed his eyes, knowing his hope was about to be dashed.

"I had Thomas follow you because it seemed unlikely that Stephen would share the results of your investigation with me."

Stephen opened his eyes to glare at her. "When I have something of interest to tell you, I will share it."

"Your definition of what's interesting seems to differ from mine."

"Given that you are here," Weston offered, "we'll share what we learned."

Abigail's expression turned to a mix of hope and curiosity. She leaned forward. "Yes?"

"Nothing," Stephen said.

"What?"

"He speaks the truth. That was supposed to be Simmons' new lodging house, but nothing of interest was there," Weston said, "unless you count the rats." He pulled the curtain aside to look out.

"Seven," Stephen added, just to be difficult.

"Excuse me?" Abigail stared at him as though he'd grown two heads.

"Seven rats in the room," Weston clarified.

"That's it? That's all you found?" She sounded appalled.

Stephen guessed that it was the lack of findings rather than the mention of rats that caused her reaction.

"I realize you think I don't tell you of our discoveries because I wish to keep them to myself." Stephen couldn't help his sarcasm. He was so angry with her. He swore he'd never recover from seeing her surrounded by those men, from the thought of what they might've done to her.

"I fear Ashbury has a point." Weston turned to study Abigail. "Many leads turn out to be of little consequence. Hence no report."

She scoffed. "Then I'd like that information as well. That's all I'm asking. Communication does not seem to be a strong suit for either of you."

Weston smiled. "Did you hear that, Ashbury? It seems we are not good communicators."

"Nor is the other person inside this carriage."

Abigail's mouth dropped open in outrage. "How can you say that?"

"Let's take an example, shall we? Perhaps the situation you were just in!" He couldn't help but raise his voice.

She sat back at his shout, her lips pursed.

He drew a slow breath, trying to rein in his temper. "I'm certain I asked you to return home."

"No. You *ordered* me to go home."

Out of the corner of his eye, Stephen saw Weston smother a smile.

"And you agreed to my request," he continued, pretending she hadn't corrected him.

Her belligerent expression made him picture her as a young, stubborn girl. "I changed my mind."

"Which you did not *communicate* with me." He enunciated the word with care.

"There wasn't time."

Weston held up his hand. "I can see we're at an impasse, so let me just add this. You're both right."

Stephen closed his eyes again, hoping it would

give him patience. But when he opened them, the urge to hit something remained.

"Miss Bradford," Weston began, "surely you can see that it is not wise, nor healthy, for you to place yourself in danger. Not only are you at risk, but you put us at risk as well, not to mention the investigation itself. I'm sure that within hours, Simmons will hear all about the ruckus outside his lodging."

Abigail's expression fell at Weston's lecture. "I didn't think of that. Nor have I forgotten what those ruffians did to Thomas."

"True. Your footman bore the brunt of the injuries today." He turned to Stephen. "Ashbury, I'm sure you can concede Miss Bradford does indeed have a valid point."

Stephen gave Weston a bland look.

"You're not a very good communicator. Never have been."

"But you are?" Stephen asked, incredulous that Weston would find fault with him.

"*I* am not under discussion at the moment."

Stephen snorted. Why had he thought he wanted Weston back in his life?

"At any rate, I think it's important to Miss Bradford that you see the error of your ways."

Abigail gave Stephen a challenging look. Did she think he wouldn't admit to it?

"I would consider being more forthcoming if Miss Bradford would better consider her personal safety as well as those of others," Stephen relented. Anything to have Weston shut up.

"Excellent. I believe we're making progress. Miss Bradford? Are you willing to change your behavior as Ashbury requests?"

She opened her mouth to disagree, Stephen was sure, but then promptly closed it as she thought better of whatever argument she'd been about to deliver. "I never meant to put anyone in danger. Certainly not Thomas nor either of you."

Stephen waited. She hadn't answered the question. Weston waited as well. Their combined silence seemed to get the better of her.

"Yes, yes. I will avoid any rash action in the future." She folded her hands in her lap demurely.

Weston didn't seem satisfied. "Perhaps we should define the term 'rash action'."

"Oh, for heaven's sake." The scowl on her face spoke of her frustration.

Stephen remained silent, for he wholly agreed with Weston. Her definition and his did not seem to agree on this term either.

They regarded her until she let out a huff. "I will not take action with which either of you might find fault." She pondered her words for a long moment. "As regards this investigation or Simmons."

Stephen was certain her qualification held a loophole of some sort, and she would use it at the first opportunity.

"Very good." Weston smiled with satisfaction. "I believe we've resolved the chance of any future encounters such as the one we just survived."

The carriage pulled to a stop in front of Abigail's home.

Weston smiled at both of them. "My work here is done, so I'll leave you to attend some business of my own. I assume you'll keep me apprised of any further developments?" His mouth curved in a small smile as he watched Stephen. "Since you've recently improved your communication skills."

Stephen didn't bother to answer.

"Good day, Miss Bradford." Weston alighted from the carriage, leaving Stephen alone with Abigail once again.

"Well then..." After a brief glance under her lashes at him, Abigail reached for the carriage door. "I'll take my leave as well—"

Stephen grabbed her wrist. "Not so quickly. You and I have far more to discuss."

CHAPTER TWENTY-ONE

Abigail froze at Stephen's words, her heart pounding a staccato rhythm. "I have no wish to be berated further." She only wanted to see to Thomas's injuries and then retire to her bed and pull the covers over her head. Anything to put this day behind her.

"Believe me, your point has been made," she added, trying dismiss the feeling of unease that crept over her.

"I don't think it has."

"How so? Are you hoping for an apology?" Those green eyes were impossible to read. "Very well." Truth be told, she did owe one to both him and Thomas. Her actions had caused more harm than good. "I'm terribly sorry I put you and everyone else in harm's way."

He leaned forward, anger emanating from him in waves, causing her to catch her breath. "Do you have any idea what could've happened if Weston and I hadn't come along?"

Guilt flooded her as she thought of Thomas's battered face, of the fear that had enveloped her as those men held them. "I'm grateful you were there. I can't thank you enough for saving us."

"Abigail."

When he said her name in that tone, it made her shiver. "I said I'm sorry." She knew she should let the matter subside, but she couldn't. "I only intended to follow you long enough to see where you were going. You are far too good at keeping secrets. I feared this would be one more you didn't intend to share. I'd wager you found more than rats in Simmons' lodgings." She waited for him to deny her claim, hoping he would.

He glanced away for a moment, and she had her answer.

Shocked, she could only stare at him in disbelief as tears filled her eyes.

"It's true then," she said, her heart sinking. "I trust you with my very life, but you don't trust me enough to share what you've learned." She bit her lip so she wouldn't say the next words out loud.

I love you but you don't love me.

How could he when he didn't even trust her?

"Listen—"

She held up her hand, hardly able to see for her tears. Her heart ached, making it difficult to draw a breath. "You've kept so many things from me. About you. About the things you've discovered." Even as she spoke, she knew how right she was. She could see it in his eyes.

"I need you to—"

She shook her head, anxious to escape before she lost the brittle hold she had on her emotions. "I don't want to hear another half-truth."

"If you'd but listen for a moment." He took her hand but she wrenched it free, unable to bear his touch.

"No." Her breath came out in a shudder, but she forced herself to continue. "I hereby release you from our agreement. I will protect my family myself as I've always done. Your assistance is no longer needed." She shoved open the carriage door and stepped down.

"Abigail!"

Her name on his lips only made her hurt more.

Tears blurred her vision as she looked at him one last time. "A footman will see you home. Goodbye, my lord."

She quickly shut the carriage door behind her, wishing she could so easily shut out the pain in her heart. She told the footman who'd come out to meet the carriage to take Thomas's place and drive Stephen home.

Numb, she turned her back on the departing vehicle. She hooked her arm through Thomas's and moved toward the steps. "Thomas," she said, her voice trembling, "I am so terribly sorry for putting you in danger." She stopped on the landing and looked at his swollen eye. "I promise you that—"

"Miss, it's me who should apologize," Thomas interrupted. "I should've kept you safe and I didn't."

Ponsford opened the front door, glancing between her and Thomas. "Miss! What's happened?"

"Can you please see to Thomas's injuries?" She patted the footman's shoulder, her guilt making it difficult to look at his swollen features.

The butler's expression was full of concern. "Are you hurt, miss?"

"I'm fine. Please see to Thomas. He can fill you in on the events of the afternoon." She dashed up the stairs toward her room before Ponsford could argue further.

Irene stepped into the hall as Abigail reached her bedroom door. "Abigail?"

Despite the concern in her voice, Abigail shook her head and held up her hand, hoping Irene understood. The last thing she wanted to do at this moment was talk. She shut her door and leaned against it.

Not since her father died had she hurt this much. Her entire body ached with an intensity that had nothing to do with the men whom she'd fought. With slow, careful movements, she moved to her bed and curled into a tight ball, trying to hold together the shattered pieces of herself even as tears poured down her face. Stephen's lack of trust tore at her. She thought he'd cared for her, that he would've done anything to protect her.

That perhaps he'd come to love her.

She'd finally found someone who could thaw the frigid core inside her. The part of herself that she'd locked away after her father's death so she'd never have to experience this level of pain again. Stephen had bypassed her defenses and stolen her heart. To learn that she meant nothing to him was more than she could bear.

She buried her face in her pillow and wept, wondering if she'd ever be whole again.

Stephen watched outside as the light of dawn revealed tendrils of fog slithering along the street. The wisps rose slowly to engulf the entire area, smothering everything until it appeared as though the world ended at his front steps.

Appropriate, Stephen thought as he rubbed his aching forehead. Fitting weather for the darkness inside him that had reared its head yet again. He closed the curtain in his library to keep out what little light the day held and turned to pace the room as he'd done for hours.

His demons had returned in the middle of the night. This time, his will to beat them back had fled.

He simply didn't care. What was the point?

Tired to his bones, he dropped into the chair behind his desk. All his efforts to help others had proved futile. He hadn't been able to save anyone—not the missing boys, not Abigail or her family. He'd given it his best and come up empty-handed.

What game had he been trying to play? He was no hero. Why did he even try? Despair filled him as he heard Abigail's words yet again. *I release you from our agreement.*

He knew she'd released him from far more than that. His relationship with her had been built on lies. One had to tell lies in order to keep secrets.

She'd obviously realized he was a fraud, playing a different game than the one she'd asked him to. How could he not try to find out who was behind Simmons? The man wasn't capable of anything more than a simple burglary.

He reached for the glass of brandy at his elbow but thought better of it and shoved it back. He'd been drinking for hours and felt no different. It hadn't numbed his pain. With his head in his hands and his elbows on the desk, he closed his eyes.

Winston and the other servants had left him to his misery last night. He knew he'd acted like a mad man, but he couldn't seem to help himself when this darkness descended.

He had to get a hold of himself. To find the determination to wade through the despair again. Yet the pain was so much worse this time and no longer confined to his head. His chest felt as though it had a gaping hole that would never be filled. He knew it was from losing Abigail. He ached at the thought of never seeing her again, of never holding her in his arms. He'd disappointed her and he didn't see how he could make it right.

Then it dawned on him.

The anguish he felt was far more than loneliness or guilt. Abigail had captured his heart. He loved her with every fiber of his being.

He thought he'd been guarding his feelings so carefully but she'd filled him with reasons to live, to trust, to love.

He'd thrown all that away, so intent on doing what he thought best that he hadn't taken enough care with her. He'd kept his secrets for so long, he'd forgotten how to share with someone...how to trust someone. He hadn't told her about the rock they'd found under Simmons' bed, hadn't told her about the boys who'd vanished from the workhouse, nor what he knew of the lunar meteorite.

He didn't deserve her. He'd known that to begin with and now he had proof.

Bloody hell. What was he to do?

With a heavy sigh, he stretched out his legs before him and rubbed the back of his neck, trying to find relief from the pain that gripped him so tightly.

The missing boys still needed him, even if Abigail didn't. That meant he had to pull himself together. The memory of Abigail's fingers on his temples, of her soft voice speaking to him made him miss her all the more. Perhaps he could try the technique she'd used to help him.

He leaned back in his chair and closed his eyes. As he drew slow, deep breaths, he tried to remember what she'd said to him. He pictured the gray space, trying to relax each of his limbs.

So tired, he thought and focused on the heavy feeling, allowing himself to sink into the chair. He lost track of time as he continued to drift through the endless gray, her quiet voice guiding him along, offering him comfort.

"What are you doing?" Light filled the room as the drapes were jerked open.

Stephen bit back the oath he'd been prepared to deliver at whichever servant had been brave enough to interrupt him only to find Weston staring at him as though he was a newly discovered oddity.

"Is there some reason for this...pose you're in?"

Stephen looked down and realized he was sitting with his arms stretched out and palms up, his legs sprawled before him. Embarrassed, he sat up in his chair, wondering how long he'd been sitting there. "It's a bit early to pay a call, isn't it?"

"Have you become a member of the Society for Psychical Research? I hear their monthly meetings are fascinating."

Stephen ignored Weston's sarcasm as he realized that he felt better. His headache had eased, the blackness had lifted significantly. "I'll be damned."

"Most likely." Weston continued to stare at him. "Care to explain?"

Stephen considered changing the subject but then remembered the damage keeping secrets had already caused. "Do you have headaches?"

"Doesn't everyone?"

"No. I mean since the experiment."

Weston watched him for a long moment. "Sometimes."

"Mine are rather severe. Very hard to function when one comes."

His friend nodded. "I know what you mean."

Stephen rose, deciding that was as much as he could share on that topic for the moment. "What brings you here so early?"

"I've found someone who might be able to help us identify the rock that you found at Simmons'."

Relief flooded Stephen. A breakthrough at last. "What are we waiting for? Let's go."

"Do you want to send a message to Miss Bradford?"

Stephen looked away as sorrow struck him anew. "Miss Bradford has terminated our...agreement."

"Agreement? That seems an odd way to describe your relationship."

"However you'd describe it, it's come to an end. Probably for the best." Why couldn't he get his heart to understand that?

"But we're so close to unraveling Simmons' scheme. Did you tell her about the missing boys? About why we think he wants the meteorite? Surely she understands that you need Simmons to lead you to the next player in this mystery, that there's some sort of connection with it all."

Stephen said nothing. He hadn't told her any of that. He'd thought he was somehow protecting her by keeping his suspicions to himself. Now he realized he'd been an idiot to do so.

"Good God, man. What's with you and your secrets? No wonder she ended it."

"Let's just say I'm not used to sharing information."

Weston sighed. "Nor am I. Perhaps we can both work on that. So what is your plan?"

Stephen considered his options. In truth, there was only one. "I intend to save her anyway. Simmons must be stopped along with the mastermind behind his plan."

"Excellent." Weston slapped him on the back. "Let's see where this path leads."

"What is on your agenda for the rest of the day, my dear?" Irene asked from the settee in the drawing room.

Abigail looked up from her tea, well aware Irene had been studying her, waiting for an explanation for her behavior of the previous day. She knew the dark shadows under her eyes told of her sleepless night, and she couldn't hide her melancholy. She'd managed to avoid her stepmother most of the day, but they always shared tea each afternoon when they were both home. "I'm staying in this evening."

"I thought you were going to the Smithby's ball." She sipped her tea, her brow puckered in concern.

"I'm not feeling up to it. I've sent my regrets."

Irene nodded, clearly waiting for Abigail to say something more.

Abigail set down her tea, deciding it best to tell her the truth. Or at least part of it. "My...ah...association with Lord Ashbury has come to an end."

"I'm terribly sorry to hear that. May I ask why?" The sympathy in her expression caused a lump in Abigail's throat.

She looked away to stare out the window, deciding how to explain it. "We didn't agree on the correct method of removing the threat of Simmons."

"Oh dear. If Lord Ashbury is no longer helping us, then who is?"

"We will have to rely on ourselves."

Irene visibly paled. "Are you certain this is wise? What about the guards he posted? Are they gone as well?"

"I suppose so, although I haven't checked." Abigail drew a shaky breath. "I intend to speak with Simmons and propose some sort of agreement with him. In exchange for the stone he wants, I'll request he leave us alone. That he never bothers us again."

"Abigail! Honestly, what are you thinking? How can you trust the word of a murderer and a thief?" Irene's voice rose as she continued, "His agreement to your trade would mean nothing. Why would you think otherwise?"

"I hope that once he has what he wants, he'll keep his distance. He'll have no reason to threaten us anymore." Abigail was taken aback at having to defend herself. Yet she had to admit the logic that had seemed sound as she'd lain awake in the middle of the night, now sounded ridiculous.

"We still don't know why he wants the stone. That makes it all the more suspicious. I think you should reconsider. What happened with Lord Ashbury? He seemed quite reliable."

Frustrated, Abigail moved to the edge of her chair. "He was never forthcoming with information and I had to constantly ask him to report new developments to me."

"For goodness sake! He's a viscount, not an employee. How can you possibly expect him to act in any other capacity?"

Abigail hesitated. She hadn't considered that.

"Darling," Irene said with a frown, "I think you should reconsider. Having a man in your life means relinquishing control, letting go of the details in some situations, trusting him."

"I did trust him," Abigail protested.

"It doesn't sound like it."

Abigail refused to consider the truth of that. "My agreement with Lord Ashbury was for him to warn off Simmons and instead, he spent his time trying to discover who else is involved."

"That makes perfect sense."

Abigail stood and paced the room, trying to gather her thoughts, to separate her emotions from logic. "I only want Simmons gone. I can't stand it anymore. If anything happens to you or the girls..." She couldn't finish the thought let alone the sentence.

Irene rose to take Abigail's hands in her own. "But don't you see? If we don't get to the bottom of what Simmons is really after, then he could come back. And if he's up to no good, then he might hurt someone else."

With a heavy sigh, Abigail closed her eyes as the truth of her stepmother's words sunk in. "You're right. We need to follow through the whole affair and stop him. But we can't simply wait to see what he does next. Action of some sort is needed."

"Then you'll get back in touch with Lord Ashbury?"

Her eyes flew open at the thought. "No." She couldn't deal with that. She hurt too much already. "There has to be another way. Someone else who could help us."

"Do you have anyone in mind?"

"Perhaps Mr. Nesbitt could be of assistance. He recently had some interaction with the police." Abigail hoped he'd formed some sort of relationship with whoever had come to investigate the break-in at his office. Maybe together they could convince the police of the threat Simmons posed. She already felt better for having a plan even though it was still forming.

"Does Lord Ashbury still have the stone Simmons wants?"

Abigail had almost forgotten that. "Yes. I'll send a message requesting he return it."

Irene tipped her head to the side, studying Abigail. "Does your riff with Lord Ashbury involve something more than this business with Simmons?"

Abigail paused, wondering how much to say. "I do have feelings for him, but I fear he doesn't return them."

"Are you certain? The other day when he was here, I thought—"

"No." So had I, Abigail thought with an ache. "Nothing of the sort. It's better if I refrain from seeing him for any reason." She couldn't risk hurting herself any further as she feared she wouldn't recover from it.

Irene gave her a warm hug. "I am sorry, darling, for I can see how hurt you are. Perhaps you'll be able to work things out."

Abigail pushed back her tears as she took

comfort in the embrace. Reconciling with Stephen seemed impossible. How could she win his love when she couldn't even gain his trust?

The expert Weston had found was a retired Cambridge professor. At first glance, Professor Embersley appeared well dressed until one looked closer. Apparently his pension hadn't provided for him very well or perhaps he couldn't be bothered with such details.

His jacket was frayed along the cuffs and collar, and bore stains that made Stephen wonder when it had last been cleaned. His balding head was partially concealed by an overly long section of white hair combed from one side to the other. When he bent down, the over comb flapped dangerously, mixing with his long white sideburns and large moustache.

The professor lived alone off High Street in a townhome stuffed to the brim with books, stacks of papers, boxes, and odd artifacts tucked in unusual places. The entryway was no longer an open hall, but merely a path from the front door to other rooms.

The piles were organized in some manner visible only to him. As soon as they'd explained the reason for their visit, Professor Embersley had gone immediately to his library to dig through a selection of books and papers.

"A bit of a maze, isn't it?" Weston muttered to Stephen as they followed the Professor to where he searched through one of the piles stacked on the floor.

"What did you say?" The professor looked up from the book he held to peer at them over the top of his smudged spectacles.

"Nothing, sir. We were admiring your...collection," Stephen offered. He elbowed

Weston in the side to reprimand him. There was nothing wrong with the old man's hearing.

"Humph."

Apparently Stephen's attempt at flattery had fallen short.

The professor straightened with a book in his hand, his spectacles sliding to the end of his nose. "Where did you say you found the rock?"

Weston raised a brow at Stephen.

"An acquaintance of ours provided it to us." Stephen didn't see any point in going through the story of where he'd found it.

"Humph." The professor flipped through the book for several long moments, muttering as he scanned the pages. "Ah. Just as I thought."

He looked up and studied the pair of them, his hazel eyes still sharp. "Attended Cambridge, didn't you?"

"Yes, sir," Stephen answered.

"I believe I remember you. There were three of you, were there not? Students of Professor Grisby's."

Stephen shared a look with Weston. "Yes, that's right."

"Terrible accident that took Grisby." Embersley shook his head as his gaze became clouded with memories. "Terrible. I retired soon after that."

"Did you find what you were looking for?" Weston asked.

"Indeed. Right here." He pointed to a place in the book. "Dr. Woolaston discovered rhodite in 1803. I've never before had the pleasure of seeing it for myself."

"Rhodite? What is it used for?" Stephen turned the reddish stone over in his hand.

"May I see it again?" the professor asked.

Stephen handed it to him and watched as he examined it.

"Apparently this particular ore is from Brazil. Dr. Woolaston developed a process somewhat similar to what he used for platinum to obtain it. The resulting powder of sodium chlorohodate is dark red in color." He mumbled as he continued reading the text. "It doesn't seem he found any particular use for it."

Stephen sighed in disappointment. He'd hoped this stone would lead to something.

"Wait. Wait. There's something else." The old man set down the book to pick up another. "Something else," he muttered and hurriedly paged through the large tomb.

Stephen and Weston waited as the professor's lips moved with his finger on the text.

"Here it is: 'This rare ore contains the ability to act as a conductor with electric machines. In fact, it carries the potential to enhance the reciprocal relationship between electricity and magnetism'."

"Interesting," Stephen said. "Professor, did you read an article last week in the newspaper about a scientist who claimed some success conducting experiments with electromagnetism?"

Embersley set down the book with a thump. "Nonsense. What sort of scientist publishes anything until their findings are complete? The man's either a braggart or a sham. Most likely both."

Stephen nodded. "We figured as much. Thought you might've heard who he is."

"No. Don't care to until he comes forward to reveal his name and his results. As a matter of fact, we were discussing it at the Association for the Advancement of Science just the other day."

"Professor, we can't thank you enough for your time," Stephen interrupted before the old man launched into a summary of the meeting.

"Of course. Happy to help. You should know that rhodite is rare and quite valuable. You wouldn't want to leave it lying around. Though not many people would recognize it."

"If you think of anything else of importance, please let us know," Weston said.

"I say, do you know what happened that night to Grisby? All sorts of rumors were flying about regarding his experiments."

How many times had they been asked this question? The only thing they'd been able to answer was a version of the truth.

"It all happened so fast. Difficult to say exactly," Weston said.

Stephen cleared his throat. "Grisby had diverse interests and electromagnetism was one of them." Even after all these years, they still had some loyalty to him. To Stephen's knowledge, none of them had offered specific details as to what Professor Grisby had been doing or what he'd hoped to accomplish.

Embersley removed his spectacles to wipe them with his handkerchief. "We all mourned his loss. Always hard to lose a colleague. Grisby had moments of brilliance."

Weston gave Stephen a wry glance. That was a very apt statement of their former professor.

They bid Professor Embersley farewell and saw themselves out, leaving the professor muttering to himself as he pulled another book from a stack.

"Moments of brilliance." Stephen shook his head as he took a seat in Weston's carriage.

"That was Grisby. How interesting that this stone could serve the same purpose as the meteorite when used with electromagnetism. But I'm not certain where that takes us."

"I'll contact the newspaper and see if they've heard anything further from our elusive scientist." Stephen wished more action could be taken. They drew to a halt before his home, and he stepped out of the carriage. "We're awaiting several other inquires but haven't heard anything yet. Do you have any suggestions?"

"My lord!"

Stephen turned to see Markus, one of his associates, approaching.

"Do you have news?" he asked the boy.

Markus's grin gave him his answer. "Only one of the boys in the workhouse was willing to talk. He says a man named Mikey offered payment to a few of the lads for a job. None of those have returned. Of late, a tall, thin man in a bowler hat was looking for boys interested in assisting with a scientific experiment."

"Excellent work, Markus." Stephen clasped him on the shoulder. "I don't suppose they knew his name?"

The boy shook his head.

"That description could fit Simmons," Weston suggested.

"I'd have to agree."

"I have someone working to see if any other buildings are leased to Leonard Smith. With luck we'll soon find where they moved to."

Stephen turned back to Markus. "Spread word that we have something the man in the bowler hat wants. Have some of the other lads help you. I want the kids in the workhouse and people down by the docks to get the message. With luck, Simmons will hear it as well."

Markus nodded enthusiastically. "You can count on me, my lord."

Stephen paid him and the boy departed.

"We're getting closer. I can feel it," he said to Weston. "Hopefully, Simmons will make contact. Then we'll persuade him to cooperate and tell us who's behind this."

"I just hope it's not too late for the missing boys," Weston added.

"Or for Abigail. Surely she won't do anything

rash." He looked at Weston, hoping for reassurance him.

But Weston remained silent, much to Stephen's dismay.

CHAPTER TWENTY-TWO

"Are you certain you want to go in with me?" Abigail asked as she and Irene arrived in Old Square to visit Mr. Nesbitt two days later.

Irene patted her hand. "Don't be so nervous, darling. I know you're used to dealing with these things alone, but I'm here to lend you my full support."

While truly grateful for her stepmother's assistance, Abigail worried about how to protect her if Simmons appeared. Her father's pistol was tucked in her pocket, just in case, thanks to Ponsford's suggestion that she bring it. The single shot it offered gave her some comfort but didn't erase the nagging unease that lingered.

She couldn't help but wonder if Irene's true purpose in accompanying her was to try to cheer her up. Ending her relationship with Stephen had dealt a blow from which she wasn't certain she'd recover. The weight of grief was heavy in her heart and colored everything she did. Not to mention the doubt. Had she done the right thing by severing their relationship?

With a mental shake, she berated herself to keep her thoughts on the task at hand. Their lives might depend on it.

Thomas opened the carriage door, his gaze casting about the area. "No sign of him, miss."

"Thank you, Thomas." She alighted with his assistance then waited for Irene while keeping watch as well. An odd feeling crept over her and she glanced around nervously, certain she was being observed. But she didn't see anyone suspicious.

She hoped Mr. Nesbitt could provide assistance in helping to convince the police to take action with Simmons. Time was of the essence as she was sure he'd strike before long. She drew a shaky breath, missing Stephen more than ever.

She and Irene were soon settled before Mr. Nesbitt's desk, but Abigail could tell from his expression that he didn't have good news.

"I'm terribly sorry, but the inspector I spoke with was of little assistance."

"Did you tell him you thought Simmons was the man who'd broken in?" Abigail asked.

"Indeed I did. But I have no evidence to tie him to the crime. They did a cursory search of the room at the lodging house of which you gave me the address but found nothing."

Irene sighed. She reached over to squeeze Abigail's hand. "Something will turn up. These criminal sorts always make a mistake that lead the police to them."

Abigail nodded. Irene's knowledge came from a recent mystery she'd read which didn't reassure Abigail in the least. By the time Simmons slipped up, it might be too late.

Mr. Nesbitt removed his spectacles to rub the bridge of his nose. "The inspector did say they'd post an extra man in that area to keep an eye on things. They have a description of Simmons. Perhaps that will lead to something."

"Thank you very much for your efforts." Disappointment flooded her. She couldn't think of any other way to stop Simmons.

They discussed a few items of business,

including a list of the improvements the bookstore owner wanted to complete, but her mind was not on what he was saying.

As quickly as possible, Abigail rose to take her leave. "Please keep us apprised of any new developments."

"Of course." Mr. Nesbitt saw them to the door and bid them goodbye.

"Now what shall we do?" Irene asked after they settled into the carriage again.

Abigail shook her head, wondering what could be done. Despite Irene's presence, she felt alone. In truth, she'd come to rely on Stephen in many ways, from his friendship to the passion she felt in his arms. And now, when she and her family were in danger, there was no one she'd rather have at her side. The reasons she'd decided to toss away all that were suddenly less clear.

After a long moment with only the creaking of the carriage to accompany her thoughts, she met Irene's gaze. "You were right."

Irene blinked. "Was I?"

"You told me that I hadn't trusted Stephen. And I didn't. How can I possibly berate him for not trusting me when I didn't trust him?" She scolded herself for not realizing it sooner. She'd let her emotions affect her thinking.

An understanding smile graced Irene's lips. "So glad I could be helpful, darling."

"I need to apologize to him."

Irene's smile grew wider. "That sounds like a marvelous plan."

Once they arrived home, Abigail stepped out of the carriage, not bothering to wait for Thomas's assistance. After she saw Irene safely inside, she would pay Stephen a visit.

As she mounted the steps, the front door flew open to reveal a frantic Ponsford. "Thank heavens you've returned!"

"What's wrong?" she asked as Irene stepped up beside her.

"Are the twins with you?" he asked.

"No." Irene paled visibly. "They're in their room."

Abigail's stomach dropped. She reached out to grip Irene's hand.

"I can't find them, my lady." Ponsford shook his head. "I've searched the whole house. They're gone."

"Were you able to follow her?" Stephen asked Markus when the boy arrived in Stephen's library that afternoon to give his report.

"Aye, my lord. She went to a solicitor's office on Old Square with her mum. I kept watch outside near the window. I couldn't hear much but it sounded like they're tryin' to get the police to help 'em."

At fifteen, Markus had served as one of Stephen's associates for over two years and had proven himself time and again. Stephen had requested the boy to keep a close watch over Abigail today.

"Shall I return to the lady's house again?" Markus asked.

While relieved to hear Abigail had done nothing more than contact Mr. Nesbitt, Stephen still worried she might do something to put herself in danger. A sense of impending doom was growing inside him. Simmons had been quiet too long. Stephen was sure he'd strike soon.

But Abigail involving the solicitor or even the police wouldn't be enough. Stephen knew *he* should be at her side, guarding her and her family. He ran his fingers through his hair, frustrated with himself.

With her.

With the situation.

In his heart, he knew she belonged to him. He hated not being with her when she needed him the most. The question was what to do about it.

Markus stared at him as he began to pace the room, but Stephen ignored the question in the boy's eyes as he considered his options.

He stopped abruptly. How many times had he told himself never to ignore his instincts? Every fiber of his being told him they belonged together. Abigail was right. He wasn't good at sharing, but he could change.

He picked up the small electromagnetic device that sat on his desk. The damned experiment had already cost him so much. Why should it cost him the chance at love as well? He might not make the best husband with his many flaws, but he could promise her love and fidelity. That was more than many men offered their wives.

At the very least, he had to tell her how he felt. If he had to beg her to marry him, he would. He'd make her see that she needed him and try not to think about how much more he needed her.

"So...should I go back to her house?" Markus repeated warily.

"Yes, yes. Go down to the kitchen first and have something to eat. You've had a long day already." Stephen set the device aside and squeezed the boy's shoulder. "I need you to be extra vigilant over the next day or two. Something will be happening soon."

Markus nodded. "We'll be on guard. Don't you worry. I'll report again soon. Ta-ra, my lord." With a quick bow, the boy departed.

Stephen had just returned to his desk when Winston appeared at the door. "My lord? Hubert is gone."

"Gone where?"

The butler shook his head. "No one seems to

know. One of the maids said he was worried about the missing boys. I can only guess that he decided to search for them himself."

"Damn!" Stephen pounded his fist on the desk. "Send word to Weston that I need him. Quickly."

Panic struck Abigail like a blow at Ponsford's words. "Are you certain?"

"No one has seen them since earlier this afternoon." The old man had aged ten years in the short time since Abigail and Irene had left for their meeting.

"Oh, dear God," Irene murmured. Abigail took her arm as she wilted at the news. "Where could they be?"

"We'll find them." Abigail tried to quell the panic rising inside her. "They can't have gone far."

Irene's hand shook as she held out her hand. "Tell me that awful man didn't take them."

Her heart broke at Irene's tearful plea. That was exactly what she feared. She prayed she was wrong. She gripped her stepmother's hand and squeezed tight. "We'll find them," she repeated, trying to find the confidence to make it so.

Irene's face crumpled as she began to cry.

Abigail could hardly breathe let alone think of what to do. With Ponsford' help, she guided Irene inside to the drawing room and sank down on the settee beside her. There had to be a logical explanation for Sophia and Olivia's absence. "Calm yourself, Mother. Let us think of where they might've gone."

"All I can think is that somehow Simmons has them." She buried her face in her hands.

Abigail closed her eyes, hoping it wasn't true. After all her efforts, surely she hadn't failed to protect her family. She'd tried so hard to do everything possible to keep them safe, but now it seemed all for naught. She had to stay calm and think.

Now more than ever, she longed for Stephen's assistance. He'd know what to do.

"When did you last see them?" Abigail asked Ponsford, forcing herself to reflect composure despite the panic roiling inside her.

"I checked on them shortly after you left. They were in their room reading." Ponsford shook his head. "Then I went down to the kitchen to see to some things. I went up again about fifteen minutes ago and the room was empty. The other servants and I have been searching, but—"

The butler's distress added to Abigail's. Irene put her fingers to her lips, her breath coming out in shaky gasps.

"Were they speaking of anything earlier today?" Abigail asked, trying to remember herself. "Perhaps something they wanted to do that we didn't allow them to?"

"They spoke of a gathering at one of their friend's homes, but I told them no." Irene looked at her with hope. "Do you think they could've gone anyway?"

"We'll send a footman to inquire." But Abigail didn't believe that was the answer. The girls would never disobey something like that. "Is there anyone else they might've gone to visit?"

Irene shook her head. "No. But I haven't been paying that close of attention with everything else going on."

Abigail felt the heavy weight of guilt. "Nor have I." In truth she should've, especially since the girls didn't realize the possible danger they were in. That alone made them easy targets.

But now was not the time for self-recrimination. She had to determine some course of action, some way to find them.

A knock sounded at the door.

Dread seized Abigail. She rose from the settee as Ponsford hurried out of the drawing room to answer the door.

He returned a moment later, his eyes glittering with anger. "It's Vincent Simmons. He wants to speak to you regarding the girls."

Abigail closed her eyes for a brief moment, unable to believe this had come to pass. Then she looked at Irene, wanting to reassure her somehow. Yet how could she when things were so terribly wrong?

She moved toward the door.

"Wait." Irene put her hand to her heart. "You must be careful. Do as he says and he'll give the girls back to us."

Abigail nodded, hoping it was true. She looked at Ponsford. "Send him in."

"He requests that you to come to the door."

With a deep breath, Abigail gathered her courage. She had to find some way to convince Simmons to return the girls.

The front door was shut. She felt Ponsford's presence behind her but motioned for him to remain out of sight. She didn't want anything to go wrong nor give Simmons a reason to do something reckless.

Please let him return the girls, she prayed. Then she opened the door. At first she saw nothing in the evening twilight.

"Shut the door behind ye." A gruff voice came from the left and she stepped toward it, leaving a narrow crack in the door with hope that Ponsford could hear their conversation.

Simmons stepped out of the shadows, his brown eyes darting between her, the door, and the street behind him.

"What do you want?" she asked.

"A better question is who are ye missing?" he asked with a smirk.

Her heart stopped beating. She was sure of it. "Are my sisters safe?"

"For the moment. For them to stay that way, I need the rock." He rolled onto the balls of his feet as though very pleased with himself.

"If you'd tell me which rock—"

"Come now. Ye know exactly what I'm looking for."

"No, I don't. I've been telling you that all along." Irritation colored her tone.

"The one yer father got in India."

Her father had traveled to India twice, the second time just months before his death. How had Simmons known that? What was so special about that particular stone? The only thing she remembered about her father's trip was how happy she'd been when he'd come home.

Simmons scoffed with impatience. "Dark gray with light stripes, 'bout so big." He formed his hands in the size of a potato.

The description matched the one Stephen had taken. Fear made her heart pound even faster. Now what was she to do? How could she possibly explain to Simmons that she no longer had the stone he wanted? He'd think she was inventing excuses.

Nothing could be done but tell him the truth and hope he believed her.

She cleared her throat nervously. "I believe I know which one you mean. Unfortunately, I don't have it at the moment."

Simmons stiffened in surprise, his face tightening into a menacing scowl. "What do ye mean?"

"An...associate of mine has it."

"Who?"

Abigail hesitated for only a moment before answering, "Lord Ashbury."

Simmons cursed and spun away, muttering

before at last turning back to her. "What did ye give it to him fer?"

"He asked to examine it in detail."

He kicked the walkway in frustration.

Now was her chance to convince him to give up on this craziness. "Please return the girls to us. We can forget this ever happened."

"No! I need the bloody rock!"

"What is so special about it that it's worth returning to prison? Are you willing to hang for a rock?"

Simmons glowered as he reached into his jacket and withdrew his knife, then reached for her arm. "Yer coming with me."

"Where?" Abigail's breath caught as she backed away.

"To get the friggin' rock! I'm not letting ye out of my sight until ye get it." He tugged on her arm.

She balked, torn with indecision. The idea of going anywhere with the man who'd killed her father caused bile to rise in her throat.

But he had her sisters.

While she had no choice, that didn't mean she had to do it on his terms. "I'll ask Lord Ashbury to give it back. Bring the girls and I'll trade you the rock for their safe return."

"No! I don't trust ye and I certainly don't trust him. He's to know nothing 'bout this."

"I won't tell him why I want it back. I—"

Simmons stepped closer, his knife inches from her face. "He's already caused more problems than I can count. If ye think I trust either of ye any further than I could spit, ye've got another thing comin'. Tell anyone and it means the end for them girls. Now let's go!"

"All right. Let me get my things and order the carriage." She'd have to go with him. Anything to save Sophia and Olivia.

"We'll take a hackney." He pulled her forward.

"Wait! At least let me get my cloak."

Simmons scowled. "Don't go farther than the doorway. Stay where I can see ye."

Abigail nodded and opened the door. Ponsford and her stepmother stood nearby, eyes wide with fright.

"It's too dangerous, Abigail," Irene whispered. "Don't go with him."

"She's right, miss," Ponsford agreed as he wrung his hands. "He can't be trusted."

"I have to get Sophia and Olivia." Abigail spoke softly, hoping Simmons couldn't hear her. "I'll be back as soon as I can."

"Hurry up!" Simmons called from the steps.

Ponsford glared over her shoulder, his lips tightening. "Do be careful, miss. Here's your cloak. You have everything else you need in your pocket, I believe."

He raised a brow, and at last it dawned on her what he meant. She still had her father's pistol in her pocket.

"Shall I alert a constable?" Ponsford murmured.

Abigail shook her head. "No. I don't want to take any risks."

"Come on," Simmons demanded from just outside.

Abigail gave Irene's hand one last squeeze to give them both strength. "I'll be back soon with Olivia and Sophia."

Irene was too distraught to reply, her trembling fingers holding Abigail's a moment longer, her tears wrenching Abigail's heart.

Simmons grabbed Abigail's arm. "Enough already." He jerked her out into the darkness of the night. "Very touchin', but we've got to hurry."

Abigail pushed back her fear, praying she'd truly return soon, and that Sophia and Olivia would be with her.

CHAPTER TWENTY-THREE

"The carriage will be here shortly, my lord," Winston told Stephen as he passed through the hall to the library.

"Thank you. If Weston arrives before I return, please give him an update."

Stephen planned to visit Abigail and tell her everything. If she'd listen. He should've done so weeks ago. From the missing boys to the connection he suspected between them and Simmons—she needed to know all of it. Perhaps she'd learned something from her solicitor that might add to the growing pile of clues.

Somehow, he'd make her believe him despite how ridiculous it all sounded. Together, they could decide how best to proceed. Together, they could overcome whatever plan Simmons had devised.

Together...

His breath caught at the thought. The time he'd spent without her had shown him just how much he needed her. The image of those blue eyes filled with hurt and tears haunted him. He could only hope she'd forgive him and allow him another chance to show her—

"My lord!"

He turned as Markus burst into the room with Winston directly behind him.

"He's got her!" the boy cried out. "Simmons has

Miss Bradford and they're on their way here. To get some rock!"

"What?" His stomach dropped to his knees. *Christ, he was too late.*

"He told her he has her sisters. Miss Sophia and Miss Olivia," Markus said between pants. He bent over, his hands on his knees as he tried to catch his breath.

A knock sounded at the front door.

Winston looked in askance at Stephen who nodded. "Let us see what he has to say."

Stephen drew closer to the hall, motioning for Markus to remain hidden. But what he really wanted to do was throw open the front door, grab Simmons by the throat and choke the truth out of him.

"Greetings, Miss Bradford," Winston said, his usual smile in place as though nothing was wrong.

"May I speak with Lord Ashbury, please?" Abigail's voice sounded strained even at this distance.

"Good evening, Abigail." Stephen stepped toward the door. "How nice to see you."

"Stephen." The way she said his name would've been enough to make him realize something was terribly wrong. But her muddy blue aura told it all. Fear was visible not only in the dim light around her head, but in every line of her face and body.

"Come inside. Please," he added, willing to beg if necessary.

She shook her head, her gaze shifting to the side, her head held stiffly. "I didn't come to pay a social call."

"Oh?" Subtly, doing his best to make the movement look natural, he stepped into the doorway, glancing around to see if he could spot Simmons nearby.

The shadows of the night combined with the

foggy mist revealed little. He wanted to pull Abigail into his arms and slam the door behind her to keep her safe. But if Simmons had her sisters, that would not be good enough.

"I've come for the rock you borrowed from my father's collection." Her blue eyes caught his, staring intently as though urging him to read her mind.

If only he could.

"Now?" He tried to think of some way to stall, to determine a plan to aid her without alarming Simmons.

"Yes. Right away, if you please." Her lips tightened. "We're—I'm in a terrible hurry."

"Is everything all right?" He needed to remember to act as though he didn't know what was happening.

"Of course. I'm merely in need of that particular stone." Her voice trembled. She looked to her right out of the corner of her eye again.

Simmons was obviously nearby, listening to every word she said. The only way Stephen could think to keep Abigail safe was do as she asked. "Certainly. Won't you come in while I retrieve it?" His hand tightened on the knob as the temptation to drag her out of danger surged.

"No, thank you. Please hurry."

"All right then. It will take me a few moments to fetch it."

She nodded stiffly. "I'll wait here."

"As you wish." He pushed the door closed to keep Simmons from seeing his movements.

He gestured to Winston to follow him into the library where Markus still waited. "Markus, are you up to another task?"

"Of course."

"Go out the kitchen door. Follow Miss Bradford and Simmons."

"Yes, my lord."

"Wait!" He thought for a long moment. Damn. He wanted to follow them himself, but Simmons would be watching for him. "I need you to leave a trail for me to follow. I've got to know where Simmons takes Miss Bradford as quickly as possible."

Markus nodded. "Simmons hired a hackney. Can a few of the servants come with me? We'll leave one along the way at each turn he makes. With luck, that will show you the way. I'll stay with them and come back for you."

"Excellent idea, but be careful. You can't be seen. The safety of several people depends on you."

"Of course, my lord."

"Winston, go with him and explain the situation to the other servants and see who'll volunteer."

The pair hurried away, leaving Stephen alone in the library. He unlocked his desk drawer and stared at the meteorite, weighing his options, painfully aware of every second ticking by. He opened another drawer to reveal his own modest rock collection, including one similar in appearance.

No matter which rock he gave Abigail, he risked the chance of never seeing her again. There was no guarantee the servants would be able to follow them. Many things could go wrong. If they lost them, Stephen had no idea where to search. The warehouse where Simmons had been remained empty. Nor had he returned to his lodgings. At the moment, no other clues existed as to his whereabouts.

Yet if Stephen didn't give Abigail the meteorite, Simmons might realize it, and Abigail would be the one to pay the price.

In truth, neither option was palatable.

Nor could he stand here and ponder the

matter. He hastily withdrew the stone from his collection as well as the meteorite and returned to the front door.

The sight of her standing there scared and shivering nearly broke him. "I'm sorry for the delay." *And for everything else.* "I nearly forgot where I put it." He handed one of the stones to her and prayed it was the right decision. "I believe this is what you wanted."

She froze as she stared at the rock he'd placed in her hand. Those huge eyes looked back up at him, full of doubt and fear.

"Trust me," he whispered.

"But—"

"Please."

She stared at him a moment longer, her fear evident. Then she gave him a single nod. "Thank you," she said in a normal tone.

He looked out at the street behind her, hoping he'd given Markus and the servants enough time to get into position. "You're sure you won't come in?"

"No. I must be on my way." She backed up.

No, his heart cried.

A shaky breath helped to rein in his emotions. He would not do anything to put her in further danger. The fog-shrouded darkness revealed nothing—not his servants, not Simmons. Somehow, he had to reassure her. "Abigail, I've been meaning to call on you. We have much to discuss, you and I."

She opened her mouth to protest and cast a nervous glance to the side again. He held up his hand. "I realize now is not the time. I'll come by to visit very soon." He hoped she understood he meant it literally.

"Goodbye." Abigail turned away, giving one last glance over her shoulder at him before she walked down the steps and disappeared from sight.

Stephen gripped the doorknob, needing to hold on to something—anything—to keep from running after her. Simmons would be watching. Markus and the servants had a better chance of following them than he would. Logically he knew that, but every fiber of his being wanted to run out that door after her and never let her go.

Now he had only to keep his sanity until one of the servants returned. Abigail's rescue was forthcoming but waiting for his plan to fall into place was one of the hardest things he'd ever had to do.

Abigail's breath hitched as she walked away from Stephen into the deepening mist. She could only pray the odd stone he'd given her wouldn't cost the lives of her sisters. When he'd whispered 'trust me', her heart had filled. In that moment, she'd realized that she trusted him completely. It didn't matter if he didn't trust her. She'd hardly given him a reason to.

Time and again, she'd moved forward without considering the consequences, thinking only of her problem while he'd worked toward solving the larger issue.

In truth, she'd ended their association to protect her heart. She hadn't let anyone close except her family since her father's death. The wall she'd built may have kept her from being hurt but also prevented her from taking a chance at love. Luckily, Stephen had found a way to breach her defenses.

What a fool she'd been, thinking she needed to be in control. What she needed was love. Stephen's love. She could only hope in time he'd return her feelings and trust her enough to let her into his life and maybe, someday, into his heart.

For now, she needed to trust in her love for him and know that he had a plan. That he cared enough to help her.

She slid the rock into her pocket, hoping Simmons wouldn't demand to examine it. The idea of not being able to save her sisters terrified her.

"See now? That wasn't so difficult, was it?" Simmons' voice startled her as he emerged from the fog to walk by her side. "Ye even managed to follow my instructions."

"I have the rock. Now take me to the girls." They'd nearly reached the hackney that waited down the street.

"Hand over the stone and I'll send yer dear sisters home to ye."

"Not until I see Sophia and Olivia for myself." She clenched her fists, prepared to fight him if necessary. He might be stronger than she, but he couldn't possibly be as determined.

The driver of the hackney remained huddled beneath his cloak, his hat low on his forehead. She knew not to expect any assistance from him. He'd already ignored their conversation on the drive here.

"Just give me the rock. I'll leave ye here and go free them. They might even arrive home before ye do." Simmons' cajoling tone was anything but reassuring.

"Take me to them. *Now*. When I see they're safe, I'll give you the rock."

"Let me see the bloody thing. How do I even know you have it? Don't force me to use this knife." He pulled the blade from his pocket.

She swallowed hard, her stomach in knots. Left with no choice, she retrieved the rock from her pocket and handed it to him. Would he realize it wasn't the right one?

He held it up to the dim light cast by the

hackney's lantern and her nerves stretched taut.

Without waiting for him to decide if he recognized it, she stepped up into the hackney and sat. She was coming with him whether he approved the rock or not. If necessary, she'd threaten him with her pistol and force him to take her to the girls, but only as a last resort. She knew too well the gun was no guarantee that her plan would go her way.

"If ye would've given this to me the first time I asked, we wouldn't be takin' this ride," Simmons grumbled as he climbed in beside her.

She breathed a shaky sigh of relief.

He glanced around as though to see if they were being followed, then ordered the driver to depart, not yet telling him their destination.

Abigail shivered. The dampness in the air seeped into her body. Or perhaps it was fear that made her tremble. She had to hope that whatever plan Stephen had would be successful for she didn't believe she could do this on her own.

The hackney made its way slowly through the foggy streets. The driver ignored Simmons' calls to hurry. When they finally drew to a halt, Abigail guessed they were somewhere near the docks, though the fog made it difficult to discern. The air smelled briny, and a fog horn sounded in the distance. She studied the unfamiliar buildings, searching for signs of occupation.

"Where are they?" she demanded.

"Pay the driver."

"Excuse me?"

"Ye 'eard me. Pay the bloody driver." Simmons jumped down from his seat. "Then I'll take ye to those sweet sisters of yers."

The way he spoke of them made her skin crawl. She stepped down then dug into her pocket to find the proper coins, grateful she carried some with her. As she reached in, the cold steel of her father's pistol reassured her.

She handed the money to the driver. His hat hid his face almost completely, but what she could see appeared much younger than she'd remembered.

"Thank ye," the driver said as he tipped his hat to her with a wink. "Ta-ra. See you soon."

She stared up at him, wondering at his words. Could he be one of Stephen's associates? Before she could ask, the hackney jolted away at a fast clip, leaving her standing by Simmons. A little flame of hope flickered inside her. She had to believe Stephen would soon know where she was and come to her aid.

"Where are my sisters?" she demanded. Sophia and Olivia must be frightened out of their wits by now.

"In here." Simmons withdrew a key from his pocket and unlocked the door of a large, dark building.

Abigail warily stepped inside the dark interior while Simmons locked the door behind them.

The strike of a match broke the eerie silence. The glow of a lantern emitted a small circle of light, easing back the darkness.

"This way," he directed her as he lifted the lamp and moved toward the rear of the building.

The large open space appeared empty except for three tall objects draped in canvas. As they passed them, the dim light revealed several doors at the back of the warehouse, most of which were shut.

Muted voices could be heard from behind the door where Simmons stopped. Abigail held her breath as she listened closely, desperate for the sound of Olivia and Sophia.

He pulled out another key and unlocked the door. With a gesture for her to go first, he held the lantern with one hand and withdrew his knife with the other. Did he expect her sisters to cause trouble or did he intend to use that on her?

"Get back, all of ye," he said in a loud voice, "else I'll be using my blade to carve out yer hearts!"

Shocked by his threat, Abigail opened the door.

Loud gasps drew her gaze as Sophia and Olivia rushed toward her. "Abigail!"

She gathered both of her sisters in her arms, relief weakening her knees. "Are you all right?"

"Yes, we're fine," Sophia said, her trembling form clinging to Abigail.

"We're so glad you found us," Olivia added, her face buried against Abigail's shoulder.

But they weren't the only ones in the small room. Far from it.

As she held the girls, others moved forward out of the dark corners. Nearly a dozen children filled the small space, all boys except for Sophia and Olivia. They ranged in age from perhaps as young as five to closer to the twins' age. All had the look of street urchins or orphans with their thin faces and ragged clothes.

"What on earth is going on?" Abigail glared at Simmons. "Why are you holding these children?"

The man watched the boys, his knife at the ready. "Stay back and none of ye will be 'urt."

"Release them at once," Abigail demanded.

"They've volunteered to participate in a very important scientific experiment."

"We did not!"

"He's tellin' ye a lie, miss!"

Abigail turned at a familiar voice to find Hubert nearby. "What are you doing here?"

"Long story, miss."

"Let us go!"

"Don't listen to 'im!" Their voices rose, all in disagreement at the claim Simmons had made.

"Here now! You filthy little—"

"Do *not* speak to them like that." Abigail refused to stand by and listen to him berate the poor boys, regardless of the knife he held. "Release them at once!"

"Not a chance," Simmons said. "They're devotin' their lives to science."

"What? Are you out of your mind?" Abigail's outrage knew no bounds.

Simmons laughed, an unpleasant sound. "Yer not the first to ask me that."

Abigail had had enough. "Children, come along. It's time to go." Fear pulsed through her but she kept an arm around each of her sisters and moved toward the door.

Simmons set the lantern outside the room and blocked their path, still wielding his knife. "None of ye are leavin'."

Sophia gasped as Olivia shouted, "You told us you'd free us when our sister arrived."

Her heart sinking, Abigail tightened her grip on the girls and addressed him. "You have the stone. Now let us go. All of us."

She phrased it as a statement, not a question. For the briefest moment, she'd forgotten of what this man was truly capable. He'd killed her father. She needed to remember that. The children's lives and her own depended on it.

"You're not goin' anywhere until my uncle has a look at the stone."

Sophia stood in front of Abigail, blocking Simmons' view of her hands. Without looking down, Abigail reached into her pocket, gripped the pistol, and cocked the hammer, easing Sophia behind her. "You're leading us out of here. Now."

Simmons' eyes narrowed as he caught sight of the gun. "Give that to me. Remember what 'appened last time. You don't want to 'urt someone again."

"You're right. I don't. Lead us out." Her heart

pounded so hard she could barely hold the gun steady. His reminder of how she'd shot Stephen made her hands shake even more.

Sophia whimpered behind her.

"Ye've been nothin' but trouble since day one," Simmons said, his disgust obvious.

"Move. Now." She gestured to the door with the pistol, her finger trembling on the trigger.

Simmons scoffed, but turned to walk out the door.

Abigail drew a breath of relief then gasped when he spun back and dove for the pistol. She gritted her teeth and tightened her finger on the trigger.

Olivia screamed and grabbed for Simmons' arm but bumped Abigail in the process. The pistol went off, the blast deafening in the small room.

"Damn you!" Simmons cursed, holding his shoulder. "You shot me." He yanked the now useless pistol out of her hand before she could stop him and tucked it in his pocket. "You and that bloody gun! Nothin' but trouble. Now you can all rot in here."

He slammed the door, leaving them in the pitch black of the small room. She heard the grate of the key turning the lock and the soft cries of one of the boys.

She pounded on the door. "Let us out of here!" With little hope, she found the handle and twisted. It didn't budge.

The sound of fading footsteps made her heart sink. Now what was she to do?

Stephen paced the front step outside his home, unable to sit inside and wait. One of the servants should've been back by now. Where the hell were they? Something must've gone wrong.

As he ran his fingers through his hair in

frustration, the rattle of an approaching carriage gave him hope. He waited, straining to see through the mist.

But he soon realized it was Weston's. Damn.

The conveyance pulled to a halt and Farley and Weston both alighted.

"I picked up Farley on my way here after I got your message," Weston said, frowning. "Thought we might need assistance. What are you doing out here?"

"Simmons has Abigail."

"Blast it all!"

"You might be overdressed for a rescue attempt." Stephen frowned at Weston's formal evening attire.

"I was on my way to a ball, but your message sounded urgent."

"Do you know where he has her?" Farley asked.

Stephen quickly told them what he knew. Before he'd finished, footsteps pounded toward them out of the fog. Relief filled him as he recognized one of his footmen. "Here are our directions now."

They piled into Weston's carriage and were off, the footman directing them.

Farley scowled. "And here I thought I'd finally see the inside of your residence."

Stephen smiled. "If we manage to save Abigail and her sisters, you're welcome to visit any time."

Soon they picked up another servant who told them where to turn next. Each servant had stopped where the hackney had turned a corner then ran back to where they'd left the previous one, leaving a trail just as Markus had promised.

In a short time, they passed a hackney whose driver hailed them. The man pulled off his hat, and Stephen was surprised to see Markus with a huge grin. One of Stephen's other servants was with him as Markus had picked him up on his way back.

"I don't know how you managed to replace the hackney driver, but I appreciate your cleverness." Stephen shook his head in amazement, grateful for the boy's resourcefulness.

Markus shrugged. "It's amazing what a few coins can buy. Simmons took her to a warehouse near Pearson's Lane, not far from the docks. A big warehouse from what I could see."

Relieved beyond words, Stephen smiled. "Well done. Show us the way."

He patted his pocket for the twentieth time. The meteorite was still there. As a last resort, he intended to offer it in exchange for Abigail and her sisters. Though he still hoped to discover who was behind this whole affair, the safety of Abigail and her family was his first priority. The last half hour of waiting had taken years off his life.

Markus turned around the hackney and they followed, the horses hooves echoing on the quiet streets until at last they halted outside a building near the docks.

"This is interesting." Weston looked around with curiosity. "I received word earlier today of another address leased to Leon Smith and I think this is it."

"With luck, we'll not only be able rescue Abigail and her sisters, but discover the identity of Mr. Smith."

Markus led the way to the entrance of the warehouse.

"The offices are probably in the rear of the building. That would be the most likely place to hold the girls," Weston said.

"You take Farley to investigate the back," Stephen said. "Markus and I will see if we can get in the front door."

Weston looked down at his elegant evening

attire and sighed. "I like this jacket, but clothes can be replaced. Let's go, Farley."

"Keep watch, Markus," Stephen bid the boy. "I'll see if I can open the door." He could only hope they'd arrived in time.

CHAPTER TWENTY-FOUR

"Vincent, what is going on out there?"

"That woman shot me!" Vincent slammed the door of a neighboring room behind him and looked down at his arm. Anything to avoid looking at his uncle's face. The sight of the scars still turned his stomach.

"Miss Bradford? How resourceful of her." Uncle Joseph stepped closer to examine Vincent's arm in the dim light of the lantern. "It appears to be merely a flesh wound. Nothing serious."

"It bloody freakin' 'urts!"

"I'm sure. There are some rags over there if you care to wrap it."

His uncle's lack of sympathy only stirred Vincent's anger more. "She's a pain in the—"

"Vincent, do you have the stone?"

It was all he could do not to throw the damned thing at his uncle. His single-mindedness was enough to make a man want to punch something. Instead, he clenched his jaw and handed him the rock. He moved to the pile of rags, searching for a clean one with which to bind it.

His uncle handled the stone with reverence, hefting it in his hand as though to determine its weight. He limped over to the table against the wall where a collection of coils, circuits, and resonators lay along with a myriad of other items

Vincent could not name.

While Vincent admired his uncle's knowledge, his obsession with electromagnetism made him uneasy. How he could waste so many years tinkering with a bunch metal parts? Nothing had yet come of the devices he'd built, or the promises he'd made Vincent.

Muttering under his breath, Vincent wrapped a long piece of linen around his arm. "Could you help me tie this?"

But his request was lost on his uncle who turned the stone over, peering at it closely. The glow of the lantern on the table lit the good side of his uncle's face.

With a sigh, Vincent managed to tie the binding one-handed with the aid of his teeth. What he wouldn't give to leave this place—the bratty kids, the blasted woman, and his obsessed uncle—and grab a pint at the pub down the street where he knew he could find a sympathetic ear. However, his uncle had forbid him from visiting such places, insisting on secrecy. Vincent had agreed at the time, but he'd had about enough of this. He hadn't survived his time in prison only to answer to Uncle Joseph's every tedious demand.

He wanted freedom but had yet to figure out a way to get it. Not without money—preferably a lot of it. Uncle Joseph was his best chance for wealth.

"This stone is quite interesting."

The proper diction of the words grated on Vincent's nerves. While he'd be forever grateful to his uncle for arranging the switch in prison, his uncle wouldn't have bothered had it not been for the unique set of skills and information Vincent possessed.

Vincent nearly smirked as he thought of his own cleverness. In reality, he'd stolen his uncle's notes and papers ten years ago, hoping to sell them, but events had prevented him from doing so. He was in sole possession of all those years of research. That bargaining chip was what had kept him useful to his uncle and forced him to arrange the switch.

Now he was returning the papers in small doses—enough to keep his uncle happy. Uncle Joseph might be smart when it came to books, but Vincent was much smarter when it came to looking out for himself.

"Unfortunately, this is not the correct stone."

"What?" Rage filled Vincent, numbing the pain.

"Can't you do anything right?" His uncle shook his head. "You're no better than your mother."

Hurt mingled with anger as his uncle's words struck an old wound, but Vincent shoved it aside. "Are you sure?"

Uncle Joseph turned to him with a 'you've disappointed me once again' sigh of which he seemed so fond. "Of course I'm certain. Let us speak with Miss Bradford and obtain the proper stone. It seems I must do everything myself."

Vincent held his tongue, knowing from experience that any protests would only bring another lecture. His uncle donned his cloak and pulled up the hood, carefully arranging it to cover most of his face, then reached for his cane. Not once did he look at Vincent's arm or ask as to his well-being. He merely pointed toward the door with his cane.

With a curse, Vincent approached the door, determined to make Miss Bradford pay for her lie.

Abigail's chest tightened as panic took hold. Several of the boys behind her whimpered and Sophia's breath hitched. The darkness was disorienting and added to her worry.

"I'm so sorry, Abigail," Olivia said. "I didn't mean to bump you. I was only—"

"It's all right. You were trying to help. Perhaps he's wounded worse than he seemed."

"I hope so," Sophia said vehemently. "He's absolutely dreadful. What are we to do now?"

Abigail couldn't think. She had no idea what she could do or say to calm the frightened children. The idea of being locked in this dark room for any length of time was horrifying.

"It's all right," she said automatically. Then she repeated it in a firmer voice, saying it for herself as well as the children. "It's all right. We simply need to devise a plan to escape. Hubert, where are you?"

"Here, miss. Did Lord Ashbury come with you?" The hope in his voice brought a lump to her throat.

"I fear not, but we must hope he'll arrive soon." They couldn't wait though. They needed to escape as quickly as possible. "Are any of you able to pick a lock?" Normally that wasn't a question she'd ask of a child, but these boys had been raised in a different world where cleverness took many forms.

"I'm pretty good at it, but I don't got no tools," claimed one of the boys.

"I've just the thing for you." She removed one of her hat pins. "Come toward my voice so I might hand it to you."

Her eyes had adjusted to the dark and she could now see vague outlines. Not much help, but better than absolute darkness. The boy touched her hand. She carefully gave him the pin, helped him locate the lock and let him start work.

She thought back to what she'd observed when she'd arrived in the room. She'd been so taken aback to see the all the boys, she'd noticed little else. Pallets were scattered on the floor for the boys to sleep on, but those were of no use.

If it was similar to the rest of the building, it had a high window. But there wasn't anything in the room upon which to stand.

"Hubert, come this way if you please." Surely giving the children something to do would provide both hope and a distraction and, with some luck, help them out of this mess.

"What can I do, miss?" he asked from her side.

"Is there a window?"

"Yes, but we can't reach it. Not even if we stack our beds."

"I've an idea. We'll need volunteers and I need your assistance in organizing them. First, someone who's strong."

"That would be me, miss," said a boy to her right.

"Stand near the window. Hubert, help me lift him on my shoulders. He might be able to reach it." She was a good five or six inches taller than Hubert and with the boy on her shoulders, he should reach the window with ease.

"But there aren't any latches on the windows to open them, miss."

"We'll break it. Sophia, hand me your shoe." She knew the girl's shoe had a small heel as she hated being shorter than Olivia.

Sophia quickly removed it and passed it to Abigail.

"Excellent. Girls, find some sort of cloth he can wrap around his hand to protect it from the glass."

Abigail heard the tearing of fabric and could only surmise that one of the girls had torn off a piece of her gown. With Hubert's help, Abigail managed to assist the boy onto her shoulders. She staggered under his weight. He was heavier than she'd expected. His boots dug into her shoulders as the shoe and cloth were handed up to the boy.

"Sam, wrap yer hand and use the heel to smash the window," Hubert urged him.

It took several tries for Sam to succeed, each movement wearing on Abigail, but at last they were rewarded with the sound of breaking glass.

"Good work," Abigail said, lurching as he shifted, balancing him with Hubert's help. "Now break off all the sharp edges with the shoe. Be careful."

Several long minutes passed as the boy completed the task. Abigail grew hot and shaky from her efforts as well as her nerves. She hoped the noise didn't alert Simmons of their impending escape.

"Can ye jump down without hurtin' yerself, Sam?" Hubert asked.

"Ahh..."

His hesitation sank Abigail's heart. It must be too far for him to jump. All this effort for nothing. She staggered, her shoulders aching under the strain.

For the first time, she was glad of the dark, for it hid her despair from the children. What else could they do? She had no other plan. The boy picking the lock still worked at it, but without success.

"There's someone below," Sam whispered from his high perch.

Abigail's stomach clenched with fear. She had a sudden vision of Simmons standing below the window, knife in hand and that horrible smirk upon his face.

"He's dressed all fancy."

"Ask him if his name is Lord Ashbury," Hubert called out.

A muffled bit of talking occurred, then the boy turned back to tell them, "Nay. He's Lord Weston and there's a Mr. Farley here as well."

Relief made Abigail's legs tremble. If they were here, Stephen had to be nearby, too.

"They've come to help us," Abigail called up to the boy. "Can you get out with their assistance?"

"I'll try."

The weight lifted from Abigail's shoulders as the boy hoisted himself up then scrambled out the window. "Hubert, do you want to go next?"

"No, miss. Take Matthew." He took the hand of the boy who'd volunteered earlier. "He's awful scared."

"Matthew, come on then. Hurry. Up you go."

The boy sniffled then crawled onto Abigail's shoulders. Though too short to reach the window by standing on her shoulders, Abigail managed to lift his small form high enough so he could pull himself onto the window ledge.

Already she was weary, her muscles protesting, and there were more children to go. But they had to hurry. Simmons could be back at any moment.

"Who's next?" She hoisted up another boy with Hubert's help and then another.

"Miss, let's get yer sisters out," Hubert suggested.

Olivia pushed Sophia forward with little argument, assisting her onto Abigail's shoulders along with Hubert's help. Sophia trembled so much that Abigail knew how frightened she was.

"Let us help the small boys out before I go," Olivia suggested. "They've been here much longer than I."

Abigail squeezed her sister's hand, proud of her for her courage. The children seemed to jump out of the window with relative ease, and she had to assume Weston and Farley were catching them. A few more minutes and they'd have them all out. She refused to worry that she'd be left by herself at the end.

Olivia at last agreed to go after Abigail told her she'd be needed on the outside to help calm the younger boys. Abigail breathed a sigh of relief knowing her sisters were safe.

"Miss, you go next. I think I can lift you,"

Hubert told her. "I'll help the rest."

"That is very brave of you, but they're going to need you out there, too." She knew the boy wasn't tall enough to lift anyone, not to mention the fact that he was still recovering from his stab wound. It was up to her to finish this.

As she lifted the next boy, the door rattled. Shaking with fright, she thrust the boy up as the door swung open. A light blinded her, and she shaded her eyes to see who'd arrived.

Simmons held a lamp aloft, a shadowy, cloaked figure behind him. Simmons' arm was in a makeshift sling. "Here now! What's goin' on?" He snarled at Abigail. "What did ye do with those kids?"

"You've no right to hold these children—"

Simmons pointed to the broken window above Abigail's head. "Get back here!"

She turned and looked up, horrified to see the little boy's legs still dangling from the window.

Simmons rushed forward, his hand reaching for the boy's foot.

Desperate to make sure the child reached freedom, Abigail shoved Simmons.

With an oath, he flailed, dropping the lamp between them as he fell. It struck the floor and shattered. Fire burst forth, the oil in the lantern erupting into a pool of flames. The sleeping pallets caught fire and the flames burned brighter.

Simmons scrambled back. The remaining boys screamed in fright.

"Run, boys!" Abigail called, pointing to the open door. "Get out!"

But they were too frightened to move, and Simmons was faster. The cloaked form was gone, leaving the path clear for Simmons' escape. He rushed to the doorway. "Ye ain't goin' nowhere!"

He was out the door before Abigail could guide the children past the fire to the opening.

"Wait! No!" she shouted.

Simmons slammed the door shut. Once again, she heard the lock turn.

Abigail rushed to the door to beat on it, yanking on the knob but to no avail. "Simmons! You can't leave us here!"

"Miss?" Hubert huddled with the four remaining boys in the corner as the flames spread.

"Oh, dear God!" Abigail pulled off her cloak and threw it on the flames, but the fire refused to be smothered. She could hardly breathe for the smoke pervading the small space. Its writhing dense mass rolled along the ceiling toward the open window. The flames licked the wooden walls, eager to devour. Time was running out.

"Let's get another of you out." She eased along the wall to the window, the heat of the fire frightening in itself. She gestured for one of the boys to step forward and lifted him up, coughing as the smoke grew thicker.

She choked and coughed, managing to get the boy out before falling to her knees. Hubert and the three other boys crowded around her, crying in fear and coughing from the smoke.

"Stay down," she told them as she gathered them close. "The smoke's worse above us." Her throat tightened with fear. The wooden beam above them now burned. How long would it hold before collapsing? She pulled the boys away from it and prayed help would soon arrive.

Her eyes stung. Her lungs burned. The heat of the fire stole every particle of air from the room. She clung to the boys, unable to believe the night—her life—might end like this.

Regret filled her at the thought of leaving Irene and the girls. And Stephen.

She hadn't yet told him she loved him.

Stephen cursed as he tried for the third time to open the lock on the front door. His normally nimble fingers refused to cooperate. The knowledge that Abigail was trapped in this bloody warehouse made his entire body tremble.

On the journey here, one thing had become abundantly clear. He couldn't live without her. He had to convince her that she felt the same way. First he had to find her.

"Want me to give it a try?" Markus's voice jolted him out of his thoughts.

Stephen gathered himself, seeing the lock in his mind as though it were broad daylight and was at last rewarded with a click.

"Good work, my lord. Perhaps you'd teach me a trick or two."

"You should not be picking locks," Stephen told him as he eased open the door. "Stay behind me. I don't want you hurt."

Markus grumbled but kept back.

Stephen peered into the darkness of the cavernous warehouse but only inky blackness met his gaze. He gestured for Markus to light the lantern they'd brought. They moved quickly through the large building, unable to make out more than several tall objects shrouded in canvas in the center of the room. Now was not the time to investigate the building or its contents. Every fiber of his being told him that he needed to find Abigail.

Markus tugged on Stephen's jacket. "Do ye smell smoke?"

Bloody hell.

He smelled it now. Flickering light shown from underneath a doorway at the far end of the building. Fear coiled deep in the pit of his stomach.

He could *not* lose her.

A form ran toward them and Stephen lunged,

tackling the man to the ground. "Markus, move the lantern over here," Stephen said as he held down his captive.

The soft glow revealed Simmons struggling against him. Yet after all these weeks of pursuing him, Stephen didn't care.

"What have you done with her?" Stephen demanded.

"Fire!" Simmons yelled as he continued to flounder.

"Where is she?" Stephen grabbed him by the lapels of his jacket and shook him with all his might.

Simmons didn't answer, but his gaze flew to the room with the light coming from under the door.

Stephen's rage knew no bounds. He shook him again. "You left her in there? Give me the keys!"

"I don't have no keys."

Stephen drew back his fist.

Simmons threw something across the floor. "Get them yerself."

Stephen struck him, his anger granting him strength. The solid *thunk* of his fist striking bone provided grim satisfaction.

"Ye knocked him out cold!" Markus scrambled for the keys and tossed them to Stephen.

"Drag him outside then guard him well, Markus." He wanted the boy in the safety of the fresh air as far away from the fire as possible.

"But—"

Stephen was already running toward the back of the warehouse. "Go! Now!" he yelled over his shoulder. "Find Weston and Farley to aid you."

He reached the door and tried the knob only to jerk his hand back at the heat. Frantic, he pounded on the door. "Abigail?"

He could hear crying from inside the room, but it didn't sound like Abigail. Studying the ring of keys in the dim light, he tried to determine which one was the most likely. His first guess was wrong, but it might've had more to do with his shaking fingers than his choice. Luckily, the lock turned with his next attempt.

He used the bottom of his jacket to protect his hand as he turned the scorching knob and threw open the door. Thick, black smoke blanketed the room, hiding any occupants.

"Abigail?" He shielded his face with his jacket to ward off the heat.

"Over here," she called out from the opposite side of the room.

Relief filled him at the sound of her voice.

"Lord Ashbury?" The young boy's voice sounded familiar.

"Hubert? Is that you?" Stephen bent down, realizing the smoke was not as thick near the ground.

Abigail huddled together with Hubert and several children across the room. The fire burned brightly between him and them. How was he going to get them out?

The flames leapt all around him as though he'd entered the fires of hell. He drew a breath then dashed across the room, using his jacket to protect his head.

"Are you all right?" he asked Abigail.

She nodded, but the fear in her eyes said differently.

"The boys are too scared. They won't go near the fire," Hubert said.

"Ashbury! Are you in here?" Weston's voice came from the doorway.

"Yes! Call out. The boys can follow your voice."

"Come this way. Hurry along." Weston's calm voice carried across the room.

"Hubert, lead the way," Stephen told the frightened boy. "Crawl as close to the wall as you can. Quickly now. I'll help Miss Bradford."

Weston continued to encourage them. "Steady on, boys. Help has arrived. Outside you go."

Stephen drew Abigail into his arms. "Let's get out of here."

She nodded, still coughing, her face streaked with soot. He threw his jacket over both their heads and drew her close, grateful to have her in his arms.

But his worry was not yet over.

The flames seemed even hotter now. The smoke so thick he didn't dare breathe.

"Hurry, Ashbury," Weston prodded as the boys finally reached him, leaving a clear path.

Coughing, his eyes watering from the smoke, Stephen stayed low, hurrying across the room until they, too, reached Weston.

"This way!" Farley called out as he helped to guide the children toward the entrance. "You're safe now. Come outside."

Abigail grasped him tightly as they followed everyone out of the warehouse. The fresh air worsened Abigail's cough but still she held on to him, which was a good thing as he didn't think he could pry his arms off her if he tried.

Together, they sank to the ground.

He wiped his stinging eyes, desperate to see her, to make certain she was all right.

"The children? The girls?" Her voice was a croak. Tears tracked down her cheeks. Her normally neat hair lay in disarray along her face, and her hat was long gone.

He'd never seen her look more beautiful. He tucked a strand of hair behind her ear then cradled her cheek with his hand, gratitude swelling through him.

"Everyone is safe." He reassured her even as he looked around to be certain he spoke the truth.

Her sisters ran toward them.

"Abigail, are you all right?" Sophia asked as they knelt beside her.

"We were scared you weren't coming out," Olivia added.

Abigail reached out to squeeze their hands. "I'm fine. Just fine now that I know you're safe."

Weston stood nearby, reassuring the boys and checking to make sure everyone was all right. Farley sent Markus to fetch the Fire Brigade.

"I still can't believe you shot that man." Sophia eyed Simmons who still lay prostrate nearby where Markus had dragged him.

Stephen turned to Abigail. "You shot him?"

"I tried to," Abigail said. "But once again, things did not go according to plan."

"It was my fault you didn't kill him." Olivia shook her head, obviously disgusted with herself.

"What happened to his face?" Sophia asked.

"It ran into my fist," Stephen said wryly.

Sophia's eyes narrowed. "I hope you broke his jaw."

"Indeed," Olivia said. "How dare he lock us in that room! Those poor boys were there far longer than us."

Stephen scanned the area, trying to determine how many boys had been held by Simmons.

"Beg your pardon, my lord," Hubert said as he moved to stand before Stephen. "I'm ever so glad you found us."

"I'm glad to see you safe, Hubert. Many helped find you." He smiled at Abigail and her sisters.

"I'm sorry I left the way I did," he told Stephen. "I heard a rumor as to where the boys might be, so I came to see if it was true."

"You should've told me. I would've helped you," Stephen gently admonished the boy.

"You've been so busy. I didn't want to bother you until I knew for certain. But then that one," he pointed to Simmons, "caught me outside the buildin' and dragged me in."

"And these other boys? Do you know them?"

"Some. They're the ones who'd gone missin' from the workhouses."

"Why was Simmons holding them?"

"He said they'd volunteered for a scientific experiment," Abigail offered, shaking her head.

A small crowd gathered as word of the fire spread; some organized themselves to help contain it until the Fire Brigade arrived.

Weston joined Stephen and Abigail. "The boys seem no worse for the wear. Simmons was giving them sleeping drops to keep them calm. They're hungry though."

"We're always hungry, my lord," Hubert told him with a smile.

"What about the other man?" Abigail asked, her voice still raspy.

"What other man?" Stephen had seen no one but Simmons.

"There was a man behind Simmons in a hooded cloak. Didn't he come out?"

"No. Are you certain?" Stephen thought that must be the man they'd been looking for all along. The mastermind with a plan that involved Simmons and the meteorite, and who intended to use boys in an experiment.

"I saw him earlier," Olivia added. "He walked with a cane."

"Can you describe him?" Weston asked.

Sophia shook her head. "His face was hidden by the hood of his cloak."

Stephen shared a puzzled look with Weston.

"I'll search for any sign of him," Weston said and hurried away.

A constable approached and Stephen spoke with him, giving him as many details as he could, pleased to see Simmons hauled away to jail.

The Fire Brigade arrived and, with impressive

efficiency and a steam fire engine, made quick work of controlling the fire. Nearly half of the warehouse still stood but the whole building continued to smolder.

Sophia and Olivia walked over to speak with the other boys, giving Abigail and Stephen a moment of privacy.

He drew her into his arms. "Abigail, I have many things to tell you. So many things."

Her eyes filled with fresh tears, and she threw her arms around his neck. "Oh, Stephen! I was afraid I'd never see you again. I'm so sorry for everything."

"I'm sorry, too. You were right. I've kept too many secrets." He pulled back to look into her eyes, those beautiful blue eyes. His heart felt as though it would beat its way out of his chest. He'd never dreamed this moment would be possible, and now that it was here, he feared she wouldn't have him. He knew he didn't deserve her. He'd given her no reason to trust him, let alone love him. Yet still he hoped. "But I have another one to confess."

CHAPTER TWENTY-FIVE

Abigail's heart squeezed painfully. After all they'd been through, she wasn't about to let a secret come between them. He had reason to distrust others after all he'd been through. It might take time, but she was determined to win his trust. Perhaps eventually his feelings for her might grow.

The best thing she could do was be honest and tell him how she truly felt. More than anything, she wanted to ease the shadows from his eyes, to lift the weight of his secrets from his soul. But it began with this one step. "It doesn't matter. I don't care what it is. I only—"

"Shh." He brought his finger to her lips to silence her as he gave her that slow smile she loved so much. The one that started in his eyes, then quirked the corner of his mouth. "I want to confess it anyway. You see, I've realized I can't live without you."

Love swelled inside her, expanding her heart so she could hardly breathe. She pressed her lips to his finger and pulled back to smile. "Shall I confess my secret as well?"

A shadow of doubt crossed his face, making Abigail realize how uncertain he was.

"Stephen, I—" her words caught in her throat. She swallowed hard and hoped she'd say the right thing to reassure him. "I love you. I love you so very much."

He cupped her face with gentle hands. His gaze held hers for a moment before he captured her lips with his own. He kissed her with an intensity that it made her lightheaded, holding her with such tenderness, such sweet regard, that it brought more tears to her already watering eyes.

He pulled back and rested his forehead against hers. "I thought I'd lost you. When I saw the fire and I couldn't get the door open—"

"Shh." She put her hands over his. "You managed, and thanks to you, we're all right. You saved us."

His shaky breath tugged further at her heart strings. "Abigail?"

"Yes?"

"I'm never, ever letting you go."

She laughed, bursting with joy. "Perfect. Because I'm not letting you go either."

He pulled back and his gaze roamed over her face. "I love you more than words can say, more than I could ever show you."

She grinned, delighted with his latest confession.

With a smile, he pressed kisses over her entire face, ending on her nose. "Darling?"

Goosebumps covered her flesh at the endearment. "Yes?"

"Will you do me the honor of becoming my wife?"

Her breath caught in her throat.

"I promise to honor your independent spirit, though it occasionally makes me crazed."

She smiled, for she knew it to be true.

"I'm not the easiest person to live with. I—"

Their intimate conversation was interrupted by Weston's return. He was out of breath.

"Nothing. Not one sign of anyone else in the

vicinity. The firemen won't let us search the structure. They don't want anyone near it yet," said Weston.

"I suppose that's understandable, but I'd like to get a look at what's in there," Stephen said as he rose and assisted Abigail to her feet.

A boy emerged from the crowd and approached them. "A man asked me to give ye this." He handed Stephen an envelope.

"Stephen, Michael, and Lucas," he read out loud then shook his head in disbelief.

"What? You must be mistaken." Weston stepped forward to read it for himself.

Abigail could see shock sweep through the two men.

Stephen unfolded the missive then cleared his throat. "The time is near for the four of us to reunite." He looked up at his friend. "It's signed 'Professor'."

They both scanned the crowd as though hoping to spot the man.

"That isn't possible." Skepticism coated Weston's voice. He turned and walked away for a moment before spinning back. "It just isn't possible."

Abigail wondered who he was trying to convince.

"No. It's not," Stephen added, but he didn't sound as certain. He put a hand on the boy's shoulder. "Do you know the man? Can you describe him?"

"Never seen him afore. To be honest, he gave me the creeps." The boy shuddered. "He wore a long black cloak with a hood. Couldn't see his face."

Weston flipped a half shilling to the boy. "They'll be more of that if you remember anything else."

"I thank ye, sir." The boy tipped his cap and

took off with a grin.

Abigail leaned closer to look at the note. "I thought your professor was killed the night of the accident."

"Yes, he was."

Weston shook his head. "He's dead. Someone is attempting to play a cruel joke on us. I highly doubt Lucas will return from Brazil any time soon."

"Indeed. I don't think he ever intends to come back to England," Stephen added.

"Whoever this man is, he has the wrong stone." Abigail smiled wryly at Stephen. "I'm not sure if he knows it or not."

Weston stared at the pair of them. "Where is the real meteorite?"

Stephen withdrew it from his pocket.

"This 'Professor' will soon be looking for us, won't he?" Weston asked with a smile.

"He will if he needs the stone," said Stephen. "This whole affair is far from over."

Abigail shivered at the worried look he gave her.

"One way or another, we'll get to the bottom of it. But now, it's late. I suggest we all go home." Weston looked over at the boys huddled nearby. "Why don't I take some of them with me?"

"Excellent. We'll determine a plan in the morning."

The Fire Brigade remained to make certain the fire was out. Stephen made sure the police would guard the building so nothing could be disturbed until he and Weston returned in the morning to have a closer look at the contents. The crowd dwindled to a few curious onlookers.

Weston filled his carriage with Farley and the other boys and drove away with a wave. Several of the boys, including Hubert, piled in the hackney along with Stephen, Abigail, Sophia, and Olivia.

Within a short while, they arrived at Abigail's where a tearful Irene gathered her three daughters in a hug as Ponsford stood nearby, sniffing inconspicuously.

"Thank heavens you're all safe. What on earth happened?" Irene asked as she looked them over from head to toe. "Was there a fire?"

The story spilled out in bits and pieces with the twins interrupting each other in their rush to tell their mother everything.

Irene shook her head, seeming amazed at all they'd gone through. She gathered them into her arms again. "I'm so pleased you're all home." She turned to Stephen. "I assume I have you to thank for this?"

"I was merely Abigail's assistant." He grinned at Abigail, and the heat in his gaze warmed her from the inside out. "May I have a moment with her?"

"Of course." Irene smiled at the pair of them. Then she put an arm through Sophia and Olivia's. "Now, while we're cleaning up the two of you, explain to me why you left the house without telling anyone."

The girls' protests could be heard as they made their way upstairs. Ponsford wiped his eyes as he departed to order the hot water for baths.

Abigail cleared her still raw throat, suddenly nervous. She gestured for Stephen to step into the drawing room.

"I wanted a moment to finish our conversation," Stephen said as he shut the door behind him. "I can't believe I almost lost you."

"And I nearly lost you." The very thought of their close call brought tears to her eyes.

He drew her into his arms and her worries slipped away. His jacket was charred in places and smelled of smoke, but she couldn't think of a place she'd rather be than in his arms.

"Yes," she said firmly.

With a frown and a small smile, he looked down at her. "What?"

"I never answered you before." She lifted up on her toes and kissed him. "I'm answering you now." She kissed him again, longer this time, putting her heart and soul into it. "Yes, I would be honored to be your wife."

He kissed her back and her heart swelled with joy.

"Abigail." He drew her name out, whispering in her ear, sending shivers down her spine. "I love you so much. But as I was trying to say earlier, I'm not an easy person to live with. The aura reading—"

She kissed him. "I know about that."

"I have these moments of darkness when nothing—"

Again she pressed her lips to his. "I know of that as well."

"This whole mystery with the man who claims to be a professor isn't over. I still have the meteorite he wants."

"I know. Together, with Lord Weston's assistance, we shall discover what that man is doing."

He ran his finger along her cheek. "I'm not good at sharing information—"

"I'll unravel your secrets. Have no worries on that."

"But I—"

"Stop making excuses or I'll think you're taking back your offer," she teased him with a smile. "Kiss me instead. That's a much better use of your time."

He laughed. "You're right. Once again, you're right. Have I ever mentioned how determined you are?"

"Perhaps once or twice." She held her hand

along his cheek. "I still don't understand where you got that impression."

"A mistaken one I'm sure." He kissed her again.

Passionately.

Thoroughly.

Until her head spun.

"Always and forever?" she asked, wanting him to be sure, needing to hear him say it out loud.

"Indeed. Always and forever." He sealed his promise with another kiss.

THE END

OTHER BOOKS BY THE AUTHOR:

COMING IN 2014, PASSIONATE SECRETS

Book II of The Secret Trilogy

A Vow To Keep
Book I of The Vengeance Trilogy

Trust In Me
Book II of The Vengeance Trilogy

Believe In Me
Book III of The Vengeance Trilogy

DEDICATION

To my Family.
Your love and support means the world to me!

ACKNOWLEDGEMENTS

Brad, Brandon and Jordan: you are my heart and soul.

Thanks and gratitude to my amazing, talented critique partners: Michelle Major, Anne Eliot, and Jennie Marts, and to my beta readers, Linda Benning, Lauren Billing and Sarah Billing. You ladies rock!

ABOUT THE AUTHOR

Lana Williams writes historical romance filled with mystery, adventure, and a pinch of paranormal to stir things up. Her medieval romances include A VOW TO KEEP, the first in The Vengeance Trilogy, followed by TRUST IN ME and BELIEVE IN ME.

Filled with a love of books from an early age, Lana put pen to paper and decided happy endings were a must in any story she created. She writes in the Rocky Mountains with her husband, two growing sons, and two dogs.

She loves hearing from readers! Contact her at www.lanawilliams.net, www.facebook.com/LanaWilliamsBooks or on Twitter @LanaWilliams28.